GAVEL TO GAVEL

The Seneca County Courthouse Series: Book One

A.X. FOSTER

Copyright © 2023 by A.X. Foster.

All rights reserved. This book or any portion thereof may not be reproduced or used in any manner whatsoever without the express written permission of the publisher except for the use of brief quotations in a book review.

Published by Paper Raven Books LLC

Printed in the United States of America

First Printing, 2023

Paperback ISBN: 979-8-9876997-0-6
eBook ISBN: 979-8-9876997-1-3

Library of Congress Control Number: TXu 2-356-853

This is a work of fiction. All names, characters, places, and incidents are the product of the author's imagination or are used fictitiously. Any resemblance to actual events, locales or persons, living or dead, is purely coincidental.

DEDICATION

Why may not that be the skull of a lawyer?
Where be his quiddities now, his quillities, his
cases, his tenures, and his tricks?
Hamlet, Act V, scene 1.

CHAPTER 1

Thursday, December 20, 2018
8:22 a.m.

Mac sat in his office, appraising the tall stack of thick homicide case files piled up on his desk. Each one a tragedy. These were the most difficult jury trials to prepare. A baby shaken to death. A patient smothered in a nursing home. A hit man who killed for cash. Evil came in many forms to Senior Assistant State's Attorney Mac MacIntyre.

The worst cases haunted him and stuck in his mind like barnacles encrusted on a ship. He'd see these victims in sweaty dreams before sunrise. An angelic teenager named Violet visited regularly. Just 14 years old, she was strangled by a jealous schoolboy. She appeared at daybreak, ghostlike, her long, cascading blonde hair swishing across Mac's mind.

He glanced at his cell phone: the text alarmed him.

> TUF CASE COMING IN. BRINGING LITTLE
> GRIL DOWN TO UR OFC NOW. SHE SAW
> 0100 OF DAD. EYE WITN. B THERE 10
> MINS. SERIOUS SHIT.

In all the years they had worked together at the Seneca County Judicial Center, ever since Andre Okoye was an undercover cop and Mac a rookie prosecutor, Mac had never received a message with such urgency. "Tough case coming in?" he said out loud to his empty office. The sound of his own voice jolted him back to reality. 0100 was code for a murder. *A little girl saw her father killed? Concentrate. Focus.* That was one of Mac's great strengths. When necessary, he could fuse all of his brainpower together to solve the puzzle or crisis looming in front of him. Before he stood to address a jury or a judge, he would write the word "FOCUS" at the top of his legal pad. It was the best advice he could give himself, better than anything he had learned in law school. Five block letters printed in red with a plastic felt-tipped pen.

His phone pinged. The second text notified him:

> CMING UP ELVTOR WITH KID. RESERVE
> CONFRNCE RM NOW.

He felt a dull pain throb in his stomach. *Not that again. Not right now.* He refused to Google "ulcer," although the instinct to do so raced through his mind.

The bright December sunlight poured through the large picture window and lit up his office. His eyes fell on a framed crayon drawing over his desk. Asymmetrical rows of square and rectangular frames displaying artwork, diplomas, various awards and newspaper articles dotted the walls: a visual roadmap of Mac's career. But the small frame directly over his desk was different, and his gaze reflexively returned to it time and time again; it gave him daily inspiration, like a talisman. It was a child's hand-drawn stick figure with a headline of scribbled words in a variety of bright crayon colors: some red, some blue, some green, in alternating serendipity. It read:

"TO THE STAIT'S ATTOURNY MAC. YOU ARE VERY NICE AND THANK YOU FOR HEPLING MY GRAMMA. LOVE MADISON."

The stick figure was the tiny girl's portrait of Mac. Even 10 years later, it was, essentially, an accurate rendering, portraying Mac as tall and thin, with a mop of bright red hair. His eyes were depicted as large crayon spirals in light green, the hue of traffic lights signaling "go."

A small flashing light on his desk phone blinked, signifying a call from the front desk. He lifted the receiver.

"Mr. MacIntyre, Detective Okoye is here to see you. He's got a little girl with him."

"Thanks, Lupe. *¿Carino que onda?* Send Andre down to the conference room. And can you please mark me *out* on the board for the next hour?"

"*Todo bien. ¿Y tu guapo?*" Lupe replied.

Mac smiled. She called him handsome every day. He never got tired of it.

"I'm good, *preciosa*," he said, knowing how infrequent compliments were around the office.

Lupe brightened at his response; then she whispered, "Hey, Mac. I gotta tell you, Fischbein's in the office already. He asked me if you were here, like he was checking up on you."

"Thanks for letting me know. Hey, keep this between us, Lupe, but The Fish is a real *pendejo*."

"Right! He got elected, like, what? Has it even been a year yet? And, so far, he hasn't bothered to learn my name, just walks right by the reception desk. Says nothing. Pretty rude for a new State's Attorney. You'd think he'd want to be nice, especially to the support staff. I called him Mr. Fish-bean by accident when he first got here, and he stopped and corrected me. He said, 'My name is Fish-byne!' He's been real mean to me ever since."

Mac looked to confirm that his door was shut and added, "Yeah, my new boss. The Fish. As I said, this guy is a born asshole."

"Maybe he's like that because he's so short? What do they call that? A Neapolitan complex or something?"

"Napoleonic."

"What?"

"Lupe, what exactly did he say? Can you remember his exact words?"

"Mr. Fischbein asked, 'Is MacIntyre here!?' Kind of angry-like. That's it. He never says please or thank you. Just letting you know."

"*Gracias*, Lupe. Thanks for looking out for me. I know how to handle this guy. Just feed his ego. For such a small man, he sure has a big mouth."

Before Mac could put down the telephone receiver, Andre texted once more:

> HERE IN CONF RM. BRING TISSUES.
> GIRL CRYING. GET HERE NOW.

Mac grabbed the box of Kleenex he always kept handy in the bottom drawer of his desk, turned, opened his office door, and jogged down the hallway.

CHAPTER 2

Thursday, December 20, 2018
8:44 a.m.

Andre was waiting outside the State's Attorney's Office's conference room. The door was closed. He peeked through the glass window in the door and turned to Mac.

"Seriously, we've got to keep this guardian lady out of the way. She's the girl's aunt. The sister of the Defendant. She's major trouble. I had to bring them both down here together, but I separated them. The little girl's in here," Andre said as he used his thumb in a hitchhiking gesture to point inside the conference room. "I stashed the aunt in the waiting area up by the front desk. I asked Lupe to keep talking to her, to keep her distracted. We need to sort this shit out, and this kid will not talk with that aunt hovering over her like a damn helicopter."

"So you got the guardian to let you talk to the girl? That's good. Let's keep them apart for as long as we can. I'll talk to the kid here and you go back to the reception area. Try to smooth-talk that woman. But first, introduce me to the little girl."

Andre nodded and looked back into the room again.

Mac noted, "So, the guardian of our key witness is the killer's sister? Damn. If she says she wants a lawyer for this kid, we're jammed. Juveniles have Fifth Amendment rights just like an adult. So, stall her as long as you can. Got it?"

"OK. I'll try to chill her out, but she's super high maintenance. The aunt's name is Linden Hale, but she goes by Lindy. The little girl is a nine-year-old. She's the daughter of the dead guy. Her name is Mandy. We need to interview her before Child Protective Services or some psychologist plants some crazy ideas in her mind and messes up this whole case. She seems pretty calm, but then, out of nowhere, she will just start crying. Obviously, this shit is traumatic."

Mac sighed. "This little girl saw her mother kill her father? Unbelievable. Has this case hit the news yet?"

"No. But it will be any minute. I called Media Services—I know Lieutenant Hyman from back when we were in the Police Academy together—and he said he has to release a statement sooner or later since it's an 0100. Plus, I heard the dead guy was famous or super rich or something. I don't know if Hyman contacted your new boss yet or not."

"God help us," Mac responded. "This is so far over The Fish's head I can't even calculate it."

Andre said, "And there's something else. I didn't really understand, but apparently, this girl, Mandy, has some kind of serious mental issue, so we need to take this one real slow."

"Right. When you go out, ask the aunt about that. What type of disability does Mandy have? Text that information to me as soon as you find out. It makes a huge difference in how I interview her. Find out if it's Asperger's, or if she's somewhere on the autistic spectrum, or what exactly."

"10-4."

Detective Andre Okoye was not one of the typical, central casting types who retired from a career as a police officer and then double-dipped as an investigator in the Seneca County State's Attorney's Office, getting a new salary while also cashing in on the police department's retirement benefits and pension. The other in-house detectives looked like ex-cops: bald and bulky, like former football players. Mac loved that Andre didn't fit that profile. His charisma and energy radiated outward from deep within. His survival skills were the product of growing up on West 127th Street in New York City. They were invaluable here in Seneca County, in the Maryland suburbs bordering Washington D.C. He had both style and swag. He wore yellow Air Jordan 5's and a black leather motorcycle jacket with a lapel pin depicting the flag of Nigeria: three vertical stripes of green and white. Of course, along with the four small hoop earrings, he had a detective's badge on his belt, and a fanny pack on his left hip holding a Glock 9mm semi-automatic. His spiky hair stood up in all directions. He would wear a suit and tie when he had to testify in court, but otherwise, he dressed casually and often stretched the office's concept of "casual."

They worked together as a team. Andre investigated major crimes and brought them to Mac to analyze. Andre was skilled: he could softly interview children, but still have the guile and courage to track down leads, no matter how deeply hidden they were, in the backstreets and alleyways of Seneca County.

Andre opened the door to the conference room and slowly walked in. Mac followed and closed the door behind him.

"Hey, Mandy. This is my friend, Mac. He's the prosecutor. We work together."

Andre slipped his small handheld Dictaphone from his leather jacket, fingered the "on" switch, and left it on the chair next to his thigh, out of view under the edge of the table. It would record automatically for a maximum of 120 minutes.

Mandy was swinging back and forth in the swivel chair. She was chewing on the collar of her shirt, and a wet stain descended to her frail chest, like a bib. She looked up and said, "What's a prosecutor?"

"I work with the police to figure out stuff when bad things happen. I talk to kids all the time. I try to make sure everyone's safe. Are you OK, Mandy?"

Mac slid into the seat next to Mandy. He tilted his head and glanced back at Andre, signaling that Andre should leave and go down the hall to make sure Mandy's aunt was not causing a scene at the front desk, or, even worse, demanding an attorney be present.

Andre left, closing the door silently behind him.

Mac turned to Mandy and said, "So, I hear something really bad happened with your mom and dad last night, is that right? Can you tell me what you saw?"

Mandy stopped chewing on her shirt and answered with no emotion, "They were fighting like always, and Mommy went into the kitchen and got this, like, big knife from the block thing. She ran back in, and she and Dad were yelling all kinds of stuff real loud and then, then..."

Mandy put her head down on the table.

Mac said, "Would you like something to drink? We have some juice in our kitchen area, or a cold bottle of water?"

Mandy lifted her head up part way and looked straight down at the polished conference room table, her reflection a mirror image. She was completely still.

"I saw Mommy punch Dad with the knife."

She leaned forward again, rested her forehead on the table, and stopped moving.

"Mandy?"

She was fast asleep.

CHAPTER 3

Thursday, December 20, 2018
9:01 a.m.

Andre appeared at the door and tapped with his knuckles on the thick glass window. Mandy didn't move. Andre opened the door and escorted a thin, frantic woman into the conference room behind him.

As soon as she entered, the woman shrieked, "Who said you could talk to my niece? Hey! This is so done. We are out of here."

Mac stood. "Good morning, ma'am. My name is Mac MacIntyre, and I'm the Senior Assistant State's Attorney assigned to the case."

"What's a State's Attorney? Same as a District Attorney?"

"Yes. In Maryland, the prosecutor is called the State's Attorney. In other places, the prosecutor is called the District Attorney, or even, in Pennsylvania, for example, the Commonwealth's Attorney. Exactly the same job, but with different names. But, yes, I'll be handling this case here in Seneca County."

"Well, that's just fine, but I don't give a shit who you are. I'm Lindy Hale. This is my niece you've got here being interrogated without an attorney. Do you always violate people's rights?"

Mandy was asleep on the table, a soft snoring sound, almost a wheeze, flowing from her lips.

"I'm sorry, Ms. Hale, but this is all very routine and what we do in every case, including this one involving your...?"

"Sister. My little sister, Rikki. You needed to lock up her maniac of a husband, Marten, not her. You probably know him—or at least know *of* him—he's Marten Van der Hook. Y'know, MVH Enterprises? That's him. He's MVH."

Mac recognized MVH immediately. It was a massive industrial manufacturing plant, one of the biggest corporations in Seneca County, with a gigantic factory which seemed to stretch a mile along the Interstate. Mac said, "Sorry, I'm unfamiliar with all the local businesses. But we can research your brother-in-law's company. We will definitely address all of your concerns. I'm happy to sit down with you and discuss everything. Can we do that?"

Parrying Mac's question, Lindy said, "No, absolutely not. We are leaving right now." She walked around the conference table and shook Mandy's shoulder.

"Mandy! Wake up! It's Aunt Lindy. Wake up!"

Mandy stirred and raised her head. She opened her eyes and yawned.

"This child has pediatric narcolepsy and needs special care. Stressful situations cause cataplexy and really make it kick in." Lindy's hands were clenched into fists. "You will not talk to her again without some kind of court order or subpoena or whatever it's called." She pulled her phone out of her back jeans pocket, tapped on the screen, and said, "My Uber is here. Let's go!"

Lindy reached under Mandy's armpits and used both of her hands to lift her halfway out of her chair. Mandy stood, wobbled, and said, "I'm thirsty."

"It's OK, honey," Lindy assured. "We will be home in a few minutes, and I'll get you a juice box, and you can rest. Don't worry. You're staying at Aunt Lindy's house for the time being. You'll be safe with me."

Mac looked at Andre, who had stayed by the door like a lookout. They made eye contact.

I need Andre to take this child and her guardian back out to the reception area. We need Mandy's full cooperation. That will be essential to win this case.

Lindy wrapped her arm around Mandy's tiny shoulders and walked her towards the door. As she left the room, Lindy turned back and said, "Call our attorney. Marcel St. Croix. I'm sure you've heard of *him*."

Andre volunteered, "Ms. Hale, I'll walk you guys out to the reception area and thank you so much again for helping us. We appreciate your assistance. And we will definitely be in touch."

Lindy escorted Mandy through the doorway. As Andre crossed the threshold, he turned back and mouthed silently to Mac, "Oh shit!"

When the three of them had turned the corner, Mac stood in the empty conference room. He closed his eyes and sighed.

Marcel St. Croix. Oh my God, this is going to be a nightmare.
He left the room and walked briskly back to his office.

CHAPTER 4

Thursday, December 20, 2018
9:45 a.m.

Andre was back at Mac's office in less than two minutes, bursting through and exclaiming, "Isn't that private attorney—the French dude, St. Croix—isn't he a total showboat?"

"He can be difficult," Mac sighed. "And he's not French. He's French Canadian, from way up there somewhere in Quebec."

"Same thing," Andre replied.

"But I can work with him. Marcel's a gentleman in his own way. He's very, very smart. But this is more important—juries seem to love him. He's extremely persuasive."

"How much would a hired assassin like St. Croix charge for a murder case? I mean, knowing that this Rikki woman is married to a multimillionaire-type guy?"

"Man, Andre, I'm sure it depends on how rich the client is. With this case being all about MVH Enterprises, I'd guess at least something like $500,000 or more. And then extra money to hire all kinds of expert witnesses. Those legal whores will say anything you want for the right fee."

"Half a million!? Damn Mac, you should quit this state's attorney shit and become a hired assassin yourself."

"Don't tempt me."

Andre slumped down on the couch. He took off his black leather motorcycle jacket and dropped it on the floor.

"So what did this Rikki Van der Hook tell you when you interviewed her?" Mac asked, letting the specter of Marcel St. Croix drift momentarily out of his mind. "What did she say? Did she confess?"

"She's so psycho. But she told me everything. This woman is cooked. We got her cold, but we need you to bring your max game. You know how child witnesses go. Something always blows up in a case like this. I don't need to tell you that."

"Copy the video of your interview with her and get it to me fast. Also, email me a copy of the SCPD-505 form. I need to double-check if you advised her of her *Miranda* rights. Marcel St. Croix will want to see the SCPD-505 first. That form needs to be perfect."

"I couldn't videotape her statement. But she completely spilled the beans, and I wrote it all down exactly, right as she was talking to me in the interview room at the 6D station after she was arrested."

Mac considered the phrase *spilled the beans* for an instant. He *hated* clichés. But he said, "Did she give a motive? Does her confession match up with what Mandy says? If we can corroborate Rikki's statement with what Mandy says, we will have this trial locked up pretty solid."

"We are good. The rest will just be icing on the ca—"
"Don't say it!"
"It's the tip of the iceb—"
"No! Not the tip! What about the whole iceberg? No one ever mentions that. We only hear about the tip."
"OK, my man. Well, trust me, this case is airtight."

Mac looked up at the clock. It was 9:59 a.m. He could hear shoes shuffling on the hallway carpet outside his office door as the assistant state's attorneys rushed to get to the courtrooms upstairs in the Seneca County Judicial Center. ASAs covered a variety of matters—daily dockets, bond reviews, pleas, sentencings, violations of probation, and jury trials—the big kills. By 10:00 a.m., everything would have already started, so there was a general air of chaos swirling around the hallways each day at this time. Mac sat still in his chair. He looked up at the crayon drawing above his desk. STAIT'S ATTOURNY. His pulse was pounding. He could actually hear it sluicing through the veins in his temples. HEPLING ME.

Andre was so sharply attuned to Mac's moods and idiosyncrasies that he sensed hesitation. Or was it apprehension?

Andre cupped his hand into the shape of the letter "C" and tapped it on his heart, signaling the American Sign Language sign for "police." He then lifted both of his hands, made two horizontal circles with his index fingers, imitating the pans in the scales of justice. He signed "prosecutor," and said, "Remember that trial we did way back with that deaf college girl who saw her roommate killed?"

Mac was staring at the crayon drawing.

Andre continued, "I remember how you learned sign language just to bond with that girl and make her feel safe. That was amazing how fast you memorized all of them signs, man. That case lit some kind of insane fire inside of you. I only remember two: the signs for 'cop' and 'prosecutor.'"

There was a moment of silence in the room, and neither man moved.

"Mac, you got this. You are the best prosecutor in Maryland. Dude, I've known you since day one. This kid Mandy really needs you. Think about it: she saw her mother murder her father. That is about as cold as it gets. This is exactly your lane. And this crazy-ass Rikki needs to be locked up in Baltimore SuperMax for like a hundred years!"

It was a pep talk, the sideline rant, the trainer urging the boxer to summon all of his remaining courage to get up off the stool. Andre could press the right buttons to get inside Mac's head and inside his heart. They had been through the wars together, going all the way back to the night when Andre nearly died.

"Anything you need, just tell me," said Andre. He dropped his voice to a lower tone and exhaled. "We've been in this shit since that drug rip bust on Rotterdam Street. No matter how much I try, I still can't get that night out of my mind. You were there for me. I swear, I'll never forget how you helped me."

Mac didn't respond. He was staring at the drawing, deep in thought.

"Mac, are you listening to me?"

CHAPTER 5

Thursday, December 20, 2018
10:03 a.m.

A drop of sweat rolled from Andre's armpit down across his rib cage. That humid summer evening, all those years before, was once again returning to haunt him. For 16 years, he had tried to blot it out, but in his nightmares, he always returned to Rotterdam Street. Back to the inside of his undercover police car. The feeling of that gun pressed tight against his temple. That terrible night—it seemed like it was only yesterday.

A second drop of sweat descended.

He closed his eyes; the whole thing flashed through his mind...

Andre saw himself wearing the Knicks jersey with "Ewing" across the back, his gold necklaces flipped over his shoulder, and his baseball cap twisted backwards. The dented unmarked car was innocuous. Seized from a drug dealer in a vehicle forfeiture, it barely ran, but it was perfect for its current purpose. The interior was mic'ed up—no cameras, but four microphones hidden in the dashboard. Other Special Assignment Team officers were listening in, two blocks away.

Then he saw him.

Swaggy T approached from the alley and opened the passenger side door. He said, "Yo, Dog, what's up?"

"You got that brick, T? I ain't playing," said Andre.

The air was moist and dense. Sweat was forming below the brow of Andre's baseball cap, and beads of liquid reflected off his dark skin, his bare deltoids shiny and wet. He reached for the unzipped fanny pack on the side of his back near his kidney. He tapped it just to reassure himself and felt comforted by its weight and solidity. There weren't many advantages to being left-handed, but this was one.

The SAT Unit had been tracking Swaggy T for months. He was one of the biggest dealers in Seneca County. He dealt mostly rock, but bricks of weed too, if the price was right. The trap was set: do the drug deal, buy the marijuana with marked Department money. Make the arrest as soon as Swaggy T exited the vehicle. Pretend to arrest Andre too, for show. Then, months later, when Andre would walk into the courtroom wearing a suit and tie to testify, the metamorphosis from drug buyer to undercover cop would be displayed.

Andre said, "Man, you got that brick or not? Answer me, dude!"

"Yeah," said Swaggy T slowly, "I got something for you…" and then he spun quickly.

Andre felt a metal gun barrel the size of an ice cube firmly pressing against his right temple. *Fuck. A rip. Help me. Think! Move slowly, don't panic. Follow your training.* Thoughts raced through his mind like a lethal, spinning roulette wheel. *Please God, don't let me die in the front seat of a broken-down undercover police car over two pounds of cheap Jamaican weed.* Incongruously, the face of his grandmother sitting on the fire escape on West 127th Street with the blue Hudson River behind her flashed through his mind, distracting him. *Move slowly. Don't panic!*

"Give me the cash, motherfucker, or I'll blow your head off!" said Swaggy T, raising his voice.

"OK, OK, OK, take it easy, man!" replied Andre, realizing that *he* was now the one caught in a trap, the roles reversed. He was now the prey, not the predator. *Where were the other SAT officers? Weren't they listening?!*

"You can have it. Don't shoot!"

Then a strong flash! A thunderously loud BAMMM! Undercover police officers were swarming the car. Swaggy T was slumped over, and all four of the car doors were being violently pulled open. Andre looked down at his sweaty right shoulder and saw bright red blood spattered chaotically on his skin, a spray of crimson dots. The front of his Knicks jersey, formerly orange and blue, was now drenched in red. The gunshot was so loud, the sound amplified by the ricocheting effect inside a closed car, that his hearing was now just beginning to come back.

"10-50! 10-50! Officer down!" someone was shouting.

As his senses returned, like a fog lifting, Andre realized he was not injured. He turned to see Swaggy T, now on the pavement, lying on his stomach, with his hands unnecessarily handcuffed behind him. There was a fist-sized hole in the back of his head—the exit wound. Plumes of blood were pumping two inches out of his skull as his heart was still beating its last few spasms of life. A large pool of blood quickly grew in a circle on the pavement beneath his face. The bullet had penetrated his left eye socket.

"You got him!" some voice enthusiastically exclaimed. But there was no gun in Swaggy T's hands or on the floor of the vehicle or anywhere. In Swaggy T's left hand was a small, black, rectangular pager. He had pressed a pager against Andre's temple in the botched robbery, and Andre had spun and shot him through the eye.

Within two hours, the media grabbed the story: a 17-year-old boy shot to death over a marijuana deal! Police brutality. Community advocacy groups calling for the indictment of Officer Andre Okoye, demanding a second-degree murder charge from the Seneca County State's Attorney's Office. Executed a boy with a pager in his hand!

But Mac MacIntyre didn't desert his friend. He saw through the politics and public pressure. Mac convened the Grand Jury and steered them through their investigation. They returned a No Bill, and the case was concluded without any charges. A justified act of self-defense. Fox News broadcast a photo of Andre in his Police Academy graduation uniform side-by-side with a photo from the night of the shooting, wearing his New York Knicks basketball jersey soaked in blood.

After the investigation ended, Mac offered him a job at the SAO as his chief homicide investigator. He'd been Mac's top guy ever since.

The desk phone rang, jolting both Mac and Andre back to reality. Mac hit the speaker button.

"Yes, Lupe?" asked Mac.

"Hey, Mr. MacIntyre, I gotta tell you something important."

CHAPTER 6

Thursday, December 20, 2018
10:05 a.m.

"What, Lupe? What?"

"Fischbein and Jo Newgrange were just here at the front desk, all frantic-like. I heard him tell her to go get you and bring you down to his office right away. She's heading to get you right now. Watch out for that lady, Mac. She kinda scares me. She's pretty, but when she smiles, it's like she has too many teeth."

"I'll be careful, Lupe. Thanks for letting me know. *Gracias. Cuidame a mis secretos.*"

"You're welcome. All your secrets are safe with me too, Mac. And good luck with Napoleon!"

"My cue to split," said Andre, who stood and shook hands with Mac and grasped him in a quick hug.

"I'll head back to the Van der Hook house right now, Mac. The Crime Scene Techs are processing the place right now.

They bagged up the carving knife she used, so I'll get that over to the Crime Lab with instructions to test it for DNA, top priority, OK? I'll come back here to the courthouse later this afternoon. Does that work?"

"Yes, perfect. Have the Techs take a lot of photos, more than they usually do. I want to have photographs of the entire place, especially from the point of view of Mandy's perspective."

"Mac, the blood splatter patterns are amazing. I've been doing homicide cases half my life, and I've never seen anything like this before."

"Really? Like what? Tell me..."

Andre pulled out his phone and clicked through his photos. "There's blood on the damn ceiling. Long crisscrosses—like X shapes—across the walls and even up above your head!"

Mac leaned over his shoulder to see.

The patterns depicted linear trails of red dots, some tiny and some thicker, the larger ones hanging down like miniature stalactites dripping to the floor below.

"Look at that shit! She stabbed this guy like 50 times. Some serious overkill."

"That always means a crime of passion," Mac responded. "Overkill. You don't need to stab someone a million times to kill them. Something's going on here more than the usual murder."

"Right."

"Someone really hated this guy."

"Is there a word for something more than overkill? Can we call this over-overkill? Remember that case we had a couple of years back with that Albanian guy who flipped out on that chick when she said she was leaving him? We need that Dr. Mossberg guy again. That's his name, right? The blood splatter expert we used before."

"Yep. Mossberg. It's called spatter, not splatter. Yes, can you reach out to him? I remember his testimony perfectly. He said the blood gets thrown *up* each time the stabber pulls the knife forcefully out. Like if you pulled a paintbrush out of a can of paint as fast as you could."

"Brutal," Andre confirmed. He texted himself as a reminder:

DR MOSSBRG BLOOD SPTTER EXPERT

"Once we have the crime scene photos back from Tech, we can have him analyze. But blood on the *ceiling*? That is bad, Andre."

"Damn straight. That shit looks like some modern art. Who's that guy who threw paint on the canvas and then sold it for a million bucks?"

"Jackson Pollock."

"What?"

"Listen, I've got some lawyer stuff to do here, administrative crap. Politics, man. Take care of the DNA sample first, get that knife to the Crime Lab now. Then meet me back here at four-thirty. We need to go over everything before this case hits the fan. Catch you later. And Andre? Thank you."

Mac lifted both of his hands and signed "prosecutor."

Andre tapped his chest directly over his heart to sign "police" in return, and said, "Love you, bro. Appreciate everything you done for me."

"But look," said Mac, gesturing towards his office window, where the sun was brightly streaming in, "the morn in russet mantle clad, walks o'er the dew of yon high eastward hill..."

"Oh, man, not that Shakespeare talk again. You always do that when you're nervous. I know you! What's that one from? *King Lear*?"

"*Hamlet*."

Andre shook his head as he zipped up his motorcycle jacket and opened the door. Mac and his quotes. He loved the guy, but man, it got annoying. He waved a hand in the air before dashing down the hallway.

CHAPTER 7

Thursday, December 20, 2018
10:17 a.m.

Mac heard the sound of high heels clacking closer and closer, a tapping like an S.O.S. in Morse code, until it was just outside his office door. He looked up at exactly the same time Deputy State's Attorney Jo Newgrange leaned through the doorway, grasping the doorframe like the handlebars of a motorcycle. She dipped her head inside, smiled, and said, "Macaroni! Hey, we gotta talk about this new homicide case! The victim is Marten Van der Hook. He's the owner and CEO of MVH Enterprises. The press has already been calling nonstop. Ari wants to meet right now to discuss. Let's go."

Ari Fischbein was the top prosecutor; he was the Seneca County State's Attorney. Jo was second-in-command, his deputy, and Mac, along with the dozen other Senior Assistant State's Attorneys, were on the next horizontal row in the office organizational chart. Technically, Ari was his boss, but Jo held all the day-to-day power.

Jo spun back around towards the hallway, a pirouette with feline dexterity, and brushed her hands against her small hips, smoothing her tight charcoal Ralph Lauren skirt. Mac lowered his eyes to assess the back of her trim triathlete's physique. Charcoal: smoky, too hot to touch. He noticed the smoothness of her skirt, not a crease. It looked fresh from the dry cleaners. He spied a solitary, misplaced white thread clinging to her flank along for a ride. He observed the way her skin crinkled up in untanned lines behind her knees, deducing that she was not wearing pantyhose. He catalogued the tautness of her calf muscles and how they subtly inflated and deflated with each step she took. There were some things in Mac's mind he could not control.

Jo turned back and said, "Enjoying the view? C'mon! Let's go! Ari's waiting."

CHAPTER 8

Thursday, December 20, 2018
10:31 a.m.

"What the fuck is this shit?" Ari Fischbein exclaimed, his cheeks flushed. "Why didn't you tell me about this situation? Don't you realize that MVH Enterprises is like the biggest conglomeration in Seneca County? This needs to be handled right, or I could lose donations to my campaign. Are you trying to make me look like a loser?!"

Jo Newgrange chimed in, "Mac, we're a new administration here. We need to be conservative and not charge recklessly. We can't afford anything radical in our first term, don't you agree?"

Mac was sitting in Ari's office. It was the largest office on the fifth floor, which housed the entire State's Attorney's Office. Ari said, "I am the one who'll be running for reelection!" even though that was three years away and he had just assumed power earlier that year.

At 34, Ari was stocky and edging towards pudginess. He stood five-foot-five—with lifts in his dress shoes. Mac was rail-thin and towered above him. Mac, sensing that Ari was jealous, purposely stood straight when they were together, extending his vertebrae to his full six-foot-three height. Ari's sparse, straw-colored blond hair was severely brushed across the top of his head in a futile attempt to cover a widening bald spot. He wore designer eyeglasses that had almost no frames, just two discs of solid glass held together with thin pieces of gold wire. He hoped no one would notice he was wearing them, but, of course, everyone did. Ari always wore a suit and tie, a tie that dangled well below his belt. A stylist for his election campaign had advised him that the longer tie would give the optical illusion that he was taller and less squat, although absolutely no one saw Ari Fischbein as dashing or athletic. The entire office—both prosecutors and support staff alike—called him The Fish behind his back.

"Listen, I was a partner in a major corporate law firm in D.C.," he said, with a tone which sounded more arrogant than proud. Gesturing to a single courtroom sketch behind his desk, Ari rambled on, "I litigated big cases in Federal Court in downtown D.C., not out here in the country. I tried a lot of cases, more cases than anyone here, that's for sure! So, I'm not going to look like a fool because of you! I *am* the Seneca County State's Attorney."

Mac glanced at the courtroom sketch and noted that Ari was the figure depicted in the extreme far left of the scene. It appeared to be a civil trial in progress, not a criminal case, and all the prosecutors in the SAO knew that civil attorneys rarely went to trial, while a busy ASA might have as many as a dozen jury trials in a year. Ari was sitting at the counsel table next to a woman who occupied the "first chair," or lead attorney's position. An older man with white hair, likely the opposing attorney, was standing in the middle of the sketch with his hands outstretched, obviously the centerpiece of the drawing. The older attorney's arms partially blocked Ari's face, covering the lower half, so you couldn't see Ari's mouth, which, Mac thought, was symbolic. Shut this Fish jerk up.

Attorneys and prosecutors loved those courtroom sketches. They were mounted on the walls of every law firm and prosecutor's office like the safari triumphs of a big-game hunter, the taxidermy of a stellar courtroom career. It infuriated Ari that Mac had four courtroom sketches, each one featuring Mac front and center in the middle of a dramatic closing argument or cross-examination. These courtroom sketches, which newspapers and TV stations still used, were archaic, more appropriate for the Lizzie Borden trial or the Lindbergh kidnapping case. But Mac loved the sketches' cartoonish quality, like a comic strip of his legal résumé.

To the right of Ari's desk, there was an elaborate set of bookshelves covering the entire rear of the office, floor to ceiling, like a theatrical set of a "law office" designed for an audience. The books—lime-green volumes in towering rows for State of Maryland cases—now functioned merely as props for The Fish Show. None of these books had been opened in decades, since legal research by pulling dusty books from a library shelf had long since become obsolete, and all legal research was now done online, using search engines LexisNexis and Westlaw.

"I've already interviewed the kid personally this morning," Mac said. "She was traumatized in a horrendous way, and the Seneca County State's Attorney's Office needs to speak for her. That's going to be us." He was going to say, "That's going to be me," but at the last millisecond switched "me" to "us," thinking it would drill down better into Fischbein's soft ego.

"I didn't come out here to this backwoods country-ass place to lose big cases," Ari replied. "And now I have that dickhead Don Morris of the fucking *Seneca Journal* hounding me. And that blonde bitch from TV, that chick with the fake boobs. What's her name? And everyone else out here in the sticks trying to make me look like a stupid schmuck!" Mac noted the inverse use of "me" and "us."

Mac decided to use the word "you" as many times as possible in his reply, "You are not going to lose. Think of it this way: when you win, you will win a huge case with national attention. A little girl watched her mother kill her father. It doesn't get any bigger than that. You will be seen as a pioneer in the use of child witnesses, Ari. I'm talking *Dateline NBC* or *20/20* big. This is going to be like you landed on the Moon. This trial will be the Bay of Tranquility major."

Ari stopped talking and, as if he had been injected with a drug, paused to digest those intoxicating thoughts.

Jo said, "Well, how do we win? I mean, explain how Maryland law works with this situation. We're used to Federal law downtown in D.C., and our firm didn't handle these kinds of things. So, how can a child who is only nine years old testify?

What's the law on competency here? And I hear this child has some rare type of mental disability, right? We absolutely cannot lose this case. So, tell us, how do we become *pioneers* in the use of a child eyewitness? How do we get a conviction?"

CHAPTER 9

Thursday, December 20, 2018
11:01 a.m.

It was curious, Mac thought, how Jo's Southern accent cropped up occasionally. "Pioneers." She could take a three-syllable word and stretch it into five. Down at Emory Law School in Atlanta, Jo's Georgia accent was used to great effect. She garnered first place in the moot court tournament and, commensurate with that honor, received a dozen offers from local law firms. Her brilliant mind was housed in a trim yoga instructor's physique, always wrapped in perfectly tailored suits. She was not tall—maybe five-foot-four—but seemed larger because of her commanding presence. Her sky-blue eyes could either sparkle or flash, depending on the situation. Her perfectly manicured nails could morph into claws at any moment. Beware of cat. There was a hint of something rakish, like a courtesan, in Jo's smile. But now, here in Maryland, all these years later, her Southern dialect had segued into an

American accent of no discernable geography. She spoke with a generic Heartland lilt, a voice rooted in perhaps Oklahoma, or Iowa, or Indiana, but not her original tone of a Confederate soldier's young widow.

Jo flipped her red hair extensions over her shoulder and thrust her chin out towards Mac, signaling with her body language that she demanded a response to her question. She was wearing a tight white cotton dress shirt, with a string of faux pearls gracefully resting around her neck. The top three buttons were unfastened.

Without moving his head even a fraction, and using just his peripheral vision, Mac noticed how her cleavage emerged as she bent forward, the channel between the two cloth halves of her shirt parting and inviting attention, her bra silhouetted and outlined through the gauzy fabric. The aqueduct between her breasts glistened slightly with perspiration, or possibly body lotion; he detected a faint scent of coconut. He also observed the galaxies of freckles on her chest. He could not see her nipples, but he could deduce their shape—yes, the thought raced through his mind, by circumstantial evidence—by gauging the large convex bumps in the shirt's white fabric exactly where they should be, at the midpoint of each globe.

Ari, listening intently, leaned forward on his desk, and cupped his chin. He had long surrendered all discussions of legal novelties to his top deputy state's attorney. She would adroitly take over from here. He'd stick to media and PR and shaking hands and making announcements—the things he was good at, particularly how it all *looked*. Most importantly, how it all reflected on him.

Mac clarified, "We will win this case. So, under Maryland law, this is how the competency of a child, even a disabled child, works..." but he was interrupted by a beeping tone from the landline telephone intercom.

Lupe's voice came through. "Mr. Fischbein, sorry to interrupt you, sir, but I've got Don Morris of the *Journal* on the line. He wants a statement for a case called Van der Hook. Should I patch him in, sir?"

"Yes! I'll explain it all to him. Send it through right now."

CHAPTER 10

Thursday, December 20, 2018
2:31 p.m.

Marcel St. Croix glided his mint condition 1978 Datsun 240Z into a visitors' parking space outside the Seneca County Detention Facility. Before stepping out, he sat in the driver's seat and looked in the rearview mirror to check his appearance. His long hair was dark brown with streaks of grey and perfectly straight. It was the hair of a college student, not a 77-year-old top criminal defense attorney. He glanced down at the passenger seat, where his legal case file rested flat. There were six blank yellow legal pads in the file. A collection of assorted pens—his red, black, and blue weapons—were neatly clipped to the outside of the file, ready for immediate use, like bullets strung together in a bandolier.

He looked up into the mirror again and stared deeply and privately into his own brown eyes. He centered his paisley necktie perfectly below his Adam's apple. He needed one final moment to prepare himself before embracing someone else's crisis.

He visualized walking into the jail and negotiating the security check. No paperclips allowed. No cell phone. Driver's license for ID. He needed another moment to sit in the car and think. The bright sunlight glinted off the large copper bracelet on his right wrist.

He didn't know much about Rikki Van der Hook. Of course, everyone knew about her husband. He was famous, well, not famous like a celebrity, but MVH was a vast company with headquarters in Seneca County. He Googled Marten before leaving his law office and confirmed that, while MVH was not a global giant like Amazon, it was comparable to similar major corporate competitors, like Home Depot and John Deere.

So this woman stabbed him 50 times?

Rikki's sister, Lindy Hale, had called him at 4:00 a.m. earlier that morning. Marcel knew from many years of experience representing criminal defendants that when his phone rang at 4:00 a.m. someone had probably just been arrested or a disaster of some magnitude was unfolding for a client on the other end of the call. Desperation was his retail trade; desperate clients had made him wealthy and prominent. He was no MVH, but he was Marcel St. Croix, the most feared and successful criminal defense attorney in Seneca County. He had become addicted to the personal rewards that came with the territory: local fame, a big stage, and a lot of money to spend on flashy things to burnish his image. He liked winning; that was addictive too.

GAVEL TO GAVEL

By tomorrow morning, the news would break, and the *Seneca Journal* and the local TV stations would air coverage of the case, so it was crucial that Marcel get his message out preemptively. Perhaps he could poison the jury pool. Everything he knew about this new murder was hearsay. Supposedly, their daughter Mandy had witnessed the stabbing. Marcel worried the police had a significant head start.

I pray they didn't interview Rikki after arresting her. I hope she was smart enough to invoke her right to remain silent. They're probably recording the little girl right now. Oh, Lord. He never wanted his clients talking. That was never helpful. After speaking with Lindy again over breakfast, he arranged for his courier to snatch the $125,000 retainer fee once it was ready. Marcel charged 25 percent of his fee up front and always required a cashier's check. Then he called Warden Stempkowski, who, thankfully, had notified the corrections officer at the entrance of the jail to accommodate Marcel's request for a private interview room, one of those designed solely for attorney/client meetings.

He took one long last look at himself in the rearview mirror and took a deep breath to steel himself.

For just a fleeting instant, his mind wandered. He saw the flickering image of his father's face. The image froze in his thoughts. His father, Alexandre St. Croix, he of mixed Mi'kmaq and Irish blood, looked at Marcel from some impossibly distant, imaginary place. The jet-black hair, the craggy, sunburned skin, the intelligence in the deep-set squinting eyes, and the strong defiance. All of those qualities had traveled down a path of mysterious genetic heritage, and, when Marcel looked at his reflection, he saw his ancestors looking back.

Alexandre St. Croix's father, Henry—going one generation even further back—had survived the shipwreck of the *Carricks*, an Irish coffin ship carrying 148 desperate immigrants fleeing the Great Potato Famine of 1847. The rickety, overcrowded *Carricks* crossed the Atlantic, steeped in typhus and dysentery, and, within sight of Canadian land, was caught in an unexpectedly fierce gale and driven into the sandy shoals, shattering into splinters just off the coast of Gaspé, Quebec.

One hundred twenty Irish men, women, and children drowned. Their bodies, along with inestimable wooden planks and shipwreck detritus, floated to the shore with the morning tide.

Henry, just a boy, washed up unconscious on the beach. He was taken in by an elderly and childless local couple, Mr. and Mrs. St. Croix, who helped him adapt, grow strong, and thrive. He learned a trade as a tanner, working leather into elaborate saddles, bridles, and belts. Bowing to social pressure, Henry became Henri, and learned French and the ways of the hearty Québécois people. At 17, he fell in love with a young Mi'kmaq woman named Naguset, and, two generations later, when Marcel looked at his reflection, he believed his own tenacity, will to survive, and charisma flowed from Henri and Naguset in some impossible-to-prove way.

Marcel's father, Alexandre, drifted south, first to Quebec City and then, further down the St. Lawrence, to the sprawling bilingual metropolis of Montreal to attend McGill

University. From there, Alexandre immigrated to Vermont, where Marcel was born.

Marcel excelled academically, both in college and law school. The complexity of human emotions inherent in criminal law cases instinctively appealed to him, so, after a short stint at the Bureau of Indian Affairs in Washington, D.C., he joined a small suburban private criminal defense firm in Seneca County, Maryland. Soon, Marcel opened his own solo law firm. His success exceeded his expectations, as his innate courage, smooth style, and tactical genius melded together to create a formidable courtroom advocate.

And now, nearly 50 years later, he was in the parking lot of the Seneca County Correctional Facility about to meet a woman charged with murder. Such unpredictability in life, he concluded. Like getting thrown in stormy ocean waves and floating to a sandy beach rather than onto the rocks.

He carefully exited his vintage sports car. It seemed to be more difficult each year to get in and out. At 77, he knew his best jury trials were behind him, but all of that accumulated experience, gravitas, and reputation clearly offset his imperceptibly diminishing power of voice and courtroom dynamism. Yes, it was his reputation—no, it was his image—that was now the key. Image was more important than any actual courtroom skills. The judges loved his towering sense of logic, and the young prosecutors feared his ability to sway a jury. Plus, in almost all of his cases now, the ASAs offered excellent plea offers just to avoid the possibility of losing, so the last decade of his career had been mostly deal making instead of persuasive jury oration and courtroom elegance.

Marcel closed the car door, turned, and walked in the icy December air to the entrance of the jail. *Christmas is next week. Perhaps I can get this Van der Hook lady out of jail and give her an early Christmas present at her bond review hearing tomorrow?*

He walked up to the counter. A young corrections officer looked up, adjusted her thick eyeglasses and said, "Can I help you, sir?"

CHAPTER 11

Thursday, December 20, 2018
3:01 p.m.

"Yes, my name is Marcel St. Croix, and I have a pre-arranged appointment for a professional visit at 3:00. I believe Warden Stempkowski has called down to facilitate things so I can interview my client?"

"Oh, yes, sir," she said, turning to her left and picking up a yellow sticky note from the desk. "What's his name again?"

"It's a she. My client is a female inmate. Her name is Van der Hook. It's spelled like three separate words: Van, der, Hook."

The jail guard reached behind her to a clipboard thick with dozens of printed pages. It was a roster of the inmates. She flipped to the very back of the pages and said, "We only have a few females. They're listed in alphabetical order. Yes, here she is, the very last name: Van der Hook."

"Excellent. Thank you."

"OK, I'll radio her down. You can go to Interview Room Four," she said, gesturing towards the far corner of the lobby, beyond the security station.

The corrections officer took off her thick glasses and looked up at Marcel.

Those glasses look just like the ones Buddy Holly used to wear. What am I thinking? No one even knows who Buddy Holly is anymore, especially this girl.

"Thank you, ma'am," Marcel replied with a kindly tone, smiling. He stepped through the rectangular frame of the metal detector. He raised his arms so she could wave a handheld wand over his front and back.

The wand made a crisp beeping noise, and she said, "Sir, please take your keys and anything else you have out of your pockets and place them in here," pointing to a blue plastic container which looked like the type of basket a cheap restaurant might serve fried chicken in.

"Oh, yes. Sorry," Marcel said, using just a fraction of his prodigious charm. Charm and polite manners were effective tools for a criminal defense attorney. "Of course, yes, ma'am. At least I remembered to leave my cell phone back in the car. That's it. My pockets are empty."

She looked into his eyes longer than necessary. She then waved the wand again, and it was silent.

"Can you please sign the Visitor's Log, Mr. St. Croix?"

He signed, tilted his head to make direct eye contact, and said, with practiced sincerity, "Thank you again."

She slipped her heavy glasses back on and studied his signature, monitoring the sign-in process.

"That's how you spell it? With an X?"

"Yes. It's a French name. The X is silent. But, now that I'm an old man, let me tell you something. I've always observed that silence sometimes attracts more attention than any words said out loud."

"Oh, yes, I know what you mean," she said, clueless to his meaning. She took off her glasses again. "If there is anything else I can do to help you, just let me know. Oh, and sir, you aren't old!"

"You have been very kind."

Marcel walked across the lobby towards the interview room. As he stepped down the hallway, he saw a cleaning crew's abandoned push cart. He stopped and tore off several sheets from a roll of paper towels balanced upright in the cart. He opened the door.

Across from him, seated in an orange plastic chair behind a wide conference room table, sat Rikki Van der Hook.

She was wearing an olive-green jump suit several sizes too large for her tiny frame. She had placed her thin arms inside the sleeves for warmth, so, at first glance, she appeared armless, like a sparrow in a nest, burrowing for safety.

As Marcel entered the room, Rikki looked up and said, "It's about fucking time you got here! I've been locked up all day!"

Marcel took a deep breath, his chest rising. Before sitting down, he quickly swiped the paper towels across the chair and crumpled them into a ball. He tossed the clump into a small metal trash can in the corner and sat opposite her.

Without prompting, Rikki asserted, "First of all, I killed the motherfucker, and he deserved it! I've wanted to kill his ass for years, and finally, I've done it."

"Wait! Don't say anything else about what happened! Please!"

"Fuck that!" Rikki counterattacked. "I'll say whatever the hell I want! You're my lawyer, and I'm paying you some ridiculous king's ransom of a fee, so I'll say whatever the fuck I want. You got that?"

Marcel notified her, "Please, you may put me in a compromised position if…"

Rikki could not contain herself. Like a soda can fizzing up, her voice started foaming over, spilling and spraying words uncontrollably.

CHAPTER 12

Thursday, December 20, 2018
4:26 p.m.

Judge Marcia Harajuku was born in Katsura, a prosperous neighborhood outside of Kyoto. When she was six years old, her father, a mostly silent, austere man, immigrated to Washington, D.C. with his family to accept a minor position in the Embassy of Japan. Her memories of her birthplace—her grandmother's onsen with the steaming hot tub, the local pachinko parlor with the rattling pinball machines—those memories were faded now, like smoke evaporating into air, unseen but with a lingering scent. Not speaking any English, she entered elementary school in Seneca County, a total stranger to American culture and language. Her teachers noted her quick mind and how she learned exponentially, and within a few months, her English was conversational and completely unaccented. Her schoolteachers would not have been surprised that Marcia

Harajuku would one day become the first Asian-American Circuit Court judge in Seneca County history.

"Anything unusual on the bond review docket tomorrow?" she called out towards her antechamber where her young law clerk, also an Asian-American young woman, Phoebe Chao, sat at a cluttered desk stacked high with new case files.

"Um, I'm just flipping through the stack now, Judge. Looks pretty average for a Thursday, but there is a first-degree murder case..." Phoebe replied.

"Really? Can you bring in that file, please?"

Judge Harajuku had seen virtually every type of criminal case, going back to her early years as a prosecutor, as well as during her time as a defense attorney, before she was appointed to the District Court by the Governor of Maryland. She had been elevated to the Circuit Court when she was only 32 years old, and now she was an established judge, known for her quick wit and, also, her impatience. She did not suffer fools gladly.

Phoebe swept her long, inky hair behind her head, trapping it in an elastic band. She opened the grassy-green cardboard cover and reached for the twin metal prongs on the inside. Adroitly, she bent the metal prongs upward, claw-like, to receive the inevitable court filings, police reports, and reams of anticipated miscellaneous paperwork that comprised a criminal case. Papers, lots of papers—the complexity, mystery and gravity of a criminal case—all reduced to a scattered stack of papers.

"Hang on, Judge, just let me punch in the Statement of Charges, and there is also a Pretrial Services Unit Report, too. One sec."

GAVEL TO GAVEL

Phoebe reached down, pulled open her bottom desk drawer, lifted out the cumbersome metal two-hole punch, slid the relevant papers ominously under the razor-sharp puncher, and, with this miniature guillotine, slammed it down with a jolt, ejecting two small twin circular paper cutouts where perforations now existed.

"Coming... the case is called *State v. Van der Hook*," pronouncing the "v." as "vee," not "versus."

Judge Harajuku sat behind a majestically large oak desk which had almost nothing on it. She preferred an organized desk totally free of clutter. Her office was called her "chambers," since she was entitled to all the archaic accoutrements of justice. She loved those black robes, which made her feel like a high priestess. Up high on her throne-like seat in the courtroom, she commanded deference. Every day was punctuated with salutations and honorifics: "Your Honor" and "Judge." Each time she heard those words, she felt a slight tremor of pride, which gently stroked her ego.

Her chambers were larger than most two-bedroom condos in the Courthouse Square, and, from her large picture windows, she had a commanding view of the old Colonial Courthouse. On her walls, she had dozens of assorted framed awards, laminated yellowing newspaper articles praising her for past accomplishments, and photographs depicting her standing next to a variety of officials and celebrities. Behind her desk was a photograph of her stiffly shaking hands with the Governor of Maryland. Another photo, with Justice Ruth Bader Ginsburg, hung by the door. Her favorite, the one of her wearing plaid shorts and a red college baseball cap standing next to Tiger Woods, was upright on the coffee table. The adjacent diplomas and awards said things like, "University of Maryland School of Law Moot Court Tournament—1st Place," and "Seneca County State's Attorney's Office Merit Award," and "Who's Who of Maryland Judiciary."

She took great pride in a framed newspaper article from her college days, a faded edition of the "Terp Times," declaring, "MD COLLEGE GIRL WINS REGIONAL CHESS TOURNEY." She had a chessboard set up and displayed on a side table. It was not an antique or fancy set, but a regulation competition set with the familiar oversized chess pieces on top of a green-and-tan roll-up mat. It was the chess set she had used to win the college tournament, which, for her alone, held a mystical symbolism. It reminded her of her innate combat ferocity, and, although she would not admit it, she enjoyed how it warned any cocky attorney or colleague who might underestimate her. For Judge Marcia Harajuku, chess had always been a great equalizer: with her intuitive logic, keen sense of strategy and tactics, and the ability to think several moves ahead, even a tiny girl could besiege castles, capture bishops and knights, and even assassinate kings and queens.

She proudly glanced at the awards and other symbols of recognition as the landmarks of her academic and professional career with pride. First this, first that. First female Asian-American Assistant State's Attorney. A wall of precedent that reminded her daily how unexpectedly her journey from Katsura had unfurled. She noted, of course, how slender and youthful she looked in those old photos. Now, she had surrendered to a mostly sedentary life, and she was constantly reminded of her physical inactivity by the daily questions from courthouse staff, "Judge, when are you sitting today?" Yes, she sat a lot now.

She reached up to pat her hair to gauge the symmetry of her hairstyle, a spherical globe of tight curls. Judge Harajuku, who naturally had perfectly straight black hair, like an Edo-era geisha, defied her Asian heritage by curling her hair, with some labor, into a tight dome that encircled her head. Once, years earlier, a young man in college, also Asian, had asked her, "Why do you curl your hair into an 'American' style?" He followed that volley with another query, "And why do you call yourself Marcia when your Japanese given name is Ryoko?" She stopped dating Asians after that, preferring not to have her fidelity to her ethnicity questioned.

Back then, she felt dual pressures and was unsure where she truly belonged. She had one foot firmly trapped in a Japanese household with strict traditions, and one foot free in America, with all the flashing lights, loud noises, and aggression. It became even more confusing when her parents insisted she speak only Japanese inside the home. Her mother made little effort to learn English, using precocious little Ryoko to translate mundane transactions at Target and Costco. Even all these years later, her mother, now tiny and grey, spoke very little English. When Judge Harajuku took her oath in the Ceremonial Courtroom, a Japanese interpreter sat next to her mother, translating every word of her Investiture.

Back in her schoolgirl days, Ryoko was the only girl from Japan. Older boys made fun of her name, teasing her about being married to John Lennon and breaking up the Beatles, which, of course, meant absolutely nothing to her. Still, she was determined to assimilate, to become an American, and TV was her portal to an endless world of Western culture, each commercial, movie, and sitcom teaching her more and more. Since her parents forbade watching television in the evenings, Ryoko raced home after school to scour several hours of reruns and old movies before her parents came home. One day, after watching *The Brady Bunch*, Ryoko decided henceforth she would be "Marcia," after her favorite character. Each afternoon, she would sit and watch reruns, mesmerized by the antics of this wholesome, blond, All-American suburban family. In tiny Ryoko's mind, that was what she wanted to be: American. In August, when school commenced for fifth grade, she was Marcia Harajuku. She couldn't change Harajuku, but that was OK. Ryoko was no more.

"*State v. Van der Hook*, that name sounds vaguely familiar," she said to Phoebe.

"It says the Defendant's first name is Rikki. I'm guessing that's a woman, but you never know. And the Commissioner is holding him or her on a No Bond status."

"It's a first-degree murder. So, that's not unusual. I'll take a look at the SOC and the PTSU Report, but it doesn't get any more serious than first-degree."

"Should I call the Assignment Office and see when they're setting the 4-215 Scheduling Conference, Judge?"

"Yes, thanks. That's helpful, Phoebe, and ask AO to notify the attorneys on the case. I see a Line of Appearance listed for Marcel St. Croix. This should be fun."

Phoebe spun her entire body towards the door, with perhaps a little more flair than was necessary, her long ponytail whipping a full 180 degrees as she stepped into her small law clerk's office.

Judge Harajuku flipped open the file. The first page was the Statement of Charges authored by the arresting police officers.

First-degree murder... domestic violence... kitchen knife.

"Phoebe, can you pull the Maryland Common Jury Instructions for homicide, please?"

Judge Harajuku leaned back and read, "An eyewitness, Amanda Van der Hook, the deceased's minor child, age nine, gave the I/O a full statement." She flipped through all the pages in the file, trying to find something important. She found it: a second Line of Appearance, this one with the name "William MacIntyre" printed as the designated Assistant State's Attorney in charge of the prosecution.

Oh, Mac. What have you got up your sleeve this time?

CHAPTER 13

Thursday, December 20, 2018
4:54 p.m.

By the time Mac got back to his office, the sun was setting. *Damn, the days are getting short. It's almost night already.*

He threw his jacket on the small couch beside his desk and sat in his swivel chair. The light on his desk telephone was blinking. He ignored the backlog of voicemails, leaned back, and took a deep breath.

The sun had descended halfway below the horizon. Dying beams came through the window and reflected off one of his framed newspaper articles from a decade ago. The article was from the *Seneca Journal*, a profile of him, called "The Gentle Giant." Mac noticed how, at sunset, the angle of the sunbeams changed ever so slightly with each passing day of the year, like a miniature Stonehenge, his office's own astronomical calendar. In June, on the summer solstice, the sun missed "The Gentle Giant" entirely.

Mac looked around. He took a moment to take an inventory of his career and his life.

On the far wall, he admired the horizontal display of the four courtroom sketches Ari Fischbein hated so much. Turning, he glanced at the wall over the couch, where he noticed the framed posters of Marlon Brando in a tuxedo, Kenneth Branagh holding a skull, and a teenage Luka Doncic in his forest green Slovenija National team jersey. His eyes rotated around the room and then settled on "The Gentle Giant" article again. Ari hated that framed newspaper article even more than Mac's courtroom sketches. Faded now from years of sunlight, the sub-headline was still legible: "Mac MacIntyre, Seneca's Top Homicide Prosecutor." Ari would sneer and say, sarcastically, "Oh, the 'Giant?'" Knowing it would annoy The Fish even more, Mac stood as tall as he could.

Mac examined the article's photograph to see if it, too, had faded further over time. Once, the photo had accurately depicted the color of Mac's bright, copper-colored red hair. Now, sunlight and time had muted the hue to a dull, brownish rust, like dried blood. Genetics. Both his old Scottish grandfather Hamish, who was uncreatively nicknamed "Red," and his father also had the same thick copper mop on top of their heads. Now, however, Mac kept his hair short, sometimes quite short, to deemphasize it. He wanted jurors listening to his prosecutorial words and following his eyes, and not distracted by the color of his hair.

He pulled out his cell phone and dialed the Seneca County Animal Rescue Center.

"Hey, Judie. This is Mac MacIntyre. How are you?"

"Oh, Mr. MacIntyre, good evening. Are you coming over tonight to volunteer? We got some strays in this afternoon."

"No, I'm sorry. Something important came up at work. But I promise I will be there early Saturday morning like always."

"Oh, it's no problem. Thanks for letting us know."

"Sure. Well, I'll see you then. Take care."

Mac grabbed his coat and walked down the hallway towards the employee coffee room. Holiday decorations were unenthusiastically draped across the refrigerator. Ari had declared that, this year, it was a "Holiday" and not "Christmas." Mac opened the fridge and pulled out the rectangular aluminum foil baking pan, which had been dropped off for him at the front desk with a handwritten note, "For Mr. MacIntyre—Thank you, Mrs. Rakash Patel."

The pan was heavy, so Mac used both hands to extricate it from the fridge. He lifted the corner of the metallic covering and was immediately rewarded with a gust of curry, cinnamon, and coriander. Chicken curry and rice.

Mac took the container home, scooped the contents into a ceramic serving dish, heated four portions in his microwave, and ate the whole thing.

Just before 9:00 p.m., fully fortified, he left his apartment and headed out.

CHAPTER 14

Thursday, December 20, 2018
6:52 p.m.

Zaria Valentina stepped out of the Public Defender's Office, walked down the hall, entered a waiting elevator, and pressed "T." No one knew what "T" stood for. Reaching the ground floor of the Seneca County Judicial Center (was that "T" for "terrace?"), she zipped up her Patagonia down jacket and headed towards the exit. The glass door was grimy with constellations of fingerprints and smudges. She loathed touching it. Using her back to lean against the door, she pried it open, feeling the cold December air splash against the nape of her neck. She needed to breathe. She couldn't stand tight places. Small rooms, elevators, the back seat of a taxi—all confined spaces caused waves of crippling claustrophobia to close in on her, making her feel like an animal with a paw caught in a steel trap.

She glanced at her watch. It was almost 7:00 p.m. The PD's Office was quiet now, not the usual chaotic place with sounds like a street bazaar. Zaria's days reverberated with loud voices negotiating things, or laughing or shouting, exclamations of all types. The human sounds were a whirlpool of American noise to Zaria's European ears.

She turned the corner and lit up a Salem Light. Now that the workday was done, she walked home, visualizing the next three inevitable events in her life: a big bowl of oatmeal with granola, the safe refuge of a hot bath, and the escape of her dreams in bed. She would leave all the lights on—she couldn't fall asleep unless every inch of her apartment was brightly lit. Her earbuds would drown out the world. Wrapping herself tightly with the unzipped sleeping bag she used as a comforter, she'd look at her phone, scrolling through travel websites, basking in the beauty of inaccessible foreign places. She'd imagine herself far away from the self-imposed misery of her bland apartment and her blunt reality. She'd look at website photos of places she'd never go and lie in bed until she fell asleep, dreaming of a life she would never experience. She'd imagine Bondi Beach, with muscular, blond lifeguards rushing out to save her from drowning in the Australian ocean. In a dream, she'd stroll through the Englischer Garten in Munich, and sit with a tableful of laughing German students, drinking Löwenbräu from enormous, two-handled, frothy beer steins. She'd float in a canal boat down the Prinsengracht in Amsterdam, watching the tiny townhouses with step-gabled roofs drift by. If she was lucky, her dreams would soothe her, and another day would be done.

She had downloaded dozens of CDs on her cell phone with environmental sounds of nature—waterfalls, waves rolling onto the shore, thunderstorms. Ah, the relaxing sound of flowing water. Swishing, gurgling, dripping. It was the only way she could stay asleep, distancing herself from the fear. Fear of something—something more sinister than just dark tight claustrophobic spaces—but she couldn't identify exactly what it was.

I will wake up and start this daily cycle again, like a swimmer caught in a paralyzing undertow, pulling and pulling, and getting nowhere. I'm 36 and should feel settled by now. Why am I so unhappy?

She stopped at the front door to her apartment building, took a final drag on her cigarette, and then dropped it on the sidewalk by her Nordstrom Rack cowboy boots. She looked down at the sparkly concrete and saw a dozen crushed cigarette butt carcasses by her feet. She tried to push the thoughts of her job out of her mind.

Yes, it was stressful work, translating for all these grieving and distraught family members of public defender clients—screaming, crying, weeping. It never became routine. The sounds of waterfalls and rainstorms temporarily washed away the pain and agony of these broken lives. There was a giant supply of Kleenex boxes in the storage closet right outside her office. Clients, defendants, respondents, and petitioners ceased having actual names and just became an endless rotation of tragedy. Like waves, the cases always kept coming.

She was a courtroom interpreter, certified to translate in four languages. Her American colleagues—the attorneys and staff in the PD's Office—were amazed at her innate linguistic talent. She was born in Yugoslavia, in the northern region of

Slovenia, in the shadow of the Julian Alps. Her mother had Italian roots, and her father, Vladimir, was Croatian. By the age of six, Zaria could speak Italian, Croatian and Slovenian fluently. Once in school, she quickly absorbed her English lessons.

An American refugee program run by exiled former Yugoslavians in Washington, D.C. sponsored her family's immigration application to enter the United States. Awarded free housing in Seneca County, Zaria and her family shared a townhouse with two other exiled international families, one from El Salvador and one from Guatemala.

Within a few years, her Spanish became fluent too. Upon graduation from high school, she easily passed her oral examinations to become a courtroom interpreter in English, Italian, Croatian and Spanish. There wasn't much need for Slovenian.

At work, however, she was quiet, efficient, and shy. Outside of interpreting, she was mostly silent, which was paradoxical since they had hired her because of her ability to translate and speak for others. That was easy, Zaria thought, speaking for other people. But she struggled to think of things to say for herself. The attorneys in the office were witty and never stopped talking, but when she tried to converse, she felt that imaginary undertow pulling her down under the crashing waves. Conversation made her feel as if she might drown.

Once, she turned the corner at the PD's Office and overheard two of the female attorneys gossiping about her. One of them, an aggressive one named Ashley, had her back turned, and, before she noticed Zaria, she said, "She's so inarticulate, you know who I mean? That tall, skinny Communist one." Zaria turned and bolted in the other direction.

While women seemed to be jealous of her, she got positive attention from men because of her striking looks. She was tall, five-foot-eleven and slender, but muscular, some might say wiry. Her skin was pale, and her hair was long and dark brown, and sometimes she dyed it black, black as a Slovenian midnight. She was drawn to a Goth look, but wasn't sure why. Her clothing choices leaned towards dark and somber. She had been told many times by both men and women that the color of her eyes was unique, a tone of such light feline blue they seemed almost grey. Those eyes could study a room subtly, like sonar scanned the depths of the ocean, and she would notice some man staring at her, transfixed. Zaria wore sunglasses all the time when not indoors and had recently started wearing reading glasses in the office, just to avoid having to make eye contact with people. She did not go on dates, and never went to a restaurant or bar alone, where, inevitably, men would approach her to tell her what beautiful eyes she had, and other stupid American-sounding prefabrications and pickup lines.

She exhaled again, reached into her coat for her keys, and said to herself, "*Sama sen in zelo prestrasena.*" Her brain unconsciously translated into English: "I'm all alone and so scared."

Suddenly, a text came through, her phone buzzing like a trapped housefly in her coat pocket. She pulled her phone out and glanced at the screen. Immediately, a warm rush emanated from deep inside, radiating outward, relaxing her. It shocked her how a simple text popping up on her screen could create a swell of physical feelings to rush over her. The feelings were incongruous: stimulating, like an adrenaline rush, but mixed with a soothing relaxant. The mix was like a junkie's cravings.

It was the one thing that made her feel confident and alive. She looked back down at the text. It said:

> IM COMING OVER AT 9. I NEED YOU SO
> BADLY. GET EVERYTHING READY, MAC.

CHAPTER 15

Thursday, December 20, 2018
8:56 p.m.

Mac parked his Jeep two blocks from Zaria's apartment in the parking lot of a strip mall outside a deserted Mr. Smoothie store. Huge gentle snowflakes were dropping from the sky, falling like an endless series of paper plates. All the shops—a Pancake House, a budget mattress store, and a vape shop—were closed for the night. He crossed the parking lot and used his key fob to enter her apartment complex. When he reached the fifth floor, he stepped out and walked the familiar path to Apartment #505. He knocked, although he knew there would be no answer. The door was unlocked. He went inside.

She was ready. The room was totally dark except for a faint ambient red light coming from somewhere—either the dishwasher or the coffeemaker in the kitchen. The smoky scent of a recently extinguished candle hovered in the air. The aroma of fir trees gently spiced the air in deference to Christmas.

It was a small studio apartment, with the main room doubling as a bedroom. There was a bathroom to the left and a tiny, functional kitchen to the right. He could see Zaria's silhouette as she sat in an oversized armchair which had been pulled to the center of the main room. Mac had never seen the room in full daylight, but, from previous nighttime visits, all of its details were clear in his mind, like a photograph frozen in time.

Thin slashes of diagonal light from the streetlamps outside sliced through the horizontal openings of the Venetian blinds on the twin windows behind her, framing her slender body like a halo. Mac's eyes adjusted to the darkness. The large, framed poster on the wall to his right depicted a blocky geometric shape. It was the outline of a fortress. She had told him the name once, and he remembered. Predjama Castle, outside Ljubljana, majestically tucked into a rocky cliff crevice.

Mac could see her sitting upright in the chair. She was not wearing any clothes. Four neckties, like streamers, splayed outward, one on each wrist and one around each ankle.

She was perfectly still, and Mac could hear her breathing rapidly.

He took two steps into the kitchen area and reached for a small, fluted glass. Yes, it was exactly where it always was, on the counter next to the sink. The glass, the shape of an inverted tulip, was filled with several ounces of Dutch jenever. The clear liquid was poured over crushed ice. He grabbed the glass from above with his extended fingers, like an owl clawing a field mouse. He shifted his prey from his right hand to his left, rattled the ice in a swirling motion, and lifted the glass to his lips. He drank half. The jenever simultaneously burned and froze his throat in a contradictory mix of pain and pleasure.

"*Hvala vam*," said Mac, softly, whispering. "Thank you."

Zaria remained seated, then shifted herself to the edge of the armchair and uncrossed her legs.

"Shhh. Do not talk," she said, barely audible.

Zaria then stood to her full height and looked intently at Mac. He saw a slight reflection of light in the whites of her eyes. She turned and faced the armchair and knelt down on the soft cushioning, arching her back, with her arms dangling down towards the floor on either side of the armchair's wings.

Mac took off his corduroy blazer and dropped it to the floor. He stepped out of his Timberland boots, shucked off both socks, and pulled his grey Champion T-shirt over his head. He stepped forward, knelt down, and secured Zaria's wrists to the two back legs of the armchair. Then, he tied her ankles to the front two legs, binding her in a kneeling position on the chair. Zaria arched her back even more, expectantly, and Mac noticed the rhythm of her breathing increasing in tempo.

He unbuckled his leather belt, and, in one motion, unzipped his jeans, and dropped them to the floor. With his foot, he slid the nest of balled-up jeans to the side to accompany his discarded T-shirt, socks, and boots.

He stepped up to the armchair and grabbed both of her hips, gripping her taut muscles. They were both ready. There was no need to wait. He thrust himself deeply into her, repeatedly, strongly, then slowly, then very slowly, then furiously, until he could hold back no longer.

Zaria rocked athletically backwards to meet his thrusts, her back glistening with sweat. As he came to his zenith, she did as well. At exactly the same time.

Mac lay exhausted on top of her back for several minutes, basking in the warm sensations, as his heart rate slowly returned from his final, delirious sprint to a normal pace. Her skin was slippery. He could feel his chest sliding through the wetness. After several moments of soaking in their mutual pleasure, Mac rose. He untied her ankles first, then her wrists. Exhausted, Zaria turned around and then slumped back into the chair. Mac pulled up his jeans, but remained shirtless and barefoot. She reached to the side table and drew her silk kimono to her lap, lifted up a sleeve, and adroitly slipped her arm through. Then she repeated the motion, with both of her long slender arms floating through the shadowy light like a dancer's *pas de deux*.

Zaria said with a tone of satisfaction, "Ah, thank you, sir. You are so good to me."

"*Hvala vam*," repeated Mac. He reached for the glass and tipped the remaining mixture of jenever and melted ice down his throat.

"Teach me the Slovenian word for addiction, Z."

"*Dipendenza.*"

Before he could repeat it, she added, "That's Italian. You'll never be able to pronounce the Slovenian word."

He smiled, crossed the room, and kissed her again, this time with less hunger and more affection.

Mac said, "You are my *dipendenza*."

Zaria felt a new wave of heat freshly radiate from deep inside her chest. Her grey eyes were wide, and the left corner of her mouth curved slightly upward, forming a crooked smile. Mac once again had satiated her in every way. She'd pulled back her own waves of pleasure until they'd crashed simultaneously on the shore at just the right time, feeling him swell larger at the exact point of his explosion.

But she was not just satisfied physically. She was satisfied somewhere else, somewhere she couldn't identify—somewhere in her *soul*. These intersections of ferocity, these shared passions, momentarily pushed away the demons which constantly tortured her. Mac was her transitory relief. She didn't want a "relationship" or a boyfriend. That was far too complicated. He didn't want a girlfriend, and he certainly was too distracted to follow all the unwritten rules of courtship. But he wanted Zaria. And Zaria couldn't live without him.

"I've got to go, Z. Big case just starting. Can you do me a big favor? I have a new homicide case. I know the Public Defenders rotate murder trials in your office. Do you know which PD is up next to take it? I have a feeling this case is going to end up with the PD's office. Just a hunch."

"Should be Santiago—Santiago Garcia."

"Ah, little Santi! One of my favorite PDs. Can you keep an eye on him for me?"

Zaria did not reply, but she nodded. She would do anything for him.

Mac stepped towards her and hugged her tightly. He could feel her rising chest, and he kissed her again, pressing his mouth delicately on her lips. He then haphazardly finished dressing, counted his possessions to make sure none of them had dropped: his keys, his wallet, his cell phone.

He stepped into the hallway, shutting the door quietly behind him, then took the elevator downstairs. He walked out into the brisk December night. He was not cold at all. As he strolled towards his Jeep, the word "symbiotic" came to mind, and he searched his endless mental catalogue of Shakespearean quotes for something using that word. He couldn't find one.

Zaria slept for 10 hours.

CHAPTER 16

Friday, December 21, 2018
8:00 a.m.

Maryland Edition

WIFE CHARGED IN VAN DER HOOK MURDER, YOUNG DAUGHTER SOLE EYEWITNESS

Newly Elected Top Prosecutor Fischbein Leads Way

By Don Morris — Seneca Journal

Seneca County State's Attorney Ari F. Fischbein (D) announced the arrest of a Maryland woman, Rikki Michele Van der Hook, who is charged with first-degree murder in the slaying death of her husband Marten Van der Hook, the prominent Dutch-American industrialist and CEO of MVH Enterprises, a Seneca County-based corporation known for the production of stand-up lawn mowers, tractors, and other patented commercial machinery.

The 34-year-old Fischbein claimed he was "thinking outside the box" by spearheading the case against Ms. Van der Hook, the 48-year-old Defendant, who is currently incarcerated at the Seneca County Correctional Facility in Riverside, MD. Judge Marcia Harajuku of the Seneca County Circuit Court set a Bond Hearing for today at 10:00 a.m.

Fischbein, who challenged the status quo during last year's election cycle, noted the case against Ms. Van der Hook reflects his personal dedication to "do whatever it takes to protect our children." Court filings allege that Van der Hook stabbed her husband multiple times in the presence of her daughter, aged 9, who allegedly witnessed the homicide. The *Seneca Journal* does not identify victims or witnesses in cases of juveniles.

Fischbein noted, "My intent is to pioneer how these types of cases, ones involving children as witnesses, are prosecuted in Maryland," but declined to specify exactly what makes this prosecution new or unique, citing ethical concerns, "We will not try this case in the press."

A copy of the Application for Statement of Charges obtained by the *Seneca Journal* charges the Defendant with the intentional homicide of her husband, resulting in a lead charge of first-degree murder, a crime which requires premeditation, planning, or deliberation.

Well-known defense attorney, Marcel St. Croix, is listed in court documents as Ms. Van der Hook's attorney. St. Croix said, "Based upon our own investigation, we look forward to clearing Ms. Van der Hook's name. We are seeking pretrial home detention and will request that Ms. Van der Hook be released on bond immediately. This is a woefully weak case."

When reached for a response, Fischbein commented, "We'll see who's weak," but did not expound further.

Newcomer Fischbein narrowly defeated former long-time State's Attorney Robert Gill in the Democratic primary. During the campaign, Fischbein raised issues of sexual harassment in the Gill administration and controversially released emails to the media that he had obtained from a former first-year prosecutor, Jennifer Princeton. Former Assistant State's Attorney Princeton alleged SA Gill had pressured her into a sexual relationship. Fischbein was unopposed in the general election, becoming the youngest State's Attorney in Seneca County since the Civil War. When asked to comment, Gill stated, "This looks like another publicity grab by Ari Fischbein to me."

Veteran Senior Assistant State's Attorney, William MacIntyre, is listed as the prosecuting attorney of record.

A trial is set for August of next year.

CHAPTER 17

Friday, December 21, 2018
9:59 a.m.

Mac stood respectfully behind the prosecution table as Judge Harajuku said flatly, in a businesslike tone, "Call the case please, Ms. Chao."

Phoebe rose from her clerk's chair next to the witness stand.

"Calling *State of Maryland vs. Rikki Van der Hook*, Case number 3016090345-C."

The Seneca County Judicial Center had been built in 1972 and reflected the monolithic, concrete architecture of the time. The courtrooms were circular instead of squared off like a proscenium stage. Everyone who litigated cases in Seneca County—attorneys, judges, and witnesses—hated that circular design. The round shape of the room meant that no matter where someone stood, they blocked someone else's view. There was a large umbrella-shaped dome-like apparatus hanging from the ceiling in the exact center of the courtroom. Ostensibly to enhance acoustics, instead of amplifying voices, the dome had the unintentionally humorous effect of noticeably increasing the volume of an attorney's voice if they spoke from the center of the room. Inexperienced attorneys, as they moved across the courtroom pontificating, might sound silly—"Ladies and Gentlemen *of the* jury…"

The carpeting was a tired, faded orange. Countless shoes had worn clear paths, like walking trails, which connected the most frequently used locations in the room: from the attorneys' tables to the witness stand, and to and from where "bench conferences" with the judge were held. These trails were accompanied by a polka-dot pattern in the carpet where innumerable coffee cups had been spilled. There was an area which resembled an audience in a theatre. It was called the "gallery." There were four doors radiating off the circular courtroom like spokes on a wheel: one to the main hallway down an aisle through the gallery; one to a small jury room; one to the judge's chambers; and one to a secure area called "lockup," where prisoners were escorted by Sheriff's Deputies in and out. In lockup, there was a back elevator that went down to a larger jail area in the building's basement. There were no windows in the entire space.

Marcel St. Croix sat in the last row of the gallery with Lindy next to him. He glanced at his oversized Tissot Chrono XL Classic wristwatch. Its shape and vulgarity balanced the copper bracelet, which was approximately the same size, on his other wrist. Mac glanced at his own watch and noted it was exactly 10:00 a.m. He was well aware of Judge Harajuku's reputation for precise punctuality.

The room's acoustics let Mac hear Marcel speaking to Lindy. Marcel said, "Stay here. I may need you to stand and talk, OK? But wait here."

Marcel stood with a confidence borne of accomplishment. A large, but justified, ego was absolutely necessary in this line of work. There were no successful defense attorneys who were shy or introverted. Marcel walked down the courtroom's center aisle. He stepped into the well of the courtroom and took two steps towards the table to the left, where a small placard read "DEFENDANT."

Across from him, at the prosecution table, Mac stood. A filthy aluminum water pitcher, marred with mysterious stains and fingerprints, sat on the table, along with a stack of Styrofoam cups. A microphone snaked upward to record everything. Resting at the base of the microphone was another matching placard, but this one said "STATE."

The judge looked towards Mac.

"William MacIntyre for the State of Maryland, Your Honor."

"Good morning, Marcel St. Croix representing the Defendant, Ms. Van der Hook, for the purpose of this hearing *only*. I assume she will appear on the TV monitor from SCCF momentarily."

When Marcel said the word "only," it rattled down Mac's ear canal sharply, as if it were a rusty nail.

Judge Harajuku looked down at a file. She didn't react.

"Gentlemen, good morning to both of you. We are here on Defendant's Motion for Bond Review. Is that correct?"

"Yes, Your Honor," said Marcel.

"Very well," the judge responded as she turned towards the TV monitor mounted high on the wall in the courtroom. Behind the screen, metal attachments descended from the ceiling, a variety of cables and wires dripping down like an electronic waterfall. She said, "SCCF? Are you there?"

The monitor showed a small room at the Seneca County Correctional Facility used for remote hearings and all bond reviews.

On the screen, Rikki stepped into view and stood behind a lectern. She was only visible from the shoulders up.

Judge Harajuku said, "Ma'am, please state your name for the record."

Rikki responded, "Excuse me? Do what?"

She wore the same oversized olive colored jumpsuit. Her hair was frizzy, and she nervously shifted her weight. Clearly, she was not sure exactly where to look. An earnest young man stepped through the doorway and stood next to her at the lectern. He had on light brown khaki pants and a rumpled dress shirt and tie, but no jacket. His sleeves were rolled up.

He looked into the camera and said, "Good morning, Your Honor, Steve Chasen for the Department of Pretrial Services Unit." He turned to Rikki and whispered, "Say your full name into that little microphone."

"Rikki Michele Van der Hook."

Chasen asked, "Does the Court have the Pretrial Services Unit report?"

"Yes, thank you. I received the PTSU report by email attachment earlier this morning. Ms. Chao, please give copies to Counsel."

Phoebe stepped around into the well of the courtroom and walked first to Mac. She handed him a multi-page collated copy of the report. She gave another one to Marcel at the defense table and then returned to her designated clerk's chair.

"First, let me hear from PTSU. Mr. Chasen, what is Pretrial's recommendation?"

The young man on the TV monitor flipped through the document quickly and stopped on the last page. Rikki looked down at the papers and then back to the camera and ruffled her hair.

"Well, we are prohibited from making a recommendation for pretrial release, as you know, because of the nature of the charges. Ms. Van der Hook is charged with first-degree murder, and that precludes us from supervision, so..." He enjoyed talking, but Judge Harajuku swiftly cut him off.

"Thank you."

Marcel stood straight; he knew he would be next. Mac sat and didn't read the PTSU report. He watched the TV monitor, zeroing in on Rikki. This was the first time he had seen her. His mind soaked in every detail he could observe about her: her demeanor, her dress, the way her eyes darted around, and, importantly, he needed to assess her lethality.

Mac was calculating.

This little woman stabbed her husband 50 times? This may not be so easy.

She seemed far too fragile and tiny to generate such ferocity. He'd have to convince a jury this tiny sparrow was a bird of prey. She didn't appear to be a hawk, eagle, or vulture.

Judge Harajuku noted, "I'm looking at section six of the report, and it says the Defendant has no prior record. Additionally, she clearly has longstanding ties to the community. While she is not employed, it appears that she has substantial assets and property in Seneca County. Further, she is the sole caregiver for a disabled child. Mr. St. Croix, is all of that correct?"

Marcel pounced. "Yes, Your Honor. That is all absolutely accurate. As the Court well knows, a recommendation from PTSU is merely advisory and not binding. We are asking you to release Ms. Van der Hook back into the community, where we will agree to have her monitored by a private supervisory company, wear an ankle bracelet, observe strict curfew, and abide by any other pretrial conditions which the Court may order. We are prepared to post a substantial cash bond as well, so I respectfully request that you allow the Defendant to return home. Her daughter needs her as she suffers from…"

The judge didn't let him finish.

"Mr. MacIntyre?"

"Your Honor, the Defendant is charged with first-degree murder." He paused, making sure that sank in. "As I'm sure the Court will agree, that is the most significant criminal charge that exists under Maryland law. She is facing life in prison without parole. Nothing could be more serious. There are two basic prongs to be evaluated at a bond review: the risk of flight, and the danger to the community. Everything Mr. St. Croix just articulated goes to the first prong, namely, risk of flight. But what defense counsel has not mentioned—what he has not uttered one word about—is the potential of danger to the community. The victim in this case was the Defendant's husband, so there are obvious elements of domestic violence. I'm told by the investigators that Mr. Marten Van der Hook was stabbed approximately 50 times, including at least one fatal stab wound completely through his skull and into his brain. The State is waiting for the pathology report, but there is no question that this was a *savage* killing."

The judge's eyes flicked towards Rikki, but her head didn't move at all.

"Furthermore, there is an eyewitness to the murder: the Defendant's own daughter. Given the brutality of the bloodshed, Ms. Van der Hook is the last person on Earth who should be taking care of a child. The danger she represents cannot be overstated. Therefore, we respectfully ask that you deny the defense's request for pretrial release."

Judge Harajuku stared intently at Mac, absorbing his allocution, analyzing it, sifting it. She turned to Marcel and asked, "What is the status of the minor? Does she have a guardian, or is she under the auspices of Child Protective Services or what?"

Marcel turned to look out at the courtroom gallery. He made eye contact with Lindy, who was now leaning forward against the row of seats in front of her, poised to jump up, eager.

"Your Honor," he said, sweeping his right hand outwards towards Lindy. "The Defendant's sister is here in court. This is Linden Hale. She has been appointed the child's guardian and has temporary legal custody. Mr. MacIntyre's concerns can be easily assuaged. We can assure the Court that my client will have absolutely no contact with the child. Further, Ms.

Van der Hook is prepared to stay at a hotel for the duration of this matter."

"But, Mr. St. Croix, if I understood the State's proffer correctly, this child is the sole eyewitness to the murder? Is that correct?"

"*Alleged* murder, Your Honor. However, from what I have learned from my own investigation, this child's testimony will be completely exculpatory and extremely favorable to the defense. And, I might add, we object to any attempts—I should say, any *further* attempts—to influence this child's testimony by the State. I understand they have already attempted to interrogate this mentally disabled child, and that is absolutely disgraceful. We object to..."

The judge interrupted again, "You object to the State investigating its own case? You object to the police interviewing an eyewitness to a homicide? Seriously?"

"Well, Your Honor..."

Judge Harajuku was not listening.

"No. I've made my decision: the Defendant will be held on a No Bond status until trial. I find for the record that there is both a risk of flight considering the serious nature of the charges, and I further find that she poses a substantial danger to the community."

Lindy stood and said, "Oh my God, you must be joking! Jesus Christ!"

One of the deputies quickly moved towards the gallery, his left palm extended up, in a "stop" gesture. His right hand was on a yellow Taser strapped to his thigh. He said, "Shhh, no talking!"

Lindy stepped into the center of the aisle. She wasn't finished.

"This is ridiculous!"

Marcel turned and held up both of his hands, attempting to quiet her.

Simultaneously, Judge Harajuku interjected sharply, "Ma'am, please sit down and be quiet, or, if you are unable to control yourself, please leave my courtroom right now!"

Lindy spun around and stormed out into the hallway.

On the TV monitor, a female corrections officer stepped into view on the screen and escorted Rikki out of the side door. Rikki had never spoken a word beyond announcing her name.

Marcel softly said, "Thank you, Your Honor. May I be excused?"

"Yes. And, sir, I would advise you to have a talk with your client's sister. This type of outburst does not impress the Court favorably."

"Yes, I understand."

"And, further, Mr. MacIntyre has every right to interview anyone he or his investigators choose in this case. Is that understood?"

"Yes, Judge."

"There are no State witnesses or defense witnesses. There are only witnesses. Neither side owns a witness. So, I expect both of you gentlemen to resolve these pretrial issues without any intervention of the court. Is that clear?"

"Absolutely," said Marcel. "Understood."

"Now, I see we have a trial date set for August of 2019. Discovery will be extended to the defense forthwith. And there is a Motions Hearing scheduled for next month. I will see you gentlemen in January. Have a nice Christmas. Thank you."

Marcel and Mac stepped outside the courtroom. They both looked up and down the hallway, but Lindy was nowhere in sight. Marcel said, "I'm out. I'm not doing this case, Mac."

"What?! Why not?"

CHAPTER 18

Friday, December 21, 2018
11:50 a.m.

"Andre, we finished the bond review. Harajuku is holding her on a No Bond status."

"Cool. Serves that bitch right."

"Where are you, man? I can hardly hear you."

"I'm at the Crime Lab down in the basement of Headquarters. Surprised I get any cell service here. I'm outside the door to the testing area, watching through the window, but they won't let me in. They are paranoid about contamination and all that shit. The Techs are wearing these ridiculous spaceman suit things."

"OK, that's good that they are processing our request so fast."

"Yeah, Lt. Hyman is a good dude. He pulled some strings, and we jumped the line. He squeezed us in ahead of some other investigations. They should have the DNA report relatively fast. Then, it looks like everyone's off for the holiday break."

"'Pulled some strings,' Lord have mercy. There you go with the clichés again, Andre."

"Sorry, man. I'm not some fancy courtroom lawyer, OK? That's how we roll on West 127."

"Hey, Andre. I've got to tell you something wild. So, after the bond review, I was standing outside the courtroom with Marcel St. Croix. He tells me he's not doing the case anymore!"

"What? That's good news. Isn't it? Get him off the case. But why is he quitting?"

"He wouldn't tell me. Said he couldn't disclose attorney/client communications. But, yes, I think it is good news. I mean, Marcel is a superb attorney, and without him, well, it's like playing the Lakers with LeBron out of the lineup."

"Hard to believe that French dude doesn't want to cash in."

"It could be a matter of finances. It's possible someone froze all of the dead guy's accounts. Like some board of directors at his company or something. She may not have any more access to money at this point." Mac shrugged. "But I'm thinking it could be something else, too. If Rikki Van der Hook told Marcel she was guilty, and then specifically said she wanted to lie on the witness stand to try to get away with the crime, then Marcel would have to bow out. The canon of ethics for attorneys controls this type of situation."

"How does that work, Mac? I mean, defense attorneys lie like rugs all the time, so there must not be a lot of ethical ones out there."

"A criminal defense attorney can't put someone up on the witness stand when they know the witness will lie. That's called 'suborning perjury.' So, if someone plans to lie, and his attorney *knows* it's a lie, the lawyer can only say, 'Tell the jury what happened,' with no follow-up questions. But most sharp attorneys, like Marcel St. Croix, they don't want the risk of dealing with the Attorney Grievance Commission and having to go through a disciplinary hearing. Not to mention the chance of getting suspended or disbarred. A guy like St. Croix, with his career almost done, he would never risk his reputation for any single case. No way. No, he'd just withdraw from the case instead."

"Yeah, I remember that lawyer. What was his name, Sleazman or Saltzman or something like that? That guy got nailed lying in court, and he was disbarred. That shit ain't worth it. None of these damn cases is worth losing your job over."

"Well, the main thing is your reputation. A distinguished attorney like Marcel is a legend around Seneca County. He was doing high-profile cases since before I even started as a rookie down in District Court. A lot of the ASAs back then were totally scared of him. Petrified. I'm serious. They'd give away the farm in a plea deal just so they wouldn't have to lose a trial against him."

"I don't see you being scared of him, Mac."

"No, I wouldn't say I was *afraid* of him, but I definitely was cautious. One time, years ago, he walks down the aisle in District Court, and the courtroom is packed. He says to me, 'My case is going to be a trial, so you better have all of your witnesses ready.' I said, 'All the cops are here, and the civilian eyewitness is sitting in the front row.'"

"That's hysterical. Called his bluff."

"Yes, so then he says, 'I was just testing you. What's your best plea offer?'"

"I swear to God," Andre replied. "These damn defense attorneys. I have no idea how you even talk to these liars."

"Well, Marcel St. Croix and I became friends. I guess I proved myself to him. He respected that I wasn't afraid to take him on. And to this day, I definitely still respect him."

"Mac, let me ask you something else about that French dude..."

"What?"

"The bracelet he always wears. That hideous, flat, orange-looking thing. It looks like a caveman pounded it out. What the hell is that thing?"

"Oh, man. Yes, that bracelet. Once I asked him about it. I said, 'Mr. St. Croix, I hope you don't think I'm being too intrusive, but why do you wear that bronze bracelet?'"

"And...?"

"He says, 'Mr. MacIntyre, it's not bronze. It's copper. It's made from melted pennies. One of my clients made it for me while he was on Death Row. Took him years. He gave it to me the night they executed him. I watched him die in the gas chamber in Baltimore. I've worn it ever since.'"

"Oh my God, really? Do you think he was telling you the truth or testing you again somehow?"

"I don't know if he was being straight with me or exaggerating. I mean, how would you get pennies on Death Row?"

"He must have liked you to tell you that, Mac. It's also possible, I guess, that he just made up the whole thing. You know how these defense attorneys just make shit up, right?"

"Well, anyway, since St. Croix is pulling out of this Van der Hook case, we have to be ready for anything—a new attorney or, possibly, a public defender."

"If a public defender steps in and takes it over, they can't lie and play all these games, like these private attorneys do. I mean, since you see the same PDs all the time and you have to work together."

"Well, that is definitely ironic. The public defenders get knocked and slammed all the time, but most of them are really experienced in court and excellent trial lawyers."

"Hey, Mac. I'm looking through the lab door right now. They are wrapping up and putting everything away. That new Tech, Leslie, is the one doing our knife. Damn, she is so hot, I can hardly concentrate. Oh, now she's unzipping her jumpsuit or Hazmat suit or whatever it's called and, man, she is looking fine. You should see how she unzips that thing. She's got on these tight jeans underneath."

"Detective Okoye! Focus. You are working!"

"True, but I'm always looking too, my man! So, which PD do you think will get the Van der Hook case?"

"I have my sources. It's going to be Santiago Garcia."

CHAPTER 19

Tuesday, May 18, 1999
8:30 a.m.

Santiago Garcia first walked into a courtroom when he was 18 years old. He was in big trouble. His attorney, Seth Jacobs, said this could derail all of his plans, his entire future.

My lawyer said I probably won't even get into college now, and law school? Don't even think about it.

Santiago's parents were furious. Mr. Jacobs had helped them refinance their mortgage, but he didn't seem to know much about criminal law. Santiago went to his tiny office, which was filled with cardboard boxes and reeked of stale tobacco. The ashtray on the desk overflowed with the slug-like remains of brown, saliva-soaked cigar stubs. Mr. Jacobs had crumbs sprinkled on his jacket and necktie: crumbs, or possibly dandruff.

All this stress for smoking marijuana outside a movie theatre? Insane.

Santiago had considered representing himself so his parents wouldn't find out, but when he asked Mr. Jacobs, the disheveled attorney said, "Are you crazy?! If you had a bad tooth, you wouldn't go into the garage, grab a pair of pliers, and tear out your own tooth, would you?!"

Santiago agreed. Naturally smart, engaging, and articulate, Santiago spoke both Spanish and English fluently and with flair. Everywhere he went, he made friends easily. He was small and chubby, with a hearty laugh, and he made people smile with his funny observations and witticisms. His family was originally from Chile, but Santiago was born here, in Seneca County, at Tomlinson General Hospital, and he grew up in a solidly middle-class neighborhood.

And now this. Arrested. Handcuffed. Brought to some solid concrete building surrounded by barbed wire called the Central Processing Unit. Then he had to talk to someone called a Commissioner and was bonded out.

What was it called? Personal recognizance? Hell of an expensive joint, and I only smoked half of it.

Mr. Jacobs explained that there were two levels of courts in Seneca County: the lower court was the District Court, and the Circuit Court was the higher level, where serious jury trials were held. Misdemeanors were settled in District Court before a judge. There, things were disorganized and crowded, a mob of people milling around. It was like a legal street bazaar, except instead of bartering blankets or fruit, the commodity inside these brown wood-paneled walls was justice, quick and simple.

Mr. Jacobs and Santiago walked into the courtroom. Scores of wildly diverse people were jammed into wooden benches set up like rows of pews in a church. The mix of people was apparent immediately; one defendant, dressed like a businessman, sat next to what appeared to be a homeless lady with shopping bags. Up front, by the judge's bench, were three flags on wooden posts: an American flag, a Maryland flag, and a local Seneca County flag. A list of defendants was posted outside on a chipped bulletin board. The cork was crumbling and missing in craters like a lunar landscape. There he was: "Santiago Garcia: POSSESSION OF CDS."

That's me. A "defendant."

"What does CDS mean?" he asked Mr. Jacobs.

"Means Controlled Dangerous Substance."

"Marijuana? That's a dangerous substance? For God's sake, *sugar* is more dangerous. White poison you'll find loaded into every Coke or Krispy Kreme donut."

Ah, those donuts, his downfall.

"Yes, Santiago, the great State of Maryland could put you in jail for up to a year for simply possessing marijuana. A natural plant. Like cigarettes, which, of course, are completely legal yet kill millions every year."

Santiago took in a deep breath. His mother was too nervous to enter the courtroom and waited on a bench outside in the hallway on the verge of tears. She couldn't bear to see her beloved son standing in front of the court like a common criminal caught pickpocketing a tourist in the Plaza de Armas. Sweet Santiago with all the other shoplifters, drunks, and trespassers.

Mr. Jacobs said, "Sit here." He walked up towards the front of the courtroom where two dark brown wooden tables were placed in front of the judge's bench, one for the defendants and one for the Assistant State's Attorney.

The public defender, a young woman, had an enormous plume of braids balanced on her head. She held a huge stack of files. Robotically, she shouted out names in alphabetical order, apparently her clients. She was meeting them for the first time on their actual court date. Santiago was thankful she wasn't his lawyer. She seemed nervous, and several of her files were sticking out of her stack dangerously on the brink of falling to the ground and scattering like litter on a windy street. Without raising her head, she yelled out, "McCartney? McCawly? McGunn?" No one responded.

A thought flashed through Santiago's mind.

Are all the white people in Seneca County Irish Catholics?

Mr. Jacobs walked up to the front of the courtroom and joined a line of men and women dressed in business attire. These were the private criminal defense attorneys who had been hired to represent clients, not like those unfortunate souls who had to depend on a public defender. The attorneys were waiting in line to talk to a young prosecutor standing at the table, a tall, thin man with copper red hair, who seemed organized and well prepared.

The prosecutor moved gracefully around the table like a fencer. His files were spread out on the desk like cards in a game of solitaire, not all piled up in a sloppy stack like the public defender's files. He was sorting them into various logical categories. He exuded confidence.

Each file had a yellow sticky note in the corner with a handwritten code resembling hieroglyphics: a "T" or a "Pl" or arrows pointing upward, downward, or horizontally.

If I have to get on a helicopter, this would be the guy I'd want flying it.

Mr. Jacobs shook the prosecutor's hand and said, "Good morning, I'm Seth Jacobs. Pleased to meet you."

⚖

"Good to meet you too. I'm Mac MacIntyre. What case are you here for?"

Ignoring Mac's question, Mr. Jacobs asked one of his own: "How long have you been with the State's Attorney's Office? I don't think we've had any cases together before."

"Started at the SAO two months ago," said Mac.

"Well, you'll be up to Circuit Court soon. District Court is a zoo."

"Which case do you have, Mr. Jacobs?"

"Oh, call me Seth. I'm here on the Garcia case."

"I have two Garcia cases. Is yours the indecent exposure or the marijuana possession one?"

"Simple possession. It's a tiny amount, almost microscopic."

Mac looked down at his solitaire arrangement, scooped up a thin file, and read a brief summary of the case he'd written the night before.

"Mac, it's my client's first contact. Ever. Nothing in juvenile court either. He's only 18 and looking to go to college and maybe even law school."

"His first offense of any kind, Seth? Not even a traffic case?"

"First ever, I swear. Like I said, it's a miniscule amount of CDS. I mean, he's just a high school kid."

Mac quickly scoured the Statement of Charges and glanced at the police report. He flipped to the last page to check the chemist's analysis. It confirmed the substance seized was indeed marijuana. He noted the amount seized was less than a quarter of a gram. He checked the Maryland criminal database print-out to confirm there were no prior convictions. He shut the file. He had read all of this information the night before and recalled it immediately.

Mac let all of those factors bounce around in his mind, and then he made a decision. "Explain to your client this is no joke, OK. I'll *nolle* it, but tell your kid I don't ever want to see him again. And I mean, for the rest of my life. Got that?"

CHAPTER 20

Tuesday, May 18, 1999
8:57 a.m.

Mr. Jacobs shook Mac's hand and turned back towards the gallery, his face red and shiny with a veneer of sweat across his forehead. He walked back to the twelfth row and shuffled in sideways, edging his body into the space on the bench next to Santiago.

"What's going on, Mr. Jacobs?"

"This new prosecutor is a good man. You're lucky, Santiago."

"Do I have to plead guilty?"

"No. He's going to give you a break. He's flat-out dropping the case. He said for you to take it as a warning. I told him you wanted to go to law school someday, and he said he'd give you a second chance. He's not prosecuting the case."

For a moment, Santiago's mind went completely blank. The urge to urinate became overwhelming, but it passed. He exhaled.

"What happens now? Can we just leave?" he said hopefully.

"No, he has to call the case once the judge gets on the bench. Then he has to announce the case is being *nolle prossed*. He has to put it on the record, as they say."

"What's it called? Not prosecuted? Same as being dropped?"

"Yes, it's Latin. *Nolle prosequi*. It's a good thing, trust me. Then, we can get this case expunged right away, son. An expungement means that it disappears completely from your record, and there's no trace of it. Gone."

"Oh, thank you, Jesus," sighed Santiago.

At exactly 9:00 a.m., the judge came in through a side door and took his position behind the elaborate wooden bench. He was an elderly man, his back crooked in the shape of a question mark from osteoporosis, walking as if carrying an invisible heavy burden. He was almost completely bald except for several strands of grey hair which were wrapped around the top of his head in a spiral shape like a silver yarmulke. Santiago could read the nameplate mounted to the judge's bench, "HON. BARRY HEFLAND." This was not a guy who looked like he had smoked a joint before.

The fossilized judge spoke, "Please be seated." A noticeable rustling sound washed across the courtroom as 100 people all sat, a whooshing sound, like a flock of seagulls rising at once.

"You are now attending a session of the District Court of Maryland. This is a misdemeanor court. The cases will be called by the Assistant State's Attorney." He paused for the prosecutor to announce himself.

"William MacIntyre for the State of Maryland, Judge Hefland."

"For some cases," the judge intoned, "you may be entitled to ask for a trial by jury, but mostly, your cases will be decided by me. If you have a trial before me and you are unsatisfied with the results, you may appeal my decision to the Circuit Court through what is called a *de novo* appeal. Mr. MacIntyre, are there any preliminary matters to call at this time?"

"Yes, Judge Hefland, thank you. State calls *State vs. Santiago Garcia*."

Mr. Jacobs nudged Santiago, and they walked up to the front of the courtroom. The overwhelming need to urinate returned, but, again, quickly faded.

When they had settled at the defense table, Mr. Jacobs said, "Seth Jacobs representing the Defendant, Your Honor."

Mac then spoke, "Judge, the State will be using its discretion in this case and will be entering a *nolle pros.*"

"OK, very well," the judge said. "That means your case is being dismissed at the State's election, young man. You may be entitled to an expungement. Please consult your attorney about that and good luck to you. Next case?"

Mr. Jacobs said to Judge Hefland, "May I have the court's indulgence, please?" Whispering, he patted Santiago on the shoulder and said, "Say thank you to Mr. MacIntyre. He's doing you a huge favor."

"Thank you, sir," Santiago said, gratefully, in as soft a voice as he could emit.

Mac stepped over and whispered, "No problem, man. Be careful. Cops are everywhere. Good luck in law school."

"Next case," the judge repeated, with a slightly irritated tone.

Mr. Jacobs put his arm around Santiago's shoulder and ushered him down the center aisle of the courtroom and out through the heavy doors. A wave of tension left Santiago's body and mind. The urge to find a bathroom now became his top priority. His mother looked up with wide eyes, her expression a mixture of joy and relief as Mr. Jacobs explained the fortuitous outcome.

Santiago wouldn't see Mac again for nine years.

CHAPTER 21

Monday, December 24, 2018
9:03 a.m.

SENECA COUNTY DEPARTMENT OF POLICE

H. Wynn Miller - Chief of Police
Martin Daalder - County Executive

SENECA COUNTY POLICE CRIME LABORATORY

FORENSIC BIOLOGY REPORT

TO: Detective Andre Okoye, State's Attorney's Office Chief Investigator

CR#: 717-252725-6

ANALYST: Leslie Janice

REPORT DATE: December 24, 2018

VICTIM: Marten Van der Hook

SUSPECT(S): Rikki Van der Hook

EVIDENCE SUBMITTED:

1. Kitchen carving knife—"Wüsthof Classic" embossed on metal blade. Marking on wood handle: "Williams-Sonoma."

2. Vial of blood from the crime scene.

3. Buccal samples (1)—from (1) suspect.

RESULTS/CONCLUSIONS

ITEM DESCRIPTION: Blood and buccal sample (A1, A2)

DNA RESULTS: Male DNA was recovered from crime scene. AI: Marten Van der Hook.

Female DNA was detected on buccal sample A2: Rikki Van der Hook.

ITEM DESCRIPTION: Kitchen carving knife (B1)

DNA RESULTS: Mixed DNA profile of three contributors; indicative of a major male contributor, a minor female contributor, and an additional minor female contributor.

CONCLUSIONS

1. The DNA profile associated with AI (Marten Van der Hook) cannot be excluded from Item B1 (Kitchen carving knife) as a major contributor.

2. The DNA profile associated with A2 (Rikki Van der Hook) cannot be excluded from Item B1 (Kitchen carving knife) as a minor contributor.

3. An unknown female DNA profile cannot be excluded from Item B1 (Kitchen carving knife) as a minor contributor.

"I hope you understand this shit, Mac, because it's confusing as hell to me."

"I got you covered," replied Mac, shifting through the pages of the DNA report which Andre had just handed him. "It's basically what we suspected. It doesn't hurt us, that's for sure."

"Break it down in, like, simple English for me, with no quotes from Shakespeare, please," said Andre, as he leaned over and looked at the report.

"OK, I'll skip over the words genotyping and alleles," Mac teased. "And, just for you, my brother, I won't say deoxyribonucleic acid. I'll just go with DNA."

"My head is already bursting. This crap is such a migraine. How do you ever explain this to a jury so they understand?"

"Well, you've just got to translate. Just like a courtroom interpreter does, translating from some foreign language into English. I admit, it takes a few DNA cases to figure it out, but hey, anything can be simplified if you just break it down into ordinary words."

Mac held up the first sheet of the report in front of his face vertically, like a handheld mirror, as if to decipher it.

"OK, Andre, so it says they got sufficient DNA from the buccal swab used on Rikki. Y'know, a buccal swab? That big Q-Tip looking thing? They just swirl it around in your mouth. Your saliva is teeming with DNA."

"That makes sense."

"They also got a strong DNA profile from Marten Van der Hook's blood taken from the crime scene, which is not surprising. Blood, saliva, and semen are the best fluids to get a DNA profile from."

Glancing further down the report, Mac said, "Then they tested the knife to see if any of their DNA was on it. Sweat isn't nearly as good as those other bodily fluids for testing, but here we go: they recovered a mixed sample on the knife. That's logical. I mean, it's a common kitchen knife that's been in the house for years."

"Mixed? Damn, I hope that's not trouble," asked Andre.

"So, DNA is super sensitive. It's everywhere, man. Your DNA is probably all over my office right now, just from touching the chair you're sitting in, or handling any objects. Your DNA is on that doorknob over there. Some surfaces absorb DNA better than others. It soaks in. They call those surfaces porous. Clothes and sheets, any fabrics, are perfect blotters for DNA. But a knife is solid, not porous. This kitchen knife is made with a wooden handle and a metal blade."

"We can test it for fingerprints, Mac. Maybe that's a better idea."

"That is an option, true. But there are probably a million overlapping fingerprints on that thing, and it would more likely have palm prints, anyway. People usually don't touch the blade of a knife at all, but they grasp the handle tightly."

"Good point."

"The Techs can pick up DNA from the tiny secretions of oil all of us naturally have on our skin, especially the stuff that comes off your fingers or the palm of your hand."

Andre held his hand up and looked at his palm as if he was an imaginary fortune teller, noticing tiny rivulets of sweat in the channels and grooves of his flesh.

Mac studied the report and said, "So, here we have Mr. Van der Hook as a 'major' contributor. That totally makes sense. I mean, his blood would leave trace amounts all over the whole thing, especially the blade and the joint where the blade goes into the wood. Microscopic trace particles in all the little nooks and crannies in the metal and defects in the wood. Then we have Rikki as the 'minor' contributor. That's exactly what we should expect. Her sweat and skin cells on the handle. But this is something we may need to figure out. We have 'unknown female' DNA as a minor contributor as well."

"Yeah, that sounds like a problem? Whose could that be? Did a female cop or one of the Crime Scene Techs touch it or pick it up before bagging it?"

Mac and Andre both stopped talking. After a moment, they looked at each other.

Mac asked, "Did Mandy hold the kitchen knife? She's nine years old."

"Not just a kitchen knife, Mac. A murder weapon used to carve up her father like a turkey on Thanksgiving Day."

"How would the child's DNA get on a nine-inch knife?"

"Are you thinking what I'm thinking? Stop. No one in the world will think Mandy stabbed her own father. Just stop."

"Is it possible she handled the knife *after* the murder? Picked it up?"

Andre said, "I have no idea. Maybe she held it prior to the murder? Maybe it's not even Mandy's DNA. It just said 'unknown.' Anyway, we can test her and see if she matches, if that becomes an issue."

"And the housekeeper. I think they even had a cook on staff too. But we can't endlessly go down all these rabbit holes, or we'll never get this case ready for trial. I don't want to turn this trial into *Alice in Wonderland*."

"Alice in what?"

"Andre, we need to anticipate everything. These defense attorneys like to throw everything against the wall and hope something sticks. All they need is one stupid juror to get a hung jury and a mistrial."

"Just explain that trace evidence scientific crap to the jury in simple words. Make it easy to understand, Mac. That's what you do! You are great at taking something complicated and making it simple."

"But, remember, Andre, this DNA stuff is all just corroboration. It backs up Rikki's confession. She admitted she killed her husband. That statement is the centerpiece of our case. All the rest is just extra." Mac's level of confidence was not overwhelming; it was more like a vein of confidence buried in a mountain of doubt, like a streak of flashy color slashing across a rocky wall deep inside a gold mine.

"Mac, you know I was a running back on the football team in high school. You knew that, right?"

"You've only mentioned it like eight million times."

Ignoring him, Andre expounded, "Sometimes, when you play halfback, the quarterback turns and hands you the ball. Everything is a blur. All 22 guys are moving. Then, in a flash, you see the field open up right in front of you. A huge hole in the line. And you burst through, running as fast as you can. All the way down the field! That's how I feel right now, Mac. I can see that touchdown right in front of us."

"Well, don't forget the other team has 11 tacklers, dude.

So, let's not get ahead of ourselves. Let's just focus on getting that statement you got from Rikki ruled admissible. I'm a little worried about that. This judge isn't the best for that issue. Harajuku can be pretty pro-defense, and she will always err on the side of the defendant. I think you should go over everything and get ready for Motions. They're coming up in a couple of weeks."

"Yeah, man. Piece of cake. I've been going for long runs down by the river every night. Helps me sleep better. I've been having some flashbacks recently. And that Harajuku, yeah, I've testified before her a couple of times. She's like a samurai warrior, so..."

"Hey! That sounds kind of racist, man. Easy. Go run some extra miles. I need you to be relaxed and sharp when we go to Motions. There's a lot at stake, and I need you to be at your best, OK?"

"I got you, bro."

"And Andre..."

"What?"

"Merry Christmas."

CHAPTER 22

Friday, January 25, 2019
9:00 a.m.

"All rise!" Phoebe Chao proclaimed in an assertive, strong voice. "The Honorable Marcia Harajuku now presiding."

The judge emerged through the side door that connected her chambers to the courtroom. She took two steps up towards her elevated bench, sat, and said, "Please be seated. Call the case."

Phoebe said, "*State of Maryland v. Rikki Van der Hook*, case number 3016090345-C."

"Thank you, Madame Clerk. Will the parties announce themselves for the record?"

Mac stood first, as was customary for the prosecutor, and calmly said, "Good morning, Judge Harajuku, William MacIntyre for the State of Maryland." He preferred to use the judge's name when he addressed the court. It was a subtle way of showing respect.

"Thank you, Your Honor, Santiago Garcia on behalf of the Defendant, Mrs. Van der Hook, who is now entering the courtroom."

Santiago gestured towards a side door, which led to a lockup area with small cells directly outside the courtroom, where prisoners waited for their cases to be heard. As Santiago spoke, Rikki came through the doorway, escorted by two beefy Sheriff's Deputies. She was wearing an olive-green jumpsuit, her arms manacled behind her back. She had a legal file grasped between her armpit and thin bicep. Her arms peeked out of the oversized garment like a pair of wiry pale straws. From the corner of his eye, Mac watched as a young muscular deputy with a blond crew cut released Rikki's handcuffs. She vigorously rubbed her wrists and nervously rotated her head, looking all around the circular courtroom.

The circular design played havoc with acoustics. Even early in his career, Mac had learned to lean against the curved wall and let the whispers and fragments of defendants' confidential conversations come wafting all the way around the courtroom like a wayward boomerang to his uninvited ears. *Caveat emptor.*

Judge Harajuku stated, "I see we are here for Motions. Mr. Garcia, you've previously filed a Motion to Suppress your client's statement. Are we prepared to handle that issue presently?"

"Yes, Your Honor," Santiago said. "The defense is ready to proceed. I've asked Mac—sorry—I've asked Mr. MacIntyre to have his witness on call to testify. He should be the only State's witness, and the rest of our time will be legal arguments."

"Mr. MacIntyre?"

"Detective Okoye is outside. Shall I bring him in?"

"Yes. Mr. Garcia, I've read your Motion. So, you are asking the Court to focus on the issue of voluntariness as it relates to the admissibility of the Defendant's statement, with emphasis on an improper advice of rights via the SCPD-505?"

"Absolutely, Your Honor. I'll be very brief and reserve the bulk of my argument, but once we've established the facts on the record, there is no way this statement comes in. I mean, my client's *Miranda* rights were trampled on, and the SCPD-505, which, as the Court well knows, is the standardized form required to advise someone in a custodial interrogation situation, wasn't properly explained and therefore..."

"OK," said Judge Harajuku, cutting him off.

"Call your witness, Mr. MacIntyre."

"State calls Detective Andre Okoye."

Phoebe activated a paging system which had loudspeakers in the hallway just outside the courtroom.

Andre walked into the room. He was not wearing the Patrick Ewing throwback basketball jersey, Jordan 5's sneakers, nor was he adorned with gold chains. Instead, he was appropriately dressed for court in a dark blue suit—the one he used every time he had to testify. He strolled confidently down the center aisle of the courtroom to the witness stand and stood holding up his right hand. This was not his first time testifying.

Phoebe stated, "Do you solemnly swear or affirm that the testimony you shall give will be the truth, the whole truth, and nothing but the truth?"

"Yes, I do." Andre sat in the witness chair, adjusted the microphone, pushed the aluminum water pitcher to the side of the table, and laid his case file down in front of him.

"Did a time come, Detective Okoye, when you interviewed the Defendant at the 6D Police Station?" Law enforcement witnesses were always "officer" and "detective" and "captain," never "mister." The accused was the "Defendant," not "Ms. Van der Hook." Using a proper name, or a salutation like "sir" or "ma'am," had a benign quality, and Mac never wanted to normalize people who had been charged with horrific crimes. When a detective grilled a defendant, it was always an "interview," and never an "interrogation." Mac's word choices were his brushstrokes, the courtroom his canvas.

After Andre relayed in careful, dignified detail the circumstances of his interview with Rikki, Mac wrapped up with, "Did you ever make any type of promise or inducement whatsoever to obtain the Defendant's statement?"

"I never—not once—made any type of promise to her about anything," Andre replied.

Santiago was leaning forward, like a cat about to pounce on a ladybug.

Judge Harajuku said, "Thank you, sir. Mr. Garcia, any questions?"

CHAPTER 23

Friday, January 25, 2019
10:37 a.m.

Santiago stood. "Thank you, Your Honor."

He strode across the courtroom, moving with purpose. Holding up a sheet of paper, he asked Andre, "You see this? It's marked Defense Number One, OK?"

Mac did not move. He smiled slightly.

Santiago continued, "Show me where on this SCPD-505 form is a check mark or any other indication which *confirms* that you properly advised my client of her rights against self-incrimination? Where?!"

Andre didn't glance at the form.

"Detective Okoye, you've been an investigator working homicide cases for a long time, right?"

"Yes."

"You are very familiar with the standard Seneca County Police Department form that lists the necessary Constitutional rights every defendant is entitled to, right?"

"I am."

"And, Detective Okoye, you know that all law enforcement officers acting on behalf of the State of Maryland—as you are in this case—all police officers who interrogate an accused person are required to advise them of all of their rights before they can be questioned, correct?"

"And I did so in this case. I fully advised her."

Santiago was fascinated with traditional bullfighting: the picador, the toreador, and the matador. The picador came first, stabbing and picking at the bull, weakening his back and shoulder muscles with a long pike. The toreador followed next. He was on horseback, and his function was to run the bull to exhaustion. Finally, the third act: the matador. He paraded with his long sword and red cape. The matador came in for the kill, driving his sturdy sword deep behind the bull's neck, severing the spinal cord and dropping 1,500 pounds of lumbering, sweaty flesh to the dirt.

Santiago was now the picador, softening up his victim. "So, you read to my client verbatim from the SCPD-505 form, correct? And you placed a check mark in the box next to each of the four specifically required rights? The first right was, 'You have the right to remain silent?'"

Andre loosened his necktie, unbuttoned the top button on his shirt, and said, "I placed a check mark next to that advice, the right to remain silent. See it there?"

Santiago became the toreador. "And you then advised my client properly of her next right. You read from the form,

'Anything you say can and will be used against you in a court of law.' I see you placed a check mark beside that one, Detective."

"Correct, Mr. Garcia."

"'You have the right to an attorney, and if you cannot afford an attorney, one will be provided for you.' I see a check by that one too. Correct?"

"Yes, sir."

Santiago was now the matador. "'No threats or promises have been used to get you to talk.'" He took a dramatic spin 360 degrees, twirling in the nearly empty courtroom as if he was brandishing a cape and a sword.

There was no one in the courtroom except for a disheveled middle-aged man seated in the last row holding a small notepad.

"So, Detective Okoye, where is the check mark next to *that* critical Constitutional right? There is none. You never advised her properly!"

"I didn't make any promises. The entire statement was voluntary. She admitted to everything. Told me how her husband took her to Vegas with some new woman, some secretary of his. She told me that the three of them had sex all together, like a threesome. She said her husband was going to leave her and how humiliated she was. She said she had sex with the secretary herself just to please her husband. She said she wanted him dead after that. She totally corroborated everything that happened and how the crime scene looked with blood dripping from the ceiling. I mean, this is ridiculous." His voice rose.

Judge Harajuku interjected, "Please respond to the question asked and don't elaborate. If Mr. MacIntyre has any follow-up questions, he will ask them of you on redirect examination."

"Defense moves in Defense Number One, Your Honor," said Santiago, walking up towards the judge's bench.

"Hearing no objection from the State, it will be received," the judge noted. "Let me see the SCP-505. I will note, for the record, there appears to be no indication, by check mark or otherwise, that the witness properly advised the Defendant of *all* of her rights."

Santiago moved to his table and said, "No further questions."

"Mr. MacIntyre, anything further on the issue of admissibility of the statement?"

"No, thank you, Judge."

Judge Harajuku spoke, "Well, it appears to be conceded by the State that the SCPD-505 Advice of Rights, which is Maryland's mechanism for upholding the so-called *Miranda* warnings, was not *fully* complied with by Detective Okoye in his role as a State agent. Therefore, the Court finds that—while I do not ascribe any malfeasance, or that he intentionally misguided anyone—even a negligently executed advice of rights has been held by the appellate courts to be flawed. I find that the confession or, I should say, the statement, is involuntary. Accordingly, it may not be used by the State at trial. Any statement made by the Defendant is suppressed."

Mac sat perfectly still, no emotion on his face.

Santiago was smiling slightly, but he wasn't gloating—you never gloated to Mac MacIntyre's sparkling green eyes. Every public defender knew that. But he was pleased with his efficiency. The case was falling apart.

Now they need that kid, and she will never testify in front of a jury. She's a basket case. Plus, she's got some mental thing. Catatonic or something. That kid will be a disaster. This case is crumbling.

"I see trial is set for the first week of August," the judge said. "I will expect your *voir dire* questions and jury instructions in my chambers by close of business on July 29th. Is that clear? We will pick the jury on Monday, August 5th."

CHAPTER 24

Monday, August 5, 2019
8:59 a.m.

Judge Harajuku glanced at the upright flap of her laptop and typed JURY SELECTION on the keyboard to create a file for her trial notes.

"Mr. Garcia, Mr. MacIntyre, please approach."

At the bench, she flipped on the "husher," a device which emitted an irritating white noise, ostensibly to drown out the confidential conversations between the attorneys and the judge up at the bench.

"This is a 10/20 strike, correct?" she confirmed.

"Yes, Your Honor," Santiago jumped in. She recognized his tendency to try to look assertive, although it was obvious to her that he was not naturally aggressive. She had been to many trial advocacy training programs as a guest instructor and had previously spotted this quality in inexperienced attorneys and law students. Whenever she tossed out a general question to both attorneys, it was Santiago who always tried to speak first, in the mode of a game show contestant. In Mac, she sensed a naturally confident air which projected to everyone in the courtroom. Santiago's demeanor was anxious, as if he was desperate to be seen as Mac's equal, like a little dog in the park yapping at a big German shepherd.

Judge Harajuku, looking down at her laptop, said, "Mr. MacIntyre? 10/20 strike?"

"Yes, Your Honor."

"Let the record reflect both the State and the defense stipulate this case is a 10/20 strike, meaning the State has 10 peremptory juror challenges, and the defense has 20. Gentlemen, are we ready to commence with *voir dire* questions? Ms. Chao, please assemble the jurors in the hallway and have them come in and take their seats, please."

Judge Harajuku reached behind her to a small shelf which held a variety of legal reference books and grabbed her well-worn copy of the Maryland Common Jury Instructions. She thumbed her way to the standard list of introductory questions she was required to read verbatim to the entire jury panel. Today's panel was 100 random citizens of Seneca County, drawn from both the voter registration list and from the Motor Vehicle Administration's compilation of licensed drivers. The questions she was mandated to ask the group—these so-called *voir dire* questions—were the same questions asked of all jury panels everywhere in Maryland to ensure consistency and uniformity statewide. Judge Harajuku always maintained strict control over this process. For all her intensity and chess-player's logic, she did not possess abundant creativity or flair for innovation. She believed rules were rules, and it was her job to enforce them, not create them. She thought of herself as an umpire who called balls and strikes, not a pitcher who threw curveballs or a batter who hit home runs.

Rikki Van der Hook entered the courtroom from lockup escorted by a Deputy and sat next to Santiago at the defense table. She wore an aquamarine designer blazer, dark slacks, and a crisp, white button-down shirt. She wore no jewelry. No earrings, nothing around her neck, and no wedding ring. Her hair was solidly dark, with several burgeoning intrusions of grey. Out of her baggy jail jumpsuit, Rikki looked larger. The jacket's sharp-angled shoulders gave her a wider, more solid frame. She had a pad of paper placed before her on the defense table to keep her occupied. Her small round eyeglasses gave her the appearance of an executive, not someone capable of slaughtering her husband.

Judge Harajuku noticed a slight commotion at the doorway connecting the courtroom to the hallway as Phoebe entered, funneling the large group of potential jurors inside. There was a shuffling sound as 100 pairs of shoes stepped through the doorway. The room was filled with people assuming their seats, like a crowd filling a theatre. Potential jurors coughed and cleared their throats. Faint stumbling sounds, mixed with assorted pleasantries—"Excuse me," and "No problem"—drifted through the air. Jurors were always uncomfortable with the process of jury selection. It was an imposition, forced upon them, to navigate these unfamiliar strange customs.

"Ms. Chao, please take the roll call of the prospective jurors."

"Yes, Judge," said Phoebe, who then relished her turn in the spotlight by slowly going down the list of all 100 jurors by number, not name, confirming the correct jurors were in attendance.

While Phoebe was counting down the 100 numbers one by one, Judge Harajuku observed Santiago furiously taking notes on his copy of the multi-page list each attorney had been given. Mac wasn't writing anything and had swivelled his chair away from his desk to watch the audience as each juror acknowledged his or her presence. He appeared to be studying the potential jurors, as if he were memorizing their faces and numbers.

"Ladies and gentlemen of the jury panel, my name is Judge Marcia Harajuku. First of all, thank you for your jury service. Participating in our system of justice as a juror is an important civic duty and an opportunity to serve your community. This case is the *State of Maryland vs. Rikki Michele Van der Hook.* The Defendant is charged with the following counts: murder in the first-degree, murder in the second-degree, and manslaughter."

As Judge Harajuku spoke, she could feel a new intensity vibrating from the crowd arrayed in front of her, as the words "murder," and "first-degree" and "manslaughter" splashed like rocks tossed into a lake, sending concentric ripples of emotion outward in all directions. She sensed the people in the audience were trying to process a jumble of disgust, fear, and curiosity. She knew a small minority of the jurors, those with born or proven leadership qualities, would also have a nascent desire to avenge these horrible accusations.

"We are now beginning the process of jury selection," the judge said. "This trial is estimated to take five days. Picking a jury begins with what is called *voir dire*. It is a French term which loosely means 'speak the truth.' As part of the *voir dire* process, I will be asking you some general questions to see if you qualify to be a fair and impartial trier of the facts in this case. When I have completed these questions, each of the attorneys will have what are called peremptory strikes. That simply means they can excuse a limited amount of jurors for their own reasons, whatever they may be. Please do not be offended if you are excused, as this is far from an exact science, and people are often excused for little or no reason. Will you all please rise and be sworn in by my clerk, Ms. Chao?"

Phoebe swore in the jury panel. The sound of shuffling feet rolled forward like waves.

"First of all, does any member of the jury panel know either of the attorneys in this case?" Judge Harajuku asked, simultaneously gesturing for Mac and Santiago to stand.

"The State is represented by William MacIntyre. He is the Senior Assistant State's Attorney. Does any member of the jury panel know Mr. MacIntyre?"

Mac slowly rose, buttoned his suit jacket, and stood poised at attention.

The judge noticed his eyes were sweeping strategically across the faces of the entire audience, as if downloading as much information as he possibly could. She knew he would be calculating and assessing those 100 seated strangers, needing 12 of them—just 12—to buy what he was selling. To establish the bond, to build the requisite trust, to consummate the sale, that process was starting right now with *voir dire* questioning.

CHAPTER 25

Monday, August 5, 2019
9:49 a.m.

Mac's gaze slowly scanned the potential jurors and then stopped and locked eyes with a young woman in the front row, who was leaning forward to peer at him. She was wearing a black hoodie and had a tattoo bearing the number "420" on her wrist. There was a prominent green streak in her blonde hair, and a silver hoop pierced her nose.

As Mac analyzed the young woman with the nose ring, and considered whether she would be inclined to follow him or not, he mentally inventoried the entire room of jurors. They reflected the wide diversity of Seneca County: young, old, Black, white. Asians, Latinos, East Indians and Middle Easterners, rich and poor, men and women. Each attorney was given a list of the potential jurors with basic information only: name, age, occupation, address, educational level; people reduced to skeletal outlines. Without more, Mac used his experience and natural powers of observation to make intelligent guesses and to decide which jurors to keep and which to eliminate. Sometimes, the tiniest clues revealed important information. A murder trial featuring a child witness would have an entirely different dynamic than a drug deal or an embezzlement or virtually any other type of crime. Typical criminal cases centered on what the police did to investigate something. This case would be about family dysfunction and understanding how the mind of a child recorded information.

In a case with a vulnerable child experiencing extreme trauma, Mac sought out female jurors. He looked for the mothers mixed in the courtroom crowd. Schoolteachers, nurses, women who had nurtured and protected children, those would be Mac's best jurors. Surely, they were scattered out there in this crowd. The trick was to find them.

Judge Harajuku said, "The Defendant is Rikki Van der Hook. She is represented by Santiago Garcia. Does any member of the jury panel know either Ms. Van der Hook or Mr. Garcia?" She paused. The courtroom was quiet. "The Court hears no affirmative response from the jury panel." She said these things out loud, as the proceedings of the entire trial were being recorded, and this was how she made a "record."

Mac barely listened as the judge methodically read the rest of the standard questions to the group. He was almost entirely focused on the jurors' responses and not Judge Harajuku's questions. Luckily, only a few people had heard any press reports about the case, and none of them had remembered the facts well. Everyone had been pre-screened for a five-day trial. No one volunteered any private reason why he or she could not be fair and impartial. There were few instances when a juror would stand up in front of 100 total strangers and proclaim that they couldn't be fair. It had happened only once in Mac's career: the young skinhead with a spider web tattoo on his face who said he couldn't be fair to an African American defendant because he hated Black people and wished they would all go back to Africa. Disgusted, Mac asked the judge to disqualify him immediately.

Mac waited patiently for the key question he knew was coming.

"Has any member of the jury panel ever been the victim of, or has experienced, domestic violence? I don't want you to speak out loud. Just raise your hand, and then we will ask you to approach the bench privately."

At least 30 hands popped up. A forest of arms. Most were female arms, but some were male. The presence of raised male hands did not surprise Mac. He had prosecuted plenty of jury trials where men had been brutalized by their spouses, and, of course, the question was broad enough to encompass children abused in their youth. Each of these raised arms was attached to a potential juror Mac wanted. Concentrating, Mac tried to memorize all the 30 jurors who had raised their hands. Jurors who had been previously victimized would be sympathetic to both Mandy and, in a larger sense, Marten Van der Hook. Those arms were guilty votes just waiting to be plucked, like ripe fruit from trees in an orchard.

"OK, ladies and gentlemen," the judge said. "Please form a line down the center aisle of the courtroom, and we will call you up to the bench individually. Thank you."

Mac and Santiago approached the bench and positioned themselves on either side, standing like sentinels. Not having Mac's natural gifts for deciphering body language, Santiago smiled just a little too widely, giving his expression a hint of insincerity, like a bank teller asking you how you were. Obviously, the bank teller didn't really care. Mac's goal right now was to find a way, even if just for a fleeting moment, to bond with a juror. This might be the only time during the entire course of the trial that he could stand right next to a juror. During these whispered exchanges, sometimes Mac had completely won a juror over with just a slightly crooked smile, fleeting eye contact, or an expert tilt of his head.

The line of jurors stretched all the way to the back of the courtroom. One by one, they approached and haltingly described, sometimes with great difficulty, violence in their personal relationships or the intimate details of their own childhood abuse. Mac had heard thousands of these sad narratives. Almost all the perpetrators in these stories had long since escaped justice unavenged.

A lady with a metal walking cane approached. Her cane was aluminum and shiny and had three prongs in a tripod configuration for balance. Her hair was pulled back into a bun. Although it was a warm summer day, she had on a long dress and was wearing a sweater vest over it. As she approached, Mac immediately noticed a small green brooch fastened to her lapel in the shape of a butterfly. It reflected brilliantly in the harsh courtroom light. He had seen that gemstone once before: in the marketplace in Taos, New Mexico, where Native American craftsmen hustled a living in the Plaza, sitting in the shade on blankets with their homemade wares spread out on the sidewalk.

What was that jewel called?

Mac couldn't immediately recall, and that distracted him.

Somewhere deep inside his brain, he felt his memory swirling around, the answer floating like a single piece of confetti inevitably drawn by gravity down to the ground; it might drift momentarily in the breeze and linger, but eventually, it would land, and Mac would grasp it.

The old lady finally made her way up to the front of the judge's bench. She took a deep breath. Clearly, she had something troubling to say.

Under his breath, so softly no one could hear, Mac said, "Malachite."

CHAPTER 26

Monday, August 5, 2019
11:49 a.m.

Judge Harajuku said, "Good morning, ma'am, what is your juror number please?"

The lady said, "My juror number?"

She unfolded the Jury Service Notification she'd received in the mail, a pink piece of paper folded into quadrants.

"I'm Number 18. Mrs. Geraldine O'Dwyer."

"Thank you, ma'am. We'll go by just the juror number for privacy. For the purpose of this trial, you'll be Juror Number 18. Is there something you wanted to let the Court know in response to the question about prior domestic violence?"

"Well, yes. But it happened such a long time ago, so I don't know if it's important..."

"Ma'am, why don't you tell us what made you respond to the question?"

"I'm 87 years old now," she began. "Well, it was a really long time ago. I was a little girl, maybe eight or nine years old. This was when the War began. I remember that. We had ration cards in those years. I can see the booklets in my mind, even now. We lived in the country, up by where the river narrows. They run a ferry across to the Virginia side there.

"That ferry's been working, taking people across the river for many, many years. I think even back before the Civil War. Well, our farm was up in that area. Still Seneca County, but near the border."

Picking up momentum, the old lady continued, "This is way before the days of television and computers and cell phones, you understand? We didn't even have a radio until I was a teenager. We were pretty isolated. Just hard-working farm folks."

Mac was standing still on her left side, careful not to disrupt her narrative. Santiago was standing on her other side, but he was smiling incongruously. As the old lady's story moved towards an inevitable tragic conclusion, his frozen smile became increasingly out of place. Mac glanced at the green butterfly brooch.

"So, most days, my father worked hard tending the fields of crops in the back acreage. And my mother stayed in the house mostly, doing her chores and laundry and cooking and such. I was just a little girl. My father worked hard, and when he came home at sunset, he started drinking. When he drank too much, he became real mean."

Mac, Santiago, and Judge Harajuku were now captivated, listening intently.

"He would hit my mother. Sometimes a slap, sometimes worse. He'd be yelling and breaking things, and I was so scared. I used to run out and hide in the barn in the hayloft and not come back until after he fell asleep. But even from the barn, I would hear my mother crying and sobbing and the sound of things breaking. To this day, all these years later, I can't stand the sound of breaking glass.

"It took me years to realize how trapped my mother was. And I have always regretted not telling anyone. I just kept quiet. I never told anyone about it. No one. Not my husband, or any of my daughters. I haven't talked about it all these years. Until today. It's been a secret buried deep inside of me my whole life. Well, that's what I wanted to tell you."

There was a prolonged silence as Mac, Santiago, and Judge Harajuku all digested the depth of her pain and sadness. It hung around them like a fog: four people clustered in a courtroom, with nearly 100 random people watching, and the fizzing sound of the husher whirring like a fan. Five full seconds passed.

"Ma'am, I need to ask you, though, one important question," said the judge. "Ma'am, the only issue is, well, the only question that needs to be answered is this: can you remain *impartial* in this case? This trial may have elements of domestic violence in it. I mean, given what you've just told us about your own past life experiences, are you certain that you can be a fair and impartial juror to both sides in this case?"

Mrs. O'Dwyer paused, then responded, "Why, yes. Yes, I can. I can be fair to both sides."

"Well, thank you, ma'am. Can you please return to your seat? I'll confer with the attorneys for a minute."

Mrs. O'Dwyer turned, buttoned her sweater vest, and slowly returned to her seat.

Up at the bench, Santiago declared, "Judge, this is obvious! I object to this juror, and I ask that the Court strike her for cause. She can't be a fair and impartial juror. With all her own childhood DV experiences? I mean, that's just so clear..."

Judge Harajuku interrupted him, "Mr. MacIntyre?"

CHAPTER 27

Monday, August 5, 2019
12:09 p.m.

Mac said, "Your Honor, she answered your key question appropriately. She directly addressed the only essential factor at issue: her impartiality. She said, with absolutely no equivocation, that she could be fair and impartial. That is the test under Maryland law, as the Court well knows. Therefore, the State's position is..."

Judge Harajuku began to announce her decision. "I agree with the..."

Santiago, with a panicked tone, interjected a final flailing argument, "But Judge! They always say that! Every juror in the history of this courthouse says they can be fair! Have you ever heard a juror flat-out just say, 'I can't be fair?' No one does that!"

"Your objection is overruled, Mr. Garcia. I'll permit her to remain in the jury pool. I will not strike her for *cause*, but

Mr. Garcia, you have your peremptory strikes. I trust you will use them wisely. Gentlemen, you may step back." They turned, Mac with a completely blank expression and Santiago grimacing. All the eyes in the jury pool were watching and wondering what the old lady had to say that could provoke such intense drama.

Judge Harajuku's expression was blank. All judges had skilled poker faces, but hers was magnificently expressionless.

One by one, the jurors approached and told tales of traumatic events, revealing their own childhood and marital secrets. Several jurors, who had convincingly demonstrated that they were not impartial, were struck by Judge Harajuku for "cause," meaning that she, in her own independent reasoning, believed they were unsuitable for service. When this process was completed, the next phase of jury selection began; now, individually, each juror stood and either Mac or Santiago, in alternating fashion, like a card game, announced their peremptory challenges.

"Please strike Juror Number 96," said Santiago, referring to a woman who had been on the long line of jurors with some previous domestic violence experience. She was a heavyset woman with bleached hair, wearing yoga pants, and an oversized T-shirt. On her juror information form, she had listed her "occupation" as "married to a police patrol officer." Judge Harajuku guessed that this juror would hate Rikki, and that's why Santiago was excusing her. The judge looked at Rikki, who was sitting at the defense table wearing her expensive, fashionable outfit, the epitome of a slender, privileged wife of a multimillionaire.

"Please excuse and thank Juror 74," Mac said, smiling at a young white man wearing a uniform of some type with his name sewn into the breast pocket: SHAWN. Judge Harajuku flipped through her own copy of the jury roster and noted that Shawn's profession was listed as "unemployed." The judge could see a trend developing: Mac needed intelligent, well-educated jurors, not jurors to whom the moneyed life in Seneca County's wealthiest zip code would only be an impossible fantasy.

Judge Harajuku, falling back on her experience as a champion chess player, viewed the process of jury selection as a strange game, a form of human blackjack, a shuffling of people instead of cards. It was really jury deselection more than jury selection. People came up in the order of their randomly assigned juror numbers, and then they were chosen or discarded like diamonds, clubs, spades, or hearts. As the defense had twice as many strikes as the prosecution, 20 to 10, she knew Mac would be careful to save his jury strikes like aces.

By 4:00 p.m., all the strikes were gone, and the jury box was filled, 12 jurors and two alternates.

Three of the 12 jurors were Latino, noted the judge, thinking that Santiago must believe that would help him.

Nine of them were women.

Santiago silently watched, without objection, as Juror Number 18 slowly marched up with her cane and sat in the jury box. She would be part of the case. Butterfly Lady with the green malachite brooch. Judge Harajuku wondered why in the world Santiago did not use one of his last strikes on her.

"Thank you, ladies and gentlemen of the jury. My clerk will now distribute parking passes to you for the Jury Parking

Lot. Kindly be here promptly at 8:30 a.m. tomorrow morning. Please assemble at the other end of the hallway, and Ms. Chao will come get you when necessary. Thank you again for your service. Have a good evening."

Another juror, the young woman with the nose ring, gazed at Mac and lingered in the jury box, slowly gathering up her backpack. Mac looked at her and made eye contact. The jurors filed out of the courtroom, each one with a maroon sticker stating JUROR across their upper left chest.

"Gentlemen, if there are no preliminary issues, we will commence with opening statements tomorrow morning at nine sharp."

"All rise," said Phoebe. Judge Harajuku stepped down from her raised platform and walked through the side door to her chambers.

When the jurors had left the courtroom, a female deputy handcuffed Rikki and escorted her out of the room through the side door, leaving Mac and Santiago alone in the courtroom.

Mac whispered across the counsel tables, "That old lady with the butterfly jewelry is going to fry your gal's ass, I promise."

"We'll see about that. My Latino crew is looking good, amigo."

"How the hell could you leave Butterfly Lady on this jury, Santiago?"

"I ran out of strikes!"

CHAPTER 28

Tuesday, August 6, 2019
8:09 a.m.

Mac waited in the atrium area of the ground floor of the Seneca County Judicial Center, shielded by a pillar. The original architects had designed the entry to the courthouse complex to be open and airy, with clusters of trees inside the building. Of course, they didn't anticipate that when the new Juvenile Court was constructed directly across the street, it would end up blocking most of the sunlight. All the trees died. Now, as inanimate replacements, garish 1960s-style abstract steel sculptures lined up where the trees had once been, giving the atrium the appearance of a dated art gallery, or even the ruins of a skyscraper, rather than a courthouse.

Mac stood off to the side of the entrance security area, which looked like an airport screening site with officers and metal detectors. He knew he could not be easily seen from this exact vantage point; it was a blind spot for anyone entering the complex. He saw the Girl with the Nose Ring and a small Latina woman who had listed her occupation as an assistant manager of housekeeping at the Hampton Inn over by the highway. He dubbed her Housekeeper. They were both wearing maroon adhesive badges with JUROR in blocky white lettering.

The two women passed through security and then walked together towards the elevators. Mac quickly followed and joined them.

"Good morning, ma'am," he said to Housekeeper, standing next to her.

"Morning," she said in return.

They all got on the elevator.

"Ninth floor," he said, pushing the button. "We're all going to the same place." His tone was relaxed and friendly. They stood silently as they ascended to the hallway outside the courtroom.

"Have a nice day," said the Girl with the Nose Ring, smiling.

"I'll see you in there," he said.

Winning the jurors over was one of the keys to victory. An attorney's art of persuasion was often more important than the strength of the evidence. Many brilliant attorneys neglected this essential goal, putting up solid cases in front of bored juries, only to lose. Mac constantly watched the jurors for clues, however tiny. He scrutinized what they were wearing and what reading materials they brought with them. He watched to see if they lined up in order, or if they were a chaotic mob. If lined up straight and orderly, they would likely harmonize and deliberate in an organized fashion. If a lone juror was late, or lost, or uncooperative, he or she would self-identify themselves as stubborn or individualistic, a rebel who might stand up against the group. The lone wolf type of juror was potentially the one to hold out against 11 others. Mac needed all 12 to unanimously agree on guilt.

A hung jury—an indecisive one—resulted in a mistrial. Mistrials were disasters for the prosecution. Even though it was permissible to retry a case ending with a hung jury, the defense would have a huge advantage. In a retrial, the defense attorney had already heard all the testimony. That was like a football team having the opponents' playbook. Retrials took away any element of surprise. A jury trial was not a stage play where dress rehearsals made for a better opening night. Mac needed to win this Van der Hook case now, not later.

He knew any random group of jurors, no matter how diverse, always subdivided themselves into two camps: leaders and followers. Mac favored citizens who were obviously powerful leaders. A juror who had an occupation like an Army General, or the CEO of a corporation, or a high school coach, those were "Type A" personalities perfect for the prosecution. If a couple of "Type A" jurors fully committed to his theory of the case, Mac would create ambassadors inside the jury room, emissaries who would promote and argue for him when he no longer could. Military types, and of course police officers, were great for the prosecution, but they were often excused by a defense attorney's peremptory strikes.

Conversely, during this juror stereotyping process, Mac knew Santiago would look for loners, drifters, nonconformists, and people who were obviously anti-authority. Jurors Mac always tried to avoid were people who seemed to be outcasts or outlaw types and ex-hippies, artists, college students still finding their way, and people with strong political left-leaning views. Those were jurors who would be distrustful of the government, and who typically hated police and prosecutors, often with good reason.

Phoebe came out into the hallway at 8:45 a.m. She immediately began the process of herding up the participants to escort them into the courtroom.

"Jurors for Judge Harajuku's trial? Please gather here," she said.

CHAPTER 29

Tuesday, August 6, 2019
8:48 a.m.

Phoebe, relishing her role, used hand gestures like a traffic cop in a busy intersection to signal, "Come this way." The jurors were obedient and shuffled into place, forming a line. Mac needed to pick a couple of them to designate as his "Ambassadors." The jurors he felt uneasy about were the "Question Marks." Those were the ones he had to keep an eye on. He needed his Ambassadors to convince the Question Marks, beyond a reasonable doubt, Rikki was guilty. Once the jury room was locked, once Mac was shut off from them, his Ambassadors would have to take over from there.

Down the hall, Butterfly Lady emerged from the ladies' room with her three-pronged cane. She was moving more confidently. She was going to be an Ambassador. She wouldn't be strong in the sense that she'd argue vociferously during deliberations. No, she wouldn't overpower anyone in the jury room, but she was a woman with a formidable, quiet power, someone who could command enormous respect, particularly if she divulged her own riveting personal story of abuse. They'd respect her with the same reverence they respected their own grandmothers. She would lead any uncertain jurors as a shepherd leads sheep: gently but firmly. Mac was certain she'd be a definite guilty vote.

A large Black man lurched to the front of the line of jurors, moving all the way to the first position. Only a leader type would make such a move. Mac assigned the moniker "Power Forward" to him, not only based on his size—at least six-foot-six and bulky—but because he seemed totally unafraid. He had revealed during *voir dire* that, yes, he had several minor convictions, including one for trespassing in a public parking lot. Mac noted the inconsistency of trespassing in a public place; it made little sense. Power Forward also had a misdemeanor conviction for "resisting arrest," a typically trumped-up charge which aggressive police officers in Seneca County had a history of charging unfairly. Mac immediately discounted the prior arrest record, as those blemishes were likely the product of Seneca County's long history of institutional and systemic racism. Maryland had been a so-called "Border State" during the Civil War, with combatants on both sides. Enslaved people had worked the tobacco fields and fished the Chesapeake Bay alongside the first Europeans who had settled here. Just recently, citizens had lobbied for the removal of a Confederate soldier monument, an infantryman with a musket, which had stood erect outside the Old Colonial Courthouse for decades.

Power Forward would be a paradox in the jury room. He'd be no friend, generally, of police, prosecutors and judges. But he would bond extremely well with Mac's lead detective, Andre. More importantly, he would hate Rikki Van der Hook on sight and would relish the unconscious reversal of leverage. As a juror, Power Forward definitely had the power. He would be another Ambassador.

The jurors marched into the courtroom. The Girl with the Nose Ring turned around and quickly glanced at Mac. She radiated mixed messages and was difficult to decipher. She would have to be a Question Mark. She was a pretty young woman with corn-colored dyed hair. The edges of several tattoos peeked out from the shirtsleeves of her frayed hoodie. Mac wondered if she was too free-spirited to assume the responsibility of rendering judgment. Outward manifestations of individuality could signal trouble. The Girl with the Nose Ring worried him. Mac decided he would flirt with her while conducting the trial. He would make plentiful eye contact, smile, and stand directly in front of her when he did his opening statement with his suit jacket opened so she could glance wherever she wanted. He'd let her mind wander to secret fantasies in order to win her over. With luck, she too might be another Ambassador.

Housekeeper also worried him. She was stocky, but appeared sturdy rather than soft, and was somewhere in her middle-aged years. She carried a shoulder bag woven from straw instead of a purse. Mac noted the words "Machu Picchu" stitched into the side of the bag. Originally from Peru, Housekeeper had been living in Seneca County for almost

30 years. She had built a promising life, raising three children who were proudly first-generation Americans. Mac strongly preferred having female jurors for any case which featured child witnesses, and Housekeeper's perspective as a woman, and as a mother, could be a major benefit. However, Housekeeper also seemed fascinated with every word Santiago spoke. Maybe Santiago unconsciously reminded her of one of her three American sons? Clearly, Housekeeper was another worrisome Question Mark.

Santiago stepped out of the elevator and said, "G'morning, bro. Damn that rush hour traffic. Just made it here on time!"

"Good morning. Thought you might never show up. The jury's seated already."

Mac looked at his watch. He added, "She's coming out of chambers in 45 seconds."

They went into the courtroom and took their respective places at the two counsel tables. Santiago dragged his rolling briefcase behind him, thumping it into his chair with a thud, causing several jurors to take notice.

Rikki had been sitting at the defense table alone, without Santiago, for a minute before the jury entered. Two deputies stood behind her. She was wearing a different tailored jacket but the same dark slacks.

When they were all perfectly in place, there was an unnecessarily loud banging on the inside of the door which led to chambers. Phoebe stepped into the courtroom and, with all the authority she could muster, announced, "All rise! The Honorable Marcia Harajuku of the Circuit Court for Seneca County now presiding! Court is now in session."

CHAPTER 30

Tuesday, August 6, 2019
9:02 a.m.

STATE OF MARYLAND
OFFICE OF THE CHIEF MEDICAL EXAMINER

900 W. Baltimore Street
Baltimore, Maryland 21223

Oliver Trayger: Chief Medical Examiner
Mike A. Morrison: Deputy Chief Medical Examiner

POST MORTEM EXAMINATION

AUTOPSY: X

JURISDICTION: Seneca County

NAME OF DECEASED: Marten Vincent Van Der Hook

AGE: 49

SEX: Male

RACE: Caucasian/White

DATE OF INCIDENT: December 20, 2018

PRONOUNCED DEAD: December 20, 2018, 4:30 a.m.

A. X. FOSTER

AUTOPSY PERFORMED: December 22, 2018

PERFORMED BY: Zubahari Williamson, M.D.

CAUSE OF DEATH: Sharp Force Injuries

MANNER OF DEATH: **Homicide**

EXTERNAL EXAMINATION

The body was that of a well-developed, well-nourished white male clad in a white "Hanes" brand T-shirt underneath a blue striped "Nordstrom" brand dress shirt, blue suit pants with label "Jos. A Bank," black socks, and black "Givenchy Oxford" leather shoes. The clothing was blood-soaked.

The body weighed 188 pounds and was 5'11.5" in height. The body was cold to the touch.

Rigor was present to an equal degree in all extremities. Lividity was present on the posterior surface of the body. The scalp hair was dark brown mixed with grey. The irises were light green/hazel in color. The left earlobe was pierced. The mouth contained two anterior lower teeth implants. A tattoo with four Japanese kanji characters was noted on the dorsal side of the left wrist. No needle marks were noted. The external genitalia was atraumatic. No evidence of medical intervention was noted.

SHARP FORCE INJURIES

A. HEAD AND NECK:

a)STAB WOUNDS TO RIGHT BACK OF HEAD (7)
There were seven ¾" to 3" deep and ½" wide stab wounds on the right side of the back of the head. The stab wounds injured the scalp and subcutaneous tissues with two (2) wounds penetrating the skull.

b)STAB WOUNDS TO THE LEFT SIDE OF THE NECK AND FACE (24)
There were twenty-four (24) 2" to 2½" deep wounds to the left side of neck and face. The stab wounds injured the skin and soft tissues, and were directed front to back and downward. The commingled stab

wound paths injured the muscles of the neck, left carotid artery (transected), left jugular vein (transected). Due to the complex and gaping nature of the wounds, the sharp and blunt edges of the blade could not be determined, but there were clear indications of serration, consisting of multiple linear parallel lines, indicative of a serrated edged weapon.

B. HANDS:

a) CUTTING WOUNDS TO RIGHT HAND (4)
There were multiple slashing injuries to the ulnar aspect of the right hand injuring the skin and subcutaneous tissue indicative of defensive wounds.

b) CUTTING WOUNDS TO THE LEFT HAND (1)
There was a deep irregular cutting injury to the palmar surface of the left hand injuring the skin and subcutaneous tissue indicative of defensive wounds.

OPINION: This 49-year-old white male, Marten Vincent Van der Hook, died of SHARP FORCE INJURIES (36 stab and cutting injuries). The stab wounds to the neck injured the left carotid artery and left jugular vein (major blood vessels), thyroid gland, and thyroid cartilage. These injuries were associated with massive bleeding and aspiration of blood into the lungs. The remaining cutting injuries further contributed to blood loss. The characteristic of the stab wounds shows parallel and linear wounds. Serration marks are noted in multiple locations consistent with a serrated edged knife. The non-lethal injuries to the hands are consistent with defensive wounds. The manner of death is: **HOMICIDE**

Zubahari Williamson, M.D.
Assistant Medical Examiner
December 22, 2018

CHAPTER 31

Tuesday, August 6, 2019
9:05 a.m.

Mac reached for the autopsy report and arranged it on his table, along with the crime scene photos and other demonstrative evidence he was about to use during his opening statement. Knowing the jury was watching his every move, he deliberately spread out the autopsy report and photographs in a logical row, silently communicating, "See? See all the evidence I have?"

Just as Judge Harajuku was about to prompt Mac to begin his opening statement, Santiago jumped up from his position at the defense table and said, "Your Honor, may we approach? I have a Motion in Limine that is extremely important. I need to address it with the Court before the State opens."

A flash of anger burst across the judge's face; she could not contain her irritation. The muscles in her jaw bulged.

"Approach!"

Mac glanced at the jurors with an intentionally perplexed expression, eyebrows raised. If there was any gamesmanship, he wanted them to know it was Santiago's fault and not his. The jurors swiveled their heads, looking at one another, seeking eye contact, and searching for a possible explanation for this strange delay.

Mac and Santiago trudged up to the judge's bench.

Judge Harajuku switched on the husher device, and white noise filled the well of the courtroom.

"What is the issue, Mr. Garcia?! The jury is seated, and Mr. MacIntyre is literally about to give his opening statement!"

"I'm sorry, Your Honor, but it is very important that we address a critical matter as a Motion in Limine. I apologize to the Court, but it must be litigated before opening statements. If not, I will not be able to effectively represent my client, and I honestly feel…"

The judge cut him off. She had heard the magic word "effectively."

"Mr. Garcia! We are not going to have a trial-by-ambush! Whatever your problem is, it should have been handled when we did Motions back in January, not on the morning of the trial as a Motion in Limine!"

"Limine" was roughly translated from Latin as "threshold." A Motion in Limine was a last-second tactic to identify or create an emergency issue just before the trial started. Slick defense attorneys strategically waited until just before a prosecutor was about to give an opening statement, and then they would try to throw up a hurdle at the last moment.

Santiago stood plaintively, his arms outstretched. Mac was frozen in place, but he had also heard the word "effectively."

Both he and the judge knew that defense attorneys tossed that word out like a hand grenade, just to disrupt the flow of a trial. "Ineffective assistance of counsel" was one of the primary appellate attacks on any conviction. Mac knew that if the judge denied hearing Santiago's last-minute Motion in Limine, Santiago would have successfully planted a future argument to make on appeal, claiming he wasn't allowed to represent his client properly or "effectively." Mac suspected the judge knew exactly what Santiago was doing, but, weighing the alternative of gifting him a future appellate argument, Mac correctly guessed that she would just let him state whatever his "emergency" was and address it now, rather than let it fester into a problem in the future. Closing any legal loophole right now was more important than interrupting his opening statement.

The husher was still swirling, and the jurors were trying to decipher what this last-second interruption could possibly be.

"OK, Mr. Garcia, what *is* your Motion in Limine?"

"Judge, I understand that Mr. MacIntyre's key witness is my client's daughter."

Mac couldn't resist. He said, "She is the victim's daughter too, Judge."

Santiago continued, "She is just nine years old. I believe she is incompetent to testify. Yes, legally incompetent. So, we ask the Court to hear us on that issue now rather than while the young child is on the witness stand. We wouldn't want to subject this minor to the stress and pressure..."

Judge Harajuku interrupted him. She flipped the husher off, turned to the jurors, and said, "Ladies and gentlemen, an evidentiary matter has arisen which requires the attorneys and

I to discuss at some length. Please, can you head into the jury room, and we will bring you back into the courtroom when we are done. It should be no more than 15 minutes. Thank you for your understanding."

Phoebe gestured with her arm in the direction of the jury room. The jurors stood and started collecting their personal items.

Power Forward, the large African American juror in the back row, said, "Should we leave our stuff here or take it with us?"

"Just leave your things on your seat. This will not take long. Thank you," said the judge.

The jurors filed out of the courtroom.

Once they were all safely sequestered in the jury room, Phoebe made sure the double doors were securely shut and then turned to the judge and said, "That's all 14, Judge," referring to the 12 actual members of the jury and the two alternate jurors.

Mac roamed back behind the State's table and sat. He leaned back and crossed his legs.

Santiago stood behind the defense table and buttoned his suit jacket.

"So, Mr. Garcia, please state your Motion for the record and make it snappy," Judge Harajuku said.

Santiago began.

CHAPTER 32

Tuesday, August 6, 2019
9:45 a.m.

"Maryland Rule 5-601 controls the issue of witness competency, Your Honor," Santiago began, holding up a Xerox copy of the rule. "And . . . and . . . I quote, 'because of insufficient memory, intelligence or ability to express oneself, or inability to appreciate the need to tell the truth, a particular witness is not competent to testify.'"

He put the copy of the rule down on his table as if it were a winning hand at the poker table.

"In this case, I'm told that my client's daughter, who is the witness the State is relying on for its entire case, is a nine-year-old child, who, Your Honor, suffers from a severe mental disability. We contend she is not competent to testify under the auspices of the rule."

Judge Harajuku said, "What exactly is the nature of her disability?"

Santiago, not expecting to be questioned, uncharacteristically stuttered, "W-well, she has, as I understand it, narcolepsy—pediatric narcolepsy—to be precise. S-some adults have narcolepsy, to be sure, but in a child, it is extremely rare. In fact, as I understand, Mandy is the only child in the entire Seneca County Public School system to be designated with this rare sleep disorder. It's so unusual they don't even have a category for it on her Individualized Education Plan. They just list her as 'otherwise impaired.' The IEP forms have categories for blindness, deafness, ADHD, and all kinds of disabilities, but she is the *only* student in a county of over one million residents who has pediatric narcolepsy."

The judge returned the volley. "It's a sleep disorder, right? She's sleepy. How does that affect her intelligence or memory or ability to express herself? How does it affect her understanding of truth versus falsity? Do you intend to present any expert testimony on this issue? Or am I just supposed to take your word on all of this?"

"Well, Your Honor, I'm happy to answer your question," he stalled, using a meaningless phrase to delay for time as he tried to think of an appropriate response. Nothing clever came to mind, so he said, "She is only nine years old..."

"So what? I've had a child witness testify before me who was four."

"But this is a child with narcolepsy! Her ability to pay attention, and even stay awake during these proceedings..."

"Enough. Mr. MacIntyre, does the State have anything to put on the record?"

As Mac slowly stood, Santiago felt like he had stepped into a pool of quicksand and was steadily sinking. He knew Judge Harajuku's question was shorthand for *he had already lost his argument*, and Mac needed only to announce a very short perfunctory objection to the Motion. The quicksand had swallowed Santiago's argument whole.

Mac said, "Judge, the State has every confidence this child witness is fully competent to testify, and, for the record, we object to Counsel's Motion. Thank you."

The judge spoke, "So, let me be clear. The defense has raised a Motion in Limine to exclude a child witness on the grounds of incompetency. They assert that because of an underlying physical disorder—and I find that pediatric narcolepsy is a physical disorder, not a mental disorder—this child will not be able to testify intelligently, that her memory is compromised, that she is insufficiently capable of expressing herself in a courtroom setting, and that she cannot appreciate the need to tell the truth. I find that there has been absolutely no evidence presented by the defense to support these assertions. None. Therefore, the Motion will be denied."

Santiago slumped down into his chair. He turned to speak to Rikki, whispering, "Well, they still have to get her up on the witness stand and talk. If Mandy falls apart, their case falls apart too."

The judge said, "Ms. Chao, please bring the jury back in to hear opening statements."

CHAPTER 33

Tuesday, August 6, 2019
10:35 a.m.

"Thank you, Your Honor, and may it please the Court. Good morning. My name is William MacIntyre, and I represent the State of Maryland."

Mac walked to the center of the courtroom.

"This case is about a killer." Mac pointed at Rikki Van der Hook.

"A killer who planned and executed a first-degree murder of her husband Marten Van der Hook. This case will take you to a dark place—somewhere you've never been—somewhere you've only heard about on the news or seen on TV crime shows. Unfortunately, however, it is a real place, not somewhere fictitious. And, in order to find justice for Marten and his surviving family, all of us will have to go to this dark, homicidal place.

"The Defendant is charged with several counts of murder. At the end of the trial, the judge will instruct you and explain what the elements of those crimes are. She will explain the differences between first-degree murder, second-degree murder, and manslaughter. She will also define the legal terms that apply. For now, it's my opportunity, on behalf of the State of Maryland, to give you an opening statement, which, I hope, will be like a road map showing you where I expect the evidence in this case will take us. Ultimately, it will take us to proof of guilt beyond a reasonable doubt.

"The evidence in this case will clearly prove that the Defendant, to exact revenge on her husband for his infidelities, and, to some extent, satisfy her own greed, deviously designed a plan to murder Marten and stage it to look like an impromptu event or, even worse, to make it appear as if she was defending herself."

Mac moved to his table and stood within arm's reach of the photographs and reports he had previously arrayed. His voice was clear, perfectly loud and commanding. Everyone in the courtroom was concentrating on his every word. He was totally in charge of the space, center stage, like a charismatic actor.

"What the Defendant didn't know, however, what she could not have predicted, was that their daughter, nine-year-old Mandy, had gotten out of bed and was watching from the top of the staircase. She was sitting on the steps, leaning against the banister, peering down from above. And from that elevated vantage point, she clearly saw the entire horrifying event unfold before her eyes. Mandy saw her mother slaughter her father.

"In Mandy's own words, and I quote, she said, 'I saw Mommy punching Dad with a knife.'

"And that, ladies and gentlemen, is exactly what happened in this case. Mandy will enter this courtroom and walk down the center aisle and take the witness stand. She will bravely tell you exactly what she saw on that fateful night. She is a resilient and brave child, and she has more courage in her small body than the coward sitting here." Mac whirled, extending his full arm, and again pointed directly at Rikki.

Mac moved to the edge of the jury box, standing directly in front of the Girl with the Nose Ring. She turned and gazed up at Mac's face as she tugged on the drawstrings of her hoodie.

"Let me take a step back and give you some background information for context. Marten Van der Hook was a prominent businessman here in Seneca County. You may have heard of him prior to this case if you follow business matters. He was a hugely successful man. Born in the Netherlands, he went to university there and excelled in engineering and mechanics. He immigrated to the United States after college to attend graduate school at the University of Maryland, where he achieved advanced degrees. Marten Van der Hook was a very creative and entrepreneurial man. He was also somewhat of an inventor. He was one of those kids born with a mechanical mind. Even as a boy, he would take apart machines, build go-carts, and experiment with engines and motors. His first job in the Netherlands, near the tulip fields, was at a garden store, where, at age 14, he worked in the garage fixing lawn mowers.

"Then Marten had an idea: he envisioned a different way to cut grass. He thought, why not *stand* on the lawn mower and cut the grass upright instead of sitting on a riding mower? So, after finishing his graduate degree in Mechanical Engineering, Marten gained U.S. citizenship and started a new life here in America. He worked tirelessly on his upright lawn mower idea, and his persistence paid off. More than 20 years later, at the time of his death, he held over 40 patents and grew his upright invention into a multimillion dollar chain of home improvement and garden stores known as MVH Enterprises. Based in Seneca County, right here in Maryland."

From the corner of his eye, using only his peripheral vision, Mac noticed a man enter the courtroom and sit in the last row, slumping down in one of the seats. He appeared disheveled, and he was not wearing a suit.

"While Marten was a graduate student at the University of Maryland, he met a young woman who he would eventually marry. At the time, she was studying theatre and acting in the Drama Department. And, yes, ladies and gentlemen of the jury, Rikki Van der Hook is an excellent actress."

"Objection!" said Santiago, jumping up from his chair.

CHAPTER 34

Tuesday, August 6, 2019
10:53 a.m.

Before Mac could even spin around toward Santiago, Judge Harajuku said, "Sustained. Let's stick to the evidence, Mr. MacIntyre."

Of course, Mac knew it was argumentative and improper for a prosecutor to comment, even obliquely, on a Defendant's credibility, but he appreciated how lucky he was that Rikki was a drama major in college. Sometimes, in a trial, little gifts were fortuitously handed to you. When that happened, the most effective strategy was to take the gift and slowly unwrap it right in front of the jury.

Perfect! I got Santiago to object. Great. Now the jury is really going to be suspicious of Rikki if she testifies. Excellent.

"Marten and the Defendant were married and, nine years ago, they welcomed Mandy into the family. Mandy is their only child. As a newborn baby, they noticed she had unusual sleep patterns. But, as new parents, they really weren't sure what to expect. Unlike most babies who wake their parents up in the middle of the night, Mandy would sleep for 12 or even 15 straight hours. Otherwise, she appeared totally normal, and she experienced developmental milestones just like every other child. She learned to talk and walk right on schedule.

"Mandy also experienced daytime drowsiness and fatigue, which greatly concerned her parents. When she was five years old, they took her to the Mayo Clinic in Minnesota for a full sleep study. There, the physicians who specialize in sleep disorders are some of the best in the world. Mandy was diagnosed with 'pediatric narcolepsy,' which is extremely rare. Some of you may have heard of narcolepsy before. It is usually portrayed in the media or in articles as a phenomenon where someone just instantly falls asleep in a flash. One minute, they're wide awake and then, snap your fingers, and they're fast asleep. Well, that is a cliché version of what narcolepsy really is. In actuality, it can be more like a chronic fatigue and constant sleepiness.

"The good news is Mandy has effective medications which help her stay awake during the day. Her doctor projects she will have an otherwise normal life. If she can successfully manage her sleep, there is no reason why she can't have a bright future.

"I mention all of this to you for one reason: I expect the defense to exaggerate and attack Mandy because of her pediatric narcolepsy. But this much is absolutely clear: Mandy saw exactly what happened to her father. She saw her mother kill him, and what she saw is corroborated by a detailed autopsy report."

Mac lifted the autopsy report for the jurors to see.

"Rikki Van der Hook stabbed and cut her husband 36 times. Yes, you heard me right: I said she stabbed and cut her husband 36 times! That is what we call overkill.

"You will hear from the investigating officer, Detective Andre Okoye. He will explain the various aspects of his investigation, including his interview with Mandy. Just remember this concise statement: 'Mommy punched Dad with a knife.' That is the entire case in six words.

"Ladies and gentlemen, the Defendant is charged with three counts of homicide. Three different forms: first-degree murder, second-degree murder and manslaughter. First-degree murder requires you to conclude she killed her husband *intentionally*, and she did so with premeditation, meaning she planned the killing and did it on purpose. The evidence you will hear in this case clearly shows premeditation and several strong motives to kill, namely a desire to avenge what she saw as marital infidelity and, concurrently, a gigantic life insurance policy. Not to mention, a vast inheritance which would pass to her upon her husband's death. If you focus on the overkill alone, you will conclude that the Defendant acted out of rage, anger, and revenge. This was not a killing caused by so-called heat of passion or a spontaneous eruption like a volcano. It definitely was *not* justified in self-defense. Significantly, the Defendant herself had no injuries of any kind, and the victim, Marten, had substantial defensive wounds to his hands.

"This was murder in the first-degree."

Mac moved behind his table, signaling that he was concluding.

"Once you have heard all of this powerful testimony, I am very confident you will agree there is an avalanche of credible evidence in this case. Marten Van der Hook, and to a lesser extent Mandy, come to you seeking justice. Marten, a brilliant and successful man, was killed in the prime of his life. And Mandy has permanently lost her father. At the end of this trial, after you've considered all the testimony and evidence, we will respectfully ask that you find the Defendant guilty. Thank you."

The Girl with the Nose Ring zipped her sweatshirt up and flipped the hood, covering her head.

CHAPTER 35

Tuesday, August 6, 2019
1:07 p.m.

"This is Warden Stempkowski, calling from the Seneca County Correctional Facility. I know you're not in your office, and you're probably tied up in court. I just got here and heard from the overnight shift that one of your witnesses—a woman, Linden Hale—well, she was locked up last night for a DUI. I took a look at her record on Case Search and saw she's been subpoenaed by you for a trial that I believe just started yesterday. If that's correct, give me a call on my cell when you get this message so we can coordinate, OK? Thanks."

The trial had broken for lunch, and Mac was alone at his desk when he heard the voicemail message.

Oh my God, this woman is a mess, and I need her this afternoon to testify about all the background information I just mentioned in my opening. She's got to be a compelling witness. The jury is going to hate her.

He dialed the warden's number, and it went right into voicemail. He left a message back: "Stemp, this is Mac MacIntyre. It's 1:09 in the afternoon, and we're on a break from the trial. You must be on your rounds or in the Observation Pod without your phone, but anyway, shoot me a text when you get back to your office. Lindy Hale is supposed to be testifying in Circuit Court in half an hour. She's the sister of the woman on trial for murder. We picked a jury yesterday and started the trial this morning. We just finished opening statements. I need Lindy down here right now. I'll send Andre Okoye up to the jail to pick her up. We will have to make some arrangements, obviously. Thanks."

How many drunk driving cases can one person have?

His mind was already racing.

Call Andre, find a set of clean clothes for Lindy, and then call one of the Crime Scene Techs as the first witness out of order to stall for time.

He autodialed Andre, who picked up the call immediately.

"What's up, Big Dog? You OK?"

"Listen, Lindy Hale was locked up for a DUI last night. This is her fifth damn DUI. She's up at SCCF right now. I just got a voicemail from Warden Stempkowski. You remember him, right?"

"Yeah, def. I remember him from that bad assault case we handled a few years ago from inside SCCF. The case where the C.O. got blinded by that Cameroon inmate. Stempkowski had just become warden then. He will remember me. Don't panic, Mac. I got this. But what exactly do you need?"

"Right. So listen, Andre. I need you to drop everything and head up there. I need you to bring that idiot, Lindy, back down here to the courthouse as fast as you can."

"I'm listening, boss. I'm already walking to the garage."

"She is supposed to be our first witness this afternoon. She is important because she's the witness who sets the whole thing up and can give the jury background, especially on Mandy's narcolepsy. She also can explain how Rikki and Marten met in college and all of that family stuff. I don't want Harajuku or the jury to know Lindy's in jail. I can stall. I'll call another witness out of order, and I'll drag my questions out until you text me Lindy is in the building, OK? I hate to switch, because it makes the presentation so disjointed, but we have no choice. So, go up to the jail and pick her up right now. Get Stemp to help with any red tape if they give you a hard time."

"I'll call him as I'm driving up the highway and ask him to smooth the way."

"OK, Andre. If you need some leverage, mention we did the Achoba case for him. He owes me a favor big time. Go Code 3, with lights and sirens, if traffic is heavy."

"Mac, if she was arrested for a DUI last night, she probably has a bond review this afternoon somewhere. Would it be in District Court or Circuit Court? What if they're transporting her to court right now? What do we do?"

"Call Lupe at the SAO as you're driving and find out which ASA is assigned bonds today. DUIs are misdemeanors, so it will be in District Court. They do them every day at three. Whoever has bonds, tell them to get a continuance and explain that Lindy has to testify in our trial in Circuit Court today. A murder trial obviously takes precedence. She probably doesn't even have a lawyer retained for the new DUI. They can deal with all of that at bonds tomorrow. Getting her presentable to testify today is more important."

"OK, 10-4, sounds good. Hey, I'm getting on the on-ramp right now. Pretty light traffic out here this time of day. Making good time."

"One other thing, Andre. Check out the condition of her clothes. The jail will only have what she was arrested in last night, and so it's probably yoga pants and a T-shirt, hopefully not drenched in vomit or urine or tequila or whatever, right? No time to change."

"No wonder the cops call you The Godfather. Are you the head of one of the Five Families?! Always thinking ahead. I dig that. Her clothes? Never crossed my mind."

"Oh yeah, Andre, another thing. When you get a chance, can you somehow figure out who the hell is taking care of Mandy? Do they have a housekeeper or maid or anything? I mean, Mandy is nine years old and can't take care of herself. And she's supposed to testify tomorrow. So after you bring Lindy to the courthouse, can you swing back up and find out what's going on with Mandy? We need her fresh and ready to roll tomorrow morning. I don't know if that means she needs to go to bed at dinnertime or what, but she needs like 12 hours of sleep, so work backwards."

"I got you. The warden owes *you* a favor. Hah! So dope! Hey, I'll be rolling into the jail in a few minutes. I'm flying up here in the HOV lane. Go do your thing and I'll call him as soon as we hang up. He'll help make this smooth. Then, I'll get her down Code 3 to the courthouse by two-thirty, Mac. Bet your life on it."

"OK, text me along the way and let me know what's happening. I'll be doing the direct of the Crime Scene Tech and getting all those photographs in evidence, and I'll lay the foundation for the DNA evidence. So, while you're driving back, I won't be able to talk, but I will feel my phone vibrating. Call twice in a row so I know it's you. That will be our signal."

"Gotcha. Later," said Andre, who clicked off his phone.

Mac had not the slightest doubt everything would get done exactly right. He picked up his phone again and texted:

STEMP, ANDRE OKOYE WILL BE AT SCCF
FRONT DESK IN 5 MINS. REMEMBER
HIM FROM THE ACHOBA CASE? PLEASE
RELEASE HALE TO ANDRE. TX, MAC.

Oh, no. Don't think about the Achoba case now! Focus.

CHAPTER 36

Tuesday, August 6, 2019
1:22 p.m.

Mac took the final bite of his bagel, glanced at his watch, and noticed he now had only eight minutes to get back upstairs to the courtroom. Before he dashed out to the elevator, he would sit still for 30 seconds in his chair with the office door closed, trying to let his heart rate calm down.

His mind flashed back to the last time he was in the Inmate Pod at SCCF: the Achoba investigation. Young kid, maybe 19, parents from Africa. Achoba had been calmly sitting in the open area of the Pod playing chess when he jumped up, and, for no apparent reason, attacked a young Corrections Officer named Donnie Barnette. Achoba punched him in the face with a chess piece, driving it deep into his left eye so hard that his eyeball actually popped out of the socket. Shrieking, and with his eyeball dangling down the side of his cheek,

Donnie lost consciousness and fell to the cement floor, blood pooling quickly beneath his face.

What made the attack so unique was that the other inmates immediately jumped in and stopped Achoba from killing him. Even Warden Stempkowski said he hadn't seen other inmates actually protect a guard in all the years he'd been working in jails and prisons.

Warden Stempkowski called Mac and asked him to personally take the case. Mac asked Stemp to arrange a tour of the exact crime scene. Stemp assured him he would be safe.

Around inmates, it was critical to show no fear and to stay absolutely, completely calm. Never let them see you were afraid. These inmates could sense fear. When Mac visited, Stemp buzzed the two of them into the Pod. Stemp was armed only with a radio, no weapons at all, and, of course, Mac armed only with a felt-tipped pen. The inmates came right up to the doorway as they approached the electronically locked, intimidating metal door. They all knew Warden Stempkowski, but who was this tall, slender white guy with the bright red hair dressed in a suit and tie?

When they were actually inside the Pod, Stemp said, "Hey, everyone. This is Mr. MacIntyre. He's the ASA handling C.O. Barnette's case, so everyone be respectful, OK?" The other inmates got up from the metal tables that were bolted down to the concrete floor and approached, huddling around and forming a cluster of large men, almost all heavily tattooed, wearing olive-green jumpsuits.

Mac stood tall and confident.

One inmate approached. He was a Central American giant, probably six-foot-eight and as wide as a football player.

He had the words "Mara Salvatrucha" tattooed across this throat and three teardrop tattoos dripping down his cheek. He said, "C.O. Donnie was a nice kid. How's his vision, man?"

"Well, Esteban," said Stemp, "Donnie lost his sight in that eye. He's got a glass one now, but you can hardly tell the difference. Thank God you guys helped him out. Good job, Pod C."

Mac inspected the exact spot of the assault and asked for permission to let his forensics crew come back to take photos and measurements and make charts. Mac would use those charts and photos before the jury as demonstrative evidence to bring the case alive and to allow the jurors to comprehend life inside the Pod.

"Well, now the inmates know exactly who the hell you are! Mac, you better not get locked up in here or you're a goner, man!" said Stemp with a hearty laugh. "I mean, if you got locked up, we'd have to put you in Seg for a week or two," he continued with the hypothesis. "But sooner or later, we'd have to get you out of Seg—can't stay there forever—and then you'd be mixed in with Gen Pop. Damn, you wouldn't last 15 minutes in Gen Pop; a skinny prosecutor like you?"

"Dude," said Mac, "are you getting senile or something? I'm the asshole who puts these killers in here. Not a guy who ends up in here myself, right?"

The giant from El Salvador chuckled, and then several other inmates around him laughed.

"Well... You never know. Seen it happen," Stemp said in a monotone, flatly, but then with optimistic animation added, "I like your fire in the courtroom. Most of the time when I've gone to court, the ASA was boring as shit. Reading from some prepared notes. Sounding fake. But you were like on a Broadway stage or something! Guys, if you ever have another case, you do not want this guy against you, trust me."

A jury took 10 minutes to find Achoba guilty and convict him of first-degree assault. The judge sentenced him to the full 25 years.

Mac sat at his desk, eyes closed. His phone buzzed, and he jumped at the sound, returning to reality from his daydream of the Achoba case. The 30 seconds of meditation sitting at his desk had expired. The bagel was gone, the wrapping from the deli crumpled up and in his trash can. He looked at his phone and read the text from Warden Stempkowski:

> WITNESS CLEARED TO GO & HAS LEFT.
> ANDRE HAS CUSTODY. GOOD LUCK W/
> UR JURY, STEMP.

CHAPTER 37

Tuesday, August 6, 2019
2:30 p.m.

"Call your next witness," intoned Judge Harajuku.

"The State calls Linden Hale," said Mac confidently. Andre had been incredibly efficient getting Lindy from SCCF and whisking her down the Interstate to the courthouse. He had texted Mac, bragging he had utilized his police equipment, lifting the red dome light from underneath his dashboard and propping it up in front of his steering wheel. This was illegal, of course, since Andre, although a retired police officer, was technically an in-house detective for the State's Attorney's Office, and did not have the authority to flash police lights. Even so, Andre must have enjoyed the rush, watching all the cars maneuver out of his path as he flew down the highway.

Before lunch, Santiago Garcia delivered his opening statement and was finished by 12:15 p.m., so the judge let the jury go to the cafeteria 15 minutes early. Santiago's speech was a combination of the usual defense ingredients—there was a presumption of innocence, and there must be proof beyond a reasonable doubt. These were nuggets of recycled arguments Mac had heard Santiago use in every case. After weaving in some facts specific to this particular case, Santiago ended the way he always ended: "At the end of the trial, when you've heard from all the witnesses and examined all the evidence, I will ask you to find the Defendant not guilty." Today, however, to personalize the phrase "the Defendant," Santiago substituted "Rikki," not even using her full name, "Rikki Van der Hook."

Mac didn't have any visible reactions or changes in facial expression as Santiago gave his opening statement, but Mac noted Santiago had made several good points. Mac had to concede that no one except Mandy had seen the crime occur, and she had weaknesses as an eyewitness. Santiago also cleverly told the jury, "You will hear absolutely no evidence that my client *ever* admitted to planning or calculating or premeditating this regrettable event, which was a completely justifiable act of self-defense." Mac knew the jury would never learn Rikki actually had confessed to Andre and, even more importantly, had specifically admitted killing Marten intentionally.

Mac didn't move a muscle and looked down at his legal pad where the block letters FOCUS appeared.

I can't believe Andre forgot to do those damn Miranda warnings right! Santiago is destroying me with this shit.

Because Rikki's confession had been suppressed before the trial at the Motions hearing, when Santiago told the jury they would "hear absolutely no evidence" of a damning admission, he was absolutely truthful, although skillfully misleading. This was the attorney's classic "half-truth," meaning it was literally a true statement, but totally disingenuous.

Rikki sat stoically at the defense table. She was wearing the same pressed white Oxford shirt, this time with a burgundy suit jacket. The jail had all kinds of strict, often illogical, pointless rules. They wouldn't allow Rikki to have a whole wardrobe to choose from—just three outfits. Since Santiago wasn't allowed to bring her a complete change of wardrobe each day, he must have gotten permission to give her a garment bag to last the whole week with one shirt, one pair of dark slacks, and three different jackets. Mac knew that was the maximum amount of clothing the jailers would allow. If the trial lasted five days, with three different colored jackets, Rikki would only have to wear two of them twice. The jury usually only noticed the jackets and not the rest of the outfit. Seated, they couldn't even see her slacks or shoes.

As Lindy entered the courtroom, Mac noticed Rikki's eyes get wide, and then Rikki peered over the top of her glasses to scrutinize Lindy's outfit. Lindy looked pale. Her skin was a shade so white that the veins in her neck branched out in thin purple spider web patterns. She was wearing light denim jeans and a large, oversized, dark blue T-shirt, which hung down below her belt. There was a small logo on the pocket of the T-shirt bearing the letters FOP. Mac immediately recognized the shirt as one of Andre's own shirts. She was wearing Reebok sneakers. Her hair was tightly pulled back and secured with a grey rubber band at the nape of her neck. Her arms were crossed, crumpled inward, making her body look concave. She looked terrified.

Mac simply said, "This way, please," and gestured towards the witness stand.

Phoebe, the Clerk, asked, "Will you please raise your right hand?"

Lindy stood in the witness box and started to raise her left hand, caught herself, then lowered it and lifted her right hand.

"Do you solemnly swear or affirm that the testimony you shall give will be the truth, the whole truth, and nothing but the truth?"

"Yes, ma'am."

Judge Harajuku instructed, "Please be seated."

Turning her head, she said, "Mr. MacIntyre..."

Over the next 45 minutes, Mac guided Lindy through several sections of testimony, starting with a short biography. While not a critical part of the case, he warmed Lindy up with a series of easy questions. So, initially, through this question-and-answer dialogue, Mac established Lindy's background: she grew up in Seneca County with her sister, currently owned a small hair salon, and was supported by obscenely excessive court-ordered alimony payments sent to her monthly by an ex-husband who now lived in Ireland, and whom she hadn't seen in seven years.

"And do you see your sister here in the courtroom right now, Ms. Hale?"

"Yes, she's right over there," Lindy said, pointing at Rikki. "Wearing the maroon jacket. Or red. Reddish, I guess."

Santiago stood and said, "Stipulate as to identity, Your Honor."

"So stipulated," Judge Harajuku unenthusiastically noted. The jurors looked back and forth with quizzical expressions.

Lindy's ghostly skin color contrasted starkly with her dark T-shirt bearing the tiny Fraternal Order of Police insignia.

"Are you aware of any physical disabilities that your niece Mandy has, Ms. Hale?" Mac asked. He cleverly used the word "physical," picking up on how the judge had made the distinction in her ruling on the Motion in Limine.

"Yes, well, Mandy is a smart girl. She's basically normal as far as intelligence goes. I mean, she has a major disability, but it's not like she's retarded or anything."

Feeling Lindy drifting away, Mac reeled her back in. He felt like he was driving a powerboat with someone waterskiing behind it, slaloming back and forth and about to crash.

"Just to clarify, she has pediatric narcolepsy, correct?" It was a very leading question, but he dared Santiago to object, knowing that fact would be simple to establish, even if he objected.

Santiago sat still.

"Yes, that's correct. Means she just sleeps a lot, and she takes a lot of medications to help keep her awake."

"Thank you. Now, I would like to ask you about an incident when your sister took a trip to Las Vegas last year. Did she ever mention that trip to you?"

Santiago shifted around and then rose. "Objection, Your Honor. This calls for hearsay."

"Overruled," said the judge. "This is what the Defendant herself said, as I understand the State's question. It would be an admission or a statement against self-interest and not hearsay."

Lindy looked first at Mac, then at Santiago, then at the judge, then back to Mac. Her head moved back and forth like a spectator at a tennis match following the flight of the ball being volleyed over the net and crisply returned.

"You may answer," Mac said. "Did your sister tell you about a trip she took with her husband to Las Vegas?"

"Yes, she did. She said Marten invited her on that trip, supposedly some kind of business conference of manufacturers or something. And when she got there, his secretary Mimi—she was from Paris and Marten said he liked European woman better than greedy American girls—was already there. Obviously, she was staying in the same suite. Rikki told me Marten convinced her, or pressured her, into having a sexual threesome with him and this trashy French girl. He said if she really loved him and wanted to be a good wife, she'd do it. Listen, I love my sister dearly, but she has struggled with some anxiety issues, which Marten knew all about. He definitely took advantage of her psychologically. I mean, he was like the world's biggest expert in gaslighting. So, how can I explain this? So... she did it to please him. And then she called me the next day crying. Said he laughed at her. Said her body was too skinny, and she looked like a skeleton. He told her, right in front of that girl. He said she didn't turn him on. She was... well, not hysterical, but really upset. She said Marten made fun of her breasts. Said they were nonexistent. Rikki promised she'd get a boob job. And Marten told her she needed a brain job instead. Horrible stuff. A month later, Marten told her he was divorcing her and taking Mandy away since Rikki was crazy. That's what she told me."

"When you heard Mr. Van der Hook had supposedly coerced her to engage in a sexual threesome, then rejected her afterwards and said he wanted to end the marriage—what was the Defendant's initial reaction?" Mac asked, stuffing several questions into one. Technically, it was a "compound question," but he knew it was not something Santiago would have the courage to interrupt, since it would be easy for Mac to break the longer question into three or four smaller ones.

Lindy hesitated and didn't answer the question. After a pause, she said, "Can you repeat that, please?"

"When you heard that Mr. Van der Hook had supposedly coerced..."

"When he cursed?"

"Coerced. Let me rephrase. When you heard he forced or tricked your sister, what was your first reaction?"

"Well, oh my God. I... I... I didn't believe it at first. I felt so humiliated for my sister, and honestly, I hated Marten. So when this whole thing happened—this accident which resulted in him dying—I knew she must have been just trying to protect herself. He used to hit her all the time."

Inside, Mac was furious. Lindy was making this up on the spot. Improvising from the witness stand. She had earlier said during pretrial preparations that Rikki was furious and full of rage. But now Lindy was talking about supposed spousal abuse? This was a disaster.

"But, honestly," Lindy rambled, "I still really don't know what happened or if Mandy even saw it or why Rikki felt she had to protect the two of them."

Mac felt the tension in the courtroom air.

Did Lindy just use the word "honestly" while lying her ass off?

The courtroom was quiet, almost silent, as she spoke. He could hear muffled sighing or belabored breathing coming from somewhere on the right side of the jury box. He saw Lindy reach up and use her thumb to steer a lone teardrop to the side of her cheek, which was now pink.

Mac turned towards the bench. "Thank you. I have no further questions."

"Mr. Garcia, cross-examination?" said Judge Harajuku without looking up from her laptop.

"Thank you, Your Honor. Yes, I do have a few questions."

CHAPTER 38

Tuesday, August 6, 2019
3:37 p.m.

Santiago pretended to rearrange some notes before he rose to cross-examine Lindy. The shuffling of his papers was intentional, as if he had so many questions, so many areas to attack, that he couldn't decide which of his many options to use first to demolish this witness. Like a construction worker in a crane armed with a huge wrecking ball tasked with destroying a flimsy shack that was already half falling down, his only decision was where to strike first? Would a single, well-targeted hit take down the whole shack? Or would it be more fun to toy with the witness, like a cat with a half-dead bird, holding it down, letting it wriggle and flap its broken wings, and then batting it across the floor only to enjoy pouncing on it again? Lots of good choices here, appraised Santiago.

He dropped his legal pad on his table, as if he didn't need any notes, and buttoned his suit jacket.

"So, Ms. Hale, let's begin where you left off with the Assistant State's Attorney, OK?"

Lindy looked terrified. Her frosty blue eyes were watery and, surrounded by her ghostly white skin, looked like two aquamarine lakes against a snowy, barren landscape. She did not speak.

Mac put his pen down and leaned forward, putting the sharp points of his elbows on the table.

Santiago said, "Let me ask you about Mr. Van der Hook's violent tendencies…"

Mac interjected, "Objection, Your Honor. Assumes facts not in evidence."

"Overruled. The State's last witness just mentioned it. So, it's proper grounds for cross. Ask another question, Mr. Garcia."

Mac's interruption did not throw Santiago off. He said, "Ma'am, you just testified on direct—in response to Mr. MacIntyre's questions—that my client, Ms. Van der Hook, told you about some issues she had in the past with her husband. Right?"

"Yes."

Judge Harajuku turned her head to look at Lindy and said, "Please speak up, Ms. Hale. We need the courtroom recording equipment to pick up all of your testimony."

"Yes. Sorry."

"Next question, Mr. Garcia."

"You said that Marten abused both your sister and your niece, Mandy. Is that correct?"

"That's what she told me. She… she… she…" Lindy replied, trailing off into an airy whisper.

Cross-examination was different from direct testimony. Questions asked on direct testimony were to build a case up, like bricks in a wall. Cross-examination questions were designed to break the opposing counsel's wall down.

Sensing Lindy drifting off track, Santiago asked, "Ms. Hale, your sister told you that her husband hit her. Is that correct?"

"Yes, sir."

"And you have no doubt that Mandy was also the target of Mr. Van der Hook's anger and abuse?"

"Uh-huh," she said, reaching for the tissue box.

Judge Harajuku interjected, "Please say yes or no, so the record is clear."

"Oh, sorry, I mean yes, Judge."

Santiago swung the wrecking ball. "So, it makes sense your sister would defend herself if Marten physically attacked her. Correct?"

"I just can't put it into words."

"Well, please try. Because that's how people communicate. With words, OK?"

Knowing that the use of repetition was effective with a jury, Santiago added, "So, it's reasonable to assume that if Marten was violent or physically abusive towards Rikki and Mandy that she would defend herself. Isn't that what she told you?"

"Um, I guess so... I think that's possible, yes."

"Thank you. You've answered the question."

Mac didn't move at all. He shifted his weight in his chair and seemed ready to stand up to object. Knowing when to object, and when to let little unimportant facts slide by, was an art. Only inexperienced prosecutors objected to every slight infraction of the rules. Juries hated these obstructions and became suspicious when prosecutors appeared to be blocking information. It was a better strategy to let a defense attorney score a slight point rather than reinforce it by rising to object. Making an objection only drew *more* attention to whatever question was being asked, and, worse, there was always the chance the judge would overrule the challenge, compounding the error. Elite courtroom advocates did not get baited into pointless small symbolic victories. It was smarter to win the war and not be distracted over insignificant skirmishes along the way.

Several jurors were looking at Mac and not the witness.

Santiago continued, "Now, let me ask you about Mandy. She's got some serious mental health problems. Isn't that right?"

"She's got a rare form of narcolepsy. So, she's sleepy all day and needs tons of sleep every night just to function normally."

"And she takes medications—a lot of different medications—to just get up and make it through a regular day, right?"

"Yes, she takes Provigil in the morning and something called Xyrem at night to regulate her sleep, and she also takes Adderall and Prozac as mood stabilizers. And another one too. I can't remember the name, but I also have that at home to give her."

"And all these strong psychotropic medications have serious side effects. Right?" Santiago moved closer to the witness stand. "Mandy is not capable of remembering things accurately or communicating in a reliable way. Isn't that true?"

"No. I wouldn't agree with that."

Santiago didn't expect that.

What the fuck is this idiot saying? We went over this on the phone last night!

Santiago's plan to trash Mandy, and make her seem like an unreliable eyewitness, just veered in an unanticipated direction. Now, Lindy was obviously improvising, making things up as they came into her head. She either couldn't keep her stories straight, which happened when a witness was lying or fabricating wildly, or she just couldn't bring herself to attack Mandy.

"But you just said that your niece—who is nine years old—has this rare mental disorder and takes multiple medications. Wouldn't that render her useless to accurately tell the truth about something she saw months ago? I mean, she wouldn't remember accurately? Isn't that true?"

"No. I wouldn't say that. She is smart, and her narcolepsy doesn't work that way. At least that's not what I've seen since she's been living with me these past eight months. Now, I agree, she doesn't really speak clearly or put words together well when she talks, but she is a marvelous writer for her age, and her reading level is way above her grade level."

"Excuse me, ma'am. I didn't ask you anything about her reading level, OK? Can you please just stick to answering my questions and not volunteer extra stuff you want to squeeze in?"

"Well, you asked me about if she could report things accurately, and I'm just answering your question, Mr. Garcia. Mandy doesn't speak well, especially in a public setting like this, but she is excellent with words in her own way. Like I said, she reads adult books at her age. John Steinbeck is one of her favorite authors. And Agatha Christie novels, all kinds of stuff."

Now it was time for Santiago to improvise. He had used Lindy sufficiently to establish what he needed. Now he had to dispose of her before she volunteered any other new information they hadn't rehearsed. Reversing strategy, now he needed to tear down Lindy's remaining credibility. He had to discredit her. First, she had helped him. Now, she was killing him.

"Ms. Hale, isn't it true that you have a drinking problem? You've been convicted of drunk driving at least four..."

Mac was up on his feet. "Judge, I object! This is not relevant!" The wrecking ball was already swinging back like a pendulum, leaving a pile of dusty planks shattered in a useless heap on the ground.

"Gentlemen, approach!"

CHAPTER 39

Tuesday, August 6, 2019
4:35 p.m.

"Mr. Garcia, what are you doing?!" said Judge Harajuku. "You know this is inadmissible. You can't ask a witness about prior convictions which do not go to veracity. Why are you asking her about DUIs?"

As Santiago approached the judge's bench, his mind snapped to attention. As he and Mac walked up, she turned on the husher, which again emitted the obnoxious, swishing noise. When they reached the bench, Santiago quickly swiveled his head back and forth, as if on a pivot, while Mac nonchalantly stood still. Mac glanced towards the jury box. The jurors were all looking up at the cluster of Santiago, Mac, and Judge Harajuku.

"Judge, I am not asking about prior convictions," Santiago said quietly. He knew that you rarely won an argument with a judge with aggression, but rather with logic. "But her alcoholism and her ability to perceive things are highly relevant. If she's intoxicated all the time, how can she know if this child can testify reliably? That's absolutely admissible, Judge."

Judge Harajuku pointed at Santiago with her index finger and said, "Well, you asked her about her convictions. I heard that clearly! In fact, you asked her if she had four arrests or something along those lines, and that is well outside the rules of evidence pertaining to witness bias, or whether she is a percipient witness or not." She turned and said, "Mr. MacIntyre? Your position?"

"Judge, this line of questioning is clearly inadmissible and threatens the integrity of the trial. I'm tempted to ask for a mistrial. Mr. Garcia cannot ask about prior convictions unless they are felonies or misdemeanors which go to veracity. A question relating to truthfulness, such as a conviction for theft or perjury or something similar. Impeachable prior convictions must be related to the witness's honesty. But DUIs are not felonies, and they do not impact on a witness's honesty or credibility. Therefore, Mr. Garcia cannot ask this witness about her prior drunk driving convictions. So, obviously I strongly object to this line of questioning, but, moreover, I would ask that you instruct the jury to disregard counsel's last question."

Santiago noted that Mac deliberately gave an extended, long-winded legal argument summarizing the law of impeachable prior convictions. He knew Mac was not only trying to make the record clear, but his speech was also cleverly designed to elongate the time from when Santiago said "four convictions" to when the jury might hear a new question. Just as a magician uses sleight-of-hand tricks to distract an audience, Santiago knew Mac was trying to misdirect the jury with his own courtroom prestidigitation.

Santiago didn't quit, jumping in with, "But Your Honor! It goes to the witness's credibility! If she's an alcoholic and sleeps all day, she isn't supervising the kid! That's an important fact for the defense to establish, Judge."

"OK, listen to me carefully," Judge Harajuku refereed. "I will not allow you to mention anything at all about prior DUI convictions. At all. I don't want to hear the word conviction, understand? Am I clear, Mr. Garcia? I remind counsel that there is something called contempt of court. So, let's not go down that road. However, you *may* ask the witness about her ability to remember events and if anything affects her ability to perceive. I do think her general memory and capacity to observe events *is* at issue, as it is with any witness. But do not press me, Mr. Garcia. Understood?"

Mac and Santiago returned to their respective counsel tables.

Santiago spun towards Lindy, "So, let me ask you this, Ms. Hale: do you have a problem with alcohol?"

Lindy said hesitantly, "Well, I used to have a problem, but I don't anymore."

"Ms. Hale, I say this with all due respect, but ma'am, you are an alcoholic. Isn't that correct?"

"That's way in the past, sir. Not now."

"You were arrested *last night*, in fact, for drunk driving, isn't that correct?" said Santiago, while he simultaneously turned to the judge and added, "It goes to her credibility! She just said she '*used* to have a problem.'"

Mac closed his eyes. He started to rise, but Judge Harajuku said, "Overruled, Mr. MacIntyre. She *opened the door* as we say."

Santiago paused. He knew the legal phrase "opening the door" referred to when a witness volunteered adverse information. Since Lindy said she no longer had a problem with alcohol, the rules of evidence allowed Santiago to counter that statement with proof to the contrary.

Santiago didn't miss his opportunity: Lindy had, in fact, opened the door, and Santiago walked right through it. "And if you're an alcoholic, who is intoxicated all day, you would have no idea about this little girl's ability to see things or remember things or her ability to understand what's going on. Isn't that also true, Ms. Hale?" Santiago raised his voice a couple of notches higher.

Lindy shivered and turned towards the bench. Speaking directly to the judge, she wailed, "I'm sorry! I'm trying my best to take care of her! All of this is just overwhelming me."

Lindy folded her arms across her chest and leaned back as far as her chair would allow.

Santiago shook his head and said, "I have no further questions."

He had made his point.

CHAPTER 40

May 18, 2019
9:00 a.m.

SENECA COUNTY POLICE DEPARTMENT
SEROLOGY LABORATORY
RESULTS OF FORENSIC EXAMINATION

TO: State's Attorney's Office

ATTN: William T. MacIntyre, Senior Assistant State's Attorney

RE: Homicide, December 20, 2018

VICTIM: Marten Van der Hook

TYPE OF EXAMINATION: *Bloodstain Pattern Analysis.* From a review of photographs taken by the SCPD, Autopsy Report, DNA analysis and a visit to the crime scene.

BACKGROUND: The victim was stabbed to death with a sharp instrument. Victim received thirty-six (36) cutting and stabbing wounds to the head, arms and hands.

Bloodstain patterns are categorized according to the velocity of the droplets and/or the mechanism that produced the pattern. **Low-ve-**

locity patterns are produced by dripping or projected blood, such as arterial spurting at low speed. **Medium-velocity** patterns are caused by striking an area already covered in blood or by casting off blood by swinging a blood covered object. **High-velocity** patterns are produced by gunshot or explosion or other very high-energy events which were **not** present in this case.

OBSERVATIONS: The nature of the multiple stab wounds to the head of Marten Van der Hook indicate a very high probability of **medium-velocity** blood spatter patterns. It should be noted that blows/stabs to the head typically are filtered because of hair coverage, which tends to collect liquids. In this case, the victim is noted at autopsy to have a full head of thick hair, which would impact the blood spatter pattern.

Photographs of the scene depict significant blood spatter patterns from medium velocity. Droplets in varying degrees of diameter, e.g., coin-sized, comparable to the sizes of dimes and quarters, can be seen on the floor, walls, ceiling, and nearby furniture. A careful review of the photographs depict well in excess of over two hundred fifty (250) individual droplets. Additionally, multiple droplets on the ceiling have dripped down to the floor, creating a partial mirror image of the patterns on the ceiling.

Large pools of accumulated blood are noted on the carpet (tan carpet with floral design) and on the wood floor, running down the length of the room and pooling in a triangular shape in the corner of the room. This pattern is attributable to gravity guiding the flow of the blood across the room due to a slightly uneven floor.

CONCLUSIONS: The amount of blood spatter patterns is massive due to the severity and multiplicity of the wounds inflicted. Although the total quantity of blood loss from the head is extreme, the quantity of blood from the victim's hands, arms and body is minimal due to clothing which acts to entrap the flow of blood and, in some instances, acts as a blotter to soak up and retain the blood. **However, the blood spatter patterns generated from the blows to the head**, due to arterial spraying/spurting, cover areas adjacent to the body including the walls, floor,

GAVEL TO GAVEL

furniture and ceiling.

Additionally, significant patterns attributable to "blowback" or cast-away patterns are noted on the ceiling and elsewhere. This is due to a sharp cutting instrument being **withdrawn** from a bloody surface rapidly, causing droplets to spray or cast in an upward arcing direction. Measurements show the ceiling is nine feet, six inches (9'6") high.

Examiner: Colin Ray Mossberg, PhD.
Director, Forensic Services Division.

CHAPTER 41

Tuesday, August 6, 2019
6:40 p.m.

Santiago sat at his desk in the PD's Office. He read through his notes to prepare for the next day's witnesses. He dug through the remains of the Chinese takeout order from the Chun Cha Fu restaurant around the corner. He poked his chopstick into the square, eggshell-colored waxy box and swirled a nest out of the remaining shredded pork and bean curd. His mind was distracted. He tried to focus on the Van der Hook trial, but his thoughts kept drifting to something else.

Santiago was a finalist for a newly opened District Court judgeship. It was a laborious process to file an application to become a judge, but Santiago figured he had all the qualifications: the requisite residency in Seneca County and plenty of trial experience. In addition, he was well liked by members of the Bar Association. He was friendly with both defense attorneys and prosecutors. Perhaps most significant, even more important than his legal acumen or career accomplishments, there was another factor in his favor: he was Latino. If the process was objective, Mac MacIntyre, who had more courtroom experience, and infinitely more natural talent, would be selected for a judgeship. But the process wasn't always objectively fair. The reality was that, as a white man, the odds were stacked against Mac being selected. This was not a meritocracy. The last four judges had either been women, Black, Asian, or Latino, or some combination thereof. Santiago visualized himself sitting high on the bench: in just a few months he could be presiding over a courtroom, wrapped in a sable robe, running the show.

However, becoming a judge in Seneca County was all about politics. You needed friends and influential people on your side more than any other single factor. You needed support from the key courthouse players, which made Santiago think of Mac.

Santiago remembered Mac telling him once about how people succeeded in the State's Attorney's Office. There were three ways to advance: one, you worked like you were on a chain gang, taking on case after case after case. Mac called these prosecutors "The Bricklayers." Mac explained there was also another category: "The Politicians." Those were the Ari Fischbein types and the lower-level prosecutors who emulated him. Everyone knew the popular ASA Laurie Chaise, who brought home-baked cookies to the office every Monday. She was noticeably nervous and self-conscious inside of a courtroom, shivering with insecurity, but everyone adored her. They'd probably make *her* a judge one day, Mac said. The cookies were excellent. Then, finally, there was the lone wolf type of prosecutor. These were "The Architects," prosecutors who were efficient, masterful in the art of trial advocacy, and lethal before a jury. They achieved career success, even if they weren't popular or politically astute. Mac was one of the very few Architects in the SAO. The Bricklayers got down on their knees and stacked bricks one by one. The Politicians shook hands, went out to lunch a lot, and sold raffle tickets to fundraisers for their kids' annoying school charities and soccer teams. Tins of caramel popcorn and tubes of Christmas wrapping paper were the detritus of December in the State's Attorney's Office. But the Architects analyzed a criminal case and saw beautiful designs in their minds.

While Santiago calculated he was more of the politician type, he knew if he could win a big case, if he could hold his own with a prosecutor as highly regarded as Mac—not to mention, if he *beat* Mac!—that would all but seal the deal. A victory in front of Judge Harajuku—herself a pioneer as the first and only Asian female judge—would significantly raise his profile. This Van der Hook case was all over the *Seneca Journal* and local TV stations. This was his perfect opportunity.

Santiago had already completed the arduous application process to become a judge, and it had been accepted by the Judicial Nominations Committee of the Seneca County Bar Association. Then, he had survived multiple layers of interviews. The original field of 15 applicants was winnowed down to eight. Now, the Committee, a small group composed of leading members of the Bar, would shrink the applicant pool to a digestible three candidates. Santiago realized that the new

State's Attorney, Ari Fischbein, was on that Committee. With Fischbein supporting his candidacy, Santiago could surely snag a spot in the final three.

So far, Santiago had already met with the Hispanic Bar Association. He killed that interview, switching flawlessly back and forth from Spanish to English. His ethnicity, and native unaccented Spanish, was a great selling feature, demonstrating he could ably serve both the Bench and the greater community. Down in District Court, where, as a new judge, Santiago would hear traffic cases and minor criminal misdemeanor trials, he could use his Spanish in a pinch to control courtroom decorum and make general announcements when an official courtroom interpreter was unavailable. As Santiago moved on to the other Bar Association committees, he realized he had a skill for politics. He sharpened his sales pitch with each interview.

There were other groups: The African American Bar Association, the Women's Bar Association, the Jewish Bar Association, even the LGBTQ Lawyers Group, which was nonexistent just two years earlier. Santiago had flawless presentations before all of them. The thought jumped into his head: it would be great to get the support from this new State's Attorney, this pompous, yet powerful, Ari Fischbein. That would help enormously. Santiago had only met him once, and it was a very awkward encounter. Fischbein had said, "*Hola, buenos dias.*" Santiago was unsure how to respond, uncertain if the greeting was a joke or just obnoxious. Either way, Fischbein's ability to speak Spanish reminded Santiago of a high school student ordering dinner at a Mexican restaurant.

Right then, Santiago realized this guy was an idiot. But, if he could somehow get his vote, that would cinch things. Get ranked in that group of the final three candidates and be the only Latino in the mix. He had to handle this guy everyone called "The Fish" like he was handling uranium: something toxic and radioactive, but also, simultaneously, something extremely valuable.

Then Santiago had a thought.

I need Mac's support, not Fischbein's.

CHAPTER 42

Tuesday, August 6, 2019
7:01 p.m.

Zaria picked up the bundle of mail from the front desk. The Public Defenders' Office received thousands of mailings weekly, hundreds each day. Motions, notices from the courts, "Lines of Appearance," endless varieties of papers with one commonality: they all related to someone's tragedy. Dozens of letters arrived in the daily afternoon mail drop. Boilerplate form letters from the SAO or handwritten, desperate *pro se* requests from prisoners begging for help. Mixed in, there would be complaints from aggrieved family members, angry with how their loved ones' cases turned out. Of course, Zaria presumed all these public defender clients were guilty.

What did these mothers expect? It was always someone else's fault. Ineffective assistance of counsel? Please, give me a break. Don't ignore the obvious: your son is a criminal. Don't complain!

The public defenders were some of the most talented attorneys in Seneca County, and definitely some of the most experienced.

Zaria took the bundle of mail from the table at the reception desk, and she went into the conference room, which was empty this late in the day. There, she took a pair of rusty scissors from the chipped mug in the center of the table and cut the twine. The stack slid to the side, like a toppled deck of cards.

It was one of her assigned tasks to sort the mail each afternoon and distribute it around the office. Zaria preferred to tackle this mundane task late in the day once most of the PDs had left the office.

Why do these people stay here so late? At least if you're going to do this disgusting work, and deal with these wild, menacing people face-to-face, you might as well go into private practice and make, what, $200,000 a year instead of the lame salaries here.

Since she was called into court to translate, she'd seen all the top PDs performing in the courtroom. She'd heard them making passionate speeches, arguing and defending killers, drug kingpins, and bank robbers who were obviously dangerous. Some of the public defenders displayed impressive acting skills. They could practically cry with emotion, pleading for a client's innocence, and then come back to the office and laugh about it like it was all a joke.

Do they offer drama classes in law school?

A jury trial was supposed to test the truth. At least that's what they told her in that boring, mandatory orientation session. But to Zaria, it resembled an elaborate American game show, where the flashiest presentations were designed to distract the jury from the reality of what actually happened. Show a lot of shiny objects. Such theatrical performances, such oratory. But then, Zaria also knew that she herself could never get up in front of people and talk like these lawyers did. That would be literally impossible.

The thought of lawyers performing in court made her think of Mac. She tried to push that distracting thought aside because in her mind she saw Mac undressed. She quickly amended this vision until now he wore a suit and stood tall in front of the jury. The times when she'd dropped in to watch him perform in a trial, he had been totally in command of the courtroom. It thrilled her to know that he had hidden, secret skills which only she knew about. In court, he belonged to everyone. In the dark, he was hers. She could only watch him for a few minutes before she lost her concentration. Then she would have to leave, go to the ladies' room, and check in the mirror to see if her blouse was soaked with sweat under her arms.

She took the rearranged bundle of mail around the PD's Office and stopped at the various doorways, preferring to drop off the paperwork on the threshold of each office. She was glad to see a dark office or a PD on the phone, so she didn't have to engage in meaningless conversation. She preferred to wave from the doorway as if to say, "Here's your mail."

"Hey, Tommy. Mail time.

"Hey, Alison. You got a bunch of Motions."

She approached one of the corner offices reserved for the more senior PDs and stopped at the doorway. The PD was on the phone with his back to the door.

"Santiago, you got some paperwork from the SAO today."

Before she could avoid any interaction, Santiago swiveled 180 degrees in his chair, hung up his phone, and said, "Hey, Zaria. I've got a question for you…"

"Oh sure, what? Sorry, I thought you were busy," she replied, wishing he hadn't spun around.

"This guy at the State's Attorney's Office, Mac MacIntyre. You know him, don't you? I mean, have you ever seen him in court?"

A flash of fear raced through her.

How could he possibly know?

"Yes. Yes, I have. Why do you ask?"

"I have a case with him," Santiago explained. "I've had tons of cases with him ever since I came up from District Court. But this case is big. A murder. Probably the biggest jury trial of my career, actually. I'm in the middle of it right now. Anyway, what do you think of him?"

"Well, I don't know. He seems confident. But I really wouldn't know. I'm not a lawyer, Santiago."

"No, you *would* know. That's exactly the type of feedback I need. I mean, the *jurors* aren't lawyers, right? So, from the perspective of the jury—who are mostly people in a courtroom for the first time—what do you think a juror would think of Mac?"

"That he is smart. Calm. But I guess, most importantly, that you could trust him."

"Yeah, I know what you mean," Santiago said in a confirmatory tone. "This guy has practically a photographic memory. He's like Google when it comes to the Maryland Rules and jury instructions and case law and anything which is written down. He notices the tiniest details. It's spooky. Did you know that, Zaria?"

"Oh, no. I didn't know that. That's kind of cool."

"Maybe it's a phonographic memory—I think that's what it's called. When you remember everything you hear. Like a record player, y'know, a phonograph. A photo-graphic memory," he paused between the syllables, "is when you remember everything you see. Maybe he's got both?"

Santiago was venting now. "He is ridiculous with trivia. History, movies, sports, pop culture. He should go on *Jeopardy*. This guy can quote lines from Shakespeare plays. Who does that? I'm in court with a bond review on some random case, and he's like quoting *Henry the Ninth* or *Much Ado About Something* or God only knows. Another thing, he sees little things a normal human would never catch."

"Really?" Zaria replied. She paused and reached out to grab the doorframe, relocating her feet beneath her.

Santiago concluded, "Dude is like a fucking machine, I tell you."

"A fucking machine," Zaria said flatly, with no emotion.

"What?"

"*Dipendenza*," Zaria immediately responded.

"What are you talking about?!"

"Oh, never mind."

"Once," Santiago rambled, "when I first started doing Circuit Court cases, we were picking a jury in a high-profile case. My client was this nasty high school drama teacher making freshmen girls give him a blowjob to get cast in the school play. You'd be shocked how many he got to do that."

"Shocking," Zaria repeated sarcastically. Santiago ignored it.

"So, he strikes this woman from the jury pool. I was thinking, wow, good thing he struck her since she would have been so pro-State. It saved me from using up one of my preemptory strikes. Later, after the trial—of course my guy was found guilty in like 20 minutes—I was just bullshitting with Mac outside in the hallway, and I asked him, 'Hey, why did you strike that juror, y'know, the schoolteacher woman from Tortola? She would have been perfect for you: a teacher in a case like this? Why'd you strike her?' Mac goes, 'Didn't you see the tattoo on her ankle?' I said 'Hell, no! What tattoo?' I tell you, how'd he even notice that?"

"What was the tattoo?" asked Zaria.

"He told me it was a word. OMINIRA. He spelled it for me."

"What does that mean?" she asked. "That doesn't sound like a Romance language or Slavic or Germanic. Is that Greek?"

"You should know. You're fluent in, like, six languages, Zaria, right?"

"No, not that many," she replied, looking down.

"It's Yoruba, a West African language. It means *freedom*. I looked that up later. Mac said that anyone with the word *freedom* tattooed on her skin probably wouldn't be a great juror to convict someone who'd go straight to jail. So, he struck her. He's super observant, that guy, and sometimes that scares the shit out of me."

"I'll try to check that out if I ever see him, Santi."

"I mean, I think I'm kicking his ass in this murder trial, but this guy always rises from the dead, like the Terminator or something."

"Well, gotta finish up. Good luck with your case. You'll be OK. Mac MacIntyre might be really smart, but all the prosecutors are smart to some degree. But he seems different to me. He seems *honest*, unlike most of them. Most of them lie all the time, cheat on discovery stuff, and hide evidence, right?"

CHAPTER 43

Tuesday, August 6, 2019
8:15 p.m.

Mac looked at the Caller ID on his cell phone and saw "JO NEWGRANGE." He tapped the screen and said, "Hey, boss. What's up?"

Jo said, "I know you started that Van der Hook trial today, but would you be able to be a guest teacher for my class tomorrow night at Seneca County Community College? I think the kids could benefit from hearing a new voice."

"OK, well, sure, what's the class?" His antennae started vibrating. She was, in effect, setting up a private meeting with him outside the office at night. Beware of cat.

"I'm teaching Introduction to Criminal Law," Jo explained. "The students in my class are mostly adults who work all day and then go to school at night. Half of the time, they're exhausted and sit there like lumps. But you have a way of being dramatic and interesting. Can you bring a bunch of your charts and photos and demonstrative evidence from some of your closed cases and—sort of—put on a dog-and-pony show for them?"

"Sure. I can do that."

"Can you do that presentation you did at the Police Academy on homicide cases? The one with all the photos? Except don't use any really gruesome ones, OK? I don't want them seeing dead babies and pictures of chopped-up people and stuff like that. That'll freak them out. That presentation you did for the police was fantastic. Can you throw that lecture together for these college kids?"

"No problem. I have all of that stuff in a box somewhere in my office."

"Don't you get sick of doing these awful murder cases? I can *easily* switch you to Economic Crimes or another post if you want to move to a different assignment within the office. There's been a lot of white collar stuff recently, embezzlements and Ponzi schemes. We just got a Bernie Madoff-type case this morning. You could do those instead?"

There was an unusual tone in Jo's voice. Was she threatening him? Or was she worried that he was burning himself out? She must know that Mac was renowned in the Seneca County legal community for his devotion to prosecuting murder cases. "I can easily switch you," she had said. That was true. He did not like her use of the word "easily."

"I love doing homicide cases, Jo."

"I can tell! Well, I'll email you the classroom number. You know where the campus is, up the Interstate?"

"Yes, I know exactly where SenCo is. I subbed for Robert Gill several times before you came to the SAO. Back when he was tied up with all of that controversy. I think I covered three classes for him then."

"Awesome, Macaroni! See you there. Tomorrow night. 7:00 p.m."

CHAPTER 44

Wednesday, August 7, 2019
6:40 p.m.

The next evening, Mac arrived at the college and found the classroom. When he arrived 20 minutes early, Jo was already at the desk inside the room. None of the students had arrived yet.

"Hey there!" she called and waved, a wide smile on her face.

He put the cardboard box of demonstrative evidence and mounted photographs on a desk. It was a collection of morbid souvenirs from his career handling murder cases: a nightmarish assemblage. The photos silently reminded him of all the victims he'd fought for and all the horrors they'd experienced. So many lives cut short, so much depravity. One photo portrayed pattern bruise injuries of a man clubbed to death with a tennis racket—the crisscross design of little squares distinctly raised against his skin. Another showed a little girl with bite marks on her arm. Mac had hired an expert in dentistry to match the bite pattern with the suspect's teeth. There was a chart of the human head, showing the layers beneath the skull: the scalp, the dura, the subdura, to illustrate for a jury the complexity of Shaken Baby Syndrome. Subdural hematomas, diffuse axonal injuries—complex medical evidence—all of it needed to be translated as if it were a foreign language. Only then could a typical juror understand what had happened. Tonight, Jo's community college class would be like one of his juries.

Jo dashed across the empty classroom. She wrapped both arms around him and squeezed him tightly. "Thank you so much for helping me!" she said, and then pecked a kiss on the left side of his face. It was not a lingering kiss, but Mac noted the exact location of where Jo's lips touched him: not fully on the cheek, but partially on the corner of his mouth. He was also fully aware that her body was flush against his front. It was not one of those hugs where each participant leaned forward to minimize body contact. He could feel her body touching him from his chest to his knees, her pelvis pressing against his thigh. She was wearing jeans, not a suit or a fashionable blazer. She did not have on one of her trademark colorful scarves. He surreptitiously glanced at her jeans. They were tight, with two deliberately symmetrical small tears, one over each knee. Not jeans bought at Old Navy, but more likely at Nordstrom.

"Thank you for helping me, Mac. I really, really appreciate it."

A young African American woman stood in the doorway. She had long braids tied in a ponytail dripping down her back.

"Oh, hi, Zenaib! You're early," Jo said. "Come on in. We will start the class when everyone else gets here."

The young woman instinctively turned her back, as if to offer a glimmer of privacy.

Mac memorized her name: "Zenaib."

CHAPTER 45

Wednesday, August 7, 2019
10:05 p.m.

Two of Jo's students napped for most of Mac's presentation, but several others seemed enthusiastic. A few stayed afterwards, clustering around to ask questions.

"How do you handle all the stress of being a homicide prosecutor?"

"What did you study in college to prepare for law school and to become an Assistant State's Attorney?"

"What's your won/loss record in court?"

Mac politely answered all the students' question, noting Jo in the corner beaming and smiling. She was rocking back and forth—what was the emotion? Pride? Something else? He had never seen her fidget like that before. He could only observe her with quick peripheral glances, trying to keep eye contact with those who seemed legitimately interested in his presentation.

In a few minutes, the classroom emptied, and Mac packed up the courtroom exhibits and photographs into the brown cardboard box. Jo slipped on a faded denim jacket that was a few tones lighter than her jeans. It was the first time he had seen her casually dressed, as her preferred courthouse look was razor sharp and tailored. Even so, this casual, collegiate outfit, Mac thought, had a premeditated and coordinated quality to it. Jo had a chameleon-like quality: when dressed in courtroom attire—expensive suits and high heels—she looked 50 years old, but in tight jeans and a matching jacket, she looked 30.

She turned, zipped up her Michael Kors purse, and slung it over her shoulder. Mac took advantage of this opportunity to scrutinize how her jeans gripped her narrow hips and slender thighs. He'd never seen Jo wearing pants before.

"Hey Jo. There's something I've always wanted to ask you."

"What, honey? Ask away!"

She had never, ever called him "honey" before. She had previously teased him around the office with several other childish nicknames, but this felt different. He noted the emptiness of the surrounding classroom, far away from the observant eyes and gossiping whispers omnipresent in the SAO. Not for a microsecond did he forget she was, technically, his supervisor. Heading down this road was unquestionably dangerous. If Jo had been a man, and he a woman, these expressions of affection and pet nicknames would have already migrated from friendliness into clear-cut sexual harassment. But with the roles reversed, would that make any difference?

"I saw that your actual first name is Josephine. How did you come to be called Jo? I mean, you use Jo even in court and on your official signature. Seems informal, which is fine. I'm not criticizing it. I'm just curious. Because I use Mac around the office, but William in court and when signing pleadings."

She laughed. It was more than a giggle, but not a full-throated laugh.

She said, "Now, Mr. MacIntyre, aren't you a clever man?! Y'know, no one's ever asked me that before. How did you find out my real first name? Oh, well, never mind. I'll tell you. When I was a little girl, my father used to call me Josephine the Serpentine, and I had no idea what that meant. I must've been 10 or 11 before I found out it means..." She trailed off into silence.

"Snake-like. Serpentine. Like a snake. Oh, I see..."

"So, every time I hear Josephine, well, I just have these annoying PTSD flashbacks to my childhood. My father was a cruel man, to be honest. He called my younger brother Dummy until he was, like, 17."

"Jo suits you perfectly. It's simply beautiful, and beautifully simple."

"Oh Mac, you actually know the word serpentine? You're so smart. Is there anything you don't know?"

"Thanks. But I'm not really that smart. I just have a thing for words. Words go into my brain differently. Now, numbers? Not so good. Someone once told me I had dyscalculia. Not dyslexia, but dyscalculia. Numbers, not letters, get all switched around in my mind." He looked into her blue eyes. "Let's just say I have a good memory. It was a huge help in law school, believe me. All the names of those endless cases they wanted you to memorize. *Gideon v. Wainwright, Mapp v.*

Ohio, Miranda v. Arizona, that kind of thing. I don't do parlor tricks, but I could probably name 250 of them right now."

"Everyone says you have a photographic memory. Is that true?"

"Well, I don't know. I just remember things. If I really want to, if I concentrate hard, I can drive something deep into my brain, and it will stay there forever. Like when I was a kid, I could memorize a random deck of cards pretty easily. That's only 52 units of information."

"Wait. You can memorize a whole deck of cards?! And say them back in order sight unseen? That is insane."

"Oh, that's nothing. My father knew where every item in the entire grocery store was. He could visualize the exact location of everything we needed. Precisely. Which aisle, which shelf. There are literally thousands of separate items in a grocery store, Jo."

She leaned towards him, with her chest only an inch from his.

"That's amazing," she whispered.

He stood still and did not respond.

She added, "Why don't you come over to my apartment, and we can continue this conversation? It's not far, about halfway back to the office…"

"That would be nice," Mac whispered back.

Her tone changed. With her customary professional, organized, compulsive-planner voice, she commanded, "We'll take two cars. Just follow me down Seneca Pike. It's only 20 minutes from here."

CHAPTER 46

Wednesday, August 7, 2019
10:31 p.m.

This is exceptionally dangerous.

Mac's mind skipped repeatedly over the word "dangerous," like an old vinyl record with a scratch, causing the same lyric to repeat endlessly. He considered the phrase "like a broken record," and realized no one under the age of 50 would even know what a "record" was. Another anachronistic cliché, destined for the history books, along with "the phone was ringing off the hook," since cell phones didn't have "hooks."

Seneca Pike, the well-traveled artery running north/south parallel to the Interstate, followed an ancient Native American hunting trail from eons ago. Now, it was a four-lane suburban road lined with fast-food restaurants, car dealerships, strip malls offering massage parlors and pho restaurants. Late at night, Seneca Pike was empty, with only an occasional car rumbling by. During the usual daytime chaos, people were out doing errands, shopping for groceries at Giant, and commuting to the courthouse complex. Mac's sand-yellow Jeep cruised down the Pike, past the 7-Eleven where there had been an armed robbery he had once prosecuted, and the little sushi joint where he would bring his files and sit alone, picking through the salmon rolls and tuna maki, while reading murder case files.

He was nearing Jo's apartment.

This is a bad mistake. This is a kamikaze run. This is a suicide mission. She's the Deputy State's Attorney! She could fire me instantly or blackmail me somehow. Think, you idiot.

He realized he had to find an escape, but he missed his chance to make an excuse back at the community college.

I should have said, "I'm sorry, Jo. I don't think this is a good idea."

But she was so emotionally volatile. Even an awkward rejection might risk setting her off. Her ego was titanic; she was extremely defensive. When something went wrong in the office, it was always somebody *else's* fault. Everyone in the SAO knew the story about longtime ASA Christian Blender, who had talked back to her at a campaign event during the election. On Jo's first day as Deputy, she called Blender into her office and, without any explanation, fired him. She told him to place his badge on her desk. Then she called security to escort him out of the building.

Mac sensed Jo loved the feeling of power: the predator chasing down the prey. It thrilled her. He needed to be careful.

He had to extricate himself from this trap without creating an enemy. So, how to negotiate this one?

His instinct as a courtroom advocate logically conjured up both sides of the argument, but, for an instant, his mind spiraled in an unhelpful direction.

Damn, those jeans looked good on her. I'd love to tear those jeans off and release some of my inner Scottish beast on her. This could be a legendary conquest. Forget Stirling Bridge. They'd remember a victory like this in the SAO forever. Nail my pretty little boss. Make her quiver and sweat. Show her who the real boss is. Who knows? If I could control her, maybe she'd get me promoted to Deputy? They've had two deputies in the office before. Why couldn't I be one too? That could set me up to run for State's Attorney down the road once Ari moved on. I'd be great at politics. After a couple of years as the SA, I could run for Attorney General or State Senate. Anything would be possible after that. Snagging Jo could be an unbelievable coup. Maybe tonight isn't a trap, but an opportunity? Wait a minute... Are you fucking crazy? I mean, literally, crazy? You can't do this.

His mind swung back to reality.

He pulled up alongside her BMW i8. How could she afford that? It was parked in a space with "#1D" stenciled on the blacktop. She rolled down her driver's side window. Cigarette smoke billowed out of her car.

She smokes? Never knew.

Jo said, "Oh, you can't park here. These are residents' spots. Park over there," she commanded, pointing to the visitors' parking spaces. Mac put the Jeep into reverse, backed up, then parked in the correct space. Jo smiled when he immediately followed her instructions. Something was pulling him *towards* danger like a powerful magnet he couldn't control. He struggled to push back against his own instincts.

A flashback burst into his mind: he was a boy standing on a high cliff with the other boys urging him to leap into the water far below.

Jump, Willie! Jump!

His whole life, he'd always jumped. He wasn't afraid of danger. If he was, he would have never chosen this profession. Risk and competition fueled him, and like Icarus with wax dripping down his wings, he willingly flew towards the sun. The perplexing part was Mac knew of his own self-destructive instincts. They had caused him much disappointment in his life and, particularly, in his relationships with people. Ever since he was a little boy, people said he was brilliant and talented, but something scared people away.

Yes, risk and danger were thrilling. But he wasn't stupid.

He shook those thoughts from his mind and remembered his survival word: FOCUS. Jo was outside her car. She beeped her remote key to lock the BMW's doors. She looked up and smiled at Mac with an expression he had never seen before, an expression somewhere between hunger and satisfaction. Her keychain dangled along her side as they walked towards the apartment building, the light from streetlamps glittering off her bouncing keys. As they walked, he noticed a small souvenir Eiffel Tower, like a charm on a bracelet, twisting on her keyring. "This way," she guided, reaching into the bend of his arm, grasping it and escorting him.

"Oh, it's hot as Hades! And humid. Worse than Atlanta up here. It's so much swampier!" she said.

"I know. You could melt on a night like this," Mac replied.

They arrived at the front of Jo's apartment building and entered the lobby. It was all glass and polished chrome. She used her key fob to enter the main doors. They walked down a quiet hallway towards her door. As they passed another apartment, a dog started yelping. Mac noted the apartment number, "1H." The door opened just a few inches, and the heavily wrinkled face of a gnome-like elderly woman appeared. She was holding a small, white dog which Mac recognized from his volunteer work at the animal shelter was a West Highland Terrier.

The lady said, "Oh, Ms. Newgrange. Sorry. Charlie was barking at the door! Didn't mean to annoy you."

"Oh, no problem. Have a good night."

The small dog growled. Jo made no introductions. There was a small name tag by a doorbell on the neighbor's door. It said "LOWE." Mac recorded four units of information in his memory: 1H. Mrs. Lowe. Charlie. Breed of dog.

Jo opened her door. Mac hesitated just slightly.

I might as well lay my head on the guillotine's block. This is insane. I'm alone in Jo's apartment!?

He stepped across the threshold. Jo shut the door behind him. He peeled off his corduroy blazer and started to drop it on the arm of the couch, but Jo intercepted it, and stepped to the nearby closet. She opened the door and hung it up.

"Even for an eggshell," Mac said.

"What?"

"Exposing what is mortal and unsure," he added.

"Oh, wow. Beautiful! I love how you can do that."

"To all that fortune, death and danger dare," he continued, with no emotion. "Even for an eggshell."

"Gorgeous. You really know how to turn a girl on! What's that from?"

"*Hamlet*. Act four, scene four."

She walked up and placed her hand against his chest, in the exact center of his body, and said, "But why are you thinking about eggshells right now?"

CHAPTER 47

Wednesday, August 7, 2019
10:58 p.m.

"Make yourself comfortable," Jo said, gesturing to a chair, unaware of how impossible her suggestion was.

She went into the kitchenette area. It was a two bedroom apartment, with a living room in the center with two small rooms, one on either side. As you entered the doorway, there was a small kitchen area on the right. It was a compact, boxy space with a refrigerator and a four-burner stove. Mac's eyes subtly surveyed the entire apartment without noticeably moving his head, instantly taking in as many clues and details as his brain could download.

The door to the bedroom on the right was slightly ajar. Mac could see a narrow slice of the interior. It appeared to have been converted into an office space. He could see the back of a leather office swivel chair—it was exactly the same make as the ones in the SAO. Had Jo taken one home? He noticed that there wasn't a TV in the main room. As he analyzed the contents of the room, his attention was drawn to a large framed color poster prominently mounted on the wall. It had squiggly lines in random, assorted colors. The lines were intertwined in some sort of logical, yet also illogical, jumble. From this angle, he could not decipher a coherent pattern to the squiggles, but his mind pulled him towards the messy chaos, instinctively trying to find order in the multicolored lines. He was powerless to control his need to make order out of something chaotic. His father and grandfather were the same way; they jokingly called it the MacIntyre Curse. Even with effort, he could never turn that instinct off. His brain subconsciously arranged everything into logical patterns. He conceded his father's DNA was controlling him, and he knew there was no way to ever escape it.

Despite the immediate danger of being trapped in Jo's apartment, the MacIntyre Curse overwhelmed him. His brain needed to solve the riddle of the squiggly lines. He stepped towards the poster and stared at it, instantly absorbing all of it. He noticed that the words LE METRO DE PARIS were printed across the top, and he read the words that appeared at eye level. Horizontally, from left to right, they read: "Champs-Élysées," "Concorde," and "Musée Du Louvre."

Satisfied, he turned, letting the power of the Curse abate. Then, feeling it pass like a puff of smoke in the wind, he continued to mentally absorb every detail he could observe in the rest of the apartment. It was exceptionally clean, he noted, with no obvious messiness or incongruity anywhere. There were many books, perfectly lined up by size, on several bookshelves. The clear glass coffee table was shiny and clean. There was a faint scent of citrus in the air, perhaps a lemon-and-lime mix. From this vantage point, he could now see a wider slice of her office. Part of her desk inside the room was now visible. There were three pens on the desk, neatly lined up in a parallel formation. The metal mesh wastepaper basket was completely empty.

Jo appeared from the kitchenette. She was holding two green bottles of Heineken.

"Here you go, Macaroni!"

"Thanks."

"You were wonderful tonight with the students! Thank you so much. Y'know, when Ari and I first came out to Seneca County, we didn't know anyone. I mean, literally, no one. It was my very first time in the courthouse, and I was the Deputy State's Attorney!"

He listened intently.

What is she getting at? Is she reminding me of her status? Trying to exert some leverage over me?

"Ari knew some of the judges already, but literally all the ASAs were strangers to us. We had never met any of them. We had no clue about our own personnel. We didn't know who was a real trial lawyer and who wasn't. We'd heard most of these prosecutors were lazy, taking a plea in every case. No fighting spirit. We didn't know who had balls. Who had ovaries. Who was loyal and who might end up a traitor. You know what I mean? So, we had to start asking around, like doing a scouting report on which prosecutors were good and which weren't. And Mac, I gotta tell you, your name kept popping up in all of those conversations."

"That's nice. Well, I've been around Seneca County a long time," he said. "I've got some friends here. Got some enemies, too. You have to be careful around the courthouse, as I'm sure you know, Jo. People here can be real backstabbers."

"Yes, that is true. Definitely. So, well, we asked people about the prosecutors. We asked judges, and we asked some of the old-time defense attorneys, and just about everyone said you were a great trial lawyer. Not specifically that you were a nice guy. Not the kind of ASA who kissed everyone's butt. Not one of those political types. They said you weren't necessarily a team player. But they said that you were a real trial lawyer. And that's what Ari and I wanted. People who could get in there and battle. Fighters. Ari said he didn't want 'nice guys.' He wanted people who would win cases. Gladiators. Killers. Hit men. Assassins. We need them to do the heavy lifting, and then we'd handle the political, I mean… the administrative part."

"A team player. I never understood that," said Mac. "Doing a jury trial is not a team sport. Where's the team? I never cared about office politics. I became a prosecutor to help people, not to play these juvenile, high-school-type social games."

She sat on the couch next to him. She took a small sip of her beer and then placed the bottle on the coffee table. She carefully arranged two coasters and placed her bottle on one. She put two paper napkins flat on the table alongside the coasters.

"And then, after our first couple of weeks here, Ari asked me to actually go to court and watch for myself to see with my own eyes each of the ASAs in court. Take a look at all of them, he said. Make assessments and then report back to him with my own personal impressions."

"I remember," Mac said. "You came inside the courtroom when I was doing a closing argument. I remember it clearly."

"No, you're wrong. I snuck in. You didn't even notice me."

He knew she was wrong, completely wrong. He *had* noticed her as soon as she appeared at the door, but he wasn't going to challenge her now on something insignificant. Actually, he also recalled with precision that she was wearing a navy-blue suit, accented with a color-coordinated beige scarf. But now was not the time for parlor tricks.

"Mac, I watched you do the closing argument in that awful Scartelli case. The one with that little girl, Antonella? I was just bowled over. It was like you were on stage performing at the Kennedy Center or something! I have never seen a prosecutor with your raw talent."

"Really? Thanks. That was a bad case."

"Yes! And I looked around the courtroom. It was jammed. There were all kinds of reporters and press there. And people were *crying*. You had that whole place in the palm of your hand. I looked at Judge Siegfried across the room, and I think even *she* was crying, or trying to hold back her tears. It was so powerful."

Mac was distracted. Scartelli. One of his worst homicide cases. Shaken Baby Syndrome. Young girl with a sadistic stepmother. She had poured boiling bacon grease on the little girl's hands as punishment for her spilling her breakfast on the floor. Ripped the child from the high chair in a rage and shook her violently. When she stopped breathing, Scartelli called 911 and said the child had tipped the high chair over, spilling the frying pan from the stove and spattering bacon grease everywhere. Mac subpoenaed the manufacturer of the high chair to prove how difficult, nearly impossible, it was to topple. In fact, they were designed and engineered specifically *not* to topple. He also brought in medical experts to prove that the child's injuries, diffuse axonal tears and subdural hematomas, were consistent with inflicted head trauma caused by severe shaking. Injuries like those could not be caused by a single fall. His closing argument to the jury? Yes, he recalled.

"Antonella will never walk down the aisle to graduate from high school. She will never walk down the aisle, a beautiful young bride, on her wedding day. Antonella will never grow up to have a life, a life of her own, with children and blessings and all that life has to offer. No, she will never have any of these things because of this Defendant's rage." Mac wheeled to point directly at Scartelli across the well of the courtroom. Jo *had* been watching. The image was clear in his memory. Seeing Jo in his mind's eye snapped him back to the present.

"Well, that was one of my saddest cases, Jo."

She seemed to move a little closer on the couch and slightly leaned in.

He decided to take his chance right now. Jump from the high cliff.

"Jo, can we be frank with each other?"

The ambience in the room immediately changed from moist and tropical to Artic with a subzero wind chill factor.

"Yes, of course, Mac. What is it?"

"I'm just going to tell you exactly how I feel, and I hope you'll appreciate my honesty."

CHAPTER 48

Wednesday, August 7, 2019
11:40 p.m.

Jo straightened up, and her sky-blue eyes intensified as Mac looked directly at her.

He had to escape, but he also had to let her down easy and not anger her. Thinking that she might respond better to compliments, Mac decided to heap them on.

"Jo, ever since I first saw you, I was immediately attracted to you. I have to be honest," he said, which was partially true. "But because I am an Assistant State's Attorney, and you are the Deputy State's Attorney, I struggled to control my feelings. I know you're divorced. I'm single. If I had met you anywhere else, I would've definitely asked you to go out with me. If only we didn't work together. I mean, we'd make one hell of a power couple."

She defensively crossed her legs, subconsciously guarding her most intimate areas, and adopted a more professional, less casual position.

With the indecision of a burglar tiptoeing inside a deserted bank hoping not to trip the motion detectors, Mac continued, "But it just wouldn't look right for either of us at the SAO. So, I'm not sure what to do… But I want you to know… I'm really drawn to you. You are such a brilliant woman, and you are extremely attractive, and, if things were different…" He artfully trailed off. Jo absorbed these confessions. She then uncrossed her legs and put both of her heels on the floor, as if to signal she had arrived at a conclusion.

"OK, I get it. You don't have to go on and on about it. I guess I just let my emotions get the best of me. But you're absolutely right about one thing: this would never work."

"It would. It could work," Mac implored. "It would be amazing. If only we weren't in the same office. Maybe someday I won't be working as a prosecutor anymore. I can't do these murder cases forever. And then we'd make such a formidable pair, you and I."

"No, no, no, what the hell was I thinking?" Another Arctic blast swept across the apartment. Icicles formed everywhere. Jo stood, gathered the two nearly full Heineken bottles from the coffee table, and rearranged the two coasters. She scrunched up the napkins and turned towards the kitchenette.

"It's late. You'd better be going."

"Yes, you're right."

The Curse reappeared. There was chaos swirling around Mac's brain. He instinctively tried to rearrange this unpredictable scene into something orderly.

He had an idea.

"Can I just use the men's room, uh, bathroom first?"

Jo gestured toward the bedroom door, but didn't speak. She tipped the two bottles over into the sink, letting the golden liquid pour down the drain, and then she ran the faucet to rinse away all traces of the beer. She tossed the bottles into her garbage can, lifted out the black plastic bag, and spun it into a spiral enclosure. Finally, she tied a knot to seal it, as if to remove all evidence of this fiasco.

While she poured out the beer bottles and noisily ran the tap water, Mac entered the bedroom and closed the door behind him, completely blocking her view. He then turned left towards the bathroom. He stood still for a moment, analyzing all of his immediate options. He heard rattling coming from the kitchen as Jo rustled the bottles in the garbage bag. Her bed was carefully made, perfectly made, with a dozen pillows assiduously arranged in a linear formation across the headboard. A sturdy wooden dresser, perhaps made by Amish craftsmen, stood by the edge of the bed.

He silently removed his phone from his pocket, activated the video function, and filmed the interior of her bedroom in a slow, sweeping, panoramic spin. Finished, he slid the phone back into his pocket. He pivoted and returned to the small bathroom. He flushed the toilet without using it. As the toilet flushed, he stepped back into the bedroom and opened the top dresser drawer. There were rows of neatly folded, colorful panties. They looked like brightly colored butterflies. He stopped and froze.

No. That won't work.

He silently closed the drawer and turned, empty-handed. He returned to the bathroom and ran the tap water in the sink.

He reached down and opened the hamper. He saw one. He fished out a tiny piece of brilliantly colored turquoise cotton fabric.

FOCUS.

He read the label: PROVOCATEUR FAWN OUVERT - SMALL. He shoved the turquoise panties into his jeans pocket, ruffled the small towel hanging next to the sink, and then turned off the water. He took two steps across the bedroom, opened the bedroom door, and said, "Well, thanks. I guess I'd better be going."

Jo was already opening the front door. She had the plastic garbage bag in one hand and his jacket in the other. Mac slipped his jacket on and started to speak, but she interrupted him.

"It's OK. You don't have to say another word. I get it. Let's just pretend this never happened. That's the best for both of us, really. And can you do me a favor, please? The trash chute is right down the hall before you hit the lobby. Thanks. See you in the office."

How symbolic. Did she really just ask me to take out her garbage? An errand suitable for a servant.

"Sure, no problem. Good night," Mac said, grabbing the topknot of the twisted bag and stepping into the hallway. Jo shut the door and double-locked it behind him. He heard the dog growling at the door from the apartment across the hallway. He walked to the lobby, pushed open the front door, and felt the hot, thick August air envelop his face. He crossed the parking lot, went to the back of his Jeep, opened the rear hatchback, and tossed the garbage bag up into the cargo area.

CHAPTER 49

Thursday, August 8, 2019
8:01 a.m.

The next morning, Mac propped his laptop up on the kitchen counter, flipped it open, and Googled "VETS SENECA PIKE." Several websites came up near Jo's neighborhood. He dialed the number of the office closest to her apartment.

"Good morning, this is Canfield Animal Hospital. Jenny speaking. Can I help you?"

"Yes, good morning. My name is Patrick Lowe," Mac said, slightly changing the pitch of his voice. "Um, I'm calling for my mother, Mrs. Lowe. She's a little under the weather today, so she asked me to call and check on Charlie's appointment today. He's a West Highland Terrier. She also wanted to make sure your records are all updated, too?"

"OK. I'll check, just a minute. Let me put you on hold for a sec."

Recorded music played while he waited.

I'm pretty sure this genre of music is called "bebop" jazz. This is either Miles Davis or John Coltrane... or maybe both together, I'm not sure.

He knew he had heard that song before, but several years earlier. His frolicking thoughts were interrupted by Jenny.

"You said Lowe? Like L-O-W-E? I checked Lowe and Low, just L-O-W, and I don't show any records for your mother? You said it was a Westie? I can cross-check by the pet's name."

"Oh, thanks. Well, let me talk to my mom when she wakes up. I'll see if I can figure it out at this end, and then, if necessary, I'll call you back, OK? Thanks, Jenny, you've been a big help."

Mac hung up. He glanced at his laptop screen with the list of local veterinarians.

He dialed the number for the next website.

"Hello, this is Putney Vet Clinic. This is Liz. Can I help you?"

"Yes, thank you. This is Patrick Lowe calling. My mother is sick today, and she said she had an appointment to bring her dog in. Just checking on that."

"OK, what's your mother's full name?"

That was unexpected.

Shit, her first name? I have no idea.

He bluffed. He said, "Mrs. Lowe," immediately adding, "And her dog is a Westie named Charlie?"

"Oh, Charlie! I love Charlie! Yes, is Mrs. Lowe OK? She's sick? I'm sorry to hear that."

Mac slid his laptop away from the Keurig coffee machine on his kitchen counter. "Thank you for asking. Well, not too sick. At least I don't think so. She's just a little sleepy today, might be her diabetes medication. That insulin is very strong stuff. Anyway, she asked me to check on Charlie's appointment... she's getting a bit forgetful these days."

"I'm looking at the chart. I don't see an appointment listed for today," Liz replied.

"Right. Well, as I said, Mom is getting a little older and mixes things up sometimes. You know how it is."

"Yes, my grandma is also... well, my family has something brewing like that too," Liz said.

At exactly the moment the receptionist said the word "brewing," Mac was coincidentally placing a Keurig coffee pod in position. As she finished speaking, he brought the mechanism down, like a guillotine, puncturing the container and triggering the ritualistic process: in seconds, boiling hot coffee streamed into his mug.

He confirmed, "Right. OK, so no appointment. Hey, while I have you on the line, Liz, can we check the information Mom gave you? I just want to make sure it's accurate. Do you have the right address? It's apartment 1H?"

"Oh, no problem. We still have 20147 Seneca Pike, Apartment 1H, Seneca County, Maryland, 20859. Is that all still up to date?"

"Yes, exactly right. And her full name is correct as well?"

"Noelle Lowe."

"Hey, Liz, thanks so much. Sorry about the misunderstanding. Let me check with my mother, and I'll call you back if we need to reschedule Charlie's checkup, OK?"

"Have a nice day."

Mac clicked off his phone, reached for his laptop, and Googled "SENECA COUNTY COMMUNITY COLLEGE REGISTRAR."

How many ways can you spell Zenaib?

CHAPTER 50

Thursday, August 8, 2019
9:33 a.m.

"State calls Amanda Van der Hook, Your Honor," announced Mac. He spun towards the rear of the courtroom, asking, "Judge Harajuku, may I please have leave of the Court to escort the witness to the stand?"

"Yes, certainly," said the judge. She glanced over to look at the jurors. As he walked away from the jury, down the center aisle of the courtroom and towards the back doors, the jurors followed him with their eyes, eager to see this little girl.

Mac strolled down the aisle with a loping gait, pushed through the double doors, and turned towards a secure witness waiting room where Mandy was safely inside with Andre and her Aunt Lindy. Mac returned quickly, guiding Mandy forward with his hand gently on her shoulder. She wore maroon corduroy pants, a plain, solid beige T-shirt, and brown moccasins on her feet. Her hair was cut in a simple short pageboy hairstyle.

Mac gestured towards the witness stand, and she climbed up the two steps to the platform. She was unsure what to do, even though she and Mac had previously practiced these exact maneuvers in the SAO's mock courtroom. She shook her dark brown bangs out of her eyes and looked up at the judge.

"Good morning, Miss," said Judge Harajuku, causing Mandy to squint slightly, a confused expression blossoming on her face, as clearly no one had ever called her "Miss" before.

"Please stand and take the oath."

Mandy looked towards Mac with an expression asking, "What does oath mean again?" Mac had also explained this part of the process the day before, but she had forgotten.

Phoebe, the law clerk, said, "Do you solemnly swear or affirm that the testimony you shall give will be the truth, the whole truth, and nothing but the truth?"

Mandy said, "Um, what? Swear? I'm not supposed to swear."

Mac stood.

"Judge, may I *voir dire*? It may be easier if I use more child-friendly language. As you know, Maryland courts have long held that it is an appropriate alternative for the State to administer the oath when swearing in a child witness."

Santiago jumped to his feet, saying, "Objection! This is not..."

The judge interrupted him, "No, overruled. The swearing-in, or affirmation, is totally within the discretion of the Court. Overruled. Mr. MacIntyre, you may administer the oath." Turning towards the little girl, the judge said, "You may be seated."

Mandy sat in the swivel chair and immediately started playing with the microphone that twisted up from the witness box. Mac lifted his right palm into a "stop" gesture, and she put her hands down.

Softly, Mac said, "Good morning," and then stopped speaking. He waited for Mandy to reply. Mac wanted to get her to speak. The direct examination would flow much more easily if he could just get her to speak. If he could just get a few words out, then just a few more, he could then create a sense of momentum, and her testimony would begin to flow naturally.

Mandy said, "Morning."

"My name is William MacIntyre. You can just call me Mac, OK?"

She hesitated, and then said, "OK, Mac."

"What is your full name?"

"Amanda Helene Van der Hook."

"How old are you?

"I'm nine, almost 10."

"And may I call you Mandy?"

"Yes."

"Good. Now, do you know that we are in a courtroom, Mandy?"

"Yes."

"And what is a courtroom?"

"It's where you decide things. If things are bad. You tell the judge and the people sitting in the box, and then they decide if it was bad or not."

"And do you know why we are here today? Can you tell us?"

"Because my mommy and dad got into another fight. A really bad fight." She raised her arm and pointed her left index finger at the defense table where Rikki and Santiago were seated. Santiago looked down, pretending to shuffle his notes. Rikki looked directly into Mandy's eyes with a calm, almost frozen gaze—it could be fear; it could be confidence. The jurors stared intently at Rikki, trying to find a hidden clue or reaction, but she was lifeless, like a mannequin. The worm-like veins on the sides of Rikki's neck were pulsating.

Mandy said, "I am here to tell what happened. What I saw. I miss my dad."

"This is Judge Harajuku," said Mac. Mandy looked up. The judge automatically smiled.

"Listen to me, please," Mac continued. "This is very important. Do you know what it means to tell the truth?" Words like "oath" and "affirm" and "solemnly" were useless when qualifying a child as a witness. Although Mandy was nine, she presented a childlike demeanor that made her seem even younger.

If an attorney said "case," a kid might think of a briefcase. Experienced prosecutors who handled juvenile witnesses were really interpreters, simplifying and translating all the words they used into terms and phrases a child could readily understand.

"Yes. The truth is when you don't lie," she answered. "It's, like, what really happened."

"OK, and what is a lie?" Mac followed up, using Mandy's own testimony to build the next question as he inched patiently toward his goal, a courtroom technique called "looping."

"A lie is when you make something up. But it's wrong, and I won't lie. I promise."

"Good. And you just said promise. What's a promise?"

"Um, that's when... when you do something you said you were going to do. Like, I make a promise to my mommy to feed the cat, and then I do feed the cat."

"So, Mandy, we are here in court today. Do you promise to tell the truth?"

"Yes."

Mac looked up and said, "Your Honor?"

Santiago started to rise, but Judge Harajuku raised her hand as if to communicate, "Don't even try." He persisted, though, and said, "May we approach?"

The judge flipped on the husher and beckoned both Santiago and Mac up to the bench.

"I must object. For the record. This is improper and wholly inadequate. The witness is incompetent to render any valid testimony. The State has not even addressed several important issues which bear on competency. We object."

Judge Harajuku waited with extreme patience to respond, knowing the jury was watching.

"Mr. Garcia, as you know, under the Maryland Rules of Criminal Procedure, the Court has wide latitude with respect to swearing in a juvenile witness. Several elements must be satisfied. One, a witness must understand the difference between truth and falsity. So, I find, in the instant case, that the witness has acknowledged and understands that difference. She articulated it in her own way, but she clearly stated the difference between the truth and a lie. Two, there must be an acknowledgement, or some type of affirmation, to remain faithful to the truth. Here, the witness, even though she is nine years old, has clearly met that burden. I may add, to the Court, she appears to be intelligent and free from any *substantial* burden, whether it be physical or mental, that would render her incompetent to testify. If you have any questions going to capacity to testify, you may ask them on cross. Therefore, Mr. Garcia, I will note your objection, but I will overrule it. Mr. MacIntyre, you may proceed."

The attorneys returned to their table. Mac remained standing.

"Mandy, do you know this lady seated here?" asked Mac, as he took two steps towards the defense table, outstretching his arm towards Rikki. As he turned, Mac glanced at the jury box to see the jurors' reactions. They were looking intently at Rikki, boring into her with their gaze.

"Yes, that's my mommy, and I love her. But why is she wearing eyeglasses today?"

CHAPTER 51

Thursday, August 8, 2019
10:11 a.m.

Mac paused. He wanted that last answer to marinate and sink into the jurors' minds. He stood perfectly still and waited. Three seconds passed.

Judge Harajuku prompted him, "Mr. MacIntyre, do you have any other questions?" She looked at Mac with an expression which conveyed she knew exactly what he was doing: pausing for dramatic effect. Mac wanted to establish Mandy did not hate or fear Rikki, which would make her upcoming testimony ring true, and not sound like it was rehearsed or prompted by revenge or retaliation. He knew that a child of this age, unlike an adult, was unlikely to have the sophistication to hoodwink an entire jury.

"Mandy, did you live with your mother and father until recently?"

"Um, yes. But after the bad fight, my mommy was sent to jail, and she's still there."

"Objection!" Santiago jumped up from his table as if he was in an aerobics class.

"Sustained," said the judge. "The jury will disregard the witness's last statement, and, further, it will be stricken from the record. Mr. MacIntyre, please proceed."

"Let the record reflect that the witness has identified the Defendant..." he said, gesturing towards Rikki, but Santiago interrupted him sharply.

"Stipulate as to identity," Santiago exclaimed. Since it was going to be easy to identify his client, it was pointless to object. In this situation, it was smarter to just agree and appear to be helpful to the jury. But now Santiago was staring at Mandy as if she could tear him to shreds. Mac noticed his demeanor and hoped, as tiny and nonthreatening as Mandy looked, that her testimony was already throwing some nasty curveballs in his direction. Could this little girl possibly destroy him so effortlessly?

The judge said, "So stipulated. Let the record reflect that the witness has identified the Defendant. Mr. MacIntyre, you may continue."

Children who testified in court were notoriously unpredictable. Anything could happen. Mac did not want any error or mishap. A single error, or a random prejudicial statement from a witness who misspoke or blurted out something inadmissible, could result in a dreaded mistrial.

"Mandy, I want to ask you a couple of things," said Mac. "And please just try to answer the question and please try not to bring in new things, OK?" This was clever. He was suggesting to the jury that potentially ominous "new things" might exist, even if they were not allowed, by some confusing rule of evidence, to discuss them.

"Let me ask you this: when you lived with your mother and father, did anyone else live in the house with you?"

"No. Just me, Mommy and Dad and Mrs. Ambrose. She comes to take care of the house and cook and stuff like that. But she wasn't there that night. She had gone home."

"I want to ask you some questions about that night. You said you saw your mother and father have what you called a 'big fight?'"

Mandy shuffled a bit in her seat, reached for the water pitcher, decided not to touch it, and then folded her hands and placed them in her lap. She looked at the jury. Her chocolate-colored brown eyes widened slightly.

Mac began the direct testimony. First, he established a series of basic facts: Mandy's age, where she went to middle school, what some of her hobbies were and her normal daily routines, all nonessential questions designed to get her to engage in a comfortable dialogue. To Mac, this process was like two tennis players warming up before a match, using simple, basic strokes, hitting the ball easily back and forth, loosening up. Once he felt she was comfortable, he would then zero in on the important testimony.

Mac reached behind his counsel table and took a large chart that was leaning against the wall. He turned it around and said, "Your Honor, may I approach?"

Judge Harajuku said, "Certainly."

He placed the chart on the easel set up in front of the clerk's seat, blocking Phoebe's view. In the circular courtroom, there was no other logical location to place it, where Mandy, the jurors, the judge and both of the attorneys could see it. Phoebe rolled her eyes, stepped away from her seat, and leaned against the wall.

Mac pointed to the chart and said, "Do you recognize this chart as a floor plan of your home's living room area?"

"Yes, those squares are the rooms. The big square is the room where Mommy and Dad fought, and that set of steps that goes up the side of the drawing are the stairs where I was sitting and watching."

He took a large marker and wrote "LIVING ROOM" in block letters.

"Mandy, I'm going to place an X where you were sitting on the steps, OK? Was it here?"

Mac, well prepared from his pretrial interview, knew exactly where she had been sitting.

"Um, yeah. I sat on the top step and could see down."

"Did something bad happen with your Mommy and Dad while you sat there?"

Mandy did not respond. First, she shivered, and then shook her head violently, her hair flopping into her face. Then her eyes rolled into the back of her head. It looked like she was trying to stand up. Her legs flexed involuntarily as she rose slightly, then collapsed as she fainted. She hit her forehead hard on the witness stand and crumpled up in a ball behind her seat.

CHAPTER 52

Thursday, August 8, 2019
11:13 a.m.

After a long recess, Mandy was ready to take the witness stand again. All the jurors were startled when she fainted, but Mac—never distracted from his goal to win the trial—knew the audible gasps and looks of horror in the jurors' eyes gave him a major advantage.

"Did you see something bad happen with your mother and father?"

"Yes. But I wasn't supposed to watch," she said. "I snuck out of my room."

"That's alright. You're not in trouble. You didn't do anything wrong. Can you tell us what happened?"

Mac moved closer to Mandy, blocking off a portion of the courtroom to create a smaller, more intimate space. He positioned himself directly in front of her, shielding her view towards the defense table where Santiago and Rikki sat. Mac did not want Rikki to intimidate or influence her daughter with any expression or intense stare.

"What did you see happen?"

"They were fighting. Mommy got mad and started yelling. She was freaking out and smashing things and throwing stuff all over the place. She broke Grandma's blue plates, the ones from Holland."

"What happened when you were watching from the stairs?"

Mac slowly rotated his head to survey the courtroom like a periscope. Judge Harajuku was leaning forward towards the witness box. The jurors were listening attentively. He noticed that his two female Ambassadors, Butterfly Lady and Housekeeper, both had their hands nervously cupping their faces, almost covering them. One juror, the muscular man Mac had dubbed Power Forward, was wearing a green New York Jets jersey and frowning. A toothpick flickered up and down in his mouth.

Mandy looked down at the witness stand and squirmed in her seat. Her eyes fluttered and started rolling back inside her head.

"What happened?"

She tipped forward, her nose almost touching the microphone. Her hair was hanging down partially hiding her face.

Butterfly Lady had both of her hands up over her eyebrows in a double salute gesture, as if shielding her vision from the sun.

Mandy looked up. Her arms were crossed, and she was grabbing her own T-shirt with two clenched fists.

Barely whispering, she said, "I saw Mommy go into the kitchen. Then she came running back into the living room where Dad was standing. She had a big knife."

Mac paused and didn't ask any questions. Sometimes silence was best. It almost forced a reluctant witness to continue with the narrative.

"Dad turned and raised his arm like this," Mandy said, illustrating by raising her elbow across her own face in a protective shield. "Mommy hit him with the knife over and over. He fell down, and she kept hitting him. I saw one punch push the knife in his head. He wasn't moving after that. Blood was spurting out everywhere. I... I was on the steps and I... r-ran back into my room and crawled under the b-bed."

She put her head down on the witness stand, her forehead touching the wood.

Mac said, "We're almost done. I just need to ask you a few more questions."

Mandy looked up. Her face was flushed, but she wasn't crying.

"So you saw your mother stab your father over and over? She stabbed him many times? Is that right?"

Santiago was squirming. This was a glaringly leading question, exactly the type prohibited by the rules of evidence. Mac had sailed these tricky evidentiary waters many times before, guiding his direct testimony with the experience of a ship's captain sailing through the unpredictability of a stormy sea. If Santiago raised an objection at this exact moment, it would be pointless. Mac would safely sail around any rocks and easily establish the essence of the crime. Santiago was rocking very slightly as he sat in his chair.

"Yes," said Mandy.

"Did you ever see your father hit your mother before she ran into the kitchen and got the knife?"

"No. No, he didn't."

"Are you sure? Absolutely sure? Your dad never hit your mother?"

"No. She hit *him*. He never hit her at all."

"And she ran *into* the kitchen, and then ran *back* to the living room? Is that right? She didn't stay in the kitchen or run away or leave the house, did she? She came back with the knife, right?"

"Yes."

"Thank you. I have no further questions."

CHAPTER 53

Thursday, August 8, 2019
4:00 p.m.

When court convened after the afternoon break, Judge Harajuku stated, "Mr. Garcia, the State has rested. Let the record reflect that the jury is in the jury room and not in the courtroom at this time, and that both counsel and the Defendant are present. Does the defense have any Motions?"

"Yes, Your Honor, we do. Well, primarily, we are asking you to grant our Motion for Judgment of Acquittal. On all charges. Does the Court wish me to articulate specific reasons or would the Court accept my general Motion on this issue?"

Judge Harajuku flinched with irritation, but caught herself. She did not want to make her emotions too obvious.

"Yes, Mr. Garcia. For the record, please state why the Court should grant your Motion for Judgment of Acquittal."

Her job was to make a record, meaning to supervise every phase of the trial to spot any potential errors in the process and to clean up any issue which could conceivably grow into a future argument on appeal should the verdict result in a conviction. Each step of the way, from jury selection to opening statements, through direct testimony and cross-examination, all the way to closing arguments, each phase of the trial needed to be preserved correctly to survive appellate review. Judge Harajuku's goal was to line up and preserve each of these legal issues like specimens in a row of bottles soaking in formaldehyde.

"OK, well, Your Honor," Santiago began to speak, slightly rattled. He was required to state each of the legal reasons why Mac had failed to prove his case and then hope Judge Harajuku would agree and toss the whole thing out in response to his Motion for Judgment of Acquittal.

Santiago said, "The competency of the State's key witness, the minor child Amanda Van der Hook, or I should say her incompetency, has prevented my client from receiving a fair trial. As the Court saw herself, this young child testified for the State in a manner which barely met the judicial requirements for testifying, but, on cross-examination, the child basically refused to speak. She just sat there mute for most of my cross and mumbled and appeared—at least it appeared to me—that she was in some sort of catatonic state. She refused to cooperate with the trial process, which includes cross-examination, one of my client's basic fundamental rights as guaranteed by the Sixth Amendment."

Judge Harajuku turned to reach for a small bookshelf directly behind her bench and pulled out a three-ring binder. She started flipping through it.

"So, for those reasons we ask that the Court grant our Motion for Judgment of Acquittal." Santiago was starting to gasp for air in his rush to get his point across.

"Additionally," he quickly interjected, not wanting the judge to respond just yet, "the credibility of the State's key witness is so highly suspect that no reasonable juror would find her truthful. The central narrative in this case hinges on the lies of a child with obvious mental health issues. For all we know, Mandy is making all of this up!

"Also, there's also no confession for the jury to consider. It's just as likely this child didn't see the event or didn't appreciate that her mother was protecting herself from this abusive husband or didn't understand what was happening or…"

Judge Harajuku had heard enough.

"Mr. Garcia, I already found that the witness was qualified under Maryland law to testify, so that argument is moot. She is a direct eyewitness to the alleged homicide. Do you understand me? Meaning, in case I am not being clear enough, that she *actually saw* the killing of the victim. You are not positing to the Court that there is no evidence establishing the necessary elements for a homicide of some degree, are you? Issues of credibility are for the jury to decide, not the Court. Further, I find for the record that the defense had ample opportunity for cross-examination. It is not up to the Court to weigh the effectiveness of the defense's questioning, but only to assure that they receive a fair opportunity to ask questions."

"Well, I understand…"

"So, why are you emphasizing the credibility of the witness, Mr. Garcia?"

"Well, Judge, whenever a mentally disabled child takes the stand and… takes the stand and…" stammered Santiago. He paused, reached down for a cup of water on his table, took a gulp, and continued, "As we all know, the State is required to prove my client's guilt beyond a reasonable doubt. We assert that their key witness lacks the credibility to establish that degree of guilt. Here, at this stage, at MJOA, they haven't done so. Therefore, we ask Your Honor to dismiss all the charges."

"Save that argument for the jury, Mr. Garcia," Judge Harajuku flatly said. "Mr. MacIntyre? Any response?"

Mac rose calmly. In a steady relaxed voice, he summarized, "Your Honor, we are at the Motion for Judgment of Acquittal phase of the trial. The State has rested. The jury heard not only from Mandy, but also from several other important corroborating witnesses, particularly experts, who supported her testimony with probative forensic evidence. We've had unchallenged DNA results admitted into evidence. There is an autopsy report and a bloodstain pattern analysis before the jury. Most importantly, even *arguendo,* without all of this corroboration, Mandy's testimony alone has established a *prima facie* case. Combined with all the other evidence, there is no doubt that the jury should be allowed to render a verdict in this case.

"We ask that the Court deny the defense's Motion for Judgment of Acquittal."

CHAPTER 54

Thursday, August 8, 2019
4:17 p.m.

That afternoon, while Mac was delivering his MJOA argument to the court, Lindy Hale discovered a diary under Mandy's mattress as she was changing her sheets. It wasn't a formal diary, but a grade school composition book. The cover was flimsy cardboard, with the familiar mottled black-and-white design.

Mandy was at Ivy Crest, her special education school down the road, and would need to be picked up soon. She had been placed in the special curriculum there for children with Asperger's Syndrome even though she didn't have Asperger's. There was nowhere else—either public or private school—that had a program for narcolepsy. She was the only child in the entire Seneca County Public School system diagnosed with pediatric narcolepsy. She was alone in her disability, with no tailored support to accommodate her needs. If she had been born blind, or deaf, or with epilepsy, she'd be welcomed somewhere. Narcolepsy was just misunderstood. But, since the kids at Ivy Crest were highly intelligent, the Van der Hooks thought it would be the best fit among the few bad choices. But, in reality, Ivy Crest was the only fit.

Lindy's head was pounding. Since testifying on Tuesday, she had been mostly blacked out on the sofa. After appearing at her own bond review for her latest DUI, and being released on her own recognizance, Lindy's routine this week had been to pick up Mandy from school in the late afternoon, bring her home, and stash her in her bedroom with an iPad. Watching videos on YouTube would knock Mandy out immediately, which was fine with Lindy, since it gave her a solid block of time to decompress and to drink at least two bottles of wine.

But that composition book!

Lindy's mind momentarily cleared up, like the sun popping through dark cumulonimbus clouds.

A diary? Well, I guess that's a typical thing for a nine-year-old girl to do, right?

Lindy couldn't decide if she should read it or not. To keep that complex thought from bouncing back and forth inside her head, she took the composition book and went downstairs to the kitchen to reconsider. There was an empty Grey Goose vodka bottle in the sink. She picked it up and dropped it into the garbage can under the sink. She grabbed an unopened bottle of wine from the cabinet and snatched the corkscrew from the drawer. She opened the bottle and poured a large glass, then sat at the kitchen table.

She opened the composition book. It was definitely Mandy's handwriting, a surprisingly steady, confident hand, written using various Magic Marker pens in assorted colors in red, green, and blue. She haphazardly flipped through the diary, absorbing various entries, word fragments, scattered phrases, and partial sentences. It was a colorful child's kaleidoscope of expression. The thought traveled across Lindy's mind that her niece's handwriting looked almost exactly like her own. The block printing, the spacing, the simple word choices. The plentiful misspellings.

Damn, this diary looks like I wrote it, not Mandy!

Then she had an idea. She needed to help Rikki.

I can't take on the responsibility of dealing with all of this myself. I just can't handle this.

She grabbed the diary and went upstairs. She looked in Mandy's small desk and found her art set tucked inside the top drawer. It was in a flat tin box with dozens of different colored Magic Marker pens, lined up in rows. Lindy flipped open the diary and found some empty pages towards the very end.

She picked up an orange pen and carefully copied Mandy's handwriting.

She wrote: "*The trial started today. I looked threw the windows in the court room door and saw Mommy sitting at her desk with the Spaninsh little lawyer guy. He looked scarred. I went in to talk. I lied the whole time. I started crying and laying on the floor. I said I was too tired and they believed me. But I didn't tell them the real truth. Mommy only hurt Dad because he took off his belt again and said he would whip her. I heard him say that. So Mommy got scarred and was only protecting herself. That's the real truth. I didn't want to make Dad look bad. So, I made the whole thing up to get back at Dad for hitting Mommy and for hitting me sometimes."*

Lindy shut the diary.

She looked up and said out loud to no one, "Oh my God. This might work."

She flipped to another empty half-page earlier in the book, selected a blue pen, and wrote: *"Dad hit Mommy again last night and said he was leaving and never coming back and giving her no allowance ever again. Then he called her a bich and lots of bad words and screamed at her. He poured a drink on her head and made her cry. I hate him!"*

Carefully, Lindy compared her own newly handwritten entries with the older, original ones. She closed the diary and held it close to her chest. The pounding in her temples was rhythmic and felt so strong that she wondered if she was actually hearing a drum beating somewhere. She listened to the sound of her own pulse for a few seconds and then snapped back to reality.

I've got to do something. But now what?

CHAPTER 55

Thursday, August 8, 2019
5:03 p.m.

"This is Don Morris of the *Seneca Journal*. Can I help you?"

"Um, well, I'm not sure. My name is Lindy Hale."

"That sounds kind of familiar. Do I know you, Ms. Hale?" Don's mind was whirling, all of his investigative reporting instincts kicking in. He looked around his messy one-room office, a rental space in a high-rise building next to the courthouse. His office was crammed down a narrow hallway next to tacky bottom-feeder law firms, cheap legal services offering things like printing and transcribing, and the notoriously dishonest Trust-T Bail Bonds office. Don sat at his desk, holding the receiver of a cracked, plastic landline telephone, which was a steady source of random tips and calls from mentally ill people telling him what an asshole he was. He regularly heard that the media lied, that he was "fake news" and other assorted nonsense, all of which came with the job of being a crime reporter in the suburbs.

"Can I help you? Are you calling about a possible crime you want to report?" Don had an excellent radar for bizarre and strange calls from the public, and his antennae started vibrating. He sensed disorder. He felt like he was looking at an incomplete jigsaw puzzle with only one piece missing in an otherwise completed puzzle. It was the empty space he would notice first, not the rest of the completed puzzle.

"They told me you were the reporter covering the case that's going on right now. It's the Rikki Van der Hook case. A murder case."

The name Lindy Hale now clicked instantly in Don's mind.

Yes, she was the aunt of the little girl who supposedly saw her mother stab her father. The skeletal blonde with the ghostly pale hair.

Yes, he remembered.

She sounded drunk when she testified in court.

She was an enigma: she spoke with an upper-class vocabulary, but in court she was wearing faded blue jeans and what appeared to be a man's large dark blue T-shirt.

Pitiful. If she gained a bunch of weight and washed up a little and shampooed her hair, she would have an acceptable look for a stripper. Sexy but defective, as if you crossed a porno star with a meth addict.

But wait a minute; he snapped his thoughts back to the present strange situation unfurling right before him.

What does this woman want with me?

"Right. I've been covering that case ever since the Grand Jury indictment, and I've stopped by the trial all week. I can't stay all day with deadlines, et cetera, but yes, I'm generally familiar with that case. What's up?"

"OK. Well, I found something that may be important to the case," she explained. "I don't know how all this court jury stuff works, but I thought maybe you could tell me what I should do?"

"You found something? Well, have you called the police or the Assistant State's Attorney? His name is Mac MacIntyre."

"I was thinking of calling his detective. The Black one with the earrings. He seems like a nice guy. Should I do that?"

"Well, what did you find?" inquired Don, his curiosity racing.

She said she found something? An item? A tangible item? Or did she mean she "found out" something? Like evidence? Proof? A secret?

"Ms. Hale, did you find a thing, or are you saying you found out some information? What did you find?"

"I found my niece's diary. She's the little girl who testified. I read it. Well, not all of it. I stopped once I saw that... Oh, it's hard to explain. I shouldn't've read it."

Don's mind was attacking this unique problem as it was unfolding, navigating these unexpected turns as if he was racing in a sports car down a twisting mountain road. His heart was thumping, but his concentration was sharpened by adrenaline and the novelty of the experience. He pulled the pen from his shirt breast pocket and started writing notes on the small reporter's pad on his desk: **LINDY HALE, WITN RIKKI VAN D H CASE, "FOUND???"**

"Hey, listen," Don said, glancing at his wristwatch. "It's around five now. Court will be over any minute. Do you want to meet somewhere to talk about this?"

"No. No. I just think I need to give this diary to somebody. I'm really not sure what to do. I've never had anything like this happen to me before."

"Ms. Hale, that's OK. Really. Don't hang up! Perhaps you should call Rikki's lawyer? His name is Santiago Garcia. You can Google his direct number. I mean, if it goes to Rikki's defense, you should let *him* know."

"OK, I'll do that. Should I search Garcia and Seneca County Public Defenders' Office?"

CHAPTER 56

Thursday, August 8, 2019
5:59 p.m.

Santiago walked through the front door of the PD's Office. He stopped at the front desk to talk to the receptionist, Na'Tasha, who was packing up her things, getting ready to leave the office for the evening.

He was venting, "Jesus, that damn judge! Letting my case go past Motion for Judgment of Acquittal! I was praying she'd end this torture. I've got all these other trials to prepare. I have another murder trial starting in three weeks. That psycho Pakistani woman who set her car on fire with the kids strapped inside." He added, sarcastically, "That should be fun."

"Wait, Santi, which jury trial is this one you're doing now?"

"That rich woman who stabbed her husband like a thousand times. That millionaire guy, the lawn mower man."

"What do you mean 'lawn mower man?'"

"The dead guy made millions by inventing the stand-up mower. The one you see on golf courses all across the country."

"Yeah, I heard about that case. Did she really murder him? What for? His money?"

"Yeah, she's guilty as shit, but I might be messing up their case pretty good. I went to Georgetown Law School to play games in court like this? Hey, Na'Tasha, if I'm going to represent these psychotic killers, shouldn't I at least get paid, right?"

"Well, you sure make more than me. And you don't have no kids. No wife or girlfriend either, from what I can see. And buy some new clothes, Santiago! You been wearing that same damn suit ever since you got here. Probably why you ain't got no girlfriend."

"I've got *two* damn business suits. That's it. I'm no slick trial lawyer like Andy Vladimir who has a new $500 suit on each time I see him. I heard he charges $500 an hour! That guy could buy eight new suits a day? Ridiculous. I need to quit this place and open up my own defense firm. Or run for that open judge…"

He cut himself off.

"Santi, you sound stressed," Na'Tasha said in a motherly tone, as she carefully arranged her things into a large shoulder bag.

"Harajuku says Mac MacIntyre proved a *prima facie* case. That's Latin for 'at first sight.'"

"I know what *prima facie* means, Santiago. I've been here 33 years."

"Well, what it really means is that the case can go forward, and the judge won't throw it out at the halfway point of the trial. Now it's up to the jury to decide. Problem is jurors hate murder cases. Once they hear someone got stabbed to death, they feel some subconscious responsibility to find someone—anyone—guilty. I have an old lady who is on the jury who said her mother was beaten by her father like a hundred years ago! She said it happened before Pearl Harbor! When's the last time you heard something like that, Na'Tasha? How can I get this woman a fair trial? We have no chance."

"Oh, you up against that Mac MacIntyre ASA? I've seen him in court. That redhead boy is fine. Mr. Ginger."

"Na'Tasha! You're not helping me!" Santiago sighed. "Doing a trial against this guy is like arguing with a dictionary. And the daughter testified. Mac got her to say she saw her mother stab the guy. We're toast."

"Yeah, well, the lawyers can only do so much. If it's a strong case, the jury will convict. If it's a weak case, they'll go not guilty. I've been here a long time—not since Pearl Harbor, but it seems like that sometimes."

Santiago wasn't listening.

"What makes this case so strong, Santi? I mean, you've done plenty of cases with kids testifying. Everyone knows kids lie all the time. Little devils, I wouldn't believe a word they say."

"That's true. I have some good facts in my favor, but I also have some bad facts which go against me."

"OK, break it down: pros and cons. What's in your favor, and what goes against you?"

"Look, let's be absolutely clear," replied Santiago. "My client is completely guilty. OK? She actually *admitted* to the police that she's been wanting to kill this guy for years. Talk about premeditated. So, the guy said he was leaving her to run off with Mimi, his hot executive assistant from Paris. Her name is Mimi, and she's really from Paris. I'm not kidding. Can't make this shit up. So, I mean, this case is a classic. These wives who are being cheated on, well, they always kill when they know they're being dumped. She confessed to the cops! But the detective messed up and didn't advise her of her rights properly, so the judge threw out her confession. The jury has no clue about that."

Na'Tasha asked, "So the jury doesn't know she admitted doing it on purpose? That's good."

Santiago added, "So, let's not play this mental game of is she guilty or not? The question is not 'is she guilty?' The question is 'can they prove she's guilty?'"

"So, how can they prove it?" continued Na'Tasha. "Your job is to get her off. Ain't your job to prove anything. It's up to *them* to prove she did it, not your job to prove she didn't."

"Well, when MacIntyre showed those nauseating crime scene photos to the jury, I thought half of them would vomit right there in the courtroom."

"Wait," said Na'Tasha. "You said what? It's a woman who supposedly planned to kill her husband? Can't you say he was abusive? That's been working for the PDs a lot now. Try to make it all sound like self-defense? That would at least knock down the crime from a first-degree murder to a second-degree, right?"

"No. If the jury thinks it was self-defense, she gets off completely. That's my goal: to see if I can get the jury to feel sorry for her."

"How much time does second-degree carry?"

"30 years. A first-degree murder is life."

"Oh, dang. 30 years? But she'll get credit for time served."

"Well, 30 years is the statutory maximum. That's the most possible time, but the Maryland Guidelines for this client would be much lower. She has no prior record. No way she'll get even close to 30 years if the jury says it was a second-degree murder."

"So, let's say she's found guilty of only a second-degree," Na'Tasha summarized. "Say the judge gives her 10 years. Then she also gets credit for time served, so take that off the top right there. And then she only has to serve half to be eligible for parole? So, you're saying she sliced the dude up and might only do like four years? Maybe she knows something we don't know! That's a pretty good deal, if you ask me."

Santiago continued listing the factors in his favor. "And check this out: the little girl got too freaked out to even testify on cross-examination. And she's supposed to be their star witness. She was a disaster, if you ask me."

"Now I'm really suspicious," said Na'Tasha. "Girl refused to testify? She is probably lying her little ass off."

Santiago absorbed that helpful observation.

"I've got to go, Santi. Gotta get to the goddamn church to pick up my granddaughter from daycare. Place is a total rip-off. Church charges a dollar for every minute you're late. Don't worry 'bout your trial: this jury will set her free. This case sounds weak as shit to me. Sounds like she's lying, that's what I think."

"See you tomorrow," Santiago said wearily, and turned to walk down the hall towards his cluttered corner office. He sat at his desk, leaned back in his chair, and began analyzing his conversation with Na'Tasha. He'd considered the "pros," and now he wanted to balance that by listing the "cons."

That nasty crime scene. So much blood. Dripping from the ceiling. Disgusting. And the guy stabbed right through the skull. But the dead guy can't testify, so we can say anything we want, and he can't refute it. Maybe I can create some reasonable doubt with these facts? Get real lucky and they'll say it was self-defense. Or maybe the jury will decide it's just a second-degree. That would be a huge win in this case. Huge. The Guidelines will be low if I can get the first-degree murder count knocked out.

What else? Mandy's testimony? That was weak. We've just got to stick to our plan. Say the girl is lying. Let the jury think she's retarded or something, and that's why she refused to answer any of my questions in court.

This one is balanced right in the middle. Could go either way. I just need something to bounce my way.

So, tomorrow we put Rikki up there on the witness stand. She's got to testify. I mean, I hate it when these clients try to lie. They usually just shoot themselves in the head. It's so risky. On the other hand, juries hate it when an accused murderer invokes the Fifth and chooses not to testify. I'll meet her in the courthouse lockup tomorrow morning before court starts and go over her testimony again. We need to rehearse this shit one last time. Well, at least I have one thing in my favor: this woman is a great actress.

The light on Santiago's desk phone was blinking, indicating a backlog of voicemails.

The sixth message announced, "Mr. Garcia, my name is Lindy Hale. You're defending my sister… Rikki Van der

Hook. I really, really need to talk to you. I have something. I found something... well, please call me as soon as you can. Thanks." She left her phone number, and the message ended.

Santiago immediately hung up the receiver and dialed.

CHAPTER 57

Thursday, August 8, 2019
6:39 p.m.

"Hello?" Lindy picked up the phone.

"Um, Ms. Hale? This is Santiago Garcia from the Public Defender's Office."

"Oh, yes, Mr. Garcia! Thank you for calling."

"What can I do for you? You said you found something?"

"Yes. I found my niece's diary. And I read it. I shouldn't have, but there's a lot of stuff in there you ought to know about."

"You're just finding it now? I mean, the trial is more than halfway over. What does it say in there that concerns you?"

"Mandy wrote that she lied in court. Let me explain: she said her father was threatening Rikki. She says her mother was only trying to defend herself from Marten."

"Mandy is lying? But how can we trust she's not making up some new stuff now?"

"I'll give this diary to you. Then you figure out if you can use it, or whatever."

"Yes, I'll come get it from you right now. I mean now. Tonight."

"No, I don't want to disturb Mandy. She's taking a bath and has been really traumatized by all of this court stuff, especially having to testify. So, I don't want to get her all riled up. Can I bring the diary down to your office early tomorrow morning?"

"OK, yes. Bring it. For now, put it in a zip lock bag? Or something else so it doesn't get messed up or damaged? Even a paper bag. Anything. Wrap it up so it looks like a normal package. And yes, our office opens up at 8:00 a.m. tomorrow. We're on the third floor of the Seneca County Judicial Center."

"I'll come down first thing tomorrow, as soon as I drop Mandy off at school."

"Thank you. Write the name Santiago Garcia on the envelope or bag, and I'll get it. Just give it to the lady at the front desk. She's a friend of mine. Thank you very much. Goodnight."

Santiago put the phone down.

Oh, my God! This will totally blow everything out of the water. Wait, I've got to call Mac and explain. I don't want him accusing me of withholding evidence or intentionally cheating. You know how the judges believe every word he says, and then he quotes from the Magna Carta *or some 1956 Maryland Court of Appeals case from memory. I've got to cover my ass and call him tonight.*

He listened to the rest of his voicemails in case Lindy had left a subsequent one.

Two voicemails later, Santiago heard:

"Mr. Garcia, this is Don Morris of the *Seneca Journal*. I'd like to get a comment on the Rikki Van der Hook case. I understand something about a diary, or newly discovered evidence, is possibly going on right now. I'm working on a deadline, and I'm writing an article about this, so would you please give me a call? Thanks."

"Oh, shit," Santiago said.

CHAPTER 58

Thursday, August 8, 2019
8:34 p.m.

"Mac, this is Santiago. Sorry to call you so late at night, but something's come up."

"Hey, man. Is everything OK?" Mac sensed danger in Santiago's tone of voice. Not the usual jokester.

"I don't know exactly, but I think, under the Maryland Rules, and I just want to be up-front and not play hide the ball with you. Y'know, for transparency, I need to tell you about a weird call I just got from Lindy Hale."

Mac knew reputation was everything in the courthouse. No case was worth losing it. The public defenders already were labeled at the SAO as sleazy cheaters, and Mac figured Santiago didn't want to be part of that crowd. Credibility and honesty were paramount, especially if you wanted to be a judge someday.

"What did Lindy Hale say?" Mac calmly said, like a Vegas poker player sitting on a weak hand and stoically waiting for his opponent to flip over his cards. "I mean, it must be similar to *Brady* material or something serious, or you wouldn't be calling me at night." All attorneys who practiced criminal law—both prosecutors and defense attorneys—knew "*Brady* material" was the term used to designate any evidence which was beneficial to the defense. Prosecutors were legally obligated to disclose such evidence immediately, no matter when they discovered it. Defense attorneys had different ethical rules, but this was getting close to that type of situation, especially since Mac had specifically requested to see all defense trial exhibits before the case began.

"Well, I'm not sure what to think. But here's what she *said*." Santiago lingered on the last word, emphasizing its unreliability. "She *said* she found a diary. The girl's diary. And she read it. And it may be exculpatory and help my client. Claims the little girl made up her testimony and lied to the police, and to you, and also lied in court. Says something else really happened the night her father was killed. So, if there *is* a diary, well, it's clearly information I should share with you. I mean, just to be up-front with you and not hide stuff."

"That's interesting. I mean, I've been dealing with this woman Lindy for months," Mac responded. "Andre Okoye and I met with her and the little girl before we indicted this case. Strange that this development is surfacing now, now that the trial's halfway over." Mac's mind was racing, looking for clues.

Was anything about a diary ever mentioned by anyone?

In his mind's eye, he pictured the SAO conference room last winter and how sleepy Mandy was and how Andre had secretly recorded her. From memory, he instantly downloaded as many details as he could summon. Fragmentary images and snippets of conversations were chaotically replaying in his mind.

She isn't sophisticated enough to lie persuasively. Or was she?

"Well, this Lindy woman said she found a diary." Santiago dangled that phrase out for Mac to reconsider.

"Correct. She *said* she found one. Which doesn't mean she actually found one. Obviously. Don't forget—she's been taking care of a disabled child for eight months. Not to mention all of Marten Van der Hook's money is apparently frozen and both Lindy and Rikki are essentially broke."

"What do you expect, man? Her sister is locked up and charged with first-degree murder. Stressful, to say the least, right?"

Mac said, "To be honest, as this world goes, is to be one man picked out of ten thousand."

"What are you talking about, man?"

"Never mind. Listen, this Lindy Hale... Have you actually seen anything purporting to be a diary?"

"No, I'm just calling you out of an abundance of caution. I mean, she could've been drunk when she called me. Hell, I'm not *vouching* for her. I'm just doing the right thing and telling you what happened. I mean, I think I'm obligated to."

"An abundance of caution. That is such a cliché, Santi. I cringe whenever I hear it." Mac appreciated that Santiago was calling to inform him of an unexpected twist in the case, and he had a fleeting instinct to say "Thank you," but he caught himself before saying it. Mac knew Santiago wasn't the typical dishonest defense attorney, but if Mac offered thanks, it would give Santiago a psychological edge.

"Well, so what's the next step?" Mac asked. "Are you sending someone to get this supposed diary?"

"Sending someone? Like who? We have one investigator for the whole PD's office. You know that clown, Weinstein? He's stoned most of the time. I've seen you cross-examine the shit out of him and humiliate him on the witness stand."

"Weinstein. Not really *summa cum laude*. He can't even spell IQ. Hard to believe Weinstein was once the fastest sperm."

"I remember the time you were cross-examining him real hard, and he said he felt sick to his stomach, like he was about to vomit. And you were such a badass, you just picked up a wastepaper basket and handed it to him and kept asking questions! That was legendary."

"You have only Weinstein to do investigations for the whole PD's Office? Heaven help you."

"I work for the Public Defender's Office. Not the glorious SAO, with your armies of detectives. Our two offices are so different, like oil and vinegar, I'd say."

"Water," said Mac.

"What do you mean water?"

"You said, 'oil and vinegar.' That's for a salad, Santiago."

"Oh, whatever, man! You know what I mean. Do you always have to correct everyone? Do you realize how annoying that is?"

Getting back on track, Mac volunteered, "Do you want me to get the diary from her?"

"No, that's OK. I was just kidding about Weinstein. I told Ms. Hale I needed the diary right away. She's bringing it here to the PD's office early tomorrow morning. Said she'd be here first thing when the doors open."

"Newly discovered exculpatory evidence. That's dangerous stuff, Santiago. Toxic. Combustible. Explosive."

"OK, Mr. Thesaurus, if in fact a diary actually exists, and this whole thing isn't just a drunken scam designed to fake me out, I'll have it by eight tomorrow. I'll look at it, and copy it—all of it, every page—and then I'll bring you a copy just before court begins at nine-thirty."

"The courthouse opens exactly at eight, Santiago. What time does your office open?"

"Same time. The receptionist and a few other support staff people have key fobs to get in even earlier through the employees' entrance, so it shouldn't be a problem. And one other thing: it's likely I'll need to recall Mandy as a defense witness now. I know you don't want her to be forced to testify again, but I may need to establish this diary is real. She'll have to authenticate the diary in court. You understand? Actually, now that I think about it—sorry, Mac, I'm just talking off the top of my head—I will have to ask Judge Harajuku for an immediate mistrial. All of this stuff is coming out of left field right in the middle of a trial. I'm going to ask her to declare a mistrial, and then we can reschedule this shit and do it over again in a couple of months. Start from scratch."

"Santiago, this little girl nearly had a psychotic episode in the waiting room. She was unable to testify. I had another case once where a kid had epileptic seizures because she was so afraid to face the guy who supposedly attacked her. Similar situation. Kid testified and freaked out. We got a hung jury and then a retrial. Court of Appeals said we could use the transcript of the first trial instead of calling her as a witness a second time because she was 'unavailable' to testify. Legally 'unavailable.' So, I'll object if you try to call Mandy as a witness. I'll fight you as hard as I can. Judge Harajuku isn't going to be happy with a scorched-earth approach. No one wants to see a disabled child get tortured in the public square, right?"

"Hey, easy, man. I'm not sure how this is going to play out. I'll have to read that case. But that doesn't sound right. Anyway, we can cross that bridge when we come to—oh, sorry, don't want to use a cliché! But I need to preserve all of my options. I mean, I represent someone who is charged with some serious shit. I have a duty to defend my client, and if it means asking for a mistrial so I can interview Mandy and call her to the witness stand, then I will just have to do it. I have to do my job. What if Mandy lied in court, and my client is innocent?"

"Seriously? Are you fucking kidding me?" said Mac, in the calmest tone he could project. "And your client *confessed* to something Mandy fabricated? Please. Save it for the jury, not me."

"Allegedly confessed. Who knows? Maybe your Zulu warrior Detective Andre Okoye made up the Defendant's statement? Why didn't he videotape this alleged confession, huh? But before you freak out on me, let's just take this one step at a time. Let's see if Lindy Hale even shows up tomorrow morning with a diary. Then, we can figure out if it looks real or fake or whatever, OK? It is what it is."

"It is what it is. Perhaps the stupidest cliché ever. God, I hate when people say, 'it is what it is.' That's even dumber than 'an abundance of caution.' Santi, can you be more original please?"

"It ain't what it ain't. Better?"

"OK, this conversation is going nowhere. I'll see you at eight-thirty outside the courtroom, and we can take it from there," Mac concluded placidly, while his mind churned furiously, like machinery gears grinding on full power. He was several moves ahead of Santiago already.

"OK, see you tomorrow morning. Goodnight," Santiago said.

"Eight-thirty. I'll be there. Bye."

Mac immediately picked up his cell phone and dialed Andre. They spoke for a minute.

15 seconds later, he dialed Zaria.

CHAPTER 59

Friday, August 9, 2019
7:15 a.m.

The sun was barely scraping over the roof of the courthouse when Zaria approached the ramp to the underground employee parking garage. She slipped around the wooden arm that blocked unauthorized cars from entering. Down here, there was only one layer of security to pass through: a solitary, ancient security guard plopped into a swivel chair behind a desk who barely glanced at IDs and buzzed people through without scrutiny. He knew all the courthouse employees.

Zaria approached the glass door and tapped on it. The glass was embedded with chicken wire for strength and was, supposedly, bulletproof. She waved through the glass to the security guard who didn't notice her. She pulled her security badge up, and began tapping it against the heavy, thick glass and said, "Hey, Officer Carrington. How're you doing this morning?"

Her ID was a large plastic tag attached to a waxy lanyard that dangled down her chest. It had her photograph and a seal of the State of Maryland. The seal was stamped across half of her face, distorting it, which, Zaria thought, was totally counterproductive. She noticed that wearing her pendulous ID allowed men to look at her body with impunity, pretending to be examining her identification, when they were actually sizing up how attractive her breasts were. She had become wearily resigned to this type of sexual micro-intrusion ever since her teenage years.

The security guard was dozing, but awoke when Zaria's taps became audible. He reached underneath the table and activated a buzzer that unlocked the door. He wheezed and shifted his hefty frame. His dark blue baseball cap bore the insignia of the Sheriff's Department, a sewn-on patch depicting the yellow and black checkerboard crest of the State of Maryland, underscored with the words, "*gardez bien.*"

Officer Carrington was an African American man somewhere around 80 years old, Zaria guessed, based on his white hair, consistently grumpy demeanor, missing bottom teeth, and his apparent inability to stand up. Zaria had passed by Officer Carrington dozens of times and had never seen him in a standing position. She once asked someone in the PD's office how the courthouse could employ such an elderly and immobile security officer, but she was told that's why he had been assigned to monitor the entrance down in the basement employee parking garage where there was no chance he would be needed to do anything. It was assumed by many that Officer Carrington was still employed in appreciation for his much earlier pioneering career as the first Black police officer in Seneca County history. Zaria asked around the PD's office if anyone knew more about Officer Carrington, and several old-time employees told her to ask the head receptionist, Na'Tasha, for more details.

Na'Tasha told Zaria that in 1961, when Carrington had first started as a motorcycle patrol officer, he was referred to as "colored." "Colored" was a major improvement over the ubiquitous and commonplace use of the "N-word," which white people used regularly in those days. Like the humidity in swampy Seneca County, overt racism came with the territory, but Carrington was legendary in his community for refusing to accept it. At the beginning of his career, he was a "colored" police officer. Over the decades, he had evolved, through absolutely no effort of his own, into a "Negro" cop, and then briefly, into an "Afro-American" cop. Then he was "black," before becoming an "African American." Now "Black" was in vogue again, but this time with a capital B. Recently, people would say he was a "man of color," which was ironically circular, since he had started out as "colored" to begin with all those years ago.

Zaria squinted and noted the "*gardez bien*" words over the brim of his cap, and subconsciously she translated the phrase, settling on "guard well," from French. Officer Carrington buzzed her in without changing his expression.

The elevator arrived. She said, "Thanks, sir. Have a nice day." He did not respond, preoccupied with his radio earpiece. As he vigorously fiddled with it, Zaria wondered if it was stuck in his ear canal like a generous clump of earwax. She let that thought fly from her mind as she pushed the button to the third floor. As the elevator ascended, she gritted her teeth and felt her anxiety rise along with the elevator. She focused all of her attention on the task at hand. In her mind, she carefully went over Mac's instructions, compelled to carry out and satisfy his orders. It was the least she could do for him. The peace and safety he gave her was invaluable and the only brief respite she had from her usual feelings of claustrophobia and insecurity. Mac was intoxicating, no, something more. He was something addictive, something necessary. Mac had simply asked her to pick up a package. She didn't ask why. That was not really such an impossible demand.

    She stepped out of the elevator and began walking towards the Public Defender's Office. Her hands were balled up tightly, her lips pressed together. She felt her body tightening like a coil. She used her badge to swipe the electronic box on the side of the PD Office's front door and pulled the door open. There was no one else there.

CHAPTER 60

Friday, August 9, 2019
7:15 a.m.

Andre had been to the PD's office dozens of times, going back to his days as a Special Assignment Team officer. Paradoxically, inside the courthouse, his best camouflage was a dark suit and tie, not the funky street clothes he would wear to blend in with the community when conducting undercover investigations. Because of his naturally gregarious personality, combined with the regularity of his presence, Andre was well known by almost everyone in the courthouse. Now that he worked for the SAO, he was in and out at all hours of the day and occasionally on weekends.

He sat in his unmarked Buick Regal cruiser, which he backed into an empty parking spot a block away from the courthouse. In his lap, he cradled his Nikon Monarch 7 binoculars, the ones with the sharp 8x42mm high-resolution magnification. He saw Zaria nonchalantly stroll across the street and walk down the ramp to the basement employee parking garage.

He placed the binoculars on the passenger seat and then slowly drove around to the front of the courthouse. His training always kicked in. He never drove too fast or too slowly, either of which could attract attention. It was a learned skill to blend expertly into the scenery and disappear. It had taken him years to master. Chameleons were highly intelligent creatures. He looked for a spot to park where he could survey the stretch of sidewalk where people exited the public parking lot. At 7:40 a.m., he saw a Nissan Pilot SUV drive into the lot. It had several stickers in the rear window: Riverside Village HOA, Kronborg Golf Club, and a faded McCain/Palin bumper sticker. Using the binoculars, he focused on the driver. She was a petite woman with platinum blonde hair, wearing a baseball cap.

Andre shifted his car from park to drive and cruised with a deliberate pace around the block. When he reached the rear employee parking entrance, he drove down the ramp and used his key fob to raise the wooden arm blocking his path. He quickly parked in his reserved parking space, which had a small sign affixed to the wall which read: SAO—Chief Investigator. He secured his Glock in the solid steel strongbox, which was bolted to the floor behind the passenger seat. Handguns were prohibited inside the courthouse, and, even if you were in a police uniform, there was a cumbersome protocol to follow, signing in and locking all handguns in a row of boxes used by law enforcement. Today, he wanted to avoid that delay.

He got out of the car and approached the glass door to the elevator vestibule. Tapping on the door, he pulled his wallet out, unfolding it with a flip to reveal an imbedded metallic bronze disc: his SAO badge. He waved to Officer Carrington and said, "Hey, OG. What's up?"

The buzzer was activated and unlocked the door. Officer Carrington said, "Oh, the sun rising and look what the cat drug in? You early to work, Chief Okoye," with a broad, mostly toothless smile.

Andre walked across the tiny elevator vestibule, saying, "Man, I ain't heard that nickname since I was on SAT." Andre cleverly mentioned the Special Assignment Team to reinforce the fact that they were both former Seneca County police officers, part of a distinct fraternity.

"Good to see you, Gangster! Stay safe," said Andre cheerfully as the elevator arrived.

He got on the elevator but did not go to the fifth floor where the SAO was located. Instead, he got off on the third floor and turned right, in the opposite direction from the Public Defender's Office. He went around a corner, and then stepped towards the men's room, which was next to the women's room, side by side, and separated by a set of aluminum drinking fountains. He slipped inside and closed the door. It was empty. He entered the largest stall, the one marked for handicapped users. He took two brown paper towels from the dispenser and vigorously wiped down the top of the toilet seat cover, despite knowing that the midnight cleaning crew had disinfected every inch of the men's room overnight. He locked the stall, looked at his phone, and tried to calculate how long it would take Lindy Hale to park her car, walk next door to the courthouse, go through security—which would be minimal if she was one of the first people in line—and then take the elevator up to the PD's office.

In less than two minutes, he heard a ping sound from the elevator area.

He was completely silent and looked at his watch for two minutes. He listened intently for another sound he expected to hear at any moment.

CHAPTER 61

Friday, August 9, 2019
8:08 a.m.

Lindy stepped out of the elevator and turned towards the Public Defender's Office. She tucked the package with the diary tightly under her arm, shivered, and then tugged on her baseball cap to pull it down slightly, hoping, for no logical reason, to disguise her identity. She walked to the double glass doors, paused to stabilize her balance, and grasped the handle. She did not open the door. She tried, unsuccessfully, to control her trembling. Looking through the glass, she noticed no one was in the reception area.

Maybe I'm too early and this Public Defender's Office isn't open yet?

The lights were on, but sometimes in these big courthouses and office buildings they left the lights on all the time. As she started to pull the door handle, she noticed a tall, slender woman in a dark shirt who was wearing flat ballet shoes, an artistic look Lindy had only seen before in her Pilates class. Although this tall woman was standing in the far corner, just barely in view, Lindy didn't sense she was hiding, but, rather, attending to some business or straightening up the chairs in the waiting area.

Lindy gave a short wave to the dark-haired woman inside, as if to signal, "Are you open for business?" The woman smiled, waved at her to come in, and stepped behind the corner of the reception desk, where she pressed a buzzer unlocking the door. Lindy pulled open the door and stepped to the counter. There was a small nameplate balanced on the reception desk which said "Robinson."

"Good morning," said Zaria. "Can I help you?"

"Oh, yes, thank you. Good morning," said Lindy. She noted the receptionist spoke with some type of slight foreign accent. Lindy glanced down at the nameplate.

"Robinson" sounds American, not European. Maybe this girl got married to someone here.

Lindy immediately pushed that thought aside. She had something else more important to do, and, with her head pounding again, it was better to stick to one goal and get it done. Multitasking was difficult.

Lindy held out a package wrapped in brown paper. It wasn't wrapped like a present. It was a lumpy square constructed from a brown paper shopping bag from the grocery store. It had been folded in two and taped shut with Scotch tape. "Santiago Garcia" was handwritten on the paper in cursive lettering, not block printing. She held the package with two outstretched hands, like an offering.

"Please make sure Mr. Garcia—he's one of the lawyers here—gets this, OK? It's real important."

"Yes, I know him. I'll give it to him myself."

Feeling uncomfortable, Lindy said, "OK, thank you. And tell him Ms. Hale stopped by."

"Sure, no problem. Have a nice day."

"Thank you," Lindy replied in a flat tone. She spun around and stepped through the doorway, wanting to get out of there as quickly as possible. The courthouse gave her a creepy feeling. Every time she'd been there, it had been because of something bad. Those DUIs. The Violation of Probation. This week had been a total nightmare, and she had been humiliated in front of all those jurors staring at her. Some people were phobic about hospitals; Lindy felt that way about courthouses. But despite her fear, she had to try to stop this nightmare trial and get everything back to where it had been before.

Get me out of here! But maybe this will work?

CHAPTER 62

Friday, August 9, 2019
8:08 a.m.

Andre opened the door to the men's room one inch wide and watched Lindy exit the elevator. He had positioned himself so that she could not see him, but he could see her reflected in the large picture window next to the elevator. He glanced at his phone to note the exact time and calculated the entire exchange with Zaria inside the PD's office should take approximately two minutes.

As he had calculated, Lindy quickly reappeared. She abruptly left the PD's office and marched up to the bank of elevators. She pressed the button on the wall, and the elevator door immediately opened. The courthouse was just opening up, and only a few people were moving around inside the building. When he heard the elevator's ping, Andre cracked open the door to watch Lindy's reflection again—an old SAT police technique. He waited until he saw her get on the elevator and the doors close. He paused another three beats to make sure the elevator didn't pop open for some unexpected reason. Satisfied, he was now certain Lindy had actually descended from the third floor.

Then, in the reflection, he glimpsed Zaria leave the PD's office and head directly towards him. As she turned the corner towards the restrooms, Andre partially pushed the door open, not even halfway. She handed him the brown paper package through the slightly open doorway. He was wearing gloves. She took three steps and entered the women's restroom. Neither spoke.

Andre turned, went back into the same handicapped stall, and locked the cubicle. The men's room was still completely empty. Taking off his dark trench coat, he hung it on the hook on the inside of the door. He then adjusted the gloves so they fit tightly. He saw the cursive handwriting and immediately knew that might be trouble. He didn't want any possible way to identify the package's origination. Ripping off the tape that secured the brown paper package, he unfolded the paper with his gloved hands and took out the black-and-white composition notebook. He slid the book down the back of his suit pants, positioning it with the elastic band of his Calvin Klein briefs. He'd hidden a Glock there many times before, so the composition book felt comparatively light and flat in the small of his back.

After tearing the brown paper into strips, he flushed them down the toilet. He glanced at his phone; it was 8:13 a.m. He slipped on his coat and buttoned it. He checked the toilet one last time to make sure all the paper strips had been flushed down the drain. He flushed the toilet a second time and then stepped out of the stall. Studying himself in the full length mirror, he turned sideways, checking to see if the composition book made any type of noticeable bulge in the small of his back. It did not. Everything was smooth. He double-checked his reflection to confirm that he looked perfectly normal. Satisfied, he left the men's room, pressed the elevator button, and took it up to the fifth floor.

"Hey, Lupe. What's up, girl? *Como estas*?"

"Detective Okoye! You look *muy* sharp today! Testifying?"

"Not sure. It might be cancelled. You know how it goes with court stuff, right? You get 50 subpoenas and end up testifying once with all these postponements and plea bargains."

"Got a conference with Mac? He must've gotten in real early. He was already in his office when I got here. He's like that when he's in trial, y'know what I mean? Super OCD, right?"

"Nah, I'm heading out to a crime scene, but I need to check with Mac for just a second. Stay hip, my Latina superstar," he said, as he casually walked down the hall to Mac's office.

Andre knocked on Mac's office door and slipped inside. He handed the diary to Mac, turned around, and left without saying a word.

CHAPTER 63

Friday, August 9, 2019
8:09 a.m.

Santiago pushed open the door to the Sheriff's Department, which was located in the courthouse's basement. He walked up to the counter, pulled out his Public Defender's ID badge, and held it up flat against the glass partition.

"Good morning. I'm here to see one of my clients in lockup, please. Are they in from the jail yet?"

A young woman sitting on the other side of the glass glanced at Santiago's ID, turned, and shouted to someone around the corner, "Corporal Shay, is SCCF here yet?" Hearing no answer, she pointed up to a wall clock and said, "The van should be here any minute. They usually get here from the jail by 8:00, but y'know how traffic is at rush hour."

"Right. Well, my client's name is Rikki Van der Hook. We're in trial in Judge Harajuku's courtroom, and I need to talk to her before we start today."

A voice shouted from around the corner, saying, "Van's here. Tell the lawyer to come through and go to Interview Room Two. I'll bring his guy down there. Which prisoner is he again?"

The young woman looked up, having forgotten the name already.

Santiago repeated, "Rikki. That's R-I-K-K-I. Van der Hook. She's a female inmate."

"We only got one female today."

She buzzed open the side door to the lockup area. There, Santiago signed the visitor's logbook and waited for Corporal Shay to pat him down. The Corporal took a handheld metal detector wand and swiped it up and down Santiago's body. The wand beeped several times.

Corporal Shay said, "You've got stuff in your pockets, Counselor. Put everything in this tray. Keys, phone, loose change. This thing is sensitive."

Santiago emptied his pockets, and they began the process over again.

Once the wand stopped beeping, the Corporal pointed towards the two tiny rooms used for attorney/client interviews. Santiago entered Room Two and took off his suit jacket. It was a small room, a compact, squared-off space, about twice the size of a typical bathroom stall. There was a cracked plastic lawn chair, grimy with fingerprints, facing a smudged window. Through the glass, there was another small space, the exact same shape and size: a mirror image. A red plastic telephone was mounted on the wall, with another, like its twin, on the wall inside the opposite room.

He reached into his back pocket and pulled out a package of sanitary wipes. He grabbed three and squished them into a cluster. He carefully wiped down the telephone. He sanitized the receiver, especially where his ear would touch, and then the mouthpiece. With the clump of wet wipes, he rubbed down the chair and the metal shelf which operated as a small desk in front of him. Finally, he cleaned the glass partition directly in front of him. There appeared to be Vaseline—or was it possibly lipstick?—smeared on the glass. He tossed the wipes into a wastepaper basket in the corner and rubbed his hands together.

There was a metallic click, and the door to the opposite cell-like chamber opened. Rikki stepped in.

Santiago waved at Rikki through the glass, lifted the telephone receiver, and said, "Good morning. How you doin'?"

Rikki waved and lifted her telephone receiver.

"So, today's the day," she said.

"Your hair looks great. Neat and trimmed. Did they let you go to the barber or hairstylist or whatever they call the person who does that in the female Pod?"

"No, it costs a lot for a haircut, and I don't have any money left in the commissary fund. My cellmate told me to volunteer for a work detail at the jail library. They have some scissors there to open boxes. The librarian lady is like a hundred years old, and the guard sits inside his booth looking at his phone for hours. He doesn't pay attention. So, when no one was looking, I just snipped my bangs and put the hair in the trash can."

"They let you have scissors in SCCF? God help us all."

"No, they don't. Just that one old rusty pair in the library. There are metal detectors everywhere."

"Are you going to wear the eyeglasses again? I mean, it was kind of awkward when Mandy pointed out you don't wear glasses, but, hey, anything that confuses the jury is good for us."

"I have them here," Rikki replied, pulling them out of the breast pocket on her shirt.

"Where'd you get them, anyway?"

"My cellie knew a woman down across the Pod. There's only seven women in right now. So, this girl let me borrow them—or 'rent' them, I should say—for a carton of cigarettes. Used up my commissary money getting them. Lindy says she has no funds to add to my account. She hasn't called me in days. Have you spoken to her? Can you ask her to put some damn money in there? The prescription for these glasses is weak, and I just look over the tops anyway, so it's not a problem seeing or anything. Do you think the jury will notice my jacket's the same as on Tuesday?"

"No. No one in the whole world would notice that. And so what if they did? We're OK. But listen, Rikki, forget about that stuff for now. We only have a few minutes, and we need to go over what you're going to say when you testify today."

"Yeah, I've been practicing all night. I know what to say. But wait: is this phone tapped? I heard from this one girl in my Pod. She told me you should never talk about anything private in here. She called these 'snitch phones.' They wiretap these calls, don't they?"

"Only the phones used for inmates to talk to their families. They tape-record those conversations, but not the calls with attorneys. That would be illegal because we have what's called attorney/client privilege. I'm not naïve. These prosecutors and Corrections Officers are corrupt as hell. But, even if they taped a confidential call, they couldn't use it in the courtroom. So, don't worry about that right now. We need to discuss your testimony, OK?"

"OK."

"Just keep it very simple and stick to the story," Santiago continued. "When I get to ask the questions, just answer them the way we planned. But the part I'm worried about is when MacIntyre does his cross-examination. Remember what I told you: whatever happens, don't get rattled. Just say yes or no and don't try to *explain* stuff. That's what he will do—ask you to describe things or get you to tell a story. Once you do that, you are playing right into his hands, see? The more you talk, the more you hurt yourself, understand? It's like he wants you to roll out all this rope and then let you hang yourself with it. So, just stick to the plan, OK, and keep all your answers real short."

"I'm ready. Like they say, everything happens for a reason."

"To hell with that shit, Rikki! I *hate* that expression. Everything does *not* happen for a reason! I despise all of that 'God' shit I get from defendants. I had a client once, told me, 'God will protect me.' I said, no, God isn't on this damn jury!"

Rikki didn't respond.

"And, Rikki, look at the jury a couple of times. Make eye contact when you talk. Jurors like that. It bonds with them and gives you credibility. I mean, don't overdo it, but try to look at them when you answer. Got that?"

"I can handle that Mac MacIntyre guy. He thinks he's so smart. Seems a little cocky and arrogant to me. I've got this."

He glanced at his watch. "I gotta go. See you upstairs. The curtain's about to come up."

CHAPTER 64

Friday, August 9, 2019
8:59 a.m.

Mac stood in the corner of the hallway outside Judge Harajuku's courtroom next to an abandoned telephone booth which was part of the original design when the Seneca County Judicial Center was constructed almost 50 years earlier. With the advent of cell phones, the telephone booth had long since become obsolete. On the wall of the booth, instead of a payphone, wires were splayed outward like multicolored spaghetti. Mac gravitated to this isolated small space; he felt hidden and safe.

Leaning against the inside wall of the booth, he watched through the open doorway as people got off the elevator and congregated in the hallway. He glanced at his phone; all four courtrooms would be open for business in half an hour, at 9:30 a.m. As he waited, a mélange of litigants, attorneys, witnesses, police officers, family members of defendants, and, most importantly, the jurors in his trial, began to arrive and cluster in groups. The jurors had been instructed to congregate on the far side of the hallway. Once all 12, plus the two alternate jurors, had assembled, they would be herded up to enter the courtroom to take their assigned seats in the jury box.

At 9:20 a.m., Mac saw the Girl with the Nose Ring exit the elevator and join a small huddle of jurors. Phoebe, the law clerk, marched down to the opposite end of the hallway and used her finger to silently count the group. Apparently satisfied, Phoebe turned and led the group back up the hallway past the phone booth towards Judge Harajuku's courtroom. Mac stepped out and casually waited a few feet from the door. He wanted them to know he had arrived early and was prepared.

Where the hell was Santiago?

As the Girl with the Nose Ring drew close, he made eye contact with her and nodded his head. She looked at Mac and smiled, exposing two rows of perfectly aligned, suspiciously white teeth. As he was calculating the unnatural brightness of her teeth, and sorting through the various ways she may have bleached them, all the jurors passed by him into the courtroom. Once they had filed by, Santiago exited the elevator, pulling his ridiculously large briefcase behind him as if he was dragging an enormous anchor.

"Hey, man. I have no idea what's going on!" Santiago said, as he swiveled his head left, then right, to ascertain if anyone was in earshot.

Mac, getting right to the point, said, "Did Lindy Hale come to your office with the diary?"

"Beats me. I checked with our front desk gal Na'Tasha, and she said no one showed up with any package or anything. So, I've been scrambling around trying to reach that Lindy lady, but she's not responding. That's why I'm late. I said I'd be here at eight-thirty, but I've been wasting time trying to track down this airhead. Harajuku will be coming out in just a few minutes," he said, short of breath, jumpy and nervous, as he switched topics five times in one sentence.

"She didn't even come to your office?"

"I don't know, man."

"Well, I can tell you for a fact that this Lindy Hale is not exactly a Rhodes Scholar," Mac responded. "Half the stuff she's told me wasn't true. I've been waiting for her to try to sabotage this case to protect her sister. She's probably sick and tired of being a guardian already, especially since she's probably got all kinds of financial pressures now that everyone's assets are frozen."

"You're probably right. She qualified for a PD, so that tells you something. But, about this diary—it's possible she made this whole diary shit up. I don't know if she's cagey enough to come up with something like that, but we PDs deal with unbalanced people all the time. Our witnesses are not cops, y'know. They're mostly desperate prisoners or mentally ill basket cases who'd do anything to avoid trial. I once had this client who kept calling in bomb threats to the courthouse. She claimed it was her First Amendment right. I can't remember that psychopath's name."

"Ramirez. Karen Ramirez."

"What?"

"That was the name of your client. I wasn't the prosecutor on that one, but I remember that case. The woman with all the bomb threats. I remember her."

"Oh, you're right. Ramirez. How could I forget that chick?"

Mac snapped Santiago's focus back to the present and asked, with a tone of seriousness, "Look, we have to go in the courtroom now. What are you going to do about this diary issue? You can't ask for a mistrial unless you confirm it even exists."

"Well, I have a duty to check it out. I can't just forget about it. I have certain ethical obligations, right? I'm supposed to zealously represent my clients, no matter how guilty they look. So, once I get the chance, I'll get the PD investigator, Weinstein, to call Lindy back and check into it. Maybe talk to that girl Mandy, too. But, I'll think about that later. I can't focus on that now. Hey, we gotta get inside and just keep plowing ahead. I spoke to Rikki in lockup. She's ready."

Mac looked over Santiago's shoulder. Being six-foot-three had some advantages. Through the rectangular glass panels in the door leading to the courtroom, he could see several jurors watching the conversation he was having with Santiago, although they were unable to hear what they were discussing. This visual, Mac calculated, was a good scenario: while he appeared totally calm and steady and relaxed, Santiago, who had arrived late, seemed rattled and bouncy, and was gesticulating wildly with both hands like a signalman flagging down a train. That would be to Mac's advantage. Jurors would think something unexpected and troublesome had developed, something damaging to the defense case, like when a driver noticed the engine light activated on a dashboard; it was never good news.

Just before entering the courtroom, Mac said, "Keep me in the loop on that diary, Santiago. I'm serious. I don't want that to create a problem."

"I will. Promise."

"So, you're actually putting Rikki up on the stand today?" Mac said. With a slightly threatening tone, he added, "I've got a couple of questions for her."

CHAPTER 65

Friday, August 9, 2019
9:31 a.m.

"The defense calls Rikki Van der Hook," Santiago confidently declared, just a tad too loudly. He had that tendency, talking just slightly louder than necessary, making his statements sound like proclamations, rather than perfunctory announcements for the trial record.

Rikki stood. She was wearing the dark slacks and a white button-down shirt she had been wearing all week. Mac immediately noticed she was wearing the same red suit jacket she wore on Tuesday, so he deduced she was rotating three jackets, a blue one on Monday, a red one on Tuesday, and a green one on Wednesday. There were inflexible guidelines governing every aspect of how prisoners were handled in the small jail lockup facility located down in the bowels of the courthouse, including several illogical rules governing what they could wear and carry into the courtroom. Every tiny aspect of that process was strictly supervised. There had been unfortunate instances where desperate prisoners had turned benign items—pens, or even shoes—into makeshift weapons. Neckties, especially, were viewed as dangerous, not just for their potential to choke, but creative prisoners had converted simple neckties into slingshots or lethal whips.

Prisoners were transported daily for bond reviews, jury trials, pleas, sentencings, and various courtroom appearances which required, under the Sixth Amendment's "confrontation clause," a right to be present for any significant development in a case. The Sheriff's Deputies who handled transportation, movement, and security of the daily parade of prisoners hated the provisions allowing defendants to wear civilian clothes before a jury. To avoid appearing in court in an olive-green jumpsuit, a defendant's family or defense attorney needed to bring a shopping bag with an outfit to the holding cell in the courthouse basement early in the morning to be searched. Since female inmates comprised such a small fraction of the total inmate population, there were extra rules for them specifically, including one that a female deputy was needed for every transport from place to place.

As Rikki stood, all focus shifted towards her. Mac noticed her hair seemed freshly cut. She had a mixed expression of both fear and arrogance, like a foot soldier prepared to charge uphill against insurmountable odds, determined not to look afraid, but, at the same time, hoping if she feigned confidence, some real courage might actually emerge. She stepped up to the witness stand.

"Raise your right hand please, ma'am, and listen to the clerk as she administers the oath," said Judge Harajuku in an automatic robotic way, as she had done hundreds, perhaps thousands of times before.

Phoebe stood and said, "Do you solemnly swear or affirm that the testimony you shall give will be the truth, the whole truth, and nothing but the truth?"

Rikki listened to Phoebe administer the oath with an excessively sincere expression, and then replied, "Yes, Your Honor, I do." Santiago had coached Rikki to address Judge Harajuku as either "Your Honor" or "ma'am," and to always address Mac as either "sir" or "Mr. MacIntyre." Upon hearing Rikki's first spoken words, Santiago felt his tension dissipate. She seemed solid, considering this was probably the most dangerous moment of her entire life.

"Please be seated," Phoebe said, with her slightly imperious tone.

Rikki sat and immediately poured herself a cup of water from a shiny aluminum pitcher smeared with many fingerprints. The deputy nearest to her was watching intently: defendants had used those metal water pitchers as weapons.

"Mr. Garcia, your witness," said Judge Harajuku, as she settled back into her elevated position overseeing the trial and the courtroom.

Marcia Harajuku loved being on the bench, literally raised to the highest altitude in the room, a loftiness that demanded deference. It had taken Judge Harajuku several years to become acclimated to the rituals of the courtroom and all of its accoutrements: the black robe, the throne-like seat, the "All rise!" when she entered from chambers. Court had some elements of a church, she concluded. The robes, the pews, the strange medieval honorifics and customs. Judge Harajuku reveled in the pomp and ceremony, but she checked herself so it didn't excessively inflate her ego. When she felt those pangs of narcissism swelling—and those feelings came regularly with the power invested in her—when those waves of ego lapped at the shore of her reality, she remembered she was essentially a girl from Japan who was very smart and, against all odds, incredibly fortunate to be sitting up high in a position of supreme authority. From up there, she commanded the playing field beneath her. Not much different than a chessboard, she thought, looking at the position of the pieces, sizing up the combatants, the jurors in the jury box lined up like pawns in a row. Then, as that analogy floated through her mind, she noticed a man sitting in the back of the courtroom, back in the gallery where members of the public could attend and watch. He was rumpled and disheveled and sitting in the last row. He had a small book, no, not a book, but something smaller he was looking at or scribbling on. She was sure she had seen him before. As she tried to decipher this minor diversion, she was distracted by Santiago standing up and clearing his throat with a gargling sound.

He said, "Ma'am, please state your name for the record?"

Rikki opened her eyes wide and, with a practiced expression of an innocent child, spoke.

CHAPTER 66

Friday, August 9, 2019
10:51 a.m.

Internally, Mac was furious, but his exterior appearance was indecipherably cool. He burned with anger, like a potbellied, cast-iron wood stove. Inside, he blazed, but outside, he was a solid metallic shell, strong enough to contain the coals.

Rikki had denied everything. If only that damn confession hadn't been ruled inadmissible because of a technicality. If only Andre had been more careful advising her. Without a taped confession, she was free to lie like crazy. A confession would give Mac all the power; with one, he could cross-examine her bit by bit, even if she dared to take the stand. He'd slice her up like a butcher in a delicatessen sliced up a ham. Slice, slice, slice, her lies scattered around the courtroom floor. But now he couldn't even mention the suppressed confession, and one wrong word—just one loose mention of it—would draw an automatic mistrial. A mistrial at this point would set Rikki free.

Fair or not, the rules of evidence prevented a jury from hearing all the facts. Mac had learned to roll with that concept, much like a professional poker player with a hand of bad cards. You made the most of what you had, and then you waited for a better hand to come along. It was often said around the courthouse that it was better to let a guilty man go free than to convict an innocent one. He gritted his teeth as he listened to Rikki effectively testify for more than an hour, lying straight to the jurors' faces.

I'll wait for some other trial to let a guilty person go free, but not this one. Whatever it takes, I cannot let this woman escape. That's not happening.

Rikki launched a two-pronged attack: first, try to destroy Mandy's credibility, and, second, demonize her husband, Marten.

First up on the chopping block was Mandy. Rikki told the jury she was a born liar and totally unreliable, if not downright defective. Narcolepsy, cataplexy, ADHD, nightmares, prone to exaggeration, bedwetting, even hallucinatory outbursts due to heavy medications. These were the defects Rikki ascribed to Mandy, one by one, in a parade of false maladies. The school records would support that misdirection, which was worrisome. The Seneca County Public School system had required an IEP—Individualized Education Plan—for Mandy when she was only five, and the school records were a compendium of behavioral and disciplinary notes. Various incidents of misconduct dated back for years. The fact she went to the Ivy Crest School was damnation alone. Many people in Seneca County, and surely one or two of the jurors, were familiar with

Ivy Crest, where kids with assorted disabilities attended. Mac had carefully reviewed the school file and IEP. She was once restrained four times in a single day.

Rikki painted a portrait of Mandy as something bestial, dangerous, and unpredictable. When she started telling stories of specific incidents, Mac felt compelled to object, which the judge summarily sustained. He preferred not to object to Santiago's questions for fear of looking like he was trying to hide the truth. He saved his objections for moments of true importance, when Rikki's answers might seriously damage his case.

"One time, Mandy pulled out a pair of scissors and threatened to cut off all of her hair and..."

"Objection!"

"Sustained. The jury will disregard," said the judge.

This technique, as Mac and every attorney who ever tried a criminal jury trial knew, was called "ringing the bell." An attorney would pose a question which was clearly improper *expecting* to generate an objection, but, by merely *asking* the question, you'd "ring the bell." Even if opposing counsel jumped up to complain, it would be too late. You would have already rung the bell and drawn the jury's attention to something they were prohibited from considering. Of course, once rung, the bell could not be "unrung."

Mac had to stop Santiago from his repeated attempts to have Rikki ring the bell. If not, once the 12 jurors were sequestered inside the inviolate jury room, some gullible juror might say something like, "That girl sounds like a lunatic!" Jurors tended to mishear things and then run away with them, if not immediately corrected.

Rikki was well prepared. Her dialogue with Santiago, while obviously rehearsed to Mac's experienced ears, sounded authentically spontaneous, and kept moving rhythmically, like a tango, although all of her testimony was, of course, one continuous lie. Mac noted Santiago controlled the direct testimony step by step, leading her like a pair of dancers spinning across a dance floor. Step, step, spin, rotate. Step, step, pause.

Stick to the script. Next up was her husband, Marten. Rikki testified he was abusive and violent and cruel. Domineering and tyrannical, he had ruled the house like a dungeon master. Everyone was terrified of him, she said. The dramatization was so exaggerated, Mac studied the jury to see if they were swallowing these fabrications.

How can they believe this horseshit?

The very best courtroom lies, Mac had concluded from experience, were lies that were 95 percent true mixed with 5 percent false.

Then came the Las Vegas trip story. A voluntary *ménage à trois* frolic? A sex slave caught in a cruel psychological trap? Or a completely fabricated lie?

And where the hell is this Mimi character? If this shit was true, they'd subpoena her to come in and testify.

Santiago asked simple questions, and Rikki replied with simple answers. They methodically presented the defense deliberately and progressively, like a workman laying down tiles on a kitchen floor in an alternating checkerboard pattern, square by square.

"Ms. Van der Hook, did you ever *intend* to kill your husband, or were you just in fear for your own life and acting in self-defense?" Santiago asked with dramatic flair, again speaking at a volume more appropriate for a larger venue.

"No, Mr. Garcia. Never! I swear to God, I was so afraid. I thought he was going to kill me!" She delivered her well-rehearsed lines effectively. Mac knew whenever a defendant used the phrase "I swear to God," it automatically meant a blatant lie would follow.

"Why in the world would Mandy say otherwise, Ms. Van der Hook?"

Mac objected, standing and interrupting, "Your Honor, this calls for speculation and, I might add, is also argumentative. I object."

The judge didn't wait for Santiago's response and quickly refereed, "No. It goes to her state of mind. I'll allow it." Mac knew that was legally incorrect, since one witness couldn't comment on the credibility of another—that was for the jury to decide—but he decided to let the issue go, knowing there was virtually zero chance of changing Judge Harajuku's mind, even though Mac was absolutely right on the technical rule of evidence, and she was wrong.

"Overruled. You may answer."

Rikki let the slightest smile appear at the corner of her mouth. She coolly poured herself another cup of water from the aluminum water pitcher.

"Well, Mandy is, well, she's a troubled girl. I mean, I should know. She's my daughter. No one in the world knows her as well as I do. I can tell when she's lying or making up a story. Always have. And, when she testified earlier this week, she lied. She lied about everything. I don't even think she was at the top of the stairs. In her little mind, she thinks she's helping her father in some confused childlike way, but I'm sorry to say she's very mixed up and in some kind of shock, if you ask me. You just can't trust her."

"No further questions, Your Honor," Santiago said.

"Gentlemen, and members of the jury, this would be an appropriate time to break for the luncheon recess," the judge declared. "I note the time is now 11:55 a.m. Please follow the directions of Ms. Chao and reassemble outside the courtroom at 1:20 p.m. Thank you."

Judge Harajuku stepped down from her elevated seat and walked out of the courtroom through the door to her chambers.

"All rise!" said Phoebe, flipping her long ponytail back over her shoulder.

CHAPTER 67

Friday, August 9, 2019
12:10 p.m.

Mac exited the elevator on Garage Level Two and stepped into the small security vestibule connected to the parking area. He could see through the heavy glass door. Andre was parked in his unmarked cruiser, with the engine running, at the curb.

"Hey, Officer Carrington. How are you doing today?" Mac said as he passed by the security area.

Officer Carrington's eyes were focused on his phone, and he continued to tap on it without acknowledging Mac's salutation. Mac stepped through the vestibule's doorway, opened the passenger side door, and said to Andre, "Harajuku said we start back up at 1:30, so we need to move fast."

"I got two boxes of tuna maki and one California roll for you, Bro. I also rolled the dice and got some exotic thing on special called salmon skin roll. I like to live dangerously," said

Andre with a wide smile. "I remember what you said. There's three kinds of sushi: the kind with the little fish cutlets on rice that's called sushi in Japanese, and the kind all rolled up and cut into like discs, which are called maki. And then if it's just a piece of fish with no rice, that's sashimi. Betcha even Judge Harajuku don't know that!"

Mac barely heard a word he said. Just minutes removed from listening to Rikki's devastating testimony, he was absorbed in deep thought and distracted, feeling like a man being tortured on a medieval rack, stretched beyond ripping point, his shoulders already dislocated.

Shaking those distracting thoughts away, Mac turned and said, "Tuna maki. If I die, I don't care if I go to heaven or hell, as long as they've got sushi. Let's go. Only got 55 minutes and then I've got to be back here."

They pulled up the ramp of the parking garage and dashed through the Courthouse Square, heading briskly towards the river, about ten minutes away. Once there, Andre drove to an obscure, empty outdoor parking lot, a secluded spot surrounded by dense trees and thorny underbrush. Mac had previously dubbed this location "The Waiting Room," code for this covert place where they always met in an emergency. No crowds, few people, and, most importantly, free from any camera surveillance. There was a beautiful panoramic view across a wide bend in the river, giving them a safety zone of privacy, a cloistered place guaranteed to have no listening devices. With so many years of undercover work under his belt, Andre had schooled Mac on security issues: never try to discuss confidential matters in a room, especially in a hotel room, or even in a car, knowing how many places the police could easily wire for audio surveillance. Nothing critical was ever spoken on a cell phone, which created a call record. In recent years, the police had learned how to establish the exact locations of where cell phone calls were both initiated and received by subpoenaing cell tower records, something few criminals realized could be done.

They arrived at "The Waiting Room" in minutes. They pulled up to the farthest parking spot, under several clustered white oaks, now, in August, full of leafy foliage, which provided ideal cover. At this location, there was a dip in the path along the waterfront, which directed any joggers, bicyclists or dog walkers even further away and safely out of eavesdropping range.

They got out of the car and walked to a rickety wooden picnic table in the far corner, using the large Buick undercover car as an additional barrier. The only people who might see them in this exact spot would either have to be watching with binoculars from across the river, or actually floating in a canoe on the water. Neither of these possibilities was remotely rational. Andre carried the two white plastic bags from Sushi Queen.

Handing one of the plastic bags to Mac, Andre said, "California roll. Tuna roll. The wasabi is in there already, and so is the ginger. Want this little thing of soy sauce?"

They sat on the worn picnic bench. Mac separated the cheap wooden chopsticks and said, "I have two problems. One, what am I going to ask Rikki on cross? She was a damn good liar. I bet sneaky little Santiago prepped her well. I already mentioned earlier in front of the jury she was a great actress.

I hope they remember that. Two, what the hell am I going to do with this diary issue?" He swirled a green, clay-like chunk of wasabi into his soy sauce, creating a murky olive-green dipping paste.

"Don't ask that liar Rikki anything. Or just ask a few questions and let it rest. But don't go over her lies. If you repeat them or emphasize them, it will only reinforce her bullshit. Better to just ask nothing than to go over it again and make it sound true by repeating it. Act like you're ignoring what she said because it's worthless."

"Right. Good point. I'm going to cut my losses, keep my cross short, and then save my ammo for my closing argument."

"You going to eat both those tuna rolls, man? If not, I'll take 'em."

"Take this tuna roll and I'll file a misdemeanor theft charge," said Mac, smiling. "I'm saving those two extra pieces for later."

Andre winked back, then said, "Did the little girl really make up a story and write it in a journal and backdate it? Man, that's pretty slick. She's only nine? Pretty hard to believe. What's that called again, recreating?"

"When a kid makes a disclosure and then retracts it, it's called recanting. It's a recantation. But this whole thing is not adding up. I'm very suspicious. I think the diary is fabricated. Forged."

"Are you 100 percent certain the diary is fake? You think that wacky aunt wrote it herself to mess up the trial? I mean, we could take it for handwriting analysis. I know a guy at the police academy who qualified in court as an expert witness. He can say if it's definitely the girl's handwriting or if it's a forgery."

"We don't have time. The trial is almost over," Mac replied. He took a deep breath and added, "We know Rikki is completely guilty because she confessed. I have no doubt whatsoever that she's guilty. The only issue is—can we prove it to the jury?"

"So, if the jury hears about this diary recantation thing, it fucks up the case?"

"Yes. Yes. I mean, this case is already on the edge. If the jury hears Mandy supposedly recanted her whole story, and wrote something totally different in her diary, that will be a disaster. Talk about reasonable doubt. But, I'm more worried about a different scenario. What's more likely is, if Harajuku even hears about a diary—fake or not—she will freak out. She will immediately call a mistrial. That's even more of a disaster, actually. If she calls a mistrial and tells us to start this whole damn trial over again, Mandy will never come back to court again. She's too traumatized. This was our one chance. Without her, we have basically no case. Bottom line: if this diary is even *mentioned* in court, it will be a mistrial. And that's the functional equivalent of a not-guilty verdict. A mistrial means we lose this case. I can't let this killer go free when I *know* she's guilty."

Agreeing, Andre said, "She is guilty as hell! Admitted it to me. Right to my face. She confessed to everything!"

"I know. But why didn't you videotape her statement?"

Completely ignoring Mac's question, Andre said, "And so she gets off scot-free? That ain't right. I don't care what the rules are. How does double jeopardy work with a mistrial?"

"Technically, when there's a mistrial, we could try Rikki again. But, like I said, Mandy will never come back and we can't force her either. We are on the edge of a disaster. And I'm not even factoring in what The Fish will do. Probably reassign me back to traffic court."

"10-4."

"The problem is this diary," Mac summarized.

"Juries have a shitload time understanding why a kid would testify, give a statement to the police when the killing is fresh in her mind, and then, later on, say it didn't happen. That psychological mumbo-jumbo is hard to figure out, man. Juries don't get it."

"I know. Either scenario messes us up: if the diary is real, we lose. If the diary is fake, we also lose."

"Can you find an expert in recantation, like that case you did last year?" Andre pleaded. "Remember the one where the girl was getting banged by the soccer coach at that ritzy school in exchange for him getting her a scholarship? And then, when it all broke loose in the media, she changed her tune under the peer pressure from all the other kids? So, suddenly, she pulls a 180 and says it never happened. Remember? That was a recantation, too? Right? You hired an expert witness. A sharp lady psychologist. I'll track her down again."

"Dr. Harrington. Brilliant woman. University of Michigan. Retired now."

"Yeah! She was good on the stand. Explained that kids recant all the time in cases involving their own families. They try to take it back 'cause it fucks up the whole family, and they wish they had just kept quiet in the first place. Why can't we go that same route? You explained it great last time. You called it a faulty recantation or a false recantation, one of those."

"It's just way too late, Andre. I needed to list all of my expert witnesses before trial, not after the Defendant testifies. I'm allowed to call rebuttal witnesses, but not an unlisted expert. Harajuku wouldn't allow it in a million years."

"Damn."

"We are way past that point now. I've already rested my case! We're doing closing arguments tomorrow. Impossible. No, there's no turning back now. We are stuck."

"You can't quit. Bitch murdered her husband for real."

Andre fiddled with his disposable chopsticks. He secured a disk of salmon roll, and dipped it in the tiny plastic shot glass of soy sauce.

"Remember that trial with the little girl in the wheelchair who was attacked?"

Mac was staring off towards the river.

"This case is way worse than even that one, bro."

Mac decided he was not going to let Rikki go free. No matter what.

"I'm not giving Santiago Garcia this diary. I'm not. I can't do it."

"Holy shit. Are you thinking this all the way through? This is dangerous."

CHAPTER 68

Friday, August 9, 2019
12:29 p.m.

Mac looked at his box of sushi, glanced at his wristwatch, looked up at the trees, took a deep breath, and said, "OK, let's play this out logically. Who knows about the diary? Let's list everyone."

"OK. Well, first there's the girl herself. Mandy. If she created untrue diary entries, then it all starts with her," Andre began.

"Right, and then her Aunt Lindy finds it," Mac added. "But if she *forged* the diary entries, then Lindy is the key player, and Mandy has no clue what's really going on."

"Then she calls the reporter guy. What's his name again?"

"Morris. Don Morris. Worst kind of voyeur in existence, thanks to the *Seneca Journal*."

"So," Andre continued, "that's Lindy Hale and Morris, and possibly Mandy, too. That's three, max."

"Yes, but Morris doesn't know if the diary is real. All he knows is what Lindy Hale told him. She could be lying, or using him for some ulterior motive, right? Listen, this reporter guy, Morris, covers criminal trials every week. He knows everyone lies. Witnesses lie. The police definitely lie. The lawyers constantly lie. Shit, even the judges lie. I've heard judges tell attorneys, 'That was an excellent presentation, Counselor,' when everyone in the courtroom knows it was awful. So, with Morris, the important thing is he's never actually *seen* the diary. So, he'll be skeptical for sure."

"Yeah, man. True. So we really need to divide it up two ways: a list of people who know for sure the diary actually exists, and a second group of people who have just *heard* there's a diary."

"Right. So, in the first group, the people who have actually seen the diary with their own eyes, would be Mandy, Lindy Hale, and, I guess, me," said Mac, realizing the group was not so large. He continued, "And then there's a second group of people who have *heard* there's a diary but haven't confirmed it actually is real. So, that would be Morris, and then, technically, there's Zaria, who I told to intercept a package. But I never told her what was actually in it—which gives her deniability. And then there's you."

"I dig what you're saying, man."

"So, when you boil it down, Andre, only four people actually know about a diary: Mandy, Lindy, me, and you," Mac summarized efficiently. "So, here's what we do: we simply say the diary never existed. We say Lindy is lying to protect Rikki. Who can disprove it? Without proof, Don Morris won't pursue this further. And then you and I and Zaria stay silent. That covers everyone."

"I guess, but that's getting awfully dangerous," Andre said, lowering his voice despite the fact there was no one anywhere in sight. "Just think, Mr. William MacIntyre, Seneca County Senior Assistant State's Attorney, says he knows nothing about a diary. Then it's Lindy's word against Zaria about dropping off a package. Cameras don't cover the reception area of the PD's office, so they can't see inside. The camera can only see the doorway. I know that for sure. But you're right. Why would anyone believe Lindy? She's got a real motive to have this case fall apart. She needs help to take care of the disabled kid. Not to mention if Rikki ends up getting millions of bucks from the dead guy, Lindy profits, too. I mean, this woman is a total mess. She's probably drunk and passed out on the sofa mostly, or in jail locked up on another DUI. So, if she says she found a diary and brought it to the PD's office and there's no proof, no one will believe her. No way."

Mac turned to look directly into Andre's eyes, but didn't speak.

After a pause, Andre said, "This is dangerous as shit. If it comes out later, you hid evidence in a homicide case..."

"I know. My reputation would be destroyed. I'd get disbarred. And I'd likely go to jail myself. Talk about obstruction of justice. I'd last 15 minutes in jail. I mean, they'd put me in Seg for a week, and then I'd be out in the open the minute I joined General Population. The first day, I'd get jumped by a gang or have my throat slit. I know what happens to former prosecutors or cops inside SCCF."

They gathered up the boxes and napkins. Mac grabbed both of the white plastic bags. He took the two extra pieces of maki and put them in one of the plastic bags, tied it into a knot, put it inside the second bag, and then stuffed the double-wrapped bag in his coat pocket. Andre dumped the containers, napkins, and chopsticks into a large, rusty metal trash can in the corner of the parking lot. They got in the car. Andre started the engine. He glanced at his watch. He realized there was something left to say.

"But Mac, you interviewed Mandy yourself. You looked into her eyes. You know she was telling you the truth. And you read Rikki's confession. You know she's guilty. How is it right if she gets a mistrial, and then gets off? How the fuck is that right?!"

CHAPTER 69

Friday, August 9, 2019
12:45 p.m.

Jo picked up her office phone. The Caller ID portion of the phone read, FRONT DESK CODE 3, which was a signal from the receptionist that a call was coming in from the public that might be significant. She had handled plenty of these so-called "CODE 3" calls before, but they were usually some loudmouthed outraged citizen griping about a police officer or one of the rookie Assistant State's Attorneys. One of Jo's greatest talents was dividing complaints into ones that needed to be addressed and ones that could be dismissed. In this way, she had divided the world with the mentality of a shark: objects she could eat, and objects she could ignore.

"Yes, Lupe, who's calling?"

"Sorry to bother you, Ms. Newgrange. I wasn't sure if I should disturb you or not, but I thought..."

"It's OK, Lupe. Who is calling?"

"That reporter from the *Seneca Journal*. Morris. He says it's real important. I know they always say that when they call, but..."

"No problem, put him through," Jo said, and then, after a beat, "and thank you."

She mentally listed all the high-profile trials in progress in the courthouse, trying to ascertain why the *Seneca Journal* might be calling.

Was anybody arrested today which might interest the press? It's probably that case from last night, the preppie kid who blew off his fingers making a homemade bomb. He had a bond review today. That must be it. His father was Undersecretary of something down in D.C. That case would get attention.

"Good afternoon, this is Deputy Assistant State's Attorney Jo Newgrange. Can I help you?"

"Hello, this is Don Morris, of the *Seneca Journal*."

"Oh, hi, Don. Good to talk to you. What's up?"

"Well, I'm calling about this jury trial before Judge Harajuku, the Rikki Van der Hook case. It's that murder case with the kid who saw it? I mean, allegedly saw it. Mac MacIntyre is the ASA."

"Oh sure, I hear it's going really well for us, don't you agree?"

"Um, well, the reason I'm calling is, well, I wanted your comment on an issue which arose yesterday. I'm writing an article for the Sunday edition, and I wanted to get a statement from you on behalf of Mr. Fischbein and the State's Attorney's Office. Is that OK?"

"Sure, no problem," she said, her antennae sharpening. Ari was OCD about the media. Any favorable publicity needed to showcase him, and anything negative was definitely not his fault. If Don Morris was probing about anything even remotely controversial or political—and everything was political in Ari's eyes—she needed to negotiate this discussion carefully.

"What's the issue?" Jo asked.

"Have you heard about a diary? The girl apparently kept a diary. Supposedly, she wrote in it that her testimony in court was a lie. The kid's aunt says she found it and was going to bring it down to the PD's office this morning. What's your comment on how the girl's diary impacts the trial?"

"That's interesting, Don. I hadn't heard that. Y'know this aunt is the child's guardian, right? Maybe there's some hidden agenda, I don't know, but that's off the record, so don't print that, OK? I'm trusting you. Please. I'll ask Mac, and I'll also talk to Mr. Fischbein, and then I'll call you back before the end of the day, by four-thirty. Promise. Hold the story until I can dig into it, OK?"

"OK, thanks. Call me on my cell. I want to be the first to break this story if it's a scoop," Don implored.

"Thanks. My lips are sealed." The wheels in her mind were churning.

Diary, Mac, eyewitness, stabbing, Ari, good press, bad press, mistrial, sanctions.

"Talk to you later."

Jo replaced the telephone receiver in its cradle and picked up her cell phone. She glanced at the time and saw that Mac would be starting his closing argument in minutes in Judge Harajuku's courtroom. Despite that, she decided that favorable press and handling the media adroitly was more important than distracting Mac just before he had to deliver a critical closing argument. She texted:

> JOURNAL ASKING ABT "DIARY" IN UR
> TRIAL. COME SEE ME AFTER COURT.
> IMPORTANT. EXPLAIN?

Mac was in the employee kitchenette when he received her text. Andre had just dropped him off in the garage, and he was rushing to get back to the courtroom on time. He skimmed the text, then opened the double-wrapped plastic bag from Sushi Queen. First, he left one bag with the leftover sushi in the refrigerator, and then stuffed the other empty white bag into his suit jacket pocket. Casually, he walked down the hall back to his office. Once inside, he unlocked his bottom desk drawer, lifted out the diary, and put it into the white plastic bag. He then placed the bagged diary back in the drawer and relocked it. From his office, he dashed to the elevators and jumped on the first one to open. Amazingly, it was empty. Pulling his phone out of his pocket, he reread the text as the elevator rose to the ninth floor. It was 1:14 p.m.

He texted:

> SORRY JO, I HAVE NO IDEA WHAT YOU
> ARE TALKING ABOUT.

He looked at his reflection in the metallic door of the elevator and said to himself, "*Lacta alea est.*"

He buttoned his suit jacket.

"The die is cast."

CHAPTER 70

Friday August 9, 2019
1:32 p.m.

MARYLAND COMMON JURY INSTRUCTIONS—HOMICIDE

FIRST-DEGREE PREMEDITATED MURDER AND SECOND-DEGREE MURDER

The Defendant is charged with the crime of murder. This charge includes first-degree murder and second-degree murder.

A) FIRST-DEGREE PREMEDITATED MURDER

First-degree murder is the intentional killing of another person with willfulness, deliberation, and premeditation. In order to convict the Defendant of first-degree murder, the State must prove:

(1) that the conduct of the Defendant caused the death of Marten Van der Hook; and:

(2) that the killing was willful, deliberate, and premeditated.

A. X. FOSTER

Willful means that the Defendant actually intended to kill the victim. Deliberate means that the Defendant was conscious of the intent to kill. Premeditated means that the Defendant thought about the killing and that there was enough time before the killing, though it may only have been brief, for the Defendant to consider the decision whether or not to kill, and enough time to weigh the reasons for and against the choice. The premeditated intent to kill must be formed before the killing.

(B) SECOND-DEGREE MURDER

Second-degree murder is the killing of another person with the intent to kill. Second-degree murder does not require premeditation or deliberation. In order to convict the Defendant of second-degree murder, the State must prove:

(1) that the conduct of the Defendant caused the death of Marten Van der Hook; and

(2) that the Defendant engaged in the deadly conduct with the intent to kill.

MARYLAND COMMON JURY INSTRUCTIONS—SELF-DEFENSE

In order to convict the Defendant of murder, the State must prove that the Defendant did not act in self-defense. If the Defendant did act in complete self-defense, the verdict must be not guilty.

Self-defense is a complete defense, and you are required to find the Defendant not guilty if all of the following four factors are present:

(1) the Defendant was not the aggressor;

(2) the Defendant actually believed that she was in immediate danger of death or serious bodily harm;

(3) the Defendant's belief was reasonable; and

(4) the Defendant used no more force than was reasonably necessary to defend herself in light of the threatened or actual force.

CHAPTER 71

Friday, August 9, 2019
1:32 p.m.

"Mr. MacIntyre, you may address the jury," intoned Judge Harajuku.

Courtrooms and casinos had much in common. Closing arguments in a jury trial were an elaborate competition, with each side laying out key facts like high-value cards in a poker game. A pair of jacks was topped by three of a kind. A straight was topped by a flush.

"Thank you, Your Honor. May it please the Court, ladies and gentlemen of the jury." It was trendy to address the jury with alternative salutations, like "women and men of the jury," but Mac preferred the classic, traditional approach.

While driving back from the river with Andre, the scent of wasabi lingering on his suit, Mac considered several options for the arrangement of his closing argument. First, he weighed the option of presenting the evidence in a straightforward, chronological order. This was the easiest presentation for a jury to follow: listing a roster of the witnesses, and using a format starting with, "First, you heard from…" and then proceeding to go down the list of the subsequent witnesses. As he and Andre pulled into the parking deck, he completely changed his mind. While presenting evidence in chronological order was easiest for the jury to track, he'd have to sacrifice the powerful impression he would make by starting with something strong, something memorable. Therefore, he decided to lead off with his strongest evidence and then surround it with corroborating testimony.

"On Tuesday, you saw some horrifying crime scene photographs which depicted blood spattered literally all around the living room of the Van der Hook household—splashed even on the ceiling. The photos have been enlarged to poster size and will be available for you to review, should you need to, as you deliberate the verdict in this case."

Butterfly Lady winced and looked down at the floor. When delivering a closing argument, Mac always tried to watch the jury and make eye contact, even though experience had shown him that a juror's reactions were frequently impossible to decipher. Some jurors, even those on his side, might glance away and refuse to peer directly into his eyes simply because of the intensity of the moment.

"You heard from the DNA expert, who conclusively proved to a scientific certainty that genetic material—likely sweat or skin cells—was lifted from the handle of the carving knife. Those samples were primarily the Defendant's DNA, which absolutely makes sense, since Rikki Van der Hook was the one holding the knife in her palm as she killed her husband Marten."

After mentioning the stomach-churning photographs, and having linked Rikki with the murder weapon, Mac drew the jury's collective focus to the trial's key question: what was Rikki's state of mind when she killed Marten? Was the murder premeditated or impulsive or, as Santiago had suggested, self-defense? Of these three options, the first two would suffice, but Mac was determined to persuade the jury, beyond a reasonable doubt, that Rikki planned to execute Marten and was now literally trying to get away with murder.

He circled back to emphasize the indisputable scientific evidence. "So, between the photographs showing the blood spatter patterns, the autopsy report, and the DNA, we know what happened. The next logical step, therefore, is to focus on *why* it happened. The central issue in this case is intent. What evidence has shown that the Defendant *intended* for this atrocity to unfold?

"Front and center, we have Mandy's testimony. Mandy described in brutally graphic imagery the horrific nature of the slaughter she witnessed with her own eyes from the top of the staircase. 'Mommy punched Dad with a knife.'

"Six words. These six short words are essentially the entire case. Yes, it's true: Rikki Van der Hook 'punched' her husband with a knife. The photos of the crimes scene corroborate that. But you did not hear Mandy testify that there was any justification or excuse for such lethal violence. No. Not one word from Mandy about Marten being threatening or aggressive.

"The only words you hear about self-defense are purely self-serving lies from the mouth of Rikki Van der Hook herself. If her lies had any basis in reality, Mandy's testimony would mirror that. Simply put, the Defendant is lying straight to your face, and Mandy is telling you the truth."

Mac paused for a few seconds until he sensed the jury was fully attentive. He lowered his voice to just above a whisper and, in a barely audible tone, said, "It would take a trained actress to lie on the witness stand and fool all 12 of you. But I know you won't let that happen."

Santiago flinched involuntarily and grabbed for his pen lying on the table, accidentally sending it skittering across his desk and over the edge, where it bounced on the carpet. The entire jury and everyone in the courtroom turned to watch the pen spin and then fall to the ground. Sheepishly, Santiago bent down and picked it up.

"Excuse me," Santiago said. The jury looked around, not sure if he had dropped his pen intentionally to disturb the rhythm of Mac's speech or if it was an accident.

Mac smiled and didn't say anything.

Judge Harajuku said, "Mr. MacIntyre, you may continue."

"Thank you, Your Honor," Mac replied. He took three steps back towards his desk, stopped, and turned back to the jury, and then said, "Imagine how traumatic it was for Mandy to watch this horrifying crime. Imagine the pain and the shock and the terror. Imagine the certain, long-term psychological damage this child has suffered and, inevitably, will continue to suffer."

Noticeably, the jurors shifted in their seats. A faint squeaking sound came from one of their chairs.

Mac sensed he was scoring a significant point with the jury, so he made a tactical decision to repeat his last point in different words, driving it further into the jury's collective conscience. He deliberately decided to use the word "suffer" again.

"Imagine the nightmares Mandy will suffer as a result of this woman's actions!" He whirled and pointed directly at Rikki.

Santiago looked down at his notes.

Every great closing argument was a combination of persuasion, theatre, and believability. Law students were taught those three concepts using the Greek words *pathos*, *logos*, and *ethos*. The best orators had command of all three. *Pathos*, like the root word for pathetic, meant the use of emotion. *Logos* was logic. *Ethos* translated loosely to ethics or credibility. Some attorneys were great public orators, but their closings were illogical. Others were logical and methodical, but boring and mundane. The very best—and Mac was one of the best—artfully combined a clear, logical set of facts, told dramatically with a beginning, middle, and end. Like a sleazy used-car salesman who sold few automobiles, an attorney without credibility would convince few juries. Prosecutors who couldn't meld personal likeability with an orderly, compelling presentation of the evidence were prosecutors who wound up with a lot of not-guilty verdicts.

"What evidence proves this was a willful, deliberate, and premeditated first-degree murder?"

Mac always tried to use the exact wording of the Maryland Common Jury Instructions in his closing. It was a clever technique to bond with the judge, who had just instructed the jury using these same words. By echoing Judge Harajuku precisely, Mac triggered the jury to subliminally group Mac with the judge, gaining enormous credibility.

"Obviously, Rikki Van der Hook was trying to kill her husband. The savagery of the slaughter is sufficient to prove that point alone. You don't need to stab someone nearly 50 times if you're just trying to defend yourself. As for premeditation, look at all of the evidence of rancor and rage and revenge that has been clearly established in this trial. The Defendant had ample motive—actually, several motives—to want Marten dead. When you go back to the jury room to deliberate, I'm sure you will be able, collectively, to list them all. If you follow Judge Harajuku's jury instructions, there can be no other alternative than to arrive unanimously at a verdict of guilty on premeditated first-degree murder.

"Another critical factor is the consistency of the testimony you heard. Testimony that changes, that shifts like sand, cannot form a sturdy or reliable foundation. However, in this case, from the very beginning, Mandy has never wavered. All of her pretrial statements were perfectly harmonious with her sworn testimony here inside the courtroom. She has continued to be perfectly consistent. She is telling you the truth. Mandy's testimony alone is sufficient to find the Defendant guilty beyond a reasonable doubt.

"The voice of a child is crying out to you. It is a cry for justice."

He watched the jury. They were all watching him and listening intently. "Consider the bravery it took for Mandy to testify as her own mother sat here in the courtroom and sneered at her!" He turned to stare at Rikki, drawing the jurors' eyes with him. Everyone in the room was watching Rikki squirm in her chair, the veins in her neck visibly throbbing with fear.

Noticing the strange expression on Rikki's face, he improvised, "Look at her right now. She's doing it again. Maybe she's sneering at *you*, ladies and gentlemen?"

Santiago exploded, "Objection!"

"Sustained," said the judge.

Mac stared directly at Rikki, holding the intensity of his gaze long enough for everyone in the courtroom to notice.

He let the storm pass, lowered his volume down a notch, and continued. Turning back to the jury, he said, "The testimony you have heard is not only proof beyond a reasonable doubt, but, I submit to you, is proof beyond all doubt. It is an avalanche of proof confirmed by a direct eyewitness to the murder."

He paused, standing still before the jury. He could hear the overhead lights buzzing.

"For these reasons, I ask you to hold this Defendant responsible. I ask that you send her a message. What she did was not just immoral or vile or—pick any word which comes to mind—it is not only all of those things, but it is something more: it is *criminal*. Rikki Van der Hook is guilty of murder in the first degree. Therefore, I ask you to return a verdict of guilty on that lead count. Thank you."

Mac spun, walked three steps, and sat behind his counsel table.

Judge Harajuku said, "Mr. Garcia?"

CHAPTER 72

Friday August 9, 2019
2:35 p.m.

Mac sat perfectly still as Santiago addressed the jury and began listing all the many flaws in Mac's case. Santiago had an old-fashioned flip easel with sheets of blank paper and a fat Magic Marker in his hand. He awkwardly turned his back to the jury to write down various reasons why he felt the evidence fell short, compiling a list of reasonable doubts. Mac tried to concentrate on his handwritten list, but was distracted by how the ink was seeping through the pages of the oversized pad. There was also a swirl of other distracting thoughts racing through his mind. The image of the diary inside a plastic bag from Sushi Queen locked in the bottom drawer of his office desk ricocheted in Mac's mind. Then he became distracted by the last text from Jo, to which he had comfortably lied. He again mentally listed the people who could betray him. Lindy Hale? No one would believe her. Zaria? Never. Andre? Impossible.

Mac noticed one of Santiago's shoelaces was loose, flopping around the courtroom floor like a lone brown worm wriggling on the worn orange carpet. Something else caught Mac's attention: he saw Don Morris quietly enter the courtroom and slither into a seat in the last row.

"So, as we make a list of reasonable doubts, and it's getting to be a pretty long list if you ask me, it becomes clear the State has not proven this case. Let me add yet another reason for your consideration..."

He was picking up momentum.

"I'm going to list 12," he continued. "12 reasons to have a reasonable doubt in this case. One for each member of the jury. OK, so first you have Mandy's lack of credibility. That's number one. I suggest you can't believe a word she says. Why did she refuse to answer *my* questions?" he rhetorically added. "She just said what the Assistant State's Attorney told her to say. But then she wouldn't even say one word when it was my turn to ask questions? You should just disqualify her and everything she said. Take her entire testimony out of this case! Then, if you take Mandy out of the equation, what do you have left?"

Mac felt his legs tighten as they prepared to propel him into a standing position to object. Saying Mandy testified to what the prosecutor "told her to say" was clearly objectionable: it was "speculative" and had absolutely no supporting corroboration. Closing arguments were required to be based on the evidence and testimony the jury had seen and heard, not speculation. Mac let his leg muscles relax and let the urge to object pass. Objecting now would only draw more attention to Mandy's refusal to cooperate. He realized it would be better to just let that comment fly by and hope the jury wouldn't place much weight on it.

"The only trustworthy witness in this entire case is Rikki Van der Hook. Her husband, Marten, was a viciously abusive husband. Not only was he physically abusive, but he tortured her psychologically. That night, Rikki defended herself. Where is the proof otherwise? Where is the proof? There isn't any. It's missing. My client, Rikki Van der Hook, is an innocent woman!

"And then there is the expert testimony of Dr. Rosenthal. You heard what she had to say late Thursday afternoon. With all of her experience and expertise. A PhD in clinical psychology from the University of Maryland and over 43 years examining patients for signs of mental disabilities and defects. You heard her testify she examined Rikki Van der Hook for 20 hours. About the abuse in the marriage. About horrifying humiliations her husband subjected her to, culminating in forcing her to have sex against her will with another woman. I mean, you heard Dr. Rosenthal call that episode debilitating, didn't you? You heard her expert conclusion, that Rikki's mental acuity was 'severely impaired' on the night of this regrettable incident. This expert testimony proves this case was not an intentional homicide. First-degree murder is off the table."

Santiago paused.

Mac knew he was, in effect, plea bargaining with the jury instead of him. By knocking out the first-degree murder charge, Santiago would claim a big victory with a conviction on just the second-degree murder. A compromise verdict greatly favored Santiago.

"Yes, this was a disturbing event, and trust me, I, like you, get no pleasure out of seeing someone lose their life," he said, jumbling up several thoughts into one sentence. The use of the phrase "trust me" was not preferred by trial attorneys, since jurors had a natural suspicion of lawyers, knowing they were among the least trustworthy of people. Mac was watching the jury's body language for clues—which points were scoring and which were off the mark. Mac noticed the Girl with the Nose Ring, seated in the front row to the right, scrunch up her face when Santiago used the word "pleasure." He had said, "I get no pleasure"—which seemed glaringly discordant when the topic of discussion was a bloodbath.

"The crime scene is graphic and shocking, no doubt," he continued, working up to a crescendo. "And that's exactly why the prosecutor took the effort to blow up the photographs as large as possible. To distract you. To appeal to your emotions and not to your sense of logic. It's an old trick. They always try to get you emotionally overwhelmed by shoving tons of gory photographs in your face and then they hope you can't think straight. Don't reward that type of obvious ploy!" He waited a full count of three seconds while watching the faces of the jurors. Most were looking down at the floor.

"Mandy is a child who is troubled with several serious mental health challenges. I will leave that for the social workers and therapists and psychiatrists and whoever else can help her get on the right track. I sincerely wish her well," said Santiago, lowering his voice almost to a whisper. The Girl with the Nose Ring shifted her full body weight when he said the word "sincerely."

"Yes, I wish her well. However, my job is to make sure this unfortunate incident does not escalate into in an even worse outcome: the unfair conviction of an innocent woman. Don't compound this incident into another tragedy. Ladies and gentlemen, we cannot let that happen!"

He continued, flipping over a page on the easel to reveal a prepared chart.

"I remind you of the jury instruction which Judge Harajuku explained to you earlier, what reasonable doubt means. This is critical, because the entire case rests on this concept."

Santiago pointed to his chart. "Judge Harajuku told you this herself—and I am referring to the Maryland Common Jury Instructions. This is the exact definition you, as jurors, are sworn to follow."

He was copying Mac's technique. By bringing the judge into his presentation to support his argument, as if she was a defense witness vouching for his argument, he wanted to claim the same ground Mac had just staked out earlier. Jurors were highly skeptical of anything defense attorneys said, correctly surmising they weren't searching for the truth, only acquittals.

"So, when I show you these jury instructions, it is not just *me* telling you—this is the judge telling you herself." Pointing to each word he had written on the easel, he emphasized, "A reasonable doubt is a doubt founded upon reason. It is not a fanciful doubt, a whimsical doubt, or a capricious doubt." Santiago tapped on each word as he spoke them, which made Mac think of those old movies where a song was playing and a bouncing ball jumped over the lyrics at the bottom of the movie screen. Trial by karaoke, Mac thought.

Santiago spun like a matador to face the jurors. "Proof beyond a reasonable doubt requires such proof as would convince you of the truth of a fact to the extent that you would be willing to act upon such belief without reservation in an important matter in your own business or personal affairs."

Mac looked at the jury. They were all reading the written text of the jury instruction on the easel.

"Without reservation!" Santiago bellowed. "Let me give you some examples. Think of something important in your own lives. Say, you hired a builder to build your dream house? You'd have to be very confident in his ability when you hired him *without reservation*. You wouldn't want to guess about his abilities, right? You would want to be sure beyond a reasonable doubt.

"Let's take another example: let's say you were about to get on a helicopter. You would have to trust the pilot *without reservation* before climbing onboard, right? You would never get in a helicopter if you had doubts about the skill or trustworthiness of the pilot.

"It's the same with Mandy. Would you trust her to fly your helicopter? Of course not! Her entire testimony was a show. A performance. She was wound up like a toy doll and placed on the witness stand to say what the prosecutor wanted her to say! She was just a big red herring!"

Mac noticed several jurors with expressions of confusion. Santiago explained, "Oh, so you want to know what a red herring is? OK, I'll tell you. It means a distraction, a diversion. It's an old English fox hunting reference. A trick to get the hounds off the trail. In olden days, they'd drag an old dead, rotten fish—a red herring—all over the field to lead the dogs astray. That's what the prosecutor is trying to do with you here with Mandy's unreliable testimony. Lead you astray and trick you. Get you off track.

"The State of Maryland is required to prove my client's intent beyond a reasonable doubt. But here, in this case, they have failed to do so. Therefore, I ask you to render a verdict of *not guilty* as to each and every count of this indictment. Thank you."

Judge Harajuku let Santiago settle into his seat and then turned to Mac, saying, "Mr. MacIntyre, rebuttal argument?"

Mac rose, walked close to the jury box, and stood directly in front of the Girl with the Nose Ring. He unbuttoned his suit jacket and began to speak.

CHAPTER 73

Friday, August 9, 2019
3:55 p.m.

Mac spoke for 45 minutes. He used half of his rebuttal to disassemble Santiago's arguments methodically, piece by piece. That was the *logos* part. Now, strategically, he reserved the remainder of his time to probe the jury's emotions. This was the *pathos* part. That was more important. Technical or logical arguments were fine, but now it was time to dig into the collective heart of the jury.

"Ladies and gentlemen, I ask you to send a message to Rikki Van der Hook. Tell her through your verdict. Let her know that what she did was not only vicious, cruel and destructive, but it was first-degree murder." Mac's tone was sincere, intense and had an electric quality—the *ethos* part—that could hold a jury spellbound.

"You have the ability to send that message. Send it not only to Rikki Van der Hook but also to Mandy. Frankly, your verdict sends a message to the entire community. Therefore, on behalf of the citizens of Seneca County, I ask that you find the Defendant guilty of all the charges."

More than anything, forensic trial advocacy was just simple storytelling. Since the dawn of humanity, when cavemen and indigenous peoples clustered around campfires, tossing buffalo bones in the dirt and shooing away docile wolves, the art of telling a compelling story remained largely unchanged. Great orators injected passion into a story, sensing that drama would keep the listener's attention. The most effective public speakers—from the cavemen to current courtroom advocates—were performers who could skillfully start a speech with an interesting beginning that hooked your attention, and then move into rising action that built to a climax, and then follow a story on a downward slope leading to a satisfying denouement or resolution. From the campfire to the jury box, not much had changed in how people told captivating stories.

Mac scanned all 12 jurors and thanked them. The two alternates would be dismissed in less than a minute, so he ignored them. They were expendable. He sought his main Ambassadors—Power Forward in the back row and Butterfly Lady up front. She was looking down at her lap, either ignoring Mac's performance, or, possibly, having already made up her mind.

He also surveyed the jury box for the two Question Mark jurors he thought might rebel against him, the Girl with the Nose Ring and Housekeeper. Both were staring right into his eyes, which was a good sign. Housekeeper's gaze had a hint of defiance. She was wearing a shawl with broad stripes in brilliant colors—orange, lime-green, and gold—woven perhaps in the Andes by native Peruvian craftsmen. This mountainous flair did not give Housekeeper the appearance of a maid at the Hampton Inn, but rather, presented her as a stocky, strong woman with DNA genetically linking her to the Mapuche peoples of the impenetrable highlands. Mac worried about her piercingly dark, hawkish eyes. He could not decipher what thoughts were obscured on the other side.

He turned and sat confidently in his seat. After some summary canned remarks about the criminal justice system, Judge Harajuku continued to offer bromides and platitudes about patriotism and the need for conscientious jury participation by all citizens. She then directed the jurors to enter the jury room, reminding them, "Please take all of your personal belongings with you."

Further, she directed, "If you have any need to communicate, please knock on the door to the courtroom, and Ms. Chao will assist you. I do not want to influence your deliberations in any way, but if you have not reached a unanimous verdict by 6:30 p.m., we will adjourn for the evening and reassemble again Monday morning. I tell you this not to speed up or delay your deliberations, but to assist you in case you have any childcare considerations. Please place your cell phones on the table here in the courtroom. Unfortunately, our rules require that you may not bring them with you into the jury room. However, I assure you they will be secure here as you deliberate. Let us know if, or when, you have arrived at a verdict by knocking on the door. Having said that, you may begin your deliberations."

CHAPTER 74

Friday, August 9, 2019
4:10 p.m.

Mac turned to face Santiago, put his hand out, and said, "Nice job, great closing."

Santiago shook his hand, and replied, "Well, now we just wait, I guess. I think I'll stay outside in the lobby for a while." Clearly, Santiago was hoping for a quick not-guilty verdict, but Mac knew even a fast verdict in a homicide trial would take at least an hour or two. Since it was already late afternoon, Mac calculated the clock was the critical factor: once dinnertime arrived, and the sun started going down, jurors would shift their focus to themselves and their own personal lives. Kids needed to be picked up from daycare, spouses were eager to hear from isolated loved ones, employers wanted to know when workers would return. Jurors wondered when this responsibility would end and they could go home. Waiting for a jury to reach a verdict had some elements of classic siege warfare. Like a medieval chateau surrounded by enemy archers, how long could the captives endure the isolation?

Judge Harajuku rose, causing both Santiago and Mac to turn towards her. They could hear faint rumblings from the jury room. Muffled noises came from behind the first set of two double doors. Sounds of keys rattling and jackets swishing trickled out into the courtroom. Phoebe stepped out as she shut both sets of double doors behind her. All but the most vitriolic yelling or shouting would be muted now.

"Gentlemen, very well done. Both of you," the judge said flatly. Mac smiled slightly, knowing she said that after every trial. She stood behind her chair and said, "If you leave the floor, please let Ms. Chao know where you are and make sure she has your cell phone numbers in case the jury comes back sooner rather than later, OK?"

"Yes, Your Honor," said Santiago, enthusiastically, especially at her suggestion a verdict might come back "sooner."

Mac notified her, "I'll be right downstairs, Judge, in case there's a jury question or if anything comes up. How late will you hold them tonight if they can't reach a verdict by, say, six-thirty?"

Rikki was escorted out of the courtroom by a large African American female deputy.

"Well, we shall see. If it looks as if they are close to a verdict, we might just tough it out and stay." She turned towards the lone remaining deputy and said, "If we go past six-thirty, we are supposed to get them pizza from the Italian place on the corner, right? Can you check with the Sheriff on that please?"

The deputy, who had a name tag which read "Feeny," was a muscular young blond man with a noticeably lazy eye. He had one eye looking north while the other one was looking west. All of his hair was shorn except for an oval patch on the top of his head. He turned with a confused expression and replied, "Yes, ma'am, I'll check with my supervisor, but that's how we usually do a late dinner, Your Honor."

Judge Harajuku turned towards the attorneys and said, "But, on the other hand, if they seem to be nowhere near a decision, I'd prefer to send them home and start fresh on Monday." She glanced at her watch. "We will give them two hours to see if they can reach a verdict and then reassess. Why don't both of you be back here at 6:30 and then we will cross that bridge when we come to it."

Staying respectfully still, Mac and Santiago stood stiffly, like soldiers at attention, as the judge went back to her chambers. Phoebe did not say "All rise!" as no one but the two attorneys and Deputy Feeny remained inside the courtroom. Mac packed up his files and notepads into the cardboard box labeled "ST. V. VAN DER HOOK." He turned towards Santiago and said, "We will cross that bridge when we come to it."

Santiago smiled.

Mac picked up the box and marched out of the courtroom, walking with purpose towards the elevators. As he got on the elevator, he pulled his cell phone from his jacket pocket. Alone and feeling a sense of privacy, he scrolled through his texts. Andre had texted him, wanting to know what time the jury went out and also to ask if Mac wanted him to return to the courthouse to accompany him as they waited in the office for news of a verdict.

He saw the text from Jo again. She'd be waiting for him in her corner office. Jo regularly camped in her office well past midnight. She preferred to be the last prosecutor to leave the courthouse. Ari Fischbein would be away somewhere, off making a speech and shaking hands, traveling around the chicken dinner circuit, stopping by the Young Democrats Club.

At least The Fish won't be in the office after hours, thank God.

Mac exited the elevator and then used his key fob to buzz his way through the locked glass doors to the SAO. The front desk area was empty; everyone had gone home for the night. He glanced left and right, like a quarterback moving up to the line of scrimmage and checking to see where his receivers were at the edges of the field.

He turned the corner and started down the hallway towards his office. As he approached, he immediately noticed his office lights were on. At 4:30 p.m. each day, the cleaning crews started their rotations around the SAO. They always flipped the lights off in each office when they were done.

Andre will be sitting there with a hot Americano from Starbucks for me. Nice of him.

When he entered his office, he saw Jo Newgrange sitting on the couch facing his desk.

CHAPTER 75

Friday, August 9, 2019
4:55 p.m.

While seated, Jo motioned for Mac to shut the door, even though the SAO was empty this late in the afternoon.

He shut the door, sat in his swivel chair, and spun 180 degrees to face her.

Something was wrong with this scenario.

She spoke first. "So, the jury's out? Is Marcia going to hold them past dinner?" Mac noticed Jo referred to Judge Harajuku as if they were on a first-name basis.

"She said she'd order pizza for them, then reassess at six-thirty. I'm not sure how to read this jury. Some jurors seem to really be on our side, but there're a couple I just can't figure out. There's this girl with tattoos and a nose ring, for example. I felt a good rapport with her during *voir dire*, but now I'm not so sure."

"A nose ring? Lordy, and you kept her on the jury? Well, I'm sure it will all work out," Jo responded dismissively.

All of this was meaningless small talk. Clearly, she was here for something else.

There was only one other time, Mac recalled, when he had entered his office to find Jo inside waiting for him. That was the night of Ari's investiture, when he was sworn in as the new State's Attorney. Afterwards, there was a lame party in the office law library—red Solo cups with cheap wine and trays of uninspiring cold cuts—to celebrate his nascent regime. That night, as the party was winding down, Mac went back to his office to get his blazer and found Jo inside. She was peering at his awards and courtroom sketches, examining them, her watery eyes gleaming. She was wobbly and stood so close to Mac that he could smell the cheap pinot noir on her breath with each exhalation. He made an excuse to snatch his jacket and leave, turning as he walked to the elevator to see her stumbling down the hallway. She was his boss now. He realized she was a potential hazard, not an overt one, but a danger nevertheless. She could not be ignored, the way a small, unchecked campfire in a dry forest could not be ignored; it threatened to consume thousands of acres.

Mac snapped back to the present.

Jo said, "Listen, I came down to your office because I got a strange call from the *Seneca Journal* about your trial. Don Morris, he covers Seneca County, y'know. He said you had an issue with a newly discovered diary in your case? I texted you about it, and you ignored me. What's the deal with the diary?"

"A diary? No, there's nothing about a diary..." he began, but she sharply interrupted him, her tone changing instantly from benign to malignant, like a knife springing out of a pretty switchblade.

"Mac, don't lie to me."

He didn't respond.

Focus.

She said, "After Morris called, I went down to Technical Services and asked them to run through some of today's footage from various security locations around the courthouse. Starting when the courthouse opened this morning. Obviously, you know this whole building is covered by cameras 24-7. I made up a story and told them I needed to review some surveillance video because we had a purse stolen from the SAO, and I wanted to see if this woman represented by the PD took it—she's a compulsive kleptomaniac."

Mac squinted and focused all of his brainpower on what she was saying. He took the key fragments of the words she had just spoken and isolated them in his thoughts, trying to rearrange them into a logical pattern: "diary," "surveillance," and "cameras 24-7." His mind was not panicking, but solving Jo's riddle in real time. It was as if she was spilling a jigsaw puzzle with a thousand pieces onto the floor and challenging him to coherently reassemble them even as they fell and bounced on the carpet.

"I watched the surveillance tapes. Yes, I was looking for a woman, but, of course, I wasn't interested in some demented kleptomaniac. I fibbed about that part. Nope. I was watching for something else. I didn't want anyone else to know what I was looking for. Just me. You'd be *amazed* at what I saw," she said. Her use of sarcasm on the word "amazed" dripped with Southern honey.

"Nothing you do would amaze me, Jo," said Mac icily. He braced himself for what was now developing into a very dangerous confrontation. All of his skills were now required.

"I saw that woman in your murder trial, the little girl's aunt, Lindy Hale. I saw her come in real early and stop at the PD's office," Jo marched on. "Oh, yes, it was definitely her. And she was carrying some kind of small package. It was wrapped, but it was the perfect size for a book. She went into the PD's office for less than a minute."

Mac rebutted, "The camera is positioned over the elevator doors and covers only the hallway. Don't think it's the right angle to actually see her once she enters the PD's office. Her sister is a PD client, so that doesn't seem strange to me. She's probably been up there a dozen times."

"Well, she was only in there a minute. Then she leaves empty handed, no package. It was as if she was dropping it off."

"Who knows?" said Mac. "Better check with the Public Defender's Office. I was already upstairs in a crowded hallway at that exact point in time. Probably 40 people could vouch for that, so I have no idea…"

Jo interrupted, "Then I saw something very interesting. The video shows that Russian slut you've been fucking—please, we've known about that forever. That anorexic girl walked out of the PD's office holding the *exact same package* Lindy Hale brought in just a moment before. It looked like she was trying to hide it."

How did she know about Zaria?

He quickly compartmentalized that unexpected diversion.

Jo smirked and continued, "And guess what? Who should then pop out from around the corner near the men's room about two seconds later? Mind you, this is at the PD's office before work hours. Andre Okoye. Your long-time friend. A dirty cop who killed a kid years ago, who just happens to be indebted for his life to our star trial lawyer, Senior Assistant State's Attorney Mac MacIntyre."

He was still, but his mind was gyrating like a windmill, whirling fast against a strong headwind, thinking, devising a counterattack.

"So," she continued, "I assume Andre took the package from your Russian whore like a running back gets a handoff from a quarterback, and then he immediately heads up here to the SAO, where the camera out by the front desk shows him saying 'Hi' to Lupe" at 8:27 exactly."

"Was he holding a package?"

"Oh, he probably had it stuffed down his shirt. I'm not worried about that part. But then he disappears. Right around the corner... towards... your... office."

"Are you wearing a wire, Jo?"

She laughed, threw her head back, and then snapped her neck forward cobra-like, sticking her face out towards him. She pounced. "Fuck no, I'm not that amateur, Mac."

Her tone became softer and less razor-edged.

"Macaroni," she whispered. "Nobody knows about the diary but me. It's our little secret." She paused. "At least for now. But, once I open this can of worms," she added, glancing at his courtroom sketches and awards, "they will be crawling up the walls in no time."

She unbuttoned the front of her blouse all the way to her waist and pulled her shirt completely open, revealing an expensive bra and a muscular bronze chest, but no wires or listening devices.

"No wire, Mac. Take a look, honey."

He didn't look. He wasn't going to give her that power.

Jo buttoned up the lower two buttons, the ones nearest to her belt, but left the top three unbuttoned. "So, I can place a hold on the surveillance tapes until midnight. Tech Services will have a guy on duty until your case is over tonight since they need to record everything in Marcia's courtroom in case there is a verdict. But if I don't place the hold, they will automatically get recycled and erased. By Monday, they'll be ancient history. I can also call Don Morris tonight and let him investigate, I suppose. He's pretty tenacious."

"Well, as you know, we prosecutors deal in hard evidence, not speculation. So, this is an interesting, imaginary theory, with several missing links. I'm not worried."

He *was* worried.

She said, "Don Morris wants to run a story on this whole missing diary caper in the *Seneca Journal*. Let's see? What will the headline say? 'Prosecutor under investigation for corruption in a murder case?' It will be easy for me to protect Ari and, of course, myself. We'll just say we were elected to clean up all these scandals here in Seneca County. There are always some rotten apples left over from the previous administration. Everyone will remember that whole freak show that broke just before the election last year. That disaster with Jennifer Princeton and Robert Gill and that whole incredibly juicy office sex affair, remember? The State's Attorney blackmailing a pretty young subordinate and appointing her to his own private perverted Special Assignment Team?"

Everything she said was undeniable. But by mentioning blackmail, Jo had unintentionally identified the exact escape route Mac was contemporaneously devising.

"Hoist with his own petard," he said flatly.

"What?"

"Act three, scene four."

"What the hell are you talking about?"

Mac did not answer.

"Never mind that nonsense," Jo announced. "Let's get to the bottom line. As I see it, we only have two options. Let me explain."

CHAPTER 76

Friday, August 9, 2019
5:25 p.m.

"First option is I report you," Jo said. "Judge Harajuku would be quite interested in a missing diary, right?"

"Alleged missing diary," Mac clarified.

"I mean, an innocent woman might get falsely convicted!" she said sarcastically.

"Innocent women don't confess to murder."

Jo countered, "Oh, right. The 'confession.' Maybe your best friend Andre made all of that up? I find it highly suspicious he didn't properly videotape it, too. After doing homicide investigations for, like, what? 20 years?"

"Think about the guy who was slashed to death. You'd really unleash this Rikki woman back on the street?"

"Whatever. I don't give a shit about that drunk. That rich bitch is nothing but white trash underneath all of that money she married into. I've seen plenty of girls just like her down in Buckhead, that's for sure. Like they say, 'you can marry more money in a day than you can make in a lifetime,' right?"

"Rich or poor, she's dangerous and capable of unbelievable violence. She stabbed her husband through his skull. You were aware of that, right?"

"Well, I don't care about that. I suppose I'll need to call Don Morris. I'll have to explain what prosecutorial misconduct means. And then all hell breaks loose at that point. So, that's my first option."

Mac's mind was racing, planning, and digging an escape tunnel out of this trap.

Jo continued, "Then, of course, you not only lose the trial and she goes free, but there will be certain other ramifications, right? The cheating prosecutor who hid critical exculpatory evidence trying to frame an innocent defendant. The *Seneca Journal* and all the TV stations, everyone will jump on *that* story.

"The Attorney Grievance Commission will be the first step towards your disbarment, Mac. Oh, your legal career is toast. That's a given. But, let's see? What criminal charges would be filed against you? Obstruction of justice, tampering, misconduct in office? Those are felonies in Maryland, aren't they? So, when the dust settles, you'd get what? Maybe 18 months? Wonder how a white guy like you'd do at SCCF with all the big boys from the 'hood and *los amigos* from MS-13? So, that pretty much covers Option One."

He stared directly at her.

That's not happening.

"But Option Number Two is so much easier. You come back to my apartment tonight so we can seal the deal, and I will just keep all of this diary business to myself. No one ever has to know anything. It will be easy to paint Lindy Hale as a liar. Come back to my apartment again tonight. I guarantee you—you won't be disappointed."

"Lindy's the sister of the Defendant. That makes her automatically biased," Mac pointed out. "Absolutely no one will believe her."

"She's also a confirmed alcoholic nut job," Jo replied. "So, here's what we can do: I simply just tell Don Morris that we've checked it out and the whole diary thing is a fabrication of the weakest kind. He's not the sharpest knife in the drawer. The courthouse TV surveillance tapes will be recycled and erased fast. By then, Rikki Van der Hook has either been found guilty or not guilty. In no time, we can all move on. Marcia Harajuku moves on to the next trial. Don Morris moves on to the next scandal. You, me, Ari Fischbein, we all move on, and no one's the wiser. So, it seems to me that Option Two is definitely the path of least resistance."

Mac added, "There's no *corpus delecti*. Absolutely no physical concrete proof a diary even existed."

Jo smugly continued, buttoning up the rest of her shirt buttons.

"Well, Mr. MacIntyre, it seems as if I, and *only* I, hold the cards in this situation. So, tell me, what's it going to be?"

Lowering her voice, her tone changed, and her Southern accent involuntarily emerged.

She said, "Maybe you should just come back to my place tonight, and we can... negotiate a settlement?"

Mac paused and looked all around his office. His eyes locked on the small framed child's drawing over his desk. He read the words again, for perhaps the millionth time: HEPLING ME. He stood and said, "I like that idea. It will be my pleasure."

Jo smiled, adding, "Mine too."

"I have to go back up to the courtroom in an hour. I need to see if Harajuku is letting my jury go home for the weekend or holding them until they reach a verdict. But stay on the floor. Wait in your office, Jo. I'll text you when I find out what she decides, and then I'll come back downstairs, and we can leave together."

She leaned back and replied, "Of course, honey. I've been waiting for this since Ari's investiture. I can wait another hour."

"As soon as I find out, I'll be back. Until then, I should go upstairs and wait outside the courtroom in case the jury comes back with a quick verdict."

Grabbing his daily planner from the desk, Mac turned towards the door, then turned back towards Jo and smiled. It was a big, broad smile with the top row of his teeth exposed.

He raced to the elevators.

I have to go with Option Three. She didn't consider that.

First, he had to deal with Judge Harajuku. Then he needed to check on some items stashed away in his Jeep downstairs in the garage. He also needed to make a call before doing anything else.

CHAPTER 77

Friday, August 9, 2019
6:14 p.m.

Santiago was at his office desk waiting for the jury verdict. Nervously, he checked his watch. Only one minute had passed since the last time he last checked. By 6:30 p.m., the jury would be anxious to reach a verdict and not be forced to return Monday morning. They had already devoted a whole week of their lives to this case. Jurors abhorred homicide cases—being thrust into a bloody world of crime scene photographs, autopsy reports and actual, not fictitious, evil. Typically, they just wanted to go home, take a hot shower, and get back to their own world as fast as possible.

Maybe this jury will say they are stuck? A hung jury would be great! That's a mistrial, and Mac will never try this case again.

A mistrial was as good as a not-guilty verdict.

He looked at his watch, for probably the fifteenth time. 6:15 p.m.

Shit, I need to go back to the courtroom.

His office phone rang. He glanced down at the Caller ID portion of the telephone. It mysteriously said, "BLOCKED." He had seen that once before, but he couldn't quite remember the context. Was it the Seneca County Crime Lab? No. Was it Police Headquarters? "BLOCKED." The cops had ways of doing that. He let it ring three times, pondering whether to just let it go to his voicemail: "You have reached Santiago Garcia of the Public Defender's Office. I can't take your call at this time. Please leave me a detailed message when you hear the tone."

His curiosity got the better of him. It was 6:16 p.m.

The elevators will be empty now. I've got plenty of time to get upstairs.

He picked up the receiver and said, "Hello. Can I help you?"

"Look inside your bottom drawer," a voice said.

Confused, he slowly reached down and carefully pulled open the desk drawer.

I hope this isn't a booby trap or a bomb about to explode. This is making me paranoid.

He looked inside.

There was a small pink-and-white cardboard Dunkin Donuts box. Through the plastic, he could see five assorted donuts.

CHAPTER 78

Friday, August 9, 2019
6:17 p.m.

"What the fuck is this?!" Santiago said, as he lifted the shiny pink box. Holding it aloft, he examined it from all angles, including the bottom. He held it so the fluorescent light above his desk reflected on the translucent plastic window. He looked carefully.

Any fingerprints on this box?

He tilted it around in the light for maximum inspection. Nothing.

"Is this some kind of joke, asshole?" He immediately realized it wasn't a very clever remark, but he didn't have time to think of anything witty. He just wanted to sound unintimidated. It wasn't working. Fear and confusion were now washing over him the way a rising tide destroys a child's sandcastle at the waterline on a beach.

"Donuts planted in my desk? Who is this? What's your point?" As he raced through a history of all his cases, both current ones and ones spanning back over his whole career, he couldn't think of anyone who would send this type of strange message.

Was this a threat or a joke?

A voice emerged from the receiver, but it sounded distorted, perhaps by some electronic means.

That sounds like when I represented that drug kingpin guy. The witness was in the protection program and had his voice altered. The police knew how to do it.

There was also a faint crackling static, as if it was a three-way call and another unidentified person was patched in.

"Listen to me, Santiago Garcia," the voice said calmly. Hearing his name triggered a new set of distracting alarms inside his head, adding to his confusion.

This person knows me. It's not some crackpot pranking me.

"Enjoy the donuts, dude. Those are a gift from a friend of mine. Next time, it won't be donuts hidden in your desk. Next time, it might be an ounce of top-grade Thai sticks, or, who knows, maybe a speedball. Heroin has a powerful effect, y'know. It startles people. The point is: I can plant whatever I want on you. So, take those donuts as a warning, Counselor. I can get inside your car easy. Or your apartment. Even inside your office desk, see? Oh, I know all about your expunged marijuana case from when you were in high school. Interesting how the PD background check missed that? You also skipped that on your judge's application, too. It would be a shame if you got a new CDS arrest right about now. Might not look too good to the Judicial Nominations Committee, right?"

Santiago's mind was spinning.

Donuts? My prior marijuana case was way back in high school. The fat lawyer, Mr. Jacobs, with the crumbs on his necktie.

He pushed that memory deep into the back of his mind and concentrated on the voice he'd just heard on the phone.

I've definitely heard that voice before. What is the point of all of this?

"What do you want?" said Santiago, his voice losing all remnants of toughness or bravado. The nightmare of his chances being ruined with the Judicial Nominations Committee, the embarrassment, the failure, it all started swirling around in his mind like a dark tornado approaching on the distant horizon, a potentially lethal threat coming directly at him.

"The trial you're in right now? The woman who stabbed her husband. Listen to me carefully: there's no diary, man. Got it? Don't mention it again, understand? Forget about it and let's all move on, bro."

The line clicked dead, and the letters "BLOCKED" disappeared from the readout on the phone.

Glancing at his watch, perhaps for the twentieth time, he realized he could still make it upstairs on time. Judge Harajuku was OCD about punctuality. He had two minutes to get there. Being late was not an option. She was one of those judges who came out into the courtroom exactly on time, and if the lawyers weren't there, she just waited in her seat and glared. He quickly stood and decided to leave the heavy, rolling briefcase. He wouldn't really need it at this point. He jogged down the hall of the Public Defender's Office and ran out into the lobby.

Luckily, an elevator was waiting on the floor, and he jumped on. He went up to the ninth floor and scampered off. He looked around for Mac and didn't see him anywhere. The entire hallway was completely empty except for a small cleaning crew huddled in the far corner who were wearing uniforms and speaking Spanish. They were not paying attention to Santiago. They were discussing the contents of a cart crowded with mops and several spray bottles of disinfectant that were clinging to the side of the cart, hitching a ride.

He took several steps toward the courtroom. In a few seconds, the judge would come out of her chambers. He looked all around. Then he saw Mac emerge from the defunct telephone booth tucked in the far corner of the hallway. Santiago realized why Mac favored that spot. It was hidden. And he used it to hide the same way a hunter uses a camouflage tree stand to trick deer into range. He imagined Mac, not as a prosecutor, but as a predator, emerging from this refuge to spy upon the open space of the hallway and, with a sniper's guile, raise a weapon and aim it at someone wandering unexpectedly into the fatal crosshairs of his riflescope.

As Mac stepped out of the abandoned telephone booth and positioned himself just outside the door to the courtroom. Santiago sensed something was out of place. Mac didn't have a carbine, but something else—something small and dusty and unexpected in his hand.

Mac held up a small white object, popped it in his mouth, swallowed, and said, "Just finishing my donut."

He brushed a faint trace of powdered sugar off his lips and turned to go into the courtroom. Santiago froze, then followed.

"Wait! I recognized Detective Okoye's voice right away," Santiago lied. "Man, so what the fuck? What's the point of planting a box of donuts in my desk?"

CHAPTER 79

Friday, August 9, 2019
6:29 p.m.

Phoebe pushed the courtroom door open and poked her head out into the hallway.

"Guys, Judge Harajuku will be on the bench in 10 minutes. She had to handle an emergency search warrant. She's Duty Judge tonight. The jury is still inside deliberating, but I can hear them yelling. Sounds like some woman is freaking out. It's definitely a female voice we can hear through the double doors. I'll come get you when the judge is ready to enter the courtroom. She wants to know if you want to stay late tonight until they reach a verdict, or recess and come back on Monday, OK?"

"Thanks, Phoebe," said Mac. "We'll hang out here in the hallway until the judge is ready. Mr. Garcia and I will discuss it, and we'll see if we can agree on something. Thanks."

Phoebe smiled at Mac and didn't even look at Santiago.

She turned and retreated into the courtroom. Santiago slumped down into one of the tired armchairs which dotted the hallway. Mac leaned back against the frame of the old abandoned telephone booth. There was no one else in the hallway. The cleaning crew was inside another courtroom at the far end of the hallway.

"You know how these undercover CDS cops are, my friend. I'd say 95 percent of the ones I work with are corrupt. I guess it's lucky for you nothing more serious than a box of donuts was in your desk. Usually, they plant drugs or guns or something else really incriminating, like obscene pictures of kids. Who knows how they do that?"

"But how did you get a copy of my application to the Judicial Nominations Commission?"

"Godfather move, Santi. Someone on the JNC owed me a favor."

"Please. Don't fuck me up. This shit isn't worth it. That possession of marijuana case I had was when I was in high school, like 15 years ago. I could just say I thought it was expunged, so I didn't have to include it on the application."

With a surprised expression, Mac said, "Well, the question on the application clearly says to list all charges and arrests even if the case was eventually expunged, so that might not fly. But it would be a disaster if you picked up a *new* charge. That would be really unfortunate."

Santiago looked at the floor.

Mac leaned closer, looming over him. Most negotiations involved a carrot and stick approach. He'd already used the stick. Now came the carrot. Calmly, with a logical tone, he said,

"You'd be great on the District Court bench, Judge Garcia. I like the sound of that. So, you know my boss Ari Fischbein? Trust me, The Fish is completely clueless. He doesn't know anyone out here in Seneca County. I'll ask him to delegate his spot on the Judicial Nominations Commission to me. He has no clue what the JNC does anyway, and he definitely doesn't want to do the work involved. He doesn't want to sit in on all those boring interviews. He only pushed to get on the JNC for political reasons, like he does with everything. He'll be happy to assign all of those meetings to me. Then, you'll be all set, Your Honor."

"What do you want from me?"

"That diary that Lindy Hale never brought to your office? I think we can all forget about that, don't you?"

"She told me on the phone that she had a diary from the little girl."

"I mean, it's not like you actually *saw* a diary, right? You just heard about one. And from a totally biased, unreliable witness. From my perspective, it's all fantasy, a fabrication from a desperate family member. She is the sister of the woman on trial, right? So, this diary—I don't need anyone even hearing about it, and start digging around, asking questions. Are you following me? It's best if we all forget about this diary. Don't mention anything about it to anyone, especially to that reporter guy from the *Seneca Journal*. Don't tell your client either. Understand?"

"And at the end of the day, you'll support me on the JNC?"

"At the end of the day. God, how I despise that expression! I literally flinch every time I hear that cliché. At the end of the day, the day ends, OK? But, yes, I will wholeheartedly support your candidacy. *Quid pro quo*."

"Well," said Santiago, warming to the idea, "that's true. That's a good point. I never saw a diary. That is absolutely true. I could swear to that. And I totally gave that Lindy woman a chance to bring it to me, and she failed. But, if you say the diary is just one big recantation, it can't really harm you, can it?"

"Man, play that out logically, step by step. So, in two minutes, you go inside this courtroom. You stand up and say, 'Judge, I have newly found evidence!' You tell her you've learned about some kid's composition book with scribbles in it. She's going to declare a mistrial for sure. I've been through that situation before. Newly discovered evidence. Maryland Rule 4-331. I once had a murder case where this defense attorney comes to my office with a bloody hammer in a plastic bag. Says he can't tell me where he got it, but he's ethically obligated to give it to me. Caused an automatic mistrial."

"Did you plead the case out? Or try it over again? What happened?"

"He ended up pleading guilty, but I agreed to go below the Guidelines. We got mitochondrial DNA from traces of blood on the hammer. Of course, we didn't need a victim to testify, since the man was dead. Think about it: victims don't ever testify in homicide cases. But here, we have an eyewitness to the actual killing. But, unfortunately for me, and lucky for you, this kid has all kinds of issues and is definitely a 'one and done' type of witness. Mandy will never testify again. She doesn't have the strength to testify twice."

"But if Harajuku declares a mistrial, we will have time to sort this shit out," Santiago unconvincingly countered.

"If Judge Harajuku sees a diary, or even *hears* about a diary, this trial is over. She's so cautious. She doesn't want to take any chances of getting reversed by the Court of Special Appeals. That's her top priority. Herself. So, a mistrial will kill this case. No. I have to take my chances right now. Tonight. I have no choice. Right now, tonight, is my only chance."

"Let me think about it, Mac."

Phoebe opened the door and said, "She's coming out of chambers in like 30 seconds."

As Phoebe turned her back, Mac said to Santiago, "Think fast."

CHAPTER 80

Friday, August 9, 2019
6:39 p.m.

Mac walked up to the prosecution desk, pulled back the swivel chair, and sat. He didn't need to bring the large cardboard box he'd been carrying all week. That was one of his theatrical touches: lugging a huge box into the courtroom with the word EVIDENCE written in massive block letters on the side. It worked well as a prop solely for the consumption of the jurors, who, naturally, assumed there must be a lot of evidence against the accused. Usually, the box held some random law books. Mac knew that even an empty box would impress the jurors. In a criminal trial, impressions were often as important as actual evidence.

"All the world's a stage, and all the men and women merely players," he whispered to Santiago.

"What'd you say?"

"Act two, scene seven."

"Oh, yeah, all the damn world is your fake-ass stage. Has anyone ever told you how pompous you sound with those fucking Shakespeare quotes, dude?"

"Smile. You're on stage right now, my friend. You think this is a jury trial? No, sir, this is a stage. 'All the men and women' are 'merely players.' You're a player, dude."

Judge Harajuku was uncharacteristically late.

Santiago sat behind the defense table. He turned to watch what Deputy Feeny was doing. Usually, there were two deputies together in the courtroom, but Feeny was alone. A faint rattling of keys clinked, and then the sound of a flushing toilet came through the door to lockup. Mac correctly guessed that the second deputy was back there, likely getting Rikki ready to enter the courtroom. Deputy Feeny was intently focused on the side door and not eavesdropping on the attorneys, who sat quietly waiting for the judge to appear. Feeny had his head tipped over sideways on his left shoulder, listening to his radio, which was positioned like a soldier's epaulet on his deltoid.

Phoebe would knock at the door to chambers any second. She was just waiting for Rikki to be escorted into the courtroom and positioned at the defense table next to Santiago. By law, the jury could not see Rikki enter from the lockup area, so each time the court convened, there was this shuffling around. Mac felt this charade was pointless, since it was obvious that Rikki was coming from somewhere, and not just materializing out of thin air. Judge Harajuku's habit, which was frequently counterproductive, was to make sure all the participants in the trial—prosecutor, defense attorney, and the defendant herself—were all seated inside the courtroom before she entered. So, sometimes she waited for several minutes just inside the doorway to her chambers, not knowing that the attorneys could hear her muffled grumbling and complaining.

Santiago looked at Mac, but only moved his head a fraction and otherwise was completely still. The courtroom was totally empty of visitors in the gallery, which created heightened acoustics. Deputy Feeny was focused on his radio. Rikki was on the other side of the door to lockup. Santiago and Mac were, in effect, completely alone. Using just the corner of his mouth to speak, in the technique of a ventriloquist, Santiago whispered, "How did you ever remember that weed case from when I got charged in high school? It was so long ago."

Whispering back, Mac replied, "I have a pretty good memory."

The door to lockup opened, and Rikki stepped into the courtroom guided by the large African American deputy with a nameplate over her shirt pocket which said, "Banks." Rikki stood at the desk as Deputy Banks unlocked her handcuffs. Rikki sat, turned to Santiago, and said, "What's happening?"

He quickly summarized, "The judge wants to figure out if we should keep the jury here to continue deliberating, or let them go home and come back on Monday to start up again."

There was a hard knock at the door, and Phoebe stepped in shouting, "All rise!" Judge Harajuku followed her immediately through the doorway, as everyone in the courtroom rose to a standing position. The judge ascended the three steps towards her chair, grabbed it by the armrest, and spun it towards her.

In the swirling action, as Phoebe, Judge Harajuku, the two deputies and Rikki were all moving simultaneously, Santiago took a small step towards Mac, who was standing right next to him. He whispered, "OK, you win. No diary. I have no idea what that nutty Lindy woman is talking about."

Mac whispered back, "Judge Garcia. That has a nice ring to it."

Judge Harajuku took her seat, cleared her throat, and said, "Please be seated. Gentlemen, let's talk about the jury and make some decisions about tonight, OK?"

CHAPTER 81

Friday, August 9, 2019
6:45 p.m.

"Mr. MacIntyre, do you have a position on the jury's deliberations, specifically whether the Court should let them continue to deliberate or excuse them for the weekend? What is the State's position?"

"Your Honor, respectfully, I would ask the Court to poll the foreperson to see if they're close to a verdict or not. If they seem close to a resolution, then I would ask you to let them keep deliberating. It's 6:45 p.m. If we can complete this trial without extending it through the weekend, well, obviously, I'd prefer to resolve things tonight. Thank you."

"Mr. Garcia? The defense's position?" Judge Harajuku turned towards Santiago, who rose from his chair. Rikki, seated next to him, was fidgeting, nervously tapping her fingers on the table.

"Your Honor, I don't think we need to pressure them into a rushed verdict." Time and delay were both in his favor. The longer the jury was out, the greater the chance grew that complex infighting among them would develop. Santiago's strategy was to drag this out as long as possible. He wanted the jurors released to go home. Who knows? Maybe one of them would get sick or hit by a car over the weekend, and that definitely would cause a mistrial.

"I suggest we excuse the jury for the night and then start fresh Monday morning," he continued. "Additionally, the weather forecast calls for severe lightning storms later tonight, so it might be best for everyone to avoid inclement…"

Judge Harajuku cut him off, saying, "Well, this is what we are going to do."

Santiago immediately assessed his comment about the lightning storm was a mistake. Not to mention he had completely fabricated it.

"We will call the jury out, and I'll ask the foreperson to give us an update as to where they stand right now, and then, depending on their response, I'll make a decision. Phoebe, what is the foreperson's number again, please?"

"Juror Number 18," said Phoebe, referring to the old woman Mac had dubbed Butterfly Lady. Phoebe ruffled through her notes, flipping them over with flair.

"Thank you. Please ask the jury to retake their seats in the box."

Phoebe crossed the well of the courtroom and opened the first of the two double doors to the jury room. As she opened the first set of doors, muffled voices, but no actual words, could be deciphered. Then someone, a woman, laughed incongruously. It was high-pitched and sharp and could be heard clearly by everyone inside the courtroom. Judge Harajuku, Mac, Santiago, and Rikki all sat frozen and listened intently for clues as to which way the jury might be leaning.

Phoebe banged on the inner door, and the jury room immediately went silent. She opened the door a crack and said, "The judge wants to talk to you. Please leave your belongings in here and take your assigned seats."

Phoebe walked across the courtroom and resumed her spot in the clerk's chair. The jurors marched out of the jury room in single file and claimed their seats.

When everyone was seated, the judge said, "Ladies and gentlemen of the jury, thank you for your service and for your careful deliberations thus far. It's nearing seven in the evening. I would like to know a little about your progress and whether collectively, as a group, you feel it would be constructive to keep deliberating tonight. We can take a break for dinner and send for pizza and soft drinks to tide you over if you'd prefer to keep deliberating. Or, in the alternative, we can suspend things for tonight and come back on Monday and start fresh. What's your pleasure, Madame Foreperson?"

Butterfly Lady slowly rose to her feet and faced forward. She then glanced backwards toward the big man behind her in the second row, as if for his approval. He was the juror Mac had dubbed Power Forward.

"Well, Your Honor, I would need to check with my fellow jurors, but we seem to be an 11 to one vote right now."

Judge Harajuku nearly shouted, "Stop! I'm sorry. I should have said something. We do not need to have a breakdown of any votes or exact numbers. I was just trying to assess if you would generally prefer to stay, have dinner, and then continue, or stop for the evening. If we continue, I will recess at 10:00 p.m. if there is no consensus. As you know, your verdict must be unanimous, meaning all 12 of you must agree on a verdict, whether it be guilty or not guilty, do you understand?"

Power Forward jumped in, saying, "We are almost done. Let's stay and wrap this thing up."

It was extremely unusual for a juror who was not being addressed directly by the judge to interject and interrupt. Only a very self-confident person with a strong personality would speak for the entire jury. Judge Harajuku flashed a glance at Power Forward that said, "Do not say another word!"

She then concluded, "OK, having heard the jury's input, I will direct all of you to head back and continue your deliberations. I will request dinner be brought to you. My law clerk will facilitate that. Thank you. You may return," as she gestured with a sweep of her hand back to the jury room.

With a little shuffling, the jurors marched back across the courtroom. Mac stood deferentially as each juror filed past the prosecution table. Santiago remained seated next to Rikki. He huddled close to her and draped his arms around her shoulders. By wrapping his arm around her shoulders, he sought to convey he was unafraid of her and she was non-threatening.

When all the jurors had crossed the threshold back into the jury room, Phoebe closed both sets of double doors and then returned to her chair where she started flipping through a menu from Coco's, the 24-hour Italian restaurant on the street corner next to the courthouse. The meals were hearty but not creative: four plain cheese pizzas, two liters of regular Coke, and two liters of Diet Coke.

After the jurors were safely sequestered, Judge Harajuku said, "OK, gentlemen. Keep your phones handy. They may have a verdict soon. In any event, I'll see you both here at 10:00 sharp, if not before then."

Santiago interjected, "Your Honor, I have a Motion!"

"And what would that be, Mr. Garcia?"

"Your Honor," he began, "the jury inadvertently mentioned to the Court they were stuck at an 11-to-one breakdown. And, as the Court knows, in the event of a deadlock, then the remedy would be a mistrial. Therefore..."

"Oh, shut up!" she said, taking two steps down towards the door to chambers. Looking back over her shoulder, she added, "Motion denied."

CHAPTER 82

Friday, August 9, 2019
7:05 p.m.

Mac got off the elevator and walked towards his office. As he approached his door, he could hear Jo's voice as one half of a phone call conversation.

"So, then I asked her, where did you get those Jimmy Choos? I mean, they cost like an arm and a..." She was speaking on her cell phone, but as he turned into the doorway, she abruptly ended the conversation. "Oh, Donna, I have to run. I have another call coming in, girl. Bye!" Mac noted how easily she lied. She clicked her phone off, turned to look at him, and smiled.

"Verdict?"

"Harajuku's giving us until 10:00. She's letting the jury continue to deliberate, but if they haven't reached a decision by then, she's letting them go home, and we'll start up again Monday morning."

"Rats!" said Jo, compressing her lips into a thin line of disappointment. Clearly, Mac realized, she was hoping he would come back to her apartment unencumbered with thoughts of the trial, or, better yet, victorious and in a mood to celebrate wildly. Jo squirmed in her seat slightly and pressed her skirt down flat on her knees.

He explained, "The jury forewoman is this antiquated old lady. She blurted out that they were 11 to one, but she didn't say which way. They'll either find her guilty or set her free tonight. This thing should be done soon."

"Well, I can wait a couple of hours," Jo suggested, with a light, persuasive tone. "Actually, that works even better. I can go home now and get things ready? I have a couple of surprises for you. So, come over at 11:00. I'll be waiting. Perhaps some festivities will be in order?"

"OK, that sounds... exciting, boss." He changed his tone to match her seductive one. "But, hey, Jo, meet me down by your car now. I have some things I need to show you. Some surprises, too. I'm parked right next to you. Can you meet me there in literally 10 minutes?"

"Yes. Surprises for *me*? How thrilling. I just need to grab my coat and check my voicemail one last time. I hope that obnoxious Don Morris hasn't left another message. That guy is so aggressive."

Jo mentioned Don Morris's name to remind him of what was at stake. She turned the mental thumbscrews another notch tighter. She also started imagining other pleasurable possibilities once she locked her apartment door.

"Sounds good," he said. "10 minutes. Downstairs. By your car."

"Oh, a man who takes control. That's sexy. But I'm the one who gives the commands. Imagine all the fun we can have if you do exactly what I say?"

"Nine minutes. Down in the garage. We need to move," he replied.

Jo walked with purpose down the hallway to her office. The SAO was now completely empty. She grabbed her Burberry raincoat from the hook behind the door and threw her Coach bag over her shoulder. Spinning with the grace of a ballerina, she stepped back across the threshold and locked her office door.

She took the elevator down to the basement, skipped out into the garage, and saw her BMW in its reserved space. Oddly, Mac was sitting in his Jeep, perpendicularly blocking her in. As she walked over to his Jeep, she bent down and, through the passenger window, asked, "Honey, what are you doing?"

"Get in," he said. "We need to get a couple of things straight." His tone was completely different from the coy, flirtatious vibe he had used upstairs in his office. This was the tone of an assassin.

"Well, whatever. Is something wrong?" she replied, as she followed his directions and got into the unlocked passenger side of the Jeep.

CHAPTER 83

Friday, August 9, 2019
7:19 p.m.

Jo continued, "Something's wrong. I can tell, Mac. What's up?" He turned to face her.

"Deputy State's Attorney Newgrange, I have considered your two options carefully. We can forget about both of them. We will take a different option. Let's call it Option Number Three. Here's how it works: you forget everything you know about a diary. Then you call Don Morris of the *Seneca Journal* before you leave this Jeep, and you tell him the whole diary thing is a total fabrication. I'm not going back to your apartment. Not tonight, not ever. Only an idiot gets caught in the same trap twice, and I'm not an idiot. Pick some other guy to satisfy your cravings, OK? Make the call to Morris and then get out of my car and go home. Then we all move forward, and it's never mentioned again. That's the option *I'm* selecting. Do you understand?"

"What the hell! Who are you to tell me what to do?! I think you forget I have all the cards, former Assistant State's Attorney, and now Defendant William MacIntyre! Or should I say soon-to-be Inmate Number 12345 or whatever number you get assigned in prison?"

"No, it's not going to play out like that. And, please, can you stop with that ridiculous Southern accent you affect? Listen up."

Jo froze, as if she had been slapped across the face. No one ever spoke to her like that. She was listening acutely, trying to recalibrate from this unexpected diversion. She felt as if she was speeding down a wintery, icy road, the car spinning out of control towards a cliff, but, if she concentrated fully, and was also lucky, she just might be able to straighten out her path to safety.

"Listen," Mac spelled out, "you and that little moron, The Fish, are new here. Just starting. I know image is everything to Ari. Remember Robert Gill and Jennifer Princeton? Before you got here, Gill was sexually harassing the shit out of that rookie. It ended up bringing his whole kingdom crashing down. Humpty Dumpty had a great fall."

Jo sat still, as if hypnotized, thinking, processing, and trying to connect these moving dots.

"Sexual harassment is extremely hot in the media right now. The last thing you and The Fish need is a huge, messy harassment case just like the one that brought Gill down. Well, I'm sure Don Morris would be very interested in hearing about a new scandal in the SAO, this time with a fresh, juicy twist: a female Deputy State's Attorney harassing a male Senior

Assistant State's Attorney. That would be a disaster for you and Ari. So, here's the deal: you forget about this whole diary issue, and I'll forget about your blatant sexual harassment."

Like a seesaw, Jo felt her previous position of power suddenly descend to the ground. She asserted, "You can't prove shit. There are no emails between us. Nothing. That will never fly! It's too little, too late."

"Do you always talk in clichés? Too little, too late. God, how I hate that expression. First of all, it's not too little. It's actually quite a lot. And second, it's not too late either. The timing is perfect."

Mac reached behind him into the area directly behind the driver's seat and pulled out a small green nylon backpack.

He zipped it open and pulled out a smaller brown paper bag. He opened the small paper bag, reached in, and lifted out a tiny piece of turquoise cloth. It was the pair of her panties.

"What the fuck is that?!" she exclaimed.

"Oh, I think you know. They're unwashed. Your DNA is all over these, soaked with it. And, yes, mine is mixed in there too. I took care of that. A good strong mix, in all the right places. People will wonder how I got them, I suppose."

"You have got to be kidding me. You stole those!" Mac carefully put the panties back in the paper bag and placed it back inside the larger backpack. He then pulled out a large, clear, gallon-sized zip lock bag.

"What's that?!" she demanded, with a mixture of confusion and curiosity.

"These are the two Heineken bottles from that night. Remember? You asked me to take out the garbage when you sent me home. Carrying your trash—literally. Sent me on an errand like I was your servant boy. Well, I found a multitude of interesting items in that trash. Fingerprints stay on a surface like glass virtually forever, as I'm sure you know. People might wonder how I got these, too."

"You could have gotten them anywhere."

Mac put the ziplock bag with the two bottles back in the green backpack and zipped it closed. He put the backpack directly behind his seat where she couldn't reach it.

"Those empty bottles pair nicely with your stained panties. C'mon, Jo, you said you had all the cards? Well, it's time to fold your hand."

Mac lifted up his cell phone. "Nice video here of your bedroom, too. Oh, one last thing: your nosy neighbor, that old snoop in '1H,' the one with the yapping Westie named Charlie? Her doorbell said, 'Lowe.' It was easy to track her down: Noelle Lowe. She's what we call in our business an eyewitness. She can unquestionably put us together at your apartment late at night."

"You are such a motherfucker."

"How do you spell Zenaib? Never mind. I figured that out too. She saw us embracing in the classroom at the college."

Jo gritted her teeth silently.

"Well, I think the press could run with all these details. But..." Mac said calmly as he patted the backpack. "Well, to quote you: we don't need to open up this 'can of worms,' do we? Maybe I should say this can of rattlesnakes?"

"Give me back my panties, and we have a deal."

"I think I'll hold on to them, Josephine. For now, at least. We might be able to renegotiate sometime. But I'm excellent at keeping secrets. Now, to seal the deal, I need you to call Don Morris. Right now. *Now.* Before you leave this Jeep."

"Right now, right this minute? I haven't even had time to think this through."

"I've got to be getting upstairs soon. Call Morris. Call him now, and we are done."

Jo stared straight ahead for five full seconds and then reached into her Coach shoulder bag. She picked up her cell phone and scrolled through her contacts. She pressed the screen to dial Morris.

Through the speaker they heard, "You've reached the voicemail of Don Morris, of the *Seneca Journal.* I can't take your call right now, but please leave me a message, and I'll get back to you as soon as I can. Thank you, and have a nice day." A beep sounded.

"Hey there, Don! This is Jo Newgrange, calling from the State's Attorney's Office. It's, um, let me see, it's after dinnertime on Friday night. So, I looked into that issue about a diary in the Van der Hook trial, and I'm afraid I can't help you. It's a dead end. I think that whole diary thing is just some fantasy of that woman who called you. So, well, I know you don't want to go to print with some wild rumor and then you have to end up retracting it. Anyway, that's the bottom line. I hope you're well, and I'll catch you on the next case, Don. Goodnight."

Mac reached behind him and rattled the canvas bag. The two Heineken bottles clinked as if performing a ritual toast. Jo turned to glare at him one final time; then she unlatched the passenger side door, stepped out of his Jeep, and walked away without turning back.

CHAPTER 84

Friday, August 9, 2019
7:39 p.m.

Mac swung his Jeep towards the back concrete wall of the garage. He backed into the farthest parking space next to an immobile dumpster that had been stationary for at least 15 years. This exact location was shielded from all security cameras. He hid the green nylon backpack inside the custom-made stainless steel lockbox bolted to the floor behind the passenger seat. Once the bag was safely secured, he pulled the carpeted cover over it to camouflage it. As he stepped out of the vehicle, his cell phone buzzed. He looked at the Caller ID: Phoebe calling from her law clerk's office upstairs on the ninth floor.

"Hello, this is Mac MacIntyre," he said.

"Sir, this is Phoebe. Come back to the courtroom. We have a verdict."

"Yes, thanks. I'm right downstairs in the building. I'll be there in a minute."

That was very fast.

He glanced at his cell phone for the exact time. 7:42 p.m. He jogged towards the elevator, at the same time adjusting his necktie and tapping the pockets on his jacket: phone, keys, and wallet. All there.

He scrambled off on the fifth floor, moving quickly, but not quite running. The SAO hallways were totally empty. He turned into his office and grabbed his daily planner. The big box marked EVIDENCE could wait. He wouldn't need that now.

He scampered back to the elevator bank and went upstairs. As he exited the elevator, he saw Santiago over by the courtroom door.

"Fast verdict!" Santiago noted, a tinge of nerves in the tone of his voice.

"You never know. I've seen it go either way on a fast verdict."

"Yeah. Me too. Usually bad news for the defense. Well, there goes my hung jury and mistrial."

They entered the courtroom. Deputy Feeny hovered by the door to lockup, fiddling with his huge set of metal keys which gave him the appearance of either a locksmith or a dungeon master. He glanced up quickly to see who was entering the courtroom, then focused his attention on his enormous keyring. He tilted his head towards the radio transmitter on his shoulder and said, "They have a verdict up here in 9W. Get that female prisoner up here ASAP."

Mac went up to the prosecutor's table, tossed his daily planner down, and then sat. He looked at Santiago and said,

"But remember, man, it's late on a hot summer evening. With a storm approaching, right? I checked the weather. Very creative, that one."

"A storm approaching. How symbolic. Is that from fucking Shakespeare too?"

Mac explained, "I've seen totally guilty defendants get acquitted just so the jury could go home. With these homicide trials, you just never know what the verdict's going to be."

Santiago did not reply.

The side door opened, and Deputy Banks escorted Rikki into the courtroom. Rikki was wearing the same dark pants she'd worn all week and, right now, the red blazer. Mac calculated this was the second time she'd worn it. She sat next to Santiago, and they immediately huddled up and had a private, whispered conversation, which Mac strained to hear.

Because the courtroom's circular design created strange swirling acoustics, Mac had learned from experience that if he moved further from the defense table—acting as if he was giving them privacy—he could actually eavesdrop more effectively. He moved a few steps away, ostensibly to give Santiago a bubble of confidentiality. From this position, he heard wisps of their dialogue travel around the curved walls: "… that was fast," exclaimed Rikki.

And Santiago replying, "… well, you never know. I still think it's a weak case, so just hang in there."

A series of loud knocks banged on the inside of the door from chambers, a thunderous crashing. It was Phoebe, pounding her fist with even more dramatic flair. A storm was approaching. The door opened, and Phoebe stepped in, saying, "All rise! The Circuit Court for Seneca County is now in session, the Honorable Judge Marcia Harajuku presiding."

Phoebe took her position by the clerk's chair as the judge stepped up to her elevated bench. Judge Harajuku turned and said, "OK, gentlemen, I understand we have a verdict. Is that correct?"

Phoebe responded, "Yes, Your Honor. The jury foreperson knocked on the door approximately 20 minutes ago and told me they had reached a unanimous verdict on both counts."

The judge said, "Let the record reflect that the Assistant State's Attorney, Mr. MacIntyre, is present, as well as the Defendant, Ms. Van der Hook, and her counsel, Mr. Garcia. Everyone is present. Madame Clerk, you may get the jury. Thank you."

Phoebe crossed over to the jury room and opened the outer doors. When she opened them, voices were audible coming from within, some nervous giggling and a buzz of small talk. Mac heard a louder voice ask, "Anyone want that last slice of pizza?" Then Phoebe knocked on one of the inner doors, and instantly, the jury room became silent.

She then opened the inner door and said, "OK, the judge is on the bench, and everyone is assembled. You can leave all of your stuff here. You'll be allowed to return in a minute. Please come out and take your assigned seats, and the judge will give you further instructions."

Mac stood and watched intently. With his peripheral vision, he could see Santiago and Rikki standing at the defense table. Mac had learned that jurors, after reaching a unanimous verdict and entering the courtroom, would usually look at the loser of the trial: if most of them looked at the defendant, then that was a good sign for the prosecutor. If they stared at the prosecutor, it was more than likely a not-guilty verdict.

Butterfly Lady emerged first. She looked directly at Rikki.

The next two jurors looked down at the carpet.

The Girl with the Nose Ring looked directly at Mac and smiled.

Power Forward looked first at Rikki, and then quickly back at Mac.

Housekeeper looked at the judge, and then directly at Santiago, and then back at the floor.

While all 12 jurors were shuffling in the jury box and claiming their correctly assigned chairs, the judge said, "Please be seated."

The two deputies closed in and positioned themselves directly behind Rikki. Deputy Feeny grasped his radio, and Deputy Banks placed both of her hands firmly on the back of Rikki's swivel chair, prepared for anything. Mac knew these deputies had seen it all: defendants flipping over the table, throwing the water pitcher at the judge, punching their own lawyers.

Judge Harajuku addressed the jury by reading verbatim from the formalized Maryland Common Jury Instructions.

The judge asked, "Madam, has the jury reached a verdict?"

Butterfly Lady said, "Yes, Your Honor, we have."

"And who shall speak for you?"

The forewoman looked confused. She turned to look at Power Forward in the back row and said, "Who shall speak? Aren't I supposed to do that?'

The archaic language and formality must have distracted her.

"She speaks for all of us. And I mean *all* of us, unanimously," said Power Forward.

"Ma'am, what is the jury's verdict as to Count One, murder in the first degree? Guilty or not guilty?"

CHAPTER 85

Friday, August 9, 2019
8:09 p.m.

Butterfly Lady lifted the Verdict Form, where she had written the jury's decision. Mac was completely still, his face expressionless, but his eyes were burning with intensity. Santiago was rocking almost imperceptibly, staring at the jury. Rikki was looking at the table, unable to face the jury, as if she was in a movie theatre watching a horror film.

"As to Count One, murder in the first degree, we, the jury, find the Defendant, Rikki Michele Van der Hook, guilty."

Mac shut his eyes and fleetingly soaked in the surprising victory. Santiago continued to rock in his chair, gritting his teeth in disappointment. Rikki dipped her head further, then reached up to loosen her shirt's top button as if it were a noose. She began shaking her head defiantly, as if to say, "No! This is wrong!"

Santiago huddled with Rikki, discussing the various unrealistic appellate options. He wrapped his arm around her shoulders, and she pulled away. The two deputies stood up and positioned themselves next to Rikki.

All the jurors, uncomfortable with the novelty of this experience, sat still with their eyes darting around the courtroom, taking in the process. Power Forward was sitting stiffly with his arms crossed defensively across his broad chest. He was staring at Rikki with an expression of disgust, as if he was looking at roadkill swarming with maggots. Housekeeper quickly made the sign of the cross, tapping both sides of her chest and looking upwards as if seeking forgiveness. The Girl with the Nose Ring had both of her hands covering the bottom half of her face, leaving only her wide eyes visible, flickering back and forth from the judge to Mac to Rikki and then to Mac again, as if seeking someone, anyone, to connect with.

The judge summed up by saying, "And, again, we thank you for your service as jurors. Yours is an essential civic duty without which our system of justice could not function. I will ask Ms. Chao to accompany you to the jury room, where you may retrieve your belongings. Since the Jury Commissioner's Office is now closed, you will receive your per diem compensation checks by mail. And, with that, ladies and gentlemen, that concludes your jury service."

Phoebe ushered the jury back into the jury room. Mac sat still and moved only his eyes, not his head. He observed every detail unfolding before him. Soon, the jurors emerged, and several looked at him as they walked across the courtroom and out through the doors to the hallway. Rikki was completely still, frozen, and she stared down at the table in a complete daze. Santiago shifted repeatedly in his seat, twitching like a cornered mouse trying to escape.

When all the jurors had been escorted out of the courtroom, Phoebe came inside from the lobby.

"They've all left the floor, Your Honor."

The judge was busy with her computer, trying to pull up her calendar.

"Gentlemen, sentencing will be set for September 16th. Are both counsel available at 9:30 on that date?"

Mac stood and said, "Yes, Judge, that's fine with the State."

"Mr. Garcia?"

Santiago slowly rose and checked the calendar on his cell phone. He tapped the screen irregularly in a distracting manner.

"Yes, uh, September 16th should be OK. 9:30?"

"Yes," said Judge Harajuku. "I will order a Presentence Investigation. Does the State have any Motions at this time?"

Taking his cue, Mac said, "Yes, thank you, Judge. We ask that the Defendant be remanded into custody and that her bond be revoked pending sentencing on the 16th of September."

"So ordered."

Deputy Feeny had already reached behind to the small of his back, where he located his pair of handcuffs on his service utility belt. Deputy Banks held Rikki's chair and whispered, "Stand up and face forward."

With the smooth dexterity of a dance partner, Deputy Feeny clicked a cuff on both of Rikki's wrists, securing her arms behind her back. Each Deputy held Rikki tightly, their hands grasping her elbows.

"Deputies, you may stand her back," ordered Judge Harajuku.

Rikki was led out of the courtroom, leaving behind her folder of paperwork on the defense table. "I'll be up to see you at SCCF, and we can talk about the sentencing," Santiago said as she was being ushered through the door to lockup.

She turned and said, "You suck."

They took her through the door to lockup.

Judge Harajuku and Phoebe left the courtroom through the door to chambers.

Santiago turned to face Mac and said, "Shit, I wasn't expecting them to come back so fast! There were so many problems with your main witness, the kid. You are one lucky son of a bitch." Santiago extended his hand graciously forward, like a defeated tennis player at the net.

Mac grasped Santiago's hand with a gentleman's firmness and then said, "Lucky? You know what, Santiago? I've found that over the years, the harder I work, the luckier I get."

The two rivals left the courtroom together and stepped into the elevator. Santiago, exhausted and emotionally drained, said with a tone of resignation, "Do you have to convict *all* of my clients? Maybe if I bug the hell out of you, you'll let me win one of these trials?"

"'Tis a foolhardy dog that barks at a sleeping lion," Mac calmly replied.

"You are so incredibly arrogant, Mr. MacIntyre. More Shakespeare?"

"No, actually. That's Sushi Queen. My fortune cookie said that today."

"Go home. You work too hard."

Mac replied, "Wish I could go home, Judge Garcia, but The Fish wants to hold a late news conference tonight to announce the verdict. He's obsessed with getting on TV. He has no clue what this trial was about, so I've got to explain everything to him."

Santiago said, "I'd rather slit my wrists."

CHAPTER 86

Friday, August 9, 2019
9:20 p.m.

Although the courthouse was closed for business late at night, the Sheriff's Department maintained a small stage in the atrium area on the ground floor for emergency news conferences. Ari Fischbein had alerted the media that he would make an announcement about the Van der Hook verdict at 9:30 p.m. There was a small elevated platform with a lectern positioned in the center. Three flags were carefully positioned as a backdrop behind the lectern: a United States flag, a State of Maryland flag, and a blue-and-gold Seneca County flag.

On the way down in the elevator with Mac and Jo, Ari asked, "So, what exactly is it about this trial that is, um, rare? The guy from the *Journal* said it was rare. He said it was highly unusual. Why? What am I going to tell the media?"

"Ari, it's a murder," said Mac. As the elevator descended, Ari looked at his reflection in the brass plate that contained the elevator buttons. He reached up and ineffectively smoothed his thinning hair across his bald spot.

"It's an unusual case," Mac continued. "The Defendant is a woman—her name is Van Der Hook, by the way—and she stabbed her husband to death. The only eyewitness was their nine-year-old daughter. So, that type of fact pattern is very 'rare,' as the reporter said."

"Oh, yeah, I remember this case. That Van der Hook guy was the CEO of MVH Enterprises. He donated a lot to the Democratic Club. Yeah, this is bad news."

Jo pressed herself into the corner of the elevator. She was unusually icy and quiet. Breaking her iciness, she volunteered, "True, but Ari, the press isn't focused on who the victim was or his standing in the community or his wealth or anything like that. The storyline for this case is that a disabled child witness was qualified to testify. We got the Court to rule she was a competent witness. It's extremely rare for a kid like that to be at the center of a big domestic violence homicide case. So, we need to talk about how we fight for kids, blah, blah, blah."

When the elevator landed, Ari exited first. It was important to The Fish that he appear to be the leader. As he stepped off, he affected a commanding posture. He marched with purpose across the atrium. Mac and Jo followed in formation, like soldiers. When they got to the podium, Ari stepped up to the lectern. Mac was a few feet away on the left. Jo stood in a geometrically equidistant position to his right, creating an isosceles triangle of prosecutors. There was a cluster of a dozen people in front of the lectern: print journalists and two TV camera crews, each with a standup remote reporter.

Ari adjusted the microphone, annoyed that he had to lower it.

"Good evening. Today is an important day for the children of Seneca County. Because of the conviction of... Ms. Van der Hook..." Ari did not know Rikki was her first name, so he simply fell back on "Ms. Van der Hook." This omission was smoothly executed and unnoticed by all except Mac and Jo.

Don Morris shook his head and scribbled something on his notepad.

"This Defendant is now a convicted murderer. And the most important thing is that the children of Seneca County will be heard. Their voices matter. This case illustrates that our office will do everything possible to protect the children of this community and to safeguard them no matter what serious crimes they may have witnessed. Under a Fischbein administration, our office pledges to fight, with every tool available, in creative and novel ways, to help children. A child is now without both a father and a mother because of this Defendant's actions. Thankfully, she will be locked up for a long, long time. We wish to thank the Seneca County Police Department for its dedication and for the joint investigation of this matter. Without their expertise, this case would not have been possible to prosecute. Additionally, at this time, I would like to recognize the excellent work of the dedicated professionals in my office. I'd especially like to recognize my Deputy State's Attorney, Jo Newgrange, for her leadership and supervision of the prosecution. Great job, Jo!"

Ari gratuitously added, "I'd also like to thank Mac MacIntyre, who assisted on the case. Thank you, Mac."

Ari waved off questions, smiled broadly, let the photographers take photos, and said, "We will be releasing an official press statement tomorrow. Thank you." Mac kept his face absolutely stone still, like an Easter Island *moai*.

When the camera crews had taken sufficient photos, Ari stepped off of the podium first, with Jo following and Mac trailing both of them.

Upstairs, Mac stopped in the staff coffee room to get something. He walked back to his office with a small, twisted white plastic bag. He then unlocked his bottom desk drawer.

CHAPTER 87

Saturday, August 10, 2019
1:05 a.m.

Mac pulled into the Visitors' parking lot at Lock 18 and looked all around; no one was there. With the Jeep's top down, he could hear the rustling of the river as the summer waves rippled against the rocks continuously, eternally, never stopping. He leaned back, paused, deeply inhaled the warm humid air, and then stepped out.

The parking lot was completely abandoned at this time of night. Just a few hours earlier, the last remaining dog walkers and joggers had gone home. Earlier in the day, children had been playing, and people had lowered boats and canoes and kayaks into the river. But now, late at night, with only the crickets chirping and the water rippling, he was completely alone.

Reaching into the backseat area of the Jeep, he flipped up the carpet section that covered his hidden safe. After unlocking the safe, he shifted the green backpack to the side and lifted out the plastic bag from Sushi Queen containing the diary. He palmed a small flashlight from his console and slipped it into his jacket pocket. He got out, walked to the rear cargo area, and picked up a small, bright red container, which he kept for emergencies. It had less than a pint of gasoline inside.

The asphalt was wet and slippery from a brief summer shower, and so he took careful steps to the far corner of the parking lot, to the obscure, secret spot where he and Andre had eaten lunch.

Peering into the rusty metal barrel, he noticed charred wood, assorted confetti-like litter, and some glimmering pieces of broken glass at the bottom. The chopsticks and Styrofoam boxes from the sushi lunch he'd eaten earlier were still there. He took the diary out of the plastic bag and dropped it into the barrel, where it landed flat. He drizzled a small amount of gasoline from the red container onto the diary, watching as concentric circles of dark stain radiated outward from the center and soaked into the pages.

He pulled a cigarette lighter from his pocket, lifted a sheet of newspaper from the barrel, lit the corner on fire, and dropped the burning newspaper.

The diary was immediately engulfed in flames. When it had fully turned to ashes, he flipped his flashlight on and pointed it down into the crusty metal barrel to illuminate the bottom. After carefully inspecting the last dying embers, he took one of the charred branches already in the barrel and stirred the remains in all directions, swirling the ashes clockwise until there was nothing left of the diary at all.

He walked away from the barrel, peering around once more, and got into his Jeep. Turning on the ignition, he shifted into first gear and drove home.

CHAPTER 88

Saturday, August 10, 2019
5:45 a.m.

Mac woke up, walked to the bathroom, and noted the dark circles under his eyes in the mirror. Skipping his shower, he got dressed, raked his hair backwards with his fingers, and pulled on his green Slovenija baseball hat to cover up the chaos of red hair. After making a cup of coffee, he removed the small knotted plastic bag from the refrigerator, which he had brought up from his Jeep the night before, and put it in his jacket pocket. With phone, keys, and wallet in hand, he lumbered, half asleep, out of his apartment, and drove to the Seneca County Animal Shelter.

Judie, the receptionist, greeted him warmly, "Hey, Mr. MacIntyre. Good morning! Gosh, you're here early! We just opened."

"Good morning to you, too. I like it when it's quiet. Plus, the cats are hungry at daybreak. Sorry if I'm in a daze, but I had a hard week at work."

"That's OK, no worries. We got two kittens yesterday. They are just to die for! The lady who dropped them off said they were brothers, but I don't think so. One is completely white, and the other is completely black. They're waiting to meet you! They are so active and social. You'll love them."

Mac hung up his jacket, washed his hands in the trough set up in the veterinary examination area, and then went around to the back of the shelter where the newly rescued animals were sorted by species: dogs to the left, and cats to the right. The feline area had separate small cages for the cats until they were examined and given shots. There was also a large, open play area for the cats to roam and enjoy a little freedom as they waited to be adopted.

There was something about cats Mac instinctively connected to. He felt camaraderie, a rapport, a bond. Mac respected feline intelligence and independence. Cats didn't care about his cases and his trials and the horrible human abuse the victims he represented suffered. Cats didn't judge him, or criticize him, or tell lies behind his back like people did. He liked dogs too, but they came in such a variety of shapes and sizes, with different personalities and levels of intelligence. To Mac, dogs branched off into what seemed like hundreds of disparate species, while cats had a more uniform, sleek similarity. He appreciated the loyalty found in dogs, but they were servile, unclean, and begged; cats were elegant and slinky and demanded loyalty. Above all, cats were mysterious, and that attracted him the most.

Mac approached the doors leading to the feline play area. His phone buzzed furiously in his jeans pocket. He ignored it. Then, just as he pulled the door open, his phone vibrated again. Even now, early on a Saturday morning, someone really needed to talk with him.

He reached into his pocket, pulled his phone out and looked at the Caller ID. It was Warden Stempkowski, calling from the Seneca County Correctional Facility. When Mac saw his name, his mind immediately snapped to attention. He tapped the screen to receive the call, now completely focused.

"Hey, Stemp. What's up? Sorry, I'm at the Animal Shelter. I volunteer here every Saturday," he said.

"Man, you're not going to believe this! I mean, I don't even know how this happened. That Rikki woman you just convicted? She's dead."

"What the fuck? What happened?"

"She was acting strange ever since she got here to SCCF. After she was transported from court, she just slept all night and wouldn't eat, and we noticed she was acting weird. And then, this morning, on the early check, the C.O. found her on the floor under her sink. She was hanging from the pipe by a cord she'd made from her bra."

"Oh my God. Have you told anyone? I mean, anyone outside of SCCF? Anyone at the SAO?"

"No, you're the first I'm calling. We rushed her to Tomlinson Hospital, and our Medical Intervention Team was doing CPR and all this recovery shit in the ambulance, but she was dead. Dead as a doornail."

"That's from Shakespeare."

"What?"

"Dead as a doornail. Comes from *Henry the Sixth, Part Two*."

"Mac! Don't start that shit, man! Listen to what I'm telling you!"

"Sorry, Stemp, I can't help that. People use lines from Shakespeare every day when they talk without even realizing it. Sorry. I can't shut that off in my mind. OK, give me a sec. That's a lot to take in. What happened? Did someone kill her?"

"Looks like she killed herself, but we always need to investigate these things. As you know, sometimes these convicted murderers are targets for a variety of reasons. Revenge. Money. Who knows? But sometimes they're set up to look like a suicide."

"Honestly, just between you and me, Stemp, it's not a great loss, right? Not like she was some major contributor to society. She got what she deserved."

"Well, I'm not going to get into all of that. I have a job to do. This makes us look bad, and I need to cover my own ass. There'll be investigations and people saying we were negligent or even that *we* killed her. You know how the press and these liberals always eat this stuff up."

"I'll back you 100 percent, Stemp, so don't worry about that. We can control the Grand Jury if it ever gets to that point. But I think you should call Jo Newgrange ASAP. I'd rather stay out of the loop. Call Jo. Do you know her?"

"I met that fake-ass bitch when they were elected. With her red hair extensions. You could see they weren't real a mile away. She and that bald dick Fischbein came out here with a news media crew talking about reforming criminal justice and saying the jail—my jail—was going to change, and he was in favor of bail reform and some other nonsense. I could tell right away he had no idea what he was talking about. Man, I feel for you, having to work for that asshole politician."

"Well, just call Jo now. I'm going to let them handle this. And Stemp, thanks for all your help with everything. I've got your back, my friend."

"OK, good luck. Love you, brother."

Mac realized he should go back to his apartment, shower, dress, and then head to the SAO. Any second, he knew, Jo or even Ari himself, would be nagging him, even though it was the weekend.

First, he had something more important to do.

He clicked off his phone and then stuffed it into his pocket. He opened the doors to the cat play area and stepped inside. The room was filled with approximately 20 cats. Some were cautiously walking around keeping a safe distance, some nibbling at the automatic feeders and some burrowed into corners and whatever tight spaces they could find for refuge.

From the corner, a black cat—totally black—scampered over. Then, on his heels, a white one followed. Mac squatted down and gently reached out. The black cat bumped his head against Mac's fist. The white one joined them, rubbing his flank against Mac's ankle.

"Hey there, little guy. What's your name?"

The black cat swiveled in a tight circle and brushed against Mac's open palm, purring.

"I'm calling you Othello. And is this your brother? He's Iago."

He stroked both cats for a minute, then said, "Guys, I have to go. But I'll be back. I'm going to take you home with me. Would you like that?"

From inside his jacket pocket, he pulled out the small plastic bag with the two pieces of tuna maki. He untied the bag, took out the two discs of sushi, and broke them apart. He put one piece of tuna down in front of Othello and one down in front of Iago.

CHAPTER 89

Saturday, August 10, 2019
7:00 a.m.

Mac raced back to his apartment and took a shower in three minutes. Even on a Saturday, with the news of Rikki's death, the SAO would be buzzing. The Fish, likely wearing a suit and tie, would be acting like he was in charge. Jo would definitely be there too, juggling calls and requests for on-camera interviews. The two local TV crews would be scrambling to get this breaking news on the noon program. Mac quickly drove the few blocks to the SAO.

Just as he parked in the garage, his phone vibrated. The Caller ID said "JO NEWGRANGE," and the message was, simply, "CODE 3," the signal for emergency. He ignored it.

He leaned back in the driver's seat and closed his eyes.

His thoughts and imagination raced haphazardly through his mind. Changing images, in non-sequential random order, flashed through his brain: Mandy asleep, her head face first on the table in the SAO conference room; Rikki's rotating jackets at trial in blue, green and red; Judge Harajuku's eyes smoldering with controlled anger; Santiago nervously bouncing like a sparrow across the courtroom floor; Jo's laundry basket filled with tiny scraps of glittery fabrics, like an aquarium with exotic tropical fish; Butterfly Lady, her hands shaking as she read from the verdict sheet; gasoline spreading in concentric circles like an archery target across the cover of the diary. All of these images swirled in Mac's mind.

He pulled out his phone to check his work voicemails, wondering how many times Ari had called. The first message was not from The Fish. A woman's husky voice said, "Hey, Mr. MacIntyre. I just wanted to tell you I think you did a really great job in the trial. I was one of the jurors. I'm the blonde who was sitting in the front row with the green streak in my hair and with the pierced nose. I'm Becky, Becky Borden. If you'd ever want to meet for coffee or something, just let me know. I also just wanted to let you know when we started deliberating the case in the jury room, well, almost everyone agreed that Rikki woman was guilty right away. The Spanish lady was the only holdout, but she caved in after a short while. We all believed the little girl. I mean, we completely believed her. It was obvious her mother was a total liar. Once that Rikki woman testified, we all knew she was guilty. So, what I'm trying to say is I'd love to discuss all of this with you further, like I said, if you want to meet up some time and... "

Mac clicked his phone, cutting off the voicemail without listening to the end of the message.

He got out of the Jeep and crossed the basement towards

the elevators. He used his fob to enter the security area. No guard was on duty on a Saturday. He pressed the elevator button and heard the ping of the elevator arrive.

He stepped inside and ascended to the State's Attorney's Office, knowing that upstairs a frantic Ari and Jo would be waiting for him. He got off the elevator and quickly turned the corner and ducked into his dark office. He needed to collect himself before dealing with them.

His cell phone buzzed again. He looked down at the text.

NEW CASE. GIRL WAS THROWN OFF
RAILRD TRESSEL. IM NOT KDDING.
MEET ME AT TOMLINSON HOSP. SERIUS
SHIT. SHES NOT 0100 YET AND MUML-
BING. HOW DOES THAT 'DYING DECLA-
RATION' THING WORK AGAIN?
ANDRE.

Mac looked up at the small framed thank-you note above his desk addressed to "THE STAIT'S ATTOURNY." Once again, he needed to look at it for inspiration. He desperately needed to draw energy from somewhere.

He looked hard at the words "HEPLING ME" written in green crayon.

A new case. Another victim to help.

He took in a massive breath of oxygen, stood, and opened the door. He had to race down to the hospital to interview a victim. But first, he walked confidently towards Ari Fischbein's corner office.

ACKNOWLEDGEMENTS

Thank you to all of those who helped to make this fanciful dream a reality. Very belatedly, I thank my original sources of influence, Ronald M. Foster, Jr. and Anne Tolstoi Wallach. Thank you to my beloved wife, Kathy Ambrose Foster, and my children, family, friends and courthouse colleagues. Much appreciation to the excellent professionals at Paper Raven Books, especially Colleen Tomlinson who has been there from Chapter 1 to the end.

GLOSSARY OF TERMS

Arguendo - Latin term meaning "for the sake of argument," e.g., "The judge said, 'Assuming, *arguendo*, that you are correct, I am still not releasing the defendant on bond.'"

ASAs -Assistant State's Attorneys.

Asperger Syndrome -A developmental disorder affecting ability to effectively socialize and communicate.

Assignment Office/AO -An office in the Judicial Center devoted to assigning and scheduling pending cases and trials.

Autistic spectrum -A broad range of conditions characterized by challenges with social skills, repetitive behaviors, speech, and communication.

Bay of Tranquility -The location of man's first landing on the Moon on July 20, 1969 by Neil Armstrong of the Apollo 11 spaceflight.

Bench conference -A meeting at the judge's bench by the participating attorneys, often when the judge calls the litigants forward to discuss an evidentiary or legal issue.

Brady **material** -A 1963 Supreme Court ruling establishing the principle that exculpatory evidence favorable to a defendant must be disclosed by a prosecutor; failure to do so is a serious violation of a defendant's due process rights, e.g., "If the fingerprints on the weapon don't match, that's obviously *Brady* material."

Brick -A term used in the drug trade to describe a compressed solid block of marijuana.

Buccal -A swab similar to a Q-tip used to collect DNA samples on the inside of a suspect's mouth.

Canon of ethics - A compendium of rules and guidelines used by attorneys to guide ethical behavior in the legal profession.

Caveat emptor -Latin for "let the buyer beware." Used to describe situations where someone buys a product or service "as is" and often used to describe situations involving an unethical seller or sale.

Cause -During the jury selection process, strikes for "cause" are used by the judge to eliminate jurors who have shown overt prejudice towards one side or a lack of neutrality. See "Peremptory strikes," which are strikes given to each side that can be used for any reason other than striking, or eliminating, a juror because of race, gender, or other characteristics.

Cataplexy -A neurological disorder characterized by the sudden loss of muscle tone while awake and often triggered by strong emotions such as laughter, fear, anger, or stress.

Case Search - A search engine used to locate and research the status of pending criminal cases via computer.

CDS -Controlled Dangerous Substances. The term used in statutes to describe illicit drugs or prescription medications.

Cellie -Colloquial term to describe a cell mate while incarcerated.

Child Protective Services -The social services agency empowered with and responsible for guarding the welfare of minors.

Circuit Court -The higher level of the two levels of criminal courts. The lower level is called the District Court. Felony cases and jury trials are handled in the Circuit Court, while minor cases and misdemeanors are handled in the District Court.

C.O. -An abbreviation for Corrections Officer, this term is used frequently in the criminal justice system, particularly by incarcerated persons.

Code 3 -A police term to describe an emergency call or situation, e.g., "He raced his cruiser Code 3 to the crime scene."

Commissioner -An early point of contact in the criminal justice system, commissioners are judicial officers who are responsible for informing criminal defendants of the charges they are facing upon initial arrest and who set the initial bond or terms of pretrial release.

Commonwealth's Attorney - A term to describe a prosecutor, synonymous with District Attorney or with State's Attorney.

Competency -A legal term used to describe the ability of a witness to testify. A court must determine each witness's competency or incompetency under guidelines set by case law/previous cases. Generally, every witness must understand the nature of the legal proceedings and the importance of truthfulness and honesty.

Dateline NBC -A television series devoted to sensational stories of criminal cases and trials.

***De novo* appeal** -A legal procedure where a defendant can immediately have his or her conviction appealed to a higher court, e.g., "She lost her case in the District Court, so we are entering a *de novo* appeal to do it all over again in the Circuit Court."

Discovery -The process whereby a prosecutor transfers evidence to the defense in a timely manner, e.g., "The prosecutor hasn't given us discovery yet, and we might file a Motion to Compel Discovery if we don't receive it soon."

District Court -Of the two levels of trial courts, District Court is where misdemeanors and minor charges are litigated. See "Circuit Court," which is reserved for felony cases and jury trials.

DNA - Deoxyribonucleic acid, the hereditary material in humans, frequently used by criminal forensic investigators to identify an assailant or suspect, e.g., "We got his DNA off the murder weapon."

Dockets -The daily calendar of cases to be heard by a court in any single session, e.g., "My case is on the afternoon docket."

Drug Rip - A robbery, or attempted robbery, of a drug dealer by a buyer who intends to steal the drugs instead of purchasing them, i.e., "rip" as in "rip-off."

Exculpatory -Evidence or testimony which tends to favor the defendant, e.g. "The prosecutor gave the defense attorney all of the exculpatory evidence in the discovery process."

Expunged/expungement -The process of erasing a conviction from a defendant's criminal record, e.g. "My attorney got my prior guilty plea expunged from my record."

Fifth Amendment -A Constitutional Amendment which guarantees the right not to be implicated by self-incriminating testimony, e.g. "You can't force a defendant to testify; that would be a violation of his Fifth Amendment rights."

Gallery -The audience area of the courtroom reserved for public spectators.

Gardez Bien -French for "to protect well," the motto of the Seneca County Sheriff's Department and part of their uniform insignia.

Gen Pop -An abbreviation for "general population," the section of the jail where prisoners other than specially protected inmates congregate.

Grand Jury -An official group comprised of 23 citizens tasked with reviewing felony cases to assess the presence of "probable cause," not guilt or innocence.

HOV Lane -High Occupancy Vehicle lane, used by vehicles on the Interstate highway who are allowed access to a faster lane if traveling with multiple passengers.

HQ -Headquarters of the police department.

Husher -A device used in the courtroom by the judge to emit a white-noise "hushing" sound, ostensibly to drown out private conversations being conducted at the judge's bench area.

Indictment -A formal document issued by the Grand Jury listing criminal charges facing a defendant.

I/O -Investigating Officer, usually the person to author a Statement of Charges contained in a standard police report.

Investiture -A formal swearing-in given when an attorney becomes a judge, e.g., "I went to his Investiture, and all of his former colleagues from the SAO were there."

Jackson Pollock -An American painter in the abstract expressionist movement of the 1940s and 1950s, he was widely noted for his "drip technique" of pouring or splashing paints.

Jury Instructions -Definitions of legal terms given by a judge to the jury explaining the issues and crimes involved in the trial.

Jury Trial -A process of determining a defendant's guilt or innocence whereby twelve neutrally-chosen members of the community decide the sufficiency of the evidence presented to them by a prosecutor and challenged by a defense attorney.

LexisNexis -A system of online legal research replacing the need for stacks of law books in a law library.

Lindbergh Kidnapping - An infamous 1932 American crime when the baby of aviator Charles Lindbergh was abducted and murdered, resulting in the controversial conviction of Bruno Richard Hauptmann (since questioned) and his subsequent execution in the electric chair.

Line of Appearance -A legal document whereby a prosecutor and a defense attorney officially enter a criminal case representing either the State or a defendant, e.g. "Have you entered your Line of Appearance in the case yet?"

Lizzie Borden -A Massachusetts woman who was tried and acquitted of the 1892 axe murders of her father and stepmother, one of the most notorious homicide trials in American legal history.

Maki -A form of sushi (raw fish on rice) rolled in dried seaweed and cut into disks.

Media Services -An office in the police department devoted to managing media and press releases disseminating information to the public about current police activity, arrests, or cases.

***Miranda* Warnings** -In the United States, a type of notification given by police to criminal suspects in police custody advising them of their right to remain silent and to have an attorney present during custodial questioning or interrogation.

Mitochondrial DNA -A type of DNA found in human cells often used to make identifications in the criminal investigative forensic process, e.g., "Recent developments in DNA identification now use mitochondrial DNA, which is much more sensitive than the older methods of identification."

Morse Code -Named after American inventor Samuel Morse, this code is a method of communicating on a telegraph using two different signal durations, called "dots" and "dashes."

Moot Court -Used mainly in law schools, moot court is a practice court where students do mock appellate arguments before professors, e.g. "He made the school's Moot Court Team because of his oral advocacy skills."

Motions -A legal procedure before a trial where litigants argue to the presiding judge, without a jury present, the various issues of evidentiary value.

Motion to Suppress -A Motion to block or prevent the opposition from using testimony or evidence, e.g., "The defense attorney's Motion to Suppress blocked the prosecutor from using his client's confession."

Motion in *Limine* -A Motion heard by the court before the opening statements, usually requested under emergency conditions.

Motion for Judgment of Acquittal/MJOA -A Motion heard by the judge after the conclusion of the State's case, requested by the defense, arguing that the State has failed to present a case and, therefore, asking that the judge dismiss one or all of the charges.

MS-13 -Also known as *Mara Salvatrucha*, an international criminal gang, based in Central America but present in many cities in the United States with Latino communities.

Napoleonic -A reference to Napoleon Bonaparte, a French military and political leader of the French Revolution.

Neapolitan -Referring to the city of Naples in Italy.

No Bill -A legal term used to describe a conclusion by the Grand Jury that no charges should be filed.

Nolle prosequi/nolle/nol pros -Latin for "not prosecuted," the term is used to describe when a prosecutor elects not to file charges or when a decision is made by the prosecutor to abandon a case, e.g., "The ASA dropped the charges by filing a *nol pros*."

Overkill -When a murder victim has sustained multiple fatal injuries, many more than are necessary to take a life, used frequently by law enforcement and police, e.g. "He was shot twenty times; that's such overkill."

PD -Public Defenders are attorneys specializing in criminal defense who are paid by the State and who represent indigent defendants for free.

Pediatric Narcolepsy - Narcolepsy is a neurological sleep disorder characterized by chronic fatigue and sleepiness that primarily affects adults but is also occasionally diagnosed in children.

Peremptory Strikes -During the process of jury selection, the prosecution and defense each have a certain number of peremptory strikes, meaning the choice to eliminate a potential juror for any reason except those involving a juror's race, gender, or other characteristics.

Pleadings -Various documentary filings before a trial begins, e.g. "She filed all the necessary pleadings on behalf of her client."

Pleas -A defendant can choose to plead guilty in exchange for some benefit, often called a "plea bargain" or "plea agreement."

PR/Personal Recognizance -A type of release from jail on bond without having to submit a monetary amount, e.g. "He was released on his own personal recognizance."

Prima Facie -Latin for "at first sight," meaning that a case or point of argument has been proved to a bare minimum and the case can proceed forward, e.g. "The prosecutor proved his case to at least a 51 percent degree. Therefore, the judge found he had proven a prima facie case."

PTSD/Post-traumatic Stress Disorder - An anxiety disorder stemming from a traumatic event or events, such as a physical injury, abuse or severe mental or emotional distress.

PSI/Presentence Investigation -A report prepared by investigators working independently for the court to provide background information on a defendant to assist the judge in rendering a fair sentence, e.g. "The judge asked for a PSI to check on his prior convictions and employment history."

PTSU/Pretrial Services Unit -The agency that conducts Presentence investigations and submits a report to the court containing background information to the court. Also the agency responsible for supervising defendants who have been released on bond back into the community.

Quid Pro Quo -Latin for "this for that," or "in exchange for." Used to describe a situation where one party receives equal value for a thing, favor or action, e.g. "Because you plead guilty, the prosecutor dropped the rest of the charges *quid pro quo*."

Rock Cocaine -A form of cocaine which appears in rock or solid form as opposed to powered cocaine and often considered very addictive and less expensive.

SA/State's Attorney -The top prosecutor in a given jurisdiction. Prosecutors who work for the State's Attorney are designated as Assistant State's Attorneys. The second-in-command in the State's Attorney's Office is usually given the title of Deputy State's Attorney.

SCCF/Seneca County Correctional Facility - The local jail where inmates who have received a sentence of 18 months or less incarceration will be housed; a sentence in excess of 18 months will result in placement in the State system, a much more serious type of prison. Defendants awaiting trial in Seneca County are held at SCCF pretrial.

SCP-505 Form -The form used by the Seneca County Police to advise individuals in custody of their rights. See "*Miranda* warnings."

Seg -An abbreviation for "segregation," the term used in the SCCF for those inmates who must be separated from those in "general population" for their own safety or for some other legitimate reason.

Sentencing -The process at the trial's conclusion where a judge determines the length of incarceration appropriate for the defendant and the crime committed.

Speedball -A dose of cocaine mixed with heroin usually taken by injection.

Statement of Charges/SOC -A document prepared by a detective or police officer which outlines the factual basis alleging a crime, usually a short narrative summary with basic facts and not a complete police report.

Statutory Maximum -The maximum time in prison proscribed by a statute which the judge can impose, although often an actual sentence is lower based on mitigating circumstances, e.g. "My lawyer said the statutory maximum is twenty years, but I'll probably get much less because this is my first conviction."

Subpoena -A formal legal document whereby an individual is ordered or mandated to report to court.

Summa Cum Laude -Latin for "highest honor," usually given to the top academic performer in a given class or school.

Super Max -Nickname for the most secure prison in Maryland, located in Baltimore.

Ten/twenty Strike -The number of potential jurors who can be eliminated from the jury pool during the jury selection process. The defense is given twice as many strikes as the prosecution.

Thai Sticks -A form of cannabis usually associated with Southeast Asia where potent marijuana is packaged in stick form.

Time Served -A type of sentence where the judge allows a defendant to be released after conviction because the time held pretrial is sufficient, e.g. "Since she was held pretrial for six months, they let her out after she plead guilty for time served."

True Bill -The heading on an indictment conveying that the Grand Jury has decided to validate the State's allegations and move the case forward to a Circuit Court prosecution.

Vehicle Forfeiture -A civil procedure, usually in drug cases, whereby the police impound a suspect's vehicle as allegedly stemming from illegal drug sales, often used in a predatory fashion by police to punish drug dealers before guilt has been established.

Voir Dire -French for "speak the truth," this term refers to the process by which potential jurors are interviewed by the judge to determine neutrality and appropriateness to serve on a jury.

Westlaw -An online service for researching legal issues and prior cases which evolved in the 1990s to, essentially, render law libraries with book stalls obsolete.

0100 -Police internal code for "homicide."

4-215 hearing -Also called a "Scheduling Conference," a pretrial court appearance attended by both the prosecutor and defense attorney to establish a defendant's right to have the trial unfold in compliance with speedy trial concerns under the Sixth Amendment.

10-4 -Police code for "message received."

20/20 -A popular television series featuring reenactments and portrayals of true crime stories.

And now a preview of

DOUBLE BLIND

The Seneca County Courthouse Series: Book Two

BY A. X. FOSTER

CHAPTER 1

July 5, 2002
2:22 a.m.

The first shot was not fatal. It skipped down the center of J'Mal's scalp from front to back, parting his hair like a comb. Blood cascaded in equal quantities down both sides of his face, curving around each of his ears like bends in a river.

The second shot killed him.

The .22 caliber bullet hit J'Mal's cheekbone, sending a hailstorm of metal slivers and bone fragments through his brain and exiting from the back of his skull. His large body crashed downward onto a glass coffee table beneath him, smashing it into pieces. By the time he hit the table, his brain had ceased functioning, and his heart, no longer receiving signals, stopped beating.

"What the fuck?!" screamed Makayla, brushing her long, stringy blonde hair from her face. She turned away, cowering and pressing her body into the corner of the room, praying she wouldn't get shot next. She protectively covered her eyes with her hands as the thin, young man with dreadlocks dashed out of the apartment and ran down the stairs to the street.

As Makayla's ears were still ringing from the sound of the two pistol shots in the small one-room apartment, she wiped her hands reflexively on her faded jeans. She took two steps forward to look at J'Mal's body lying on the floor on top of the smashed coffee table. He was on his side, and his eyes were open. A splinter of sharp broken glass was embedded in his right eye. Underneath J'Mal's body, she saw part of a silver gun camouflaged in the glinting glass shards.

Oh my God! Oh my God! I gotta get out of here!

Then she noticed a small plastic sandwich bag with a twisted, knotted top near his left hand. Inside the plastic baggie was a collection of white, irregularly shaped rocks, jumbled together like a bag of dice. She leaned down and grabbed it. She stuffed it into her front pocket, turned, and sprinted to the door, still swinging open, back and forth, in the summer rainstorm. Even with the door open, she did not notice it was raining. She hurried down the stairs and stumbled out onto Rotterdam Street, looking both ways to see if anyone was rushing towards her. No one was. She glanced down the street to look for cars, and, seeing none, she dashed across the wet pavement to the other side. Her Converse sneakers splashed rhythmically in the puddles as she ran.

Jesus, no one heard that? You've got to be kidding. That was so loud. OK, get your shit together. I've got to call Harp!

Makayla stopped and used the window of the QuikStop convenience store as an impromptu mirror. Her reflection was staring back at her: a tall, thin woman with a nest of disheveled, wet hair and green eyes bulging with fear. She ineffectively smoothed the jumble on top of her head, pulled her damp T-shirt from the waistband of her jeans, and arranged it to hang down to her thighs. The logo on her shirt said: WORLD SERIES CHAMPION ARIZONA DIAMONDBACKS. She patted her pockets.

Money, ID, keys, and the baggie with all that crack. I gotta call Harp! This is a disaster! That dude shot J'Mal! I'm in so much trouble now!

She went inside the QuikStop. Luckily, it was open 24/7. She shivered like a wet dog, crossed her arms across her chest, and approached the counter. The store was empty. No one but the sales clerk, a familiar elderly Latina woman, was inside.

"Ana, can I use your cell phone, please? It's an emergency."

Ana smirked and, with exaggerated effort, pulled a pair of headphones from her ears. She stood up from her stool, put her portable CD player on the grimy counter, and pulled a Motorola Razr flip phone from her back pocket, saying, "Girl, you gotta get your own damn cell phone one of these days. Everyone's got one now. I ain't Verizon, y'know."

Taking the flip phone from Ana, Makayla thanked her. "I'll just be a minute. It's super important. I really appreciate it!"

Makayla stepped towards the rear of the convenience store, looked back to see if Ana was paying attention, and then pulled the door open on the floor-to-ceiling cooler compartment. It was filled with an assortment of colorful, unhealthy, cold drinks. She saw Ana had put her headphones back on her head and was now looking down at a cracked plastic *R.*

Kelly CD cover in her hand. She was examining it carefully, as if looking for clues. Ana began bobbing her head.

Makayla reached as far back into the cooler as she could and took out a bright pink Watermelon Splash Gatorade from the last row of bottles positioned in the top rack. She reached into her pants and took out the baggie and stuffed it in the back of the cooler in the space where the last bottle had been. She would get that tomorrow.

Satisfied no one could hear or see her, Makayla pushed the buttons on the cell phone.

"Harp! It's me."

"What phone is *this*? Our unit has Caller ID now. I can tell everyone who calls. What's going on? Did he make the buy? We're two blocks away."

"No! He shot J'Mal and ran! He shot him and stole the baggie!"

"Jesus Christ! Are you kidding? Me and Sergeant Ricky will be there in three minutes. Where exactly are you?"

"I'm in the QuikStop on Rotterdam across the street from J'Mal's apartment. I'm in the back of the store. Hurry!"

"Look, Makayla, if you're going to do these undercover informant jobs for us, you gotta pay attention and set these buys up better than this! I thought you knew this guy who wanted to score some drugs."

"I'm sorry. I'm *sorry*! He was just some random guy on the street who came up and asked me where he could get some rocks. So I took him up to J'Mal's because you and Sergeant Ricky wanted me to help you catch someone. I was just trying to help. And then all *this* happened."

Makayla started to cry.

Harp ignored that and said, "Did you get a good look at the guy who shot him?"

"Yes, I mean—I think so. I'm not sure."

"Well, you better be sure! If you wanna get paid, you've got to do better than that, Makayla. Right now, you're an accomplice to a homicide, and who knows how the State's Attorney's Office will think about this."

Makayla sat down on the floor of the QuikStop.

"We're pulling up now. Give the phone back to whoever you borrowed it from and come outside. We will think of something."

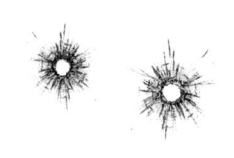

Printed in Great Britain
by Amazon